REESA HERBERTH
MICHELLE MOORE

Riptide Publishing
PO Box 1537
Burnsville, NC 28714
www.riptidepublishing.com

Detour

Cover art: Kanaxa, www.kanaxa.com
Editors: Carole-ann Galloway and Chris Muldoon
Layout: L.C. Chase, lcchase.com/design.htm

ISBN: 978-1-62649-744-3

First edition
May, 2018

Also available in ebook:
ISBN: 978-1-62649-743-6

REESA HERBERTH
MICHELLE MOORE

RIPTIDE
PUBLISHING

For Nick and Ethan, who've stuck with us for twenty years and fifteen different storylines. Cheers, gentlemen.

TABLE OF Contents

CHAPTER One

Arlington, VA

Ethan dropped the duffel bag full of food into the trunk and slammed it shut.

"I can't believe you're leaving me here with the *babies* all summer." Suze's face crumpled. "I hope you pick up a hobo and they dismember you and leave your body in a cave."

"Suzanna Marie Domani! What a terrible thing to say." His mom put an arm around Suze's neck and noogied the top of her head. "Your brother is much smarter than that." She caught Ethan's gaze, eyebrows raised meaningfully. "Aren't you?"

Ethan grinned at both of them. "Of course. I won't drive near any caves if I pick up a vagrant."

Suze glanced between Ethan and their mom, pale eyebrows lifting in kind. "Right. So, can I have his room?"

"No. What we want your brother to take away from this is that he shouldn't pick up any strangers. It's dangerous."

He managed to get both his mom and Suze in a hug at the same time. "I promise I'll be careful. No picking up hitchhikers, no sleeping in rest areas, and I'll check in every other night."

He yelped at the poke and gave his mom an accusing stare.

"*Every* night, thank you very much."

Ethan opened his mouth to protest, then stopped. The fear in her eyes hurt, but there was no denying the twinge of resentment it caused. He nodded, deliberately softening his voice. "Yeah, okay. Every night."

It helped that he'd said goodbye to everyone else already. Dad hadn't been any better at hiding his worry, and dealing with both paranoid parents would've frozen him in place. He'd already spent enough time frozen for two lifetimes.

"Love you, kiddo. Love you, Mom." He gave them both another hug each, then pulled himself away before home could suck him back in.

Ethan settled himself into the familiar seat of his inherited Subaru Outback, unable to stop the reflexive glance toward his passenger seat. He ducked down, popping open the glove compartment to check for the third time that he'd remembered to put Scott's little wooden box in there with the taco sauce and hand sanitizer.

He backed out of their driveway into the narrow, tree-lined street he'd grown up on, navigating around Mrs. Kim's minivan and the street hockey net someone (probably his brother David) had left sitting too far out from the curb. One last look in the rearview mirror and he was free.

Ethan and Scott had been planning their after-graduation road trip since sophomore year, the very second Scott had burst into Ethan's bedroom waving his newly minted driver's license. Taking the trip alone hadn't been part of the equation, but Ethan had learned a lot about adjusting his expectations in the past year.

He flipped on the radio as he crossed into Fairfax County on I-66, taking his first deep breath away from the well-meaning confines of his family. The road stretched out in front of him, four lanes of freedom and experience beckoning him away from home. From the past eighteen years, twelve of them with Scott. From the past year without him.

Ethan sailed down the interstate, music he wasn't listening to cranked to cover the noise in his head. He didn't want to think about anything but the drive.

He was doing sixty-five when the car in front of him slammed on the brakes, and everyone around it followed suit. Ethan cut his speed in time to avoid hitting anyone, though he was pretty sure he heard the crunch of buckling metal a few cars back.

Once he'd stopped freaking out about how close he was to starting off his epic road trip with an accident less than ten miles from his house, he punched the radio over to the traffic and weather station.

"—heavy thunderstorms may have been a contributing factor. Three drivers are being medevaced to Fairfax Hospital. The two tractor trailers are blocking all westbound lanes of I-66 in Manassas, with backups already extending to the Beltway. Hazardous material cleanup crews are en route, but drivers should expect delays of up to an hour—"

And then it started to rain.

Six hours deep into his month-long road trip, Ethan was lost. Not *lost*-lost, but there was no way he could find his way back to anything approximating a highway. It didn't help that what had started as a mere thunderstorm had become a full-force monsoon. He didn't remember turning on the "avoid any road with more than one lane" setting on his GPS, but he hadn't seen another car in the past ten minutes. He squinted, trying to make out where the shoulder ended and the ditch next to it began, and bit back a startled gasp when his headlights panned over someone walking down the side of the road.

He was on the person too fast, and Ethan stomped on the brake pedal with all his weight. The car fishtailed, the rear end sliding sickeningly close to the ditch, before he got control again. By that point, he was a good hundred feet past the dark figure. Ethan smacked the button for his emergency flashers and pulled as far to the side of the road as he dared while his heart tried to resume a normal rhythm. There'd been no tell-tale thump, and the car hadn't rolled over anything large. If luck was on his side, he hadn't just killed someone in the dark backwoods of West Virginia.

No matter how hard he squinted at the mirrors, he couldn't make out anything more than a few feet behind the car. Sighing heavily, Ethan reached for the door handle, then paused. Too many horror movies started this way.

A flash of lightning illuminated the dark road for a few seconds— long enough for him to catch sight of the pale face outside the driver's-side window. And scream.

Like a goddamn adult.

His fingers clenched involuntarily, including the ones still on the handle, and the door caught a gust of wind and blew open.

This time the scream wasn't his. Scream or shout of pain, it was hard to tell over the drumming rain. There was no denying the hunched-over person in the middle of the road, though, or the steady stream of obscenities that *were* audible over the monsoon.

"Are you okay? I'm so sorry!" Ethan scrambled out of his car, the water rushing over the pavement soaking into the hems of his jeans. Adrenaline spiked again when he didn't get an answer, and he reached for the person hunched over next to him, catching their shoulder. "Are you crazy? You're going to get run over out here!"

As if to prove Ethan's point, the first car he'd seen in fifteen minutes drove past in a flurry of honking, flashing high beams, and standing water that crested over them like a wave. Thunder rolled in its wake, drowning out Ethan's angry shout.

"Fucking asshole," Ethan muttered, wiping muddy water out of his eyes. The person next to him turned their—her?—his head to watch the car drive off. The same dirty water dripped down his face, rivulets running under his chin from his crew cut.

"Yeah, jeez, he could've at least stopped after almost running us over," the boy said. His smile was replaced almost instantly by a somewhat blank look.

"It's the polite thing to do," Ethan said staunchly. "We should probably get out of the road." Driver's Ed had taught him he should keep the car between himself and the road. Given that his car was sitting dangerously close to the slope leading down to the ditch, passenger-side tires riding the edge, that probably wasn't the best idea. He opened his mouth, closed it, and then sighed. In for a penny, in for a pound, his gram had always told him. "Why don't we get in the car? At least we'll be out of the rain."

"Pretty sure I remember hearing something about not getting in cars with strangers."

Ethan snickered as he opened the door. "I heard that this morning, but here I am picking up a stranger. If I promise I'm not a mass murderer, does that help?"

Ethan's damp friend didn't say anything else, but he moved toward the passenger side, edging carefully along the muddy embankment as Ethan slid into the driver's seat and yanked the door shut.

Ethan was soaked to the skin, and the air-conditioning hit him like an unwelcome slap on the ass. Turning on the heat seemed a little excessive but, since his passenger was shivering hard enough to shake the whole car, maybe not a bad idea.

"Are you heading anywhere in particular?" Ethan finished fiddling with the temperature controls and looked up in time to catch a fleeting expression of fear.

"That way." He nodded toward the road in front of them. "Or anywhere, really. Somewhere that isn't here."

Laughing, Ethan turned off his flashers and started rolling forward, letting his old Subaru find its footing before he tried to gain speed. "I can manage that. My GPS says there's a town about ten miles from here, and I think I'm done for the night. Almost killing someone will really do a number on your nerves."

Ethan did his best to keep his eyes on the road in front of him, only sneaking glances a few times before he licked his lips and tried to entice more conversation. "I'm Ethan, by the way." The guy jumped at the sound of his voice, and Ethan cringed.

"Oh. Um. Nick. Thanks for the ride."

"Pretty much the least I could do after almost running you over. I didn't see you at all." *Because you were standing there in the dark, in the road.* But he kept that last bit in his head. Nobody would've been out in this weather by choice, and Nick looked miserable enough already.

Nick shifted in the seat, holding his hands in front of the warm air blasting out of the vent. "Yeah, I appreciate that too. The not-running-over-me part, I mean."

"So, I gotta ask. What were you doing out in the middle of this?" Ethan had to raise his voice to be heard above the rain and the heater. "It's fucking horrible out."

There was a long pause in place of an answer, and Nick seemed at a loss for words. He coughed into the sodden sleeve of his hoodie, pulling the cuffs over the tips of his fingers and not looking in Ethan's direction at all. "Pissed off some carnies." Nick shrugged, water dripping off his head. "They hold a grudge. You win one too many goldfish at that ping-pong ball toss, suddenly you're walking the lonely roads in a hurricane." He shrugged again. "You know how it is."

It was such a blatant lie that Ethan couldn't help laughing to let Nick off the hook. Obviously Nick didn't want to talk about it. They'd known each other for about five minutes, so Ethan wasn't sure what the social conventions were when it came to prying. His mom's voice niggled in the back of his head anyway, and he ventured one more question to shut it off. "Just promise me you're not going to kill me and hide my body in a cave, okay?"

Nick swung his gaze away from the window, staring at Ethan for a beat before he laughed. It sounded rusty, jagged, like it almost hurt. "I promise I won't murder you and hide your body in a cave or harm you in any other oddly specific way you might come up with."

"That one I can blame on a paranoid younger sibling. She was certain I was going to be dismembered by a hobo and dumped in a cave."

That earned Ethan a raised eyebrow. "Like I said, oddly specific."

Things were quiet for a few moments, except for the thunder, the engine, the vents blowing, and his windshield wipers trying to beat themselves to death holding back the rain. Ethan jumped when Nick spoke up again.

"I can't be where I was anymore. I'm not fleeing a crime scene or anything."

The Outback's headlights swept over a road sign ahead of them, the giant white letters reflecting faintly as they got closer. Ethan giggled nervously, lifting a hand to point at the sign.

STATE CORRECTIONAL FACILITY AHEAD. DO NOT PICK UP HITCHHIKERS.

Nick's tired laugh sounded less painful this time. "Well, see? You picked me up a good five miles back, so we're golden."

"Geography saves the day." Ethan shivered as a drop of water rolled down his spine. The storm blew them down the road, farther from places neither of them could stand to be anymore.

Downtown Beaver, West Virginia, was so dark Ethan wondered if they'd lost power. Pitch-black hardware store, pitch-black diner, pitch-black something that looked like a liquor store. No streetlights, and the one stoplight was flashing yellow.

"I guess they roll up the sidewalks at five around here." Ethan slowed down at the stoplight, peering out between the windshield wipers. "I was really hoping for a place to stay and something to eat."

"There's a motel over there." Nick pointed down one of the cross streets.

Ethan pulled cautiously through the main intersection, heading toward the lighted sign he could barely make out through the rain. The lobby entrance was protected by a huge stucco overhang, and apparently it was the only place in town willing to waste money on excessive lighting. He felt like he was driving into an operating theater. The rest of the two-story motel stretched out on either side of the central lobby, doors facing into the parking lot. As only options went, it didn't seem *too* skeevy.

Nick reached for the door handle before the car had even stopped rolling. "Thanks for the ride. I really appreciate it." His other hand was curled around the strap of the backpack he'd tucked under his feet, and he looked ready to bolt.

"No problem. Really. Sorry I'm not going farther." Ethan put the car in park, letting it idle in the loading zone directly in front of the automatic glass doors to the lobby. "Um . . . Do you have somewhere to go tonight? I mean, somewhere to stay in town here? It's not any of my business. Just. Anyway. Do you?" Ethan examined the floor of his car, hoping a previously unnoticed black hole had opened and was ready to swallow him.

Nick hadn't been particularly forthcoming before, but now his face closed off entirely, expression going blank. "I'll be fine."

"Right. Okay." Where the *hell* was that black hole? "Good luck, then." Great. If Ethan got any more awkward, he wouldn't be able to walk without tripping over his own feet.

Nick opened the door the rest of the way and slipped out. "Thanks again." He shouldered his backpack, closed the car door, and disappeared into the darkness beyond the awning before Ethan had time to react.

"Yeah, no problem." Ethan shook his head, turned the car off, and pocketed the keys as he walked into the lobby.

The older man hunched over a newspaper, elbows on the desk, didn't bother looking up as the doors swished open. Ethan cleared his throat and finally got an annoyed glance.

"Kinda late to be getting a room."

Caught by surprise, Ethan bit his lip. "Yeah, I was supposed to be in Bristol tonight, but with the traffic and the storm . . ."

"Couple months late for the race, kid." At least the guy seemed vaguely amused now.

"I'm going to see the recording studios and stuff. It sounded like a cool place to stop." Ethan pulled his wallet out, flipping through to the shiny new airline-points card he'd gotten for the trip. "I'd like whatever your cheapest room is tonight, if you've got one free."

As far as Ethan could tell, all the rooms looked free, but pretending the guy was doing him a favor couldn't hurt. A few grunted questions and a swipe of his card later, he headed back out to his car and moved it a few spaces down to park in front of room 107.

His room was right next to the stairs up to the second level, and he could make out the bulk of an ice maker and a couple of vending machines in the wide pan of his headlights.

"Dinner is served," he muttered, killing the engine.

The rain marched a drumline over his head as he popped the hatch and reached into the back of the car for his bag. He dashed from the parking lot to the narrow concrete sidewalk, bag clutched protectively to his stomach while he hunched over to keep the worst of the damp off it. The limited protection of the second floor walkway above his door wasn't much against the gusting wind that seemed intent on pouring water down his neck. It was a relief to let himself into the cold, musty motel room.

The room itself was nothing to write home about. It held two double beds covered by scratchy polyester bedspreads, a counter-slash-table-slash-dresser on the opposite wall, and a TV older than Suze. There was a small closet next to the sink, and a door he hoped like hell was hiding a toilet and somewhere he could shower long enough to get warm. Something about sitting in damp clothes had gotten under his skin despite the warmth of late June.

With horror stories about bedbugs dancing in his head, Ethan hung his backpack on one of the weird nonremovable hotel hangers before going to investigate the shower. It looked clean, and there was free shampoo. Considering the state of the bathroom he shared with his younger brother and sisters at home, he wasn't going to complain. He left his wet clothing in the sink and stepped into the tub. A few seconds of fiddling with the taps managed to adjust the temperature to his liking, but there was no saving the pressure, which alternated between a half-hearted splash and a pulsing, needlelike spray. After he'd scrubbed enough to rid himself of the clammy feeling, he gave up and turned the shower off.

Once he'd accomplished warm and dry, his stomach pushed itself to the forefront. He couldn't even remember lunch, it had been so long ago. He skipped socks and shoved his feet into his tennis shoes, grabbed his wallet, then headed toward what was sure to be a delectable dinner of off-brand Doritos and stale cheez crackers. Sure, he had half a Trader Joe's in his trunk, but it was his first night out in the world as a semiadult. He didn't want to eat snacks his mommy had packed for him, no matter how plentiful.

The wind whipped the door out of his hand when he opened it, pushing him back into the motel. Head down, Ethan fought his way out into the cement wind tunnel. His room offered decent soundproofing, since he hadn't been able to tell it was still raining, much less that the wind and thunder had gotten worse. He'd stopped just in time, then. He tried not to imagine that the weather was telling him to go home.

As he fed a few slightly damp dollar bills into the vending machine, he silently thanked his older brother for giving him the roll of cash as a graduation present. Who knew there were still places that didn't take cards? Robert had probably meant for him to use the bills on lap dances by cute go-go boys, but oh well. Loaded down with dill pickle potato chips, Ho Hos, and strawberry licorice (because fruit!), he turned to walk back to his room and caught sight of a person huddled in the shelter provided by the partially enclosed staircase leading to the upper walkway. Between the ratty backpack and the purple hoodie, dark with rain, it didn't take a genius to figure out where "fine" had gotten Nick.

"Hey!" Ethan had to yell to be heard over the wind roaring through the breezeway. Nick either didn't hear him or hoped he'd go away. Dinner tucked in the crook of one arm, he climbed the stairs. Nick's shoulders shook, but that was about all the indication Ethan had that he wasn't dead.

"Nick?" Ethan touched Nick's shoulder lightly. "Are you okay?"

The kid who looked up from the depths of Nick's hood was missing all the anger and bravado that had marked his earlier departure. Nick's dark-blue eyes were bloodshot and ringed in the kind of purple bruises that only a lack of sleep or a heavy crying jag could cause. Ethan had seen his own in the mirror after more than a few sleepless, unhappy nights. Nick's knees were pulled up under his chin, and it seemed like only the bricks he was leaning against were keeping him upright. The startled, unseeing quality to Nick's expression made Ethan wonder if he even recognized him.

"Nick? Do you need help?"

Nick's throat worked, Adam's apple bobbing as his mouth opened, but no sound came for a moment. He finally seemed to look at Ethan, rather than through him.

"It's . . . It's my fucking *birthday*."

Ethan held his hand out, sympathy clawing through the cracks in his chest. "Come with me, okay? You can get warm inside, and we can celebrate."

Ethan thought Nick would refuse, was afraid he would, but he finally reached up. Hand wrapped around Nick's icy fingers, Ethan pulled him upright, tripping backward a step when Nick stumbled.

"Sorry," Nick muttered, voice barely audible over the drumming rain.

Ethan didn't let go, not with the way Nick was swaying. "Think you can make it down the hall?" He kept his voice deliberately light. "Trust me, you don't want to miss out on the spectacular accommodations here." One careful step, then another, watching to make sure Nick wasn't going to collapse on him.

When they finally arrived at his door, Ethan dropped Nick's hand long enough to fumble the key card out of his pocket. This time, the door flying open worked in his favor as he herded Nick through, then slammed it closed behind him.

The sudden silence felt like cotton in his ears, and he shook his head, groaning at the rain droplets that went flying. "I don't know about you, but I'm *done* with this weather."

Nick didn't answer him. The air conditioner was silent, and the only sound, aside from Nick's sodden clothes dripping on the floor, was the ragged breathing of someone trying desperately to remember how air worked.

Ethan dropped his food on the bed, maintaining a careful distance. Not too close, in case Nick was afraid of him—or people in general—but not too far away, in case . . . in case. He kept his voice calm and friendly, like all the voices he'd hated hearing but wouldn't have known what to do without. "I think maybe you're in shock. If I promise that you're safe here, would you feel comfortable taking a shower to warm up and putting on some dry clothes?" He flashed a smile at Nick, hoping it hid how freaked out he was. "If you want a reference, I can call my mom. She'll tell you about my merit badge in bugling and how many orphaned baby squirrels I tried to save when I was a kid."

His poor attempt at a joke earned a poor attempt at a smile, cut short by another aching breath and a sharp nod. "Okay. But I'm not a squirrel."

Ethan rubbed the tips of his fingers together, trying to keep himself calm. They couldn't *both* lose their shit. "That's true. Spiky hair, slightly upturned nose—you're clearly a hedgehog."

Nick's shudder started at the top of his head and rolled through him like an earthquake, but it seemed to leave him a little more grounded in its wake. "Been called a little prick before, but that's new." He edged around the bed, closer to the bathroom. "I'm . . . I'm going to lock the door."

It wasn't quite a question, despite the hesitation, but Ethan chose to treat it as one. "Yeah, of course. I mean, not that I would bust in to grab my toothbrush or anything. I'll leave you some clothes on the counter so you can put them on when you're done." He stayed in place, barely daring to breathe as Nick took the last few steps to the bathroom. He got another nod before Nick closed the door, followed by the unmistakable sound of the lock clicking into place.

Knees suddenly giving way, Ethan dropped onto the bed. This road trip was never going to be what he'd planned a million years ago, but this level of weirdness was a little more than he was prepared to deal with. Suddenly, calling his mom didn't seem like the worst idea.

Except it was. She'd make some reasonable argument about helping Nick by taking him to an ER or something, and Ethan would acquiesce to keep her from worrying. And sure, that would probably help future-Nick, but Ethan couldn't stomach the idea of leaving present-Nick somewhere to deal with whatever else fate wanted to hand out. The Nick showering in his bathroom had hollow eyes and that same need Ethan did—to get away, as far and as fast as he could. Ethan wasn't going to dump him somewhere, any more than he'd have left him on the side of the road. There was doing the smart thing, and then there was betrayal.

In the end, it was a sudden noise from the bathroom that unfroze him. He'd made that noise before, that choking drag of sound as fear and grief and nothingness scraped him hollow from the inside out. It didn't matter if he was fleeing or giving Nick some privacy. Either one got him out of the room, away from remembering how that sound felt. He barely remembered to toss a pair of sweats and a T-shirt on the counter next to the sink before he left.

He found himself standing in front of the vending machine again, feeding it bills and picking things that looked comforting or filling. A package of oatmeal cookies, a bag of nuts, and two Snickers bars. The drink machine supplied a couple of bottles of Coke. Ethan glanced up the now-empty stairs, biting his lip as he juggled the food around and fished another dollar out of his pocket. He added the package of chocolate cupcakes to the top of his pile and headed back to the room. Birthdays meant cake. It was the universal constant.

Or was that was gravity? Whatever.

Conversation with Scott Raines
Ethan: *I did it. I left home without you.*
Ethan: *I found this guy*
Ethan: *Which sounds weird, but I actually found him*
Ethan: *Like in the middle of the road during a torrential rainstorm*
Ethan: *I think he needs help*
Ethan: *You know how good I am at being there when someone needs me*
Ethan: *I miss you*
Ethan: *I don't know how to do this without you*
Ethan: *But I guess that's the point of trying*

CHAPTER Two

Beaver, WV

Nick stood under the inconsistent shower spray and tried to silence the countdown in his head. He got two minutes to shower. Two minutes under icy-cold water trying to leech away all the warmth in his body while he scrubbed his skin raw with powdered soap. Nobody bothered anybody in the showers—probably because it was nearly impossible to find your own dick when it had crawled back into your body to avoid frostbite.

All the scalding water in the world pouring down over him couldn't unclench his jaw as he shivered. Not until the countdown ticked through, and he could maybe convince himself that he wasn't *there* anymore. Ten seconds, nine, and the water would cut off. Tyler would drag him across the slick tile if he didn't move fast enough. Five seconds before he had to stake himself out in the locker room. End of the bench in the back row, on the aisle so he was in plain sight, but facing the back corner to make sure nobody was messing with the younger boys.

Tyler had reminded him of that on the way out. *"Who's going to keep them safe now? Your behavior is disappointing."*

With perfect hindsight, Nick thought, *Isn't that your job?* but for now there was hot water hitting his skin, and he was a second past the cutoff, and back to reality.

Reality, where he had nowhere to go and nobody who cared anyway.

Nick ducked his head under the water, leaning into the cold comfort of the tiled wall and burying his mouth against the crook of his arm. He wasn't sure the sound he made was even human, and he swallowed it as fast as he could. He knew better than to hand his weakness to anyone.

The shower felt safe, at least. He'd locked the door between the bathroom and his rescuer, and he still had his clothes. He'd be okay if he changed his mind and decided to make a run for it.

Nick let the water run over him for so long he couldn't tell if he'd zoned out or not. Eventually, he fumbled the little bar of soap open, scrubbing the institutional funk away and watching it swirl down the drain, gray and thin. The faucet spat out a few last, resentful drops of water as he turned it off and reached for the scratchy white towel that smelled overwhelmingly of bleach. At least that meant it was clean.

After shuffling across the tile floor using another towel as a bathmat, he knocked on the inside of the door. Sure, he could have put his cold, wet clothes back on, but now that he was warm, it really wasn't an enticing option. When no one answered, Nick cautiously unlocked it and stuck his head out, ready to slam it in Ethan's face if he was waiting to jump him. This was the danger zone: post-showers, pre-clothes. Maybe not here, but *there*, it was a vulnerability. And maybe here too. Nick didn't know anything about Ethan except he was too nervous to drive in a thunderstorm and his arm felt like a comforting anchor. So nothing, really—except that he didn't want to find out Ethan was after something he wasn't offering.

Ethan wasn't in the room when he looked out. There was a pair of sweatpants and a T-shirt waiting for him on the counter next to the door. Nick grabbed the clothes and ducked back into the bathroom to put them on behind a locked door.

The heat in the bathroom dissipated rapidly, and he was shivering by the time he pulled the shirt over his head. Unlike the towel, it smelled clean without burning his nose—fabric softener and detergent that hadn't come out of a fifty-gallon barrel.

A quick knock jarred him out of his laundry-induced fugue state. "Nick? Are you okay?"

"Fine," he said, twisting the doorknob. "Thanks for the clothes."

Ethan stepped back as the door opened, his hand dropping to his side as he smiled. "Awesome. You look like you feel a little better. Want something to eat?"

Nick's stomach lurched at the thought of food. It felt like months since he'd known the difference between hunger and nausea. Breakfast had been plain oatmeal forever ago, and lunch had been Tyler and Reverend Hill screaming in his face that he was wasting the lessons the program had taught him. Wasting his parents' money. Wasting the space he took up. Both had gone down about the same.

Ethan stood safely out of Nick's space, watching Nick with concern blooming on his face. "Hey," he said, so quiet it was almost a whisper. "I don't know what's going on for you, but whatever you need . . ." He trailed off, head tipping. "A lift somewhere? I'm not— I don't really have plans. So if you need to get home or something, I can help."

Nick's answering laugh felt less like it was crawling out of his throat this time. "I don't. I mean, I've got nowhere to be. I . . . Food sounds good." Maybe eating something would hold down the overwhelming panic. He could focus on the moment until he figured out if he had a future to worry about.

"Nowhere to be but here right now, since I've got a virtual cornucopia of deliciousness." Still keeping a safe distance, Ethan waved his hand toward the plethora of bright wrappers and two soda cans on the bed closest to the bathroom. "Take your pick."

Nick grabbed one of the sodas and a candy bar, then edged past Ethan to sit on the end of the other bed. He hadn't had any candy in months, soda in even longer. It didn't matter how oversweet they were. They were contraband, and they tasted all the better for it. He'd finished half the candy bar and a few greedy gulps of the soda before he even glanced up again. Ethan was holding a chocolate cupcake out to him with a single lit match shoved into the frosting.

"Happy birthday."

It sounded more like a question, the words turning the food already in his mouth to a lump of sawdust as he tried to swallow. Nick took another drink, then met Ethan's smile with one of his own. "Wow. I mean . . . Wow. Thank you." His perch on the mattress was suddenly precarious, the floor tilting when he tried to stand up.

Ethan met him halfway, crossing the short space between them and setting the cupcake in his hand. Nick blew the match out with a shaky breath, squeezing his eyes shut as he tried to remember what wishing felt like. "Fuck," he whispered, dropping his head to stare at the floor so Ethan wouldn't see him cry. Ethan took the soda from his limp fingers before he could drop it, and set it on the weird, flowery carpet near his feet. Nick stared at the cupcake, his eyes blurring. "*Fuck*."

He was too lost not to accept the hesitant touch of Ethan's hand curving around the back of his neck. Ethan's fingers ruffling through the short fuzz of his hair was the first kindness he'd felt in months, the first touch he'd wanted since before his parents had sent him away. He gulped air as greedily as he had the soda, and Ethan didn't ask him for anything else, stroking his head in accepting silence.

Eventually it became too much, got too close to the place inside him that wanted nothing more than to beg for any scrap of care he could get. Nick twisted his head away, holding the cupcake aloft between them with a smile that probably looked as forced as it felt. "There's usually two of these, right? We should share my birthday cake."

If Ethan was hurt by Nick pulling away, he hid it well. "Are you sure? I don't want to deprive you of any of the prepackaged artificially flavored goodness."

"I think I'll survive it." He took a tentative bite, chewing slowly. No sense admitting how good that prepackaged artificially flavored birthday cake was, and that was without the emotional wrapping. Nick watched Ethan pick up the other cupcake.

"I love these things," Ethan said around a mouthful of stale cake and cracked frosting. "It's like being six years old again or something."

"From all the crumbs, I take it being six was good."

Ethan brushed at the front of his T-shirt, face flushing a little. "I'm trying to stay young."

Nick grinned despite himself. "Here's to staying young forever." He might have been lost in his own head, but it was impossible to miss the way Ethan's open, cautiously happy expression clouded up for a second.

"It's not everything it's cracked up to be." Ethan glanced away for a second before shaking his head. "But I guess youth has some perks."

Nick had his doubts, but he had no problem keeping them to himself.

He finished his cupcake, swallowing around the thick lump in his throat. The cream filling left an oil slick on his tongue, and the unfamiliar grease felt cloying after going so long without. His stomach ached already, but his instincts warred with reality—if he didn't eat more now, he had no idea what might be available later. Digging through the pile of snacks, he chose a baggie of nuts. The plastic seam gave way when he tugged it open, peanuts spilling into his hands and serving as a convenient distraction while he tried to get himself together.

"I'm not crazy. I mean, I probably am, but not like this. Usually." Nick focused on splitting all the whole nuts into halves, chasing them around the palm of his hand so he wouldn't have to look at Ethan. "I think you're probably the only good thing that's happened to me today. Thanks." The speech left him almost too exhausted to chew, but at least Ethan didn't seem inclined toward more conversation, if the stunned look was any indication.

"I . . . Thank you?" Ethan smiled weakly. "Glad I could help?"

They both jumped as the room blazed bright and another clap of thunder rattled the glass in the windows. The lamp between the beds flickered dangerously as the thunder faded away, and Nick pointedly put his feet back on the floor, uncurling from his involuntary flinch.

"So, why were you driving through the middle of Nowhere, West Virginia, during this freak land hurricane?"

Ethan looked a little spooked, running a hand through his straw-blond hair. "Post-graduation, pre-college road trip. I was supposed to be in Bristol tonight, but traffic sucked so bad I decided to try back roads. Then it started to rain, and then I almost sideswiped a hitchhiker." Laughing ruefully, he shook his head. "If you add to that waiting six whole hours before breaking my solemn vow not to pick up any vagrants, I'm pretty sure it's the setup to a really terrible gross-out comedy."

"Or a really bad horror movie," Nick said without thinking. Trying to catch himself, he nodded toward his backpack. "Good thing I can't fit a chainsaw in there."

"Maybe not, but there's plenty of room for a meat hook and a couple of switchblades." Ethan lifted the bed skirt with his foot. "And plenty of room to store a body. I've read those urban legends. Unless you're planning on taking a kidney instead?"

His next rusty laugh came with the realization that it had been a while—sixteen months, five days, and eight hours a while—since he'd *felt* like laughing. "Was the ice machine working? I'd leave you in a tub of ice water. I'm not a *monster*, you know."

"That's so sweet." Waving a hand at the surfeit of snacks, Ethan did an impression of innocence. "I totally promise none of that candy was poisoned."

Nick shook a salt-covered finger at Ethan, his broken-down sense of humor kicking over in a feeble attempt at life. "High-fructose corn syrup is nothing to joke about. That stuff'll—"

Then the lights went out, a flare of blinding white searing through the room, burning everything into ghostly afterimages that danced across his vision in the dark, and whatever he'd been about to say turned into a stifled squawk of surprise. Terror, really, but it was his birthday, so he was going to be generous with his self-assessments.

"So I guess we're not watching *Colbert*." Ethan's voice floated out of the blackness somewhere to his right.

His own voice sounded thin and shaky to his ears when he replied. "Damn. I haven't seen that in . . . uh, a long time."

Ethan sounded cautious, but Nick only had his tone to go on in the pitch-black room. "It's not the same with him on network TV. I miss all the old Comedy Central stuff."

As disappointments went, it didn't even rank in Nick's top ten, but it still felt like another anchor had come unmoored. It wasn't the shows. It wasn't even that he hadn't watched TV or seen a movie for over a year. Mostly, he didn't know what he was going to tell people when they clued in to all his missing time. "Oh, I, uh, stay a couple of seasons behind on shows. Just a habit I got into when it seemed like everything I liked got canceled."

"I can actually see that. Maybe I should start doing that to save myself some grief."

Nick pictured Ethan nodding, the small line between his eyes already familiar enough to imagine. His own eyes had begun to adjust to the lingering darkness, but not enough to make out details. The block of dim ambient light on the far wall had to be the window, which was at least an upgrade from the dark rooms he was used to spending time in.

The sound of someone banging on the door was incongruous enough to stand out over the noise of the storm outside. The beam of a flashlight swung past the window, and the sudden rustle of fabric made Nick almost certain they had both jumped.

"Management! Power's out!"

"No fucking shit," Nick muttered.

Ethan giggled, the sound cutting off abruptly, like he'd covered his mouth.

"I've got a flashlight for you, if you want one."

Ethan moved past Nick, pausing before he got to the door. "You probably shouldn't be in here? Maybe?"

"Bathroom." Nick got to his feet, trying not to step on anything he'd want to eat later. The bathroom was pitch-black, even with the door cracked. He passed the time with his eyes closed, counting the seconds in silence by tapping his tongue against the back of his teeth.

The manager's voice was muffled, Ethan's slightly clearer, especially when he called, "Thanks, I'll get this back to you in the morning." The door closed with a solid *thunk*, followed by the sound of the chain lock sliding into place. "It's cool to come out now."

Nick stepped out into the blinding glare of a flashlight beam in his eyes.

"Shit, sorry!"

The light dropped down to the floor, illuminating a pack of cookies. Nick bent to pick it up, then held it out to Ethan. "If I give you these, will you promise not to blind me?"

"I think I can manage that. I'm really sorry." Ethan turned the light toward the wall. "I can do some shadow puppets to make it up to you."

Maybe it was the darkness, or the clarity of hiding in the bathroom. Nick shook his head, even though Ethan probably couldn't see it. "I can't tell you how much I appreciate the shower and the food, man. You're right though—I'm not supposed to be in here. You shouldn't start off your epic road trip by getting kicked out of a motel, so I'm gonna go."

"Nick." Ethan's disappointment and concern combined into a kind of sincerity Nick hadn't been faced with in years. Ethan had mom-voice down pat. "I wish you'd stay."

He'd been calm enough for the past few minutes, but panic didn't seem far off suddenly, and he scrambled for his backpack. "You don't want—"

"I wasn't supposed to be doing this alone." The shadows cast by the flashlight hollowed out Ethan's cheeks and turned his hair to ash, the raw note to his words sounding a little desperate. "My . . . Scott was supposed to come with me. I've got six siblings. I don't even know how to spend a *day* by myself, much less a month. Don't tell me what I want, okay? I want to know you're sleeping someplace warm and dry tonight. That's it."

Nick swallowed, his fingers tight around the nylon straps of his bag. "Why'd Scott ditch your trip? It sounds like fun."

Ethan looked away from him, the flashlight beam swaying across the floor as his shoulders slumped. "He died."

CHAPTER *Three*

Beaver, WV

The sun came through the opened curtains, hitting Ethan dead in the face, and he groaned and pulled a pillow over his head. He must've dropped off to sleep at some point during the night, hours after lying stiffly in bed, staring at the ceiling with dry, burning eyes. He suspected Nick had been awake every bit as late—he'd shared a bedroom enough in the past to know what someone's breathing sounded like when they were asleep.

It was quiet now, though. No breathing, no rustling. Ethan rolled over in a sudden panic. The other bed was empty. His feet hit the floor with a solid thump before he even realized he was moving. Two steps toward the door and he got tangled in the straps of Nick's backpack, and stumbled into the corner of the dresser. His knee connected with a *crack*, and for a second or two he couldn't catch his breath through the pain. He was still hobbling around between the beds, clutching his knee and cursing, when the door eased open and Nick slipped back into the room.

"Uh . . . food?" Nick held out a grease-stained fast-food sack like Ethan might bite off his hand. The smell of coffee wafting from the tray balanced against his hip made Ethan's mouth water.

"Food is good, but coffee is best." Ethan took the bag and set it down on the end of his bed, wiggling his fingers in the universal "gimme" gesture at the cups Nick was withholding.

"Oh. Oh!" Nick offered Ethan the tray and a smile that seemed bashful, before he ducked his head to stare at the floor. "Sorry, I didn't know if you'd want cream and sugar, so it's in the bag."

Ethan figured it was better to let Nick get over whatever was making him feel awkward, and he spent a good little while fixing his coffee. Truth be told, he wasn't at his best with eye goobers and a case of morning breath, and while coffee wouldn't fix either of those, it would at least give him something to do with his hands. "Thanks for getting breakfast. I mean, you could have woken me up. You didn't have to carry it back for me."

Nick shrugged from his cross-legged seat on his bed where he was picking open a sandwich wrapper and looking faintly guilty about it. "It's okay. I'm used to being awake really early, and I didn't want to wake you before the sun was up. Didn't seem like a good idea, the way you were snoring." He looked up long enough to grin. "I went for a walk and found food while I was out. I thought you'd probably be hungry after dinner from the vend-o-rama."

"So you're really not an escaped convict?" Ethan gulped down a mouthful of surprisingly warm coffee, waving his hand in small circles while he swallowed. "If you're showing your face on the security feed at Hardee's, I mean."

"I told you—carnies on my tail. I'm safe as long as I don't try to win anyone a stuffed animal."

"That's too bad." Ethan sighed, shaking his head. "I really had my eye on a giant pink unicorn. Guess I'll have to take a chance on my own skills."

The sandwich in front of Nick was untouched, though Nick kept fussing with the wrapper. Ethan tried to figure out what could be causing his reluctance, eventually coming down to the single cup of coffee. That he was drinking, instead of Nick. "Did I take your coffee? Dude, I'm sorry. You should have said."

Nick's head snapped up. "What? No, I'm not allowed to have coffee. It's fine. I bought it for you. I got orange juice too, if you want that."

"'Not allowed'? Are you Mormon?" He knew before he was even done asking the question that his eyebrows were squinching together in an expression that Robert said made him look like a constipated golden retriever. "I mean, that's cool."

"Uh, no." Nick didn't elaborate, but there was no mistaking his puzzled expression.

The other option sent off warning bells in Ethan's head. He was notoriously bad at judging age . . . He'd once insulted Robert's girlfriend-of-the-day by thinking she was his mom's friend. It would be his luck that Nick was an underage runaway from some controlling backwoods militant family that would end up coming after him with a shotgun.

Nick gave him one of those half smiles. "Just because I'm not going to drink it doesn't mean you can't."

"Right, yeah. More caffeine for me." Ethan took a sip to appease Nick, then gestured at Nick's rapidly cooling breakfast with the cup. "You're allowed to eat though, right?"

"I . . . Yeah. Yeah, I am." Nick finally took his first bite, and the look of blissful concentration on his face was uncomfortably interesting. Ethan did his best not to imagine how that kind of focus would translate to things that weren't dripping with cheese.

However reticent to eat it, Nick definitely hadn't held back when he'd ordered breakfast. Ethan helped himself to a sandwich and some hash browns, eating them slowly while Nick polished off another sandwich, two breakfast burritos, and something that looked like a mutant cinnamon roll.

There had definitely been sausage in the two burritos, so that knocked out a strict orthodox Jewish sect. Not Mormon, not Jewish . . . and guessing Nick's background had somehow become a game. Maybe one Ethan could keep playing, because he couldn't imagine what Nick was going to do here in Beaver. He waited until Nick swallowed his last bite before saying anything.

"Ever been to Bristol? Which, now that I say it out loud, sounds like the worst pickup line ever." Ethan shook his head, running his hands over the scratchy motel quilt. "How about it, though?"

Nick tilted his head, watching Ethan for a beat before he answered. "Sir, are you asking me to straddle state lines with you? We've only just met."

"No, no! Of course not. No straddling on a first date. I was thinking about using the HOV lanes, and I left my blow-up doll at home."

"I don't need to know about your kinky sex habits. At least not on that first date."

So far, so good. Nick was joking, but not outright refusing Ethan's offer. Ethan wasn't sure why he cared so much, but he did. It wouldn't be right abandoning Nick; there was something entirely too vulnerable about him. Walking away wasn't an option.

Nick rubbed his head, looking hesitant but hopeful. "That would be awesome. You're sure you don't mind me tagging along?"

"If you want, you can think of it as balancing the car." Ethan concentrated on cleaning all the ketchup out from under his fingernails. "Maybe it'll stop me from turning around and going home because I'm too chickenshit to make it by myself."

Nick crumpled his wrappers and got to his feet to retrieve the empty paper bag. On his way to the trash can, he patted Ethan's shoulder gently. "You rescued a stranger in the middle of a hurricane. Twice in one night, even. That's something, but it's not chicken. I'll go check if my clothes are dry, then I'm good for whatever."

The words warmed Ethan, and he stared after Nick with a big stupid grin on his face. He was pleased enough that he kept cracking a smile without warning while he got ready, dripping foamy white toothpaste into the sink and splashing soapy water into his mouth accidentally. He'd recovered by the time Nick came back, dressed in his own clothes and looking a little worse for wear.

Nick brushed ineffectively at the wrinkles in his shirt. "Turns out this fine establishment doesn't provide an iron."

Ethan pursed his lips, giving Nick a critical once-over. "Are you okay riding in the back seat? Or maybe the trunk? With a blanket over your head to hide your shame, of course."

Hefting his backpack, Nick shrugged. "Sure. I mean, you've got to have standards."

"At least one of us does." Ethan unhooked the chain on the door, swinging it open and standing aside for Nick to go out first. "Shit, wait." He darted back inside and grabbed the loaned flashlight off the nightstand. He brandished it at Nick as he stepped outside. "Don't want to get charged for this or anything, since I'm guessing I could buy a dozen at Home Depot for the markup."

Last night's storm had blown itself out, leaving sunshine and cooler temperatures. Ethan shivered a little in his T-shirt as he unlocked the car door. "I might have to take that blanket back."

"Wait, you don't have heated seats? I'm rethinking this friendship already."

Ethan opened the back door on the driver's side and tossed his bag onto the seat. Nick was surveying the parking lot, one hand over his eyes to shield them from the morning sun. His dark buzz looked wet where the light hit it, and his shoulders were thrown back as he stared up at the sky.

Ethan followed his gaze. "If you're watching for incoming helicopters hunting you down, can you let me know now? I'd like advance warning so I can hide." He was kidding. Kind of.

"The carnies don't have that kind of budget. But the Quaker mafia . . . that's a different story. That oatmeal is big business."

It had to be his job not to laugh. If they were going to do this, he needed to treat the absurd like a friend. Pursing his lips to keep from breaking into a smile, Ethan made a noise of agreement. "I thought all that fiber would keep things on an even keel, but I guess not. I have to go check us out." He paused, one hand resting on the top of the car while he tried to keep his voice light. "Don't get kidnapped by the Amish or whoever while I'm gone, okay?"

There was a different person working when he dropped the key card and flashlight on the counter, a smiling woman who didn't look like she'd lost her sense of humor in 1978. He waited while she printed out his receipt, and his eyes lit on a rack of postcards in the niche that served as a gift shop. He gave the rack a spin until he found one that said *Hello From Beaver, WV!*

The hotel employee finished his paperwork, and Ethan hesitated for a second before picking up the card and carrying it to the counter. If he was going to use this trip as a chance to let go of a future he didn't have anymore, maybe he needed to do something he was afraid of. Something that *wasn't* texting Scott's old number, waiting for an answer he knew would never come. "I'll take this too, if that's okay. Do you guys sell stamps?"

She smiled at him in the dubious way of all customer-service employees who *could* do something, but really didn't want to. "I'm sure I've got one around here somewhere. You need me to add them to your bill?"

"I can pay cash if that's easier. I want to send a postcard to . . ." Ethan hesitated for a second, at a loss for what to call Scott's mom now that Scott wasn't there to connect them anymore. "My aunt. She likes getting mail."

"Whatever you want, sweetheart. Why don't you write your card and leave it with me, and I'll put it out with our mail later?" Her tone took on a friendlier lilt, one he recognized from countless relatives and acquaintances of his parents', who all thought he was "such a nice boy."

Ethan smiled at her, willing to benefit from her indulgence. "Thank you. I'll be done in a minute."

If he thought too hard about what to write, he'd never do it at all. Gripping the hotel pen, he scratched out a message to Scott's parents and thrust it back across the counter. "Thanks," he said around the strange catch in his throat and fled back outside.

Dear Mrs. Raines,
We got lost on the way to Bristol.
I wish he was here.
Love,
Ethan

To say he was relieved to find Nick sitting in the car when he got back was an understatement. He apparently didn't hide it very well, either.

Nick raised an eyebrow as Ethan slid into the driver's seat. "Did you get the room comped?"

"No, why?"

"You look really cheerful. Thought maybe you got the room free because there was no cable."

Ethan started the car before replying. "I'll have you know it takes more than something that pedestrian to make me happy. I've got standards."

Nick snorted. "Given the fact that you pick up strangers, I'm not sure they're particularly *high* standards..."

The silence was oddly comfortable as Ethan navigated the confusing array of one-way streets that would eventually get them out of town.

"So was there an overarching theme to this epic road trip? Food? Music, since Bristol's the next stop?" Nick asked as they spotted a sign for 81.

Ethan gripped the steering wheel tight enough to hurt, then forced himself to unclench his fingers. "I wouldn't go that far. We..." He trailed off, caught in the memory of afternoons sprawled on the floor with maps and Scott's laptop. "We planned it out pretty extensively, but I don't know that we had a theme." Keeping his eyes straight ahead made it easier to talk. "Food, yeah. And those crazy things you see in the Weird America books."

"I've always wanted to go to the House on the Rock." Nick sounded almost wistful.

"Neil Gaiman fan?" Ethan glanced over in time to catch Nick nodding. "Cool. We definitely had a Wisconsin swing-by planned on the way back."

"Anything else cool on the agenda?"

"There's this creepy-ass Clown Motel in Nevada that overlooks an old cemetery. Because, y'know, who doesn't want to have the shit scared out of them? That one was more me than Scott. He was all about the six-ton prairie dog in South Dakota."

"That, uh . . ." Nick's lips twitched in a grin. "That sounds interesting. It's not edible, is it?"

"Oh my God, I can't imagine anything more disgusting."

"My mom's from Peru. We went to visit once and got to dress up guinea pigs in tiny costumes. Then we ate them. I went vegetarian for a month."

"Whoa, wait. You dressed them up and then *ate* them?"

"Well, they weren't the *same* guinea pigs."

Ethan turned to stare. "That's cold. My sister has guinea pigs . . . They're cute. You shouldn't eat cute things."

"Piglets are pretty cute, but bacon is tasty. Therefore, tasty trumps cute." Nick's hand slipped over his shorn hair, like maybe he didn't quite know where it had gone, or what to do without it. "Besides, I didn't know ahead of time. My cousins thought it was hilarious."

Ethan snorted. "That sounds like cousins." His own had pulled some epic shit over the years.

"So, Tennessee?" Ethan toyed with his phone, ready to plug anything Nick said into the GPS. There were dozens of places he'd planned to go, but he got the feeling Nick wasn't enjoying the same sense of freedom he was. It seemed more like Nick felt lost. Ethan knew from experience that any direction was good when you were lost, just to keep moving.

Nick dropped his hand from his hair to his lap, curling it around the strap of his backpack. "Sure. Wherever."

Ethan smiled as he started the navigation app, ignoring the unread texts from his mom. The car felt more balanced with someone weighing down the passenger seat, and the road out of town beckoned.

CHAPTER *Four*

Bristol, TN

Nick passed his phone from hand to hand, catching his thumb on the power button every so often but not turning it on. Hell, it had been sixteen months since he'd charged it, so he probably couldn't turn it on if he wanted to. Ethan was focused on the road, fingers tapping along to music in his head, and he started a little when Nick cleared his throat to break the silence.

"Can I borrow your phone charger?"

"Oh, sure." Ethan freed a hand from the wheel and reached for the cord dangling from the front of his aftermarket stereo. Nick took it gingerly, raising an eyebrow at the pink electrical tape wound around it like Band-Aids in a couple of places.

"Did the dog try to eat it?" He slotted the cord into place and the phone buzzed in his hand as the battery indicator started filling up.

Ethan snorted. "No, my nieces, actually. My brother Robert told me it was my own fault for letting them near anything they could chew on." He looked over at Nick for a second, the same polite curiosity he'd been restraining since they met washing over his face again. "If you need to make a call before it charges, you're welcome to use my phone."

Nick shook his head, looking out the window to avoid meeting Ethan's eyes. "Nobody to call, but thanks." No guarantee that someone wouldn't try to call him, though . . . He doubted Tyler was going to let go that easy. Nick quickly thumbed off the ringer.

When Ethan's phone rang instead, they both jumped. Ethan took his eyes off the road long enough to glance at the screen and sighed. "Sorry, I need to take this."

"Yeah, no problem. I think I can keep myself entertained for a few minutes."

"Good to know." Ethan laughed, then answered the phone. "Hey, Suze. What are you doing calling now? Aren't you in nerd class?"

Nick felt weird listening in on the conversation, but it wasn't like he could step out or something. Of course, it probably felt weird because he was super tuned-in to privacy. Funny how a complete lack of it for over a year did that to you.

"Of course I'm still alive. And no, I haven't picked up any dangerous vagrants." Ethan glanced over at Nick and winked.

Nick stifled a snicker and nodded. "Your secret's safe with me," he mock-whispered.

Ethan rolled his eyes, continuing. "Yeah, I'm sorry I didn't call last night. I know I promised." He paused, a guilty look crossing his face. "I didn't mean to scare you. You still can't have my room. There was a really bad storm, and it got me all off-kilter . . ."

It was Nick's turn to feel guilty. Just because he didn't have family worrying about him didn't mean other people didn't, and it wasn't the storm that had kept Ethan from checking in. That blame rested solidly on him.

"Yup, I'll call tonight so you and Mom don't worry. Now put your phone away and get back to designing killer robots. Love you too, brat. Talk to you soon." Ethan set the phone back in the console, then turned to give Nick a rueful grin. "Remind me to call home tonight? It might keep them from sending the state police after me."

"Only until they find out you *did* pick up a vagrant."

"Damn, good point. Can you keep the Beyoncé lip-synching to a minimum while I talk to them? That might help."

"When the Bey fills you, you can't contain it." Nick stuck his tongue out, shimmying his shoulders in a horrible seat-dancing approximation of all the single ladies. "Maybe you should set an alarm."

"Probably a good idea. Nice moves there, Queen B." Ethan wiped the screen of his phone on his jeans and held it out to Nick between his fingers. "Sure you don't need to call anyone? I'm not trying to push or anything . . . There's got to be someone worried you didn't come home last night."

Nick hadn't been home in over a year. He wasn't even sure he was welcome there anymore, especially after ditching out on the Camp Calamity experience. No, actually he was pretty damn sure he *wasn't* welcome. But it hadn't felt like home for a lot longer than that, not with Drew gone.

Nick took the phone anyway, staring at the screen as he mumbled an answer. "I want to tell you something better than the truth. The truth has never worked for me. But I don't want you to feel like you can't trust me."

"So lie to me."

Nick turned to look at Ethan fast enough that his neck twinged, and he found the same careful, worried expression he'd been getting used to for the past twelve hours. He pursed his lips but wasn't sure how to reply, and after a long, silent minute, Ethan repeated it.

"I'm serious. Lie to me. There's shit you don't want to talk about, but maybe you still want to *talk*, so make it up as you go along. Make it better." Ethan stared out the windshield, giving Nick a view of his throat as he swallowed hard. "I think I could use the same out sometimes."

Nick tapped Ethan's phone on his knee, rolling it from side to side. "I can't go home because I'm a spy. I'm with the Canadian Intelligence Agency, and I've been working deep undercover with the maple syrup cartels. It's very hush-hush."

Ethan snorted. "Thank God you told me. That Quaker-mafia story was a little hard to believe, man."

"Laugh it up. I'll be checking the trunk for contraband grade B. And woe unto you if I find anything, because I'll have to take you in. Trust me, you don't want to spend time in a Canadian prison. The only TV channel shows 24/7 Hockey Night in Canada."

"I play hockey. Maybe I'd fit right in." The clicking of the turn signal punctuated Ethan's exaggerated eyebrow wiggling as they passed a Honda plastered with NRA stickers. "Maybe I'm from *Vermont*."

"Shit. Well, I guess my cover is blown, so I'd better head south." Nick set Ethan's phone in one of the cup holders between their seats. "I'm going to have to ask you to pull over, sir, so I can exit the car."

"Oh, sorry, this is the Bristol express. No stops until we see a building shaped like a guitar."

"You might regret that more than me, but it's your upholstery. Since we're going that way, who's your favorite country singer?"

Ethan shuddered. "I hate country music."

"You hate . . . You *do* realize that Bristol is the birthplace of country music? Seems a little weird to be making the trek if you hate the music."

Silence stretched on for several long seconds, Ethan staring straight ahead. "Actually, June Carter is my great-grandmother. I'm making the trip in her memory. Promised her over Silver's body."

"Silver was the Lone Rang— I don't think . . ." Nick reached for his phone. A few moments later, he located the track he wanted and music filled the car. "Might as well listen to your great-grandpa."

Nick let Johnny Cash lead them a little farther down the highway, watching covertly as Ethan's grip on the steering wheel relaxed from bruising to merely firm. Rolling his music into shuffle mode, he bumped the volume down a couple of notches, low enough he could be heard over it.

"How 'bout you take the same deal you offered me, okay? Lie to me. If it gets too big. Tell as much of the truth as you can, and just lie about the rest."

Ethan tipped his head back against the headrest, pushing his straw-blond hair up as he sank lower in the seat and snorted. "What, did you think I was really related to June Carter? She was the only name I could remember from the stupid website Scott made me look at." Heaving a sigh, he sat up straight again, eyes dead ahead on the road. "Thanks. You might have to keep reminding me. I'm much better at the 'bottle shit up and smile' version of lying."

"We can remind each other. The next time you need to start talking about dead, stuffed horses, I'll be sure to tap you out." Nick hoped it would be easier to spot in someone else than in himself, especially since he'd been through the "repress it and shut the fuck up" school of training himself. He couldn't remember how many times

Tyler had put him on voice restriction for disrupting the therapeutic environment.

"Scott was a big country-music fan," Ethan said to the road in front of them. "Old stuff, mostly, but new stuff that sounded old too. Bluegrass, folk music. He could play the banjo." His lips curved in a smile that looked sad around the edges. "He was a huge dork."

Nick was quiet, weighing his words, wanting something that wasn't a platitude. "How long were you guys friends?"

Tapping his fingers on the steering wheel, Ethan didn't answer him for a second. "Practically forever. We met the first day of kindergarten, and we got married by the end of recess on the second day."

He couldn't help the laugh that burst out of him, but he suspected Ethan was hoping for one anyway. "Well, it's good you waited. You don't want to rush into a relationship."

Ethan's fingers stilled, his smile stretching and pushing a dimple into the cheek Nick could see. "Yeah, well, it still took us until we were fourteen to figure out there was probably a reason neither of us ever wanted to kiss Amy Nakamura." Ethan glanced nervously in Nick's direction. "You're, uh, not going to turn out to be some militant church person or something, are you? My mom always warned me I talk too much." Ethan's smile dimmed noticeably.

Out of all the things Ethan could have confessed, that wasn't one Nick had expected. "No," he said, quick enough that he almost stumbled over the words. "Not at all. It, uh, would be kind of self-defeating?"

Nick hadn't meant for it to sound like a question, but he'd never been the second person in a car to come out.

"Huh." Eyebrows pinching together, Ethan bit his lip before saying anything else. "You're not . . . Your parents . . . You didn't get kicked out on your birthday because you're gay, did you? Or, I mean, bi or trans. Or whatever."

"I can honestly say, being queer is the least of my problems at the moment." It wasn't funny, or it shouldn't have been, but suddenly Nick felt a giggle bubbling out, followed by another, until he was stifling a horrible, wheezy gale of strained laughter. "Oh my God, Tyler would die if he heard me say that."

"Who's Tyler?"

That brought a swift end to his mirth. "Eh, just this asshole I used to know."

Ethan shot him another sideways glance. "Carnie?"

"Guy who ran the funhouse. Super creeper." Exhaling slowly, Nick linked his fingers together and pushed out to stretch his arms. They passed a sign, and he tried not to feel like the miles left between them and Bristol were going by too fast. "Hey, I think our exit is coming up." The pang of regret when Ethan nodded and moved over a lane was crazy. They weren't going to keep driving forever.

"Lie to me," Ethan had said. Nick plastered on a smile and returned to swiping through his music. "I'm looking forward to seeing the giant guitar."

There. He could lie with the best of them.

Downtown Bristol was cute. Quaint? Pretty, anyway, and there were a lot of cool brick buildings. Ethan snapped pictures of a couple of them and of the sign in front of the Bristol-Taylor Hat Company declaring it the birthplace of country music. He texted one to his mom and dad, and a goofy picture of himself kissing a brass dog statue to Suze.

Suze: *How'd u get som1 so cute to kiss u*

Ethan: *Shared my snausages*

Suze: *Ur gross*

His snort of laughter earned a raised eyebrow from Nick, and Ethan waved his phone. "One of my sisters. Kids these days got no respect for their elders. It's sad."

"'One of'? How many sisters do you have?"

That, at least, was something Ethan felt okay talking about. Mainly because it came up in almost every conversation he had with a new person, and familiarity was comfortable. "Four sisters, two brothers, three older siblings, three younger." He waited for the shocked exclamation, usually followed by the Catholic question.

"Wow, the wait for a bathroom in your house must be as bad as a Nationals game."

"At least the floors are cleaner." His phone slid easily into the back pocket of his jeans, and he noticed Nick noticing. Words poured out of him to cover for the flustered feeling in his stomach. "It wasn't bad once my older siblings moved out. My oldest sister, Clara, is ten years older than me; Whitney's eight; and my brother Robert is almost six. I was supposed to be the baby, until Suze showed up accidentally seven years after me. I guess Mom and Dad figured they might as well see if they could fill out a full baseball team, so David and Janey came after her." He scratched the back of his head, shrugging. "It's loud. But fun. It's weird being the youngest, the oldest, and the middle child, all to different members of my family."

"I . . . Wow." *There* was the stunned look Ethan had been expecting, but then Nick laughed. "That's a hell of a lot of responsibility for one person. A lot of pressure."

Except he'd always had Scott, and he'd never had to be anything to Scott but Ethan. He didn't know how to explain that, though.

He jumped when Nick bumped his arm, focusing on the world around him again. "Sorry—"

Nick cut him off, shaking his head. "Hey, Ethan? Lie to me."

He took a deep breath, then exhaled slowly. "Dude, look at these shoulders." He pretended to flex. "Standing up under all that pressure has made me almost a superhero. Where else can you get a body like this?"

"Abercrombie & Fitch material, for sure."

Nick's appraising look made Ethan laugh, at least until he remembered they were standing on a street corner in Tennessee. "Uh, maybe eye-fucking me in the street isn't a great idea. I'd rather not get arrested on the second day of my trip."

"*Pffft.* They have *NASCAR* here. *Eye*-fucking is probably the least of what this street has seen." Jumping onto the low wall of the planters that lined the street, Nick held out his arms and tiptoed across the narrow brick ledge. "At least we're sober."

"For another two years, as far as my parents know," Ethan said solemnly.

Nick's steps faltered, his shoulders hunching before he regained his balance and spun around to face Ethan. Ethan folded his arms, watching the lowbrow circus performance and wondering if there might be a little truth to the whole carnie thing. The look on Nick's face was hard to place, but Ethan settled on pained, and he was offering an out before he knew it. "Your turn. Lie to me."

Nick hopped back and forth, switching feet as he jumped from brick to brick, and his voice dipped as he moved. "I have absolutely, positively, never been so drunk I forgot my own name. *Or* public decency laws."

"You should probably talk to Robert, then. He's pretty sure I'm going to do both, and he'll be stuck bailing me out." There was nothing wrong with inserting a little truth into the conversation. "You can be the good influence I'm so sadly lacking in my life."

"I don't think so." Nick held his hands up. "That would be a spectacularly bad idea."

"Damn it. I always have to play good cop."

They slowly meandered toward the end of town, Nick jumping up and down off the long planter as it suited him. Sometimes they commented on bits of musical interest, sometimes they were silent for long stretches. His mom and sisters would have loved the place, full of kitschy boutiques and tiny cafés, but other than a music store Nick seemed interested in, and a bookstore filled with little kids in paper crowns, Ethan didn't feel a huge pull to spend a ton of time in Bristol.

Nick looked up from the record-store window, his fingers ghosting across the glass as he turned back toward Ethan. "So what do you think? Is Bristol everything you thought it would be?"

"I think I'm missing most of what makes it cool, honestly. I mean . . ." Ethan stopped himself, the sudden, infuriating ache of missing Scott hitting him like a blow. "I don't know what he wanted to feel while he was here. I . . . I think I'm fucking it up."

"You can't . . ." Nick paused, seeming to weigh his words. "You can't live what someone else wanted. Or feel what they would've felt. And as much as it sucks, that's okay."

"It's *not* okay! It wasn't supposed to be like this. We were going to do this *together*!" Ethan had to fight through the words. "Without him, it . . . Fuck." Ethan shrugged angrily. "It doesn't matter."

The same hand Nick had trailed longingly over the music-store window fell lightly on his arm, squeezing so briefly Ethan barely registered its presence before it was over.

"Are you looking for him here? Are you trying to figure out how to keep him in your life?"

Ethan sucked in a breath. He'd heard some version of that question from his parents for over a year, but it had never hurt as much as it did now. Maybe because it was coming from an outsider, and that suddenly made it real, instead of his family trying to make him "better."

"I don't know if I want my life to happen without him," he whispered around the lump in his throat, finally saying out loud what he never could to his family, his friends, or the disastrous therapist he'd hated on general principle.

"Well, that sucks," Nick said succinctly, without trying to talk him out of it.

Ethan pulled up a smile. "It fucking does. Know what else does? The fact that the ice cream truck only plays music when it's out of ice cream."

"Is that a hint that it's time for ice cream?"

"It's always time for ice cream. I once hiked to Dairy Queen in the middle of a snowstorm to get a cherry Blizzard."

"As you do. Looks like there's an ice cream place up the street. Loser has to buy." Nick took off, Ethan's outraged cry chasing him down the block.

CHAPTER *Five*

Bristol, TN

"So where are you heading next?" A drip of cherry-chocolate fudge graced Nick's chin, tempting enough that Ethan almost reached over to wipe it away. Almost. The imperfection made it easier to believe Nick wasn't a hallucination he'd cooked up to counter his own loneliness. The trash next to the curb they were sitting on helped a little too.

He only realized he'd been staring for too long when Nick tapped his hand. "I didn't realize it was that hard a question. Should I start with something easier?"

"Uh, sorry," Ethan said quickly. "You're going to laugh, but it's Dollywood."

Nick put a slender hand to his chest, fingertips pressed over the faded band logo. "I would *never* mock a man's sincere affection for Dolly Parton. What kind of jerk do you think I am?"

"Good to know. I'd hate to think you were secretly judging me." He sighed, pulling back the chocolate-soaked napkin wrapped around his cone. "I'd rather see the *Titanic* reenactment."

"There's a *Titanic*— Never mind. You want to see that, then you should see it." Nick nodded decisively. "In all its morbid glory. Does the band play while the ship pretends to sink?"

"Want to come with me and find out? We could probably squeeze it in after Dollywood."

It looked like Nick had a sudden brain freeze, the way his face wrinkled up, but it didn't stop him from taking another bite of his ice cream. He shook his head, rubbing a hand over his short hair before he spoke. "Ethan. Do *you* want to go to Dollywood?"

He froze too. Suddenly it was easier to look anywhere except at Nick. "I can do both."

"But do you *want* to do both?"

"I turned down a multibillion-dollar contract on the pro lacrosse tour to make this trip. They're holding a spot for me, but I have to join them by December first, or it drops to a multimillion." Ethan pointed at Nick. "And I had to promise to give up dairy, so if you could avoid mentioning this little slipup, I'd really be in your debt."

"Silence is golden." Nick stood in one smooth motion, leaving him behind on the curb. "I kind of thought the point of lying to each other was that we didn't lie to ourselves."

Ethan crammed another bite into his mouth to avoid answering, even though it didn't seem like Nick was demanding he recant. Probably good, since he didn't have the words for it.

"Anyway, you don't owe me an explanation for where you want to go. You've been way more awesome than the average hitchhiker has any right to expect." The obscene slurping noises Nick made as he sucked melted ice cream out of the remains of his cone had to be for show, but Ethan snickered obligingly anyway. Nick dumped the last little stump of cone, over Ethan's squawk of protest. "I don't like the glue-y parts." He shrugged, shoving his hands into his pockets. "Come on, I'll take a picture of you straddling the state line. I have to get my backpack out of your car before you leave anyway."

"You want to take the keys and grab whatever you need out of your backpack? I'll get a couple more pictures and wait for you here. And properly finish my ice cream."

Their fingers touched when Nick took the keys from Ethan's outstretched hand, and Nick pulled away like he'd touched a hot stove. "I'll be right back." He spun on one heel and headed down the block, stopping a few steps away to look back over his shoulder. "You know, you really shouldn't hand your car keys to strangers. I'm just saying."

Ethan resisted the urge to stick his tongue out. There was a limit to his immaturity, it turned out, despite Robert's belief to the contrary. "I wouldn't say you're a stranger. Strange, yeah, but not a stranger."

Nick flipped him off from behind his back and kept walking, but Ethan heard him laugh.

The ice cream lost its appeal now that he was alone. He dumped the rest of his cone in the trash and dragged a napkin through the mess he'd undoubtedly made on his face. His mom swore he'd never once eaten ice cream without wearing half of it.

"What the hell am I doing?" He turned in a slow circle, surveying the street around him while the dizzying, unmoored feeling he'd been swimming in for the past year tunneled his vision down to a narrow window. Smaller and smaller, until all he could see was a slice of the street so thin that it cut a woman with a camera in half.

Swallowing hard over the ice cream that wanted to crawl back up his throat, Ethan closed his eyes.

"Are you all right?"

The unexpected voice sounded like a shot, and the hand on his arm broke the last thin strand of control. He made an inarticulate sound and flung himself backward, barely aware of the wide-eyed shock on the older woman's face, her own hands flying up to ward him off.

Run. He needed to run. With the panic attack. Away from it. Through it. Toward the one bit of stability pure chance had thrown his way. He took looping, stumbling steps away from the mumble of voices behind him, toward the car, and Nick. Vision still a tight corridor in front of him, he made it half a block before he had to stop and catch his breath.

"Fuck, fuck, fuck." Hands on his knees, Ethan let the mantra run through him. Not the one the therapist had suggested, but nothing made him feel less in control than talking to himself in the middle of a panic attack. At least if he was swearing, people thought he was angry, not crazy. Once his breath had slowed, he started walking, deliberately placing his feet as a meditation using his body until he spotted his car at the end of the block.

Nick slammed the car door, backpack in hand, and looked up, startled, as Ethan stopped in front of him. "I was kidding about stealing the car."

"I—" Ethan took another breath, leaning forward to brace himself against the car. "I was afraid you were going to leave."

Nick's guilty look said it all.

"You were." Ethan's voice sounded strangely flat, even to his own ears.

"I was going to leave your keys on the tire and a note under your wiper. I wouldn't have made you look for—"

"You were going to *leave*," Ethan said, a high, frantic lilt on the last word. Self-loathing swamped him, his heart beating a counterpoint against the repulsive tide of desperation he'd been holding off since . . . since Scott had left. Since Scott had died. Sometimes he didn't remember if there was a difference. "What did I do?"

Nick crossed both arms over his stomach, cradling his bag like a shield. "'Do'? You didn't do anything wrong, dude. You've got a whole summer planned out, all kinds of stuff to do, and this is as good a place as any for me to get lost." Nick glanced down at his scuffed backpack, hefting it a little higher before he looked up. "This is it. I've got twenty bucks, a change of underwear, and a cell phone with no charger." A tremulous smile stole across his mouth, a flash of humor sparking in his dark-blue eyes. "And I cheated when I raced you for ice cream so you'd have to buy."

"The only thing I've got is this stupid fucking trip that was supposed to be . . . be everything we ever wanted. Years in the making. The stuff everybody wishes they'd done. And now it's nothing." Ethan angrily wiped a hand across his eyes. Of all the times to lose his shit, this one ranked among the worst: when he desperately needed to get his point across. "At least it felt like nothing, until you jumped out in front of my car."

Nick snorted but remained thankfully silent otherwise.

"Then it kinda meant something again, like maybe it could be fun. Like I still had a reason to go on. So if you could not get lost, that would be really great."

Except Nick looked terrified, backpedaling a step as Ethan fought down his stupid, stupid *feelings*.

"I'm not anybody's reason to go on. We barely even know each other!"

"I know, I know. Fuck. I meant . . ." Exposed and inept, Ethan's life sheltered at Scott's side suddenly felt less like a blessing. "I meant go on the trip. Because, look, it's only been a day, and I already met someone interesting." Ethan sucked his upper lip into his mouth, teeth making sharp impressions while he wavered between the truth and something that let him seem a little less pathetic. "Come on—if you ditch me, the odds of me picking up a hitchhiker who kills me in an oddly specific way are only going to go up. Can you live with that kind of guilt?"

Nick didn't laugh, but he stopped backing away, and Ethan counted that as a win.

"I swear I'm not crazy. Or as pitiful as I seem. I'm lonely. My best friend died, and he was always the one who made it seem like doing amazing things was going to be easy."

Nick loosened the death grip he had on his bag, but he still hadn't said anything.

Ethan took a step back, trying to tone down the intensity to something below abject begging. "It was easy to give you a ride. I think it could be easy to keep going. Until you decide you've gone far enough. Or all the way to California, if you want. But at least come see the *Titanic* with me?" He tried for a grin. "If it's not everything I've built it up to be, I'll drive us to Dollywood and buy you a funnel cake. Or shave ice."

"It'll take more than a funnel cake to buy off my disappointment if the *Titanic* is boring." Nick didn't crack a smile—really, it was closer to a scowl—but that didn't stop the jump of hope Ethan didn't even bother denying.

"Right, so a funnel cake, shave ice, and a couple of corn dogs, then?"

"And you don't mind me blowing truckers in the back seat to pay for all that?" Flipping his backpack over his shoulder in one slick move wasn't really an answer to Ethan's question, but Nick's scowl eased to a wrinkle of dismay, so there was some progress at least. "I'm serious, Ethan. I'm dead broke. I can't afford dinner at a McDonald's with a flooded toilet, much less a dinner show on the *Titanic*."

"Pretty sure that dinner show didn't end well for anyone. And I don't know if you've looked, but I've got enough food in the trunk to last me through the zombie apocalypse. Not sure my mom will ever trust me to feed myself. And Scott's parents . . ." He had to stop and cough, to clear the tightness in his throat. "They gave me a shitload of money for graduation. I think . . . I think it was the money they were going to give Scott for the trip."

"I'm not going to take your money—"

"No!" Time to backpedal, at least verbally. This emotional up and down shit was exhausting. Pretty soon he was going to run out of words completely, instead of only coming up with the stupid ones. "I meant that I have enough money for three or four people to make this trip. So if you're interested in seeing some weird shit that doesn't involve hairy trucker balls, I got it covered."

"How are you real?" Nick's obvious fear seemed to leave him in a rush, until all that remained was confusion and the faint sadness that clung to him like a shadow. "Yesterday I was . . . It doesn't even matter. How the fuck did I meet the nicest guy on the planet in the middle of nowhere? My luck doesn't work like that."

Anyone else saying that would've pissed him off, given he'd heard it his whole life: *"That Ethan is just so nice." "What a nice young man."* Except hearing it from Nick didn't sting. Nick sounded bewildered, like he hadn't encountered a lot of nice people and wasn't certain he could trust the turn of events.

Ethan had unloaded quite enough already, so he weighed his words, deciding to go for light. "What can I say? You're lucky. And about to get luckier. You're going to Titanic Land! It's not Disney, but close."

"That's the problem with Disney. Not enough frozen bodies bobbing past on Small World. You can't even get people-shaped ice cubes in your drink there."

"Yeah, but you know what you *can* get? A *Titanic* stuffie. Come on, think of the sweet dreams you could have with that." He took a step closer to the car, resting a hand on the door handle. "What do you say? If we get on the road now, you could have that pillow by bedtime tonight."

"I'd settle for a toothbrush, actually." Nick winced, shoulders folding in toward his chest. "I don't know if I can handle that kind of excitement today. I don't want to hold you up if you've got a schedule."

Ethan rested a hand on the roof of his car, letting the warmth of the metal seep into his fingers. "No schedule. We can find a Target, get you a toothbrush and some underwear, and figure out if we can get to Pigeon Forge today when we're done."

Incongruously, Nick's buzzed hair looked blacker in the bright sun, and his blue eyes were lost when he squinted at Ethan for a few long seconds. "Clean underwear *and* a mysterious benefactor? Careful, dude. This is edging up on too good to be true."

"Oh, believe it. And I don't know if you noticed, but when it gets hot in the car, it smells like pizza. And like a hockey team died in their uniforms in the trunk, but also like pizza."

"I have so many questions," Nick said, but he was smiling again, and Ethan could work with that.

Brave words were all well and good, but when it came to standing in line at Target with various personal items being paid for by someone else, it was weird. Nick watched the underwear, toothbrush, socks, and a postcard slide by on the conveyer belt. Ethan reached into the cart for the pair of jeans and T-shirts he'd snagged off the clearance rack, but Nick grabbed his arm to stop him before they joined the rest of the stuff. "Dude, I can't—"

"We're going places. With people. Pants are kind of a requirement."

Nick shifted uncomfortably, pulling away. He had to stop touching Ethan. Except he *didn't*, now that he was out in the real world again. He could touch anyone he wanted to, now. Tyler wasn't going to pop up behind the impulse-buy rack to escort him to the Reflection Room. He wasn't going to spend a day with his arms duct-taped to his sides again. Ever.

"Sorry. I'm gonna hit the bathroom before we go, okay?" Curling his fingers around the back of his neck, he chuckled self-consciously. "And I'm not trying to ditch you, I swear."

Ethan set the jeans on the check-out belt and waved him away with a free hand. "I'll meet you at the front door."

Not trusting himself to say something appropriately lighthearted, Nick gave Ethan a short nod and scooted behind him to escape the register line. The bathroom was on the way out of the store, and it smelled like lemon disinfectant and apathetic employees. He bypassed the urinals and locked himself in a stall, balancing against the door so he wouldn't have to touch anything else.

The green light indicating a new text had started blinking while he was looking for the cheapest package of boxer briefs he could find, making the already strained shopping trip that much worse. He thumbed in his pass code on pure muscle memory.

Dad: *Nick, where are you?*

Hard to tell if his father was annoyed or worried. There'd been a lot of times when Nick couldn't tell the difference.

Dad: *The school called. They said you left without permission. You need to call home immediately.*

He snorted, unable to contain his contempt for the polite phrasing. Camp Cornerstone wasn't a school, it was a psychological battlefield with Bible quotes painted over the doors and bars on the bunkhouse windows. And home? He didn't know where that was anymore, but he knew it wasn't the house he'd grown up in. Staring at the messages, he tried to come up with something to say. Eventually the screen went dark.

The bathroom door banged open against the wall, and Nick jerked back to himself. He could stand in here and get sucked into a quagmire of miserable memory, or he could go find Ethan. Ethan, who for some inexplicable reason, seemed to want to spend time with him. Shrugging to himself, he shoved the phone into his back pocket and unlocked the stall.

It took him a minute to find Ethan. A panicked minute where every doubt about his worth as a human being, much less as a traveling companion, pushed to the forefront. But Ethan was still there, sitting at a table in the snack bar, and Nick took a deep breath to slow his heart.

"Hey." Ethan looked up and smiled. "Give me a second to finish this postcard, and we can hit the road for *Titanic* excitement."

"Take your time. Gotta psych myself up for the excitement anyway." Nick dropped into the seat across from him, swinging the round stool gently back and forth with his foot.

Nodding, Ethan turned back to his postcard. The tight line between his eyes as he hunched over the table told Nick he was deriving no pleasure from the process. Nick started to ask, then stopped himself. Ethan deserved privacy, and besides, it wasn't like Nick was real practiced in Normal Conversation 101 these days. Nick tapped the table and stood up, earning a half smile from Ethan before he went back to scribbling. Ethan had terrible handwriting.

The register closest to the snack bar was closed, and Nick spent a few minutes inspecting the racks of candy, batteries, and condoms. He lifted a pack of gum without thinking, shook his head, and dropped it back into the box before it wound up in his pocket. There was no point in stealing candy now—it had been Drew who'd gotten a thrill out of being a vicarious "bad kid," giggling every time Nick handed him an illicit Snickers behind their mom's back.

His days of boosting snacks from the corner convenience store were a few years behind him. That didn't mean the skills were gone, though. He glanced at Ethan, making sure to let his gaze linger enough that anyone watching would see he was waiting for someone. Deliberately smirking, he unhooked a couple of boxes of condoms, flipping them over like he was reading the back of the carton. When he finally saw Ethan get up in his peripheral vision, he slid one of the boxes back onto the hook and the other into his pocket.

Ethan's generosity seemed real. As much as he wanted to believe in the grand fantasy of a summer road trip full of drive-ins, abandoned roadside attractions, and macabre dinner theater, the road only went so far. Summer was going to end. Nick wasn't exactly itching to hit his knees in a truck stop bathroom, but he wasn't going back to Cornerstone, and it wasn't like a GED and his plucky attitude were going to get him very far. He was planning ahead. Tyler would be proud.

Interlude
ETHAN DOMANI'S PHONE

Conversation with Scott Raines

Ethan: *I don't know what you were looking for in Bristol*

Ethan: *I wanted to hear you somewhere*

Ethan: *Nick wanted to go to this music store but I was afraid they'd be playing something you loved*

Ethan: *Or I'd hear something and wouldn't know if you would have liked it or not*

Ethan: *Nick's the guy I picked up btw*

Ethan: *I think you'd like him*

Ethan: *But God, I almost don't know anymore and that's the scariest part of all of this*

Ethan: *I used to know everything about you, and now I don't even know where you are*

CHAPTER Six

Pigeon Forge, TN

Ethan fell into the driver's seat, waving a brochure at Nick, who looked barely more awake than he had an hour ago when their alarm had gone off. "The front-desk guy gave me coupons. Titanic Land *and* Dollywood!"

He wasn't sure if his enthusiasm was enough to carry both of them or not, but Nick mustered a tiny smile, so that was something. "I'm going to vote Dollywood first, because rides. And besides, the menu at the *Titanic* looked pretty good."

Nick sat up straighter, eyebrows rising. "The last dinner, like when the iceberg hit?"

"Yeah. And they actually have a violin that was recovered from the wreckage, and if we're *really* lucky, we might get to hear somebody play it."

"I don't want to hurt your feelings or anything," Nick said, shaking his head, "but has anybody ever told you you're a little . . . odd? I mean, this whole death-fascination thing. Do you really think it's healthy?"

Ethan opened his mouth for a scathing comeback, but caught himself when he saw Nick's smirk.

"I wouldn't call it a 'fascination.' What's that other f-word . . . fetish, maybe?"

Nick's sly look faded into something more like shock, his mouth dropping open. Ethan couldn't help noticing that he'd bitten his lip bloody sometime during the night. "Did . . . did you mean to imply that you're into necrophilia?"

Ethan forced his eyes wide in an expression his mom had always called "too good to be true." "I don't know *what* you could be talking about. I was trying to expand my vocabulary."

Nick muttered something in what sounded like Spanish, then switched to English. "So why are you even going to Dollywood, if you're this excited about the *Titanic* thing?"

"We're here, and it seems silly to not take advantage of both." Ethan tried to keep the defensiveness out of his voice; Nick wasn't questioning his decision, not really. "Besides, it's an amusement park. Rides and food."

"Do you *like* rides?"

Now that sounded like a leading question. "Depends on the kind. I have a problem with motion sickness, so maybe the ones that don't, you know, move too much."

Nick shook his head. "So you don't like rides."

"No, but that's not the point." Ethan concentrated on starting the car, and not on Nick's silence.

That silence stretched past the point of awkwardness before Nick finally cleared his throat. "I'm down for whatever. I guess I thought you didn't want to do the Dollywood thing, is all. If you want to, that's cool."

"I don't *not* want to. Maybe if I skip it, I'll be missing out on something amazing." Time to change the topic of conversation, even if he couldn't pinpoint exactly why it was making him uncomfortable. "I know I took advantage of the extremely stale packet of coffee in the hotel room, but I'm pretty sure all the caffeine leached out of it six or seven years ago. Mind if we stop somewhere and get something real?"

"Best idea ever," Nick said with a smile, sinking lower in the passenger seat. "Think we can get coffee in one of those mugs shaped like Dolly's chest?"

"Boob coffee? I guess we could, if you really wanted . . ."

"Maybe they have a mug shaped like someone's ass in a pair of jeans for those who can't appreciate the bustier option."

"I'm just surprised you're looking to wrap your lips around a ceramic boob. I didn't think they were your . . . chosen vessel." Ethan poked at his phone until it coughed up a list of local cafés.

Unfortunately, the only coffee place nearby was a Starbucks. Not really known for controversial drink cups, unless you counted the Christmas kerfuffle.

Nick giggled, slapping a hand over his mouth to keep the sound in until he'd recovered enough to speak. "I'll drink out of any mug that gets set in front of me. I have no bias against shapely ceramics."

"That sounds like a challenge." Ethan's villain cackle wasn't everything it could be, but that meant he threw in a little more volume.

"Statement of fact, my friend. I accept beverages in whatever cup they happen to arrive in. My thirst can be quenched by any number of liquids. All caffeine is worthy—"

"Nick. Nick! Do you want to go in, or will you be embarrassed to be seen in public with me, given my sad preference for only one kind of drink? I can do the drive-through if you don't want to be associated with me." Ethan fixed his traveling companion with a pointed look, wondering how long Nick might have gone on if he hadn't been stopped.

Nick sighed heavily. "I guess we can go in. But . . . what kind of drink? Am I going to have to stand next to someone whose order makes me blush?"

"Vanilla latte. And if you've got a problem with that, I'll call my mom and she can read you the riot act about how everyone is allowed to love the drink of their choice."

"Jesus, dude." Nick undid his seat belt and reached for the door handle. "I didn't know you'd get so worked up about coffee."

"We all need to have something to believe in, a cause to support." Ethan mustered as much dignity as he could manage. "You should work on that. Otherwise, people are gonna think you're shallow."

"There are puddles deeper than me. Now lead me into this den of sin and fetch your demon juice so we can get to Dollywood."

Nick slipped out of the car first, which left Ethan free to screw up his face while he got out and locked the car. He caught up at the front door. "So what's your poison? Chai latte? Caramel macchiato? Or are you strictly a drip?"

"Wow, way to toss out the insults. Like I said, I don't really do coffee anymore." The yawn that punctuated Nick's statement didn't lend it a great deal of authenticity, especially not when he closed his eyes and inhaled.

Ethan glanced at the board, away from the trembling flutter of Nick's thick eyelashes against his cheeks, but he couldn't look away for long. "Do you want tea or cocoa instead? It's not a heart condition or something, is it? I don't want to get to the top of a log ride and find out you're going to die on the way down."

"I'm not . . . I'm not allowed." Nick's eyes snapped open, fast enough that he had to have caught Ethan staring. "Except fuck that. I'll have a large mocha. That has a lot of caffeine and sugar, right?"

"Yeah, it should wake you right up. But you need to order a venti, not a large. Don't want to look like a total newbie."

"How about if I order a twenty ounce? I don't feel comfortable giving in to that bourgeoisie naming system."

Ethan blew out something between an amused snort and a sigh as they reached the counter. Smiling at the barista, he pulled out his phone and opened his app to pay. "I'd like a grande vanilla latte, and my snobby companion will have a venti mocha with an extra shot."

The young woman took their order, trying to hide an answering smile as Nick made a noise of vague protest behind him. They shuffled over to wait at the counter, Nick glancing around like he was waiting for someone to jump out at him. Ethan clenched a hand at his side when he wanted to reach out, taking in the hunched slope of Nick's shoulders and the sudden, nervous way he was rubbing the tips of his fingers together. They might not have known each other long, but Ethan understood that touching wasn't something Nick was comfortable with.

"'Venti' is just Italian for 'twenty,' you know. In case that's what you're worried about."

"Nah, my Italian is passable." Nick straightened up enough to reach across the counter and grab a coffee sleeve. "I'm more worried about you having to peel me off the roof of the car."

"You can always run along beside the car if you need to. I promise I'll drive real slow." Ethan flushed a little as the barista handing over Nick's coffee tried to conceal her laughter.

She popped a lid on Ethan's vanilla latte and handed it to him. "Hey, as long as you don't put him on a leash, I won't call the authorities."

Nick took a drink, looking up over the edge of his cup. "He told me I'd have to ride in the trunk if I spilled anything. Does that count?"

"Anyone who's smelled my car would know that's not something I've ever said. I'm pretty sure I've had more hockey team sweat on my seats than you could fit in that cup anyway." When Nick and the barista both made varying faces of disgust, Ethan grinned. "I found a tooth in my footwell once!"

Nick tipped his cup in Ethan's direction. "Dude, I'm seriously worried about that degree of enthusiasm."

"Well, it wasn't *mine*."

"You boys have fun now," the barista said, clearly hoping they'd move their discussion somewhere she wasn't.

Taking her hint, Ethan led them outside. Nick paused next to the car, the look on his face catching Ethan's attention.

"Thank you." Nick bit his lower lip, gaze drifting back to his coffee cup. He wrapped both hands around it, voice quiet below the hum of traffic and parking lot noise. "I don't . . ."

"Lie to me," Ethan told him, helpless against the pain and anxiety that seemed bent on swallowing Nick alive.

"I had to stick to maple products the whole time I was undercover with the cartel. It's . . . really hard not to feel like I'm going to get caught and tossed in the Reflection Room for breaking the rules." Hand clenched tight around the white-and-green cup, Nick pulled it toward himself and took a defiant drink. "But to hell with the Canadians anyway, right?"

As lies went, it was way too easy to spot the parts that were true, but Ethan had made a promise and he was sticking to it. "You're lucky I'm a die-hard Caps fan, buddy, or those would be fighting words."

"Always hockey with you, huh?"

"Only until lacrosse season." Ethan smiled across the roof. Nick's second gulp of coffee seemed to go down easier, and in Ethan's head, the crowd cheered.

"You're *sure* about this?" Nick's eyebrows pinched together, his concern obvious and . . . kind of annoying, really.

"Dude, I didn't wait in line for forty-five minutes to stand on the mom platform and wave at you while the ride leaves. I'm sure." It had been at least five years since Ethan had tried a roller coaster of any kind. Maybe puberty had cured him of his motion sickness. His acne had faded away a few years ago, so there was always hope.

Ethan was saved from further questioning by the return of one of the coaster cars. He winced in sympathy as a little kid tripped unsteadily onto the opposite platform, leaning against the railing with his eyes closed. Turning to find Nick watching him again, he bristled, stepping into the empty row of seats like it was an act of defiance.

"Remember to look cool for the picture on the way down," Nick said, and Ethan forced a laugh past his gritted teeth. He took a deep breath through his nose as an enthusiastic park employee tried to crush him with the seat harness, and then they were beginning their ascent. Ethan kicked his feet idly where they hung loose below, then considered the possibility of killing someone with a rogue New Balance (size 12) and hoped he'd tied his laces tight that morning.

"Come here often?"

He barely registered the light touch of Nick's fingers on his arm, the teasing question, and then the edge of the world dropped away under them, and he was too busy trying to scream and laugh at the same time to respond.

Ethan had less than a second at the bottom of the drop to catch his breath before the car swung hard to the right, tipped at almost a ninety-degree angle. Then it immediately went left, swinging ninety degrees in the other direction, and the coffee he'd finished an hour ago started sliding back up his throat.

Nick shouted something that might have been "This is awesome!" but Ethan's ears were ringing too loudly to be certain. He thought about nodding but then dismissed it as a terrible idea. Closing his eyes only made everything worse.

Inertia tried to pull him out of the coaster, and the final round of loops and turns bashed his head back and forth in the harness, bouncing both ears hard against the padded bar. By the time they arrived back into the platform, Ethan was sure puberty had *not* cured his motion sickness. He barely managed to wait for the attendant to lift the safety bar before scrambling out, probably stepping on Nick's feet in a mad dash for the railing that separated the covered ride shack from the shrubbery beyond it.

By the time Ethan was done throwing up, his ears hurt even more, his throat burned with bile, and he thought there might have been vomit dripping out of his nose. He remained hunched over the railing while a park employee asked him if he needed anything, until a warm hand settled on his back, rubbing slow circles between his shoulder blades.

"It's okay. Here, lean on me, and we'll find a bathroom."

Miserable and certain he was the only person who'd ever hurled on their first ride at *Dollywood*, of all places, Ethan let Nick guide him down the ramps and out of the ride. For a guy who looked like he could maybe bench press a box of Kleenex on a good day, Nick was surprisingly strong.

They made it to a bathroom, and Ethan didn't want to look up as Nick politely asked if his friend, who was "a little sick" could cut the line to get to a stall. Nick left him leaning against a stainless steel bathroom partition, returning a few moments later with a bunch of wet paper towels. "Here. Press them over your face. It'll make you feel better."

It did help, if only because it gave Ethan an excuse to hide for a second. He wasn't sure which was worse—puking on a ride little kids could handle or how bad his head hurt. It felt like he'd popped something in his eyeballs.

"Do I have demon eyes?" He lowered the paper towels and forced his eyes open wide. Nick, to his credit, studied Ethan very seriously before answering.

"Eyes are a little bloodshot, but I don't think anyone's going to mistake you for a stoner or one of hell's minions. Your breath, on the other hand . . ." He raised his hand, fanning it back and forth. "Might want to rinse your mouth, if you think you're not going to toss again. Hang on."

Nick darted out of the stall before Ethan could glare at him. He wiped his face, surreptitiously checking to make sure he hadn't gotten any puke on his shirt. Nick came back, holding up two sticks of gum. "I asked the lady sitting outside with the giant backpack. It seemed like she probably had a little of everything. Wintergreen okay?"

"Sure. Let me rinse my mouth and give someone else the stall."

"I'll meet you outside." Maybe because they were looking at each other this time, Nick stopped short of touching him, backing out of the stall and winding his way out of the bathroom instead. Ethan watched him go, then found an empty sink and cupped some water to his mouth, rinsing a few times until he couldn't taste the vestiges of bitter humiliation anymore.

An amusement park in summer was great for people watching but not so great for people *spotting*. He looked around for Nick outside the bathroom, but the crowds were too thick to see more than a few yards away. The nervous jump of his heart was stupid—it wasn't like Nick had run off and left him. Ethan saw an empty spot on the edge of a rock wall to sit and took it, scanning the crowds until Nick finally returned a few minutes later. He held out a drink to Ethan, the straw paper ripped down to a little cap to keep the end clean.

"I got you a Sprite. They didn't have ginger ale."

He accepted the cup, jumping a little at the cold contrast against his sweaty hand. "Thanks," he muttered, not looking up at Nick. He really wanted to press the cup against his face, but he settled for taking a drink instead. Never a fan of Sprite, it still tasted heavenly going down. "I'm really sorry about all this . . ." Ethan waved his free hand, not looking up.

"Nah, it's okay. I'm gonna make a suggestion though." Nick paused long enough that Ethan preemptively winced. "No more rides today."

Ethan choked out a laugh. "Damn it, and I was looking forward to that indoor roller coaster in a fire thing."

"If that's your plan, I need to know enough in advance so that I'm sitting in front of you on the ride."

"That's totally fair. I'd do the same thing."

Nick waited until Ethan finished another swallow. "So what do you think? Have you had enough of the Dollywood experience?"

"Me and Scott . . . We were supposed to play all the stupid arcade games and win the biggest stuffed animal in the—" Ethan caught himself and stopped, swallowing hard. "I think I'm done," he finished.

"I did win a stuffed giraffe in the ring toss in second grade. If you think those skills are applicable here, we can go see what rigged games

Miss Dolly has up her sleeve. Or tucked into her ample bodice." Nick's black T-shirt stretched across his chest as he made a show of winding up his arm. "Of course, everyone knows the games with the bottles are rigged, and most of the time the beanbag games are too. It's all about shooting the water pistols and popping balloons with darts." He grinned at Ethan, looking completely at ease for the first time in their acquaintance. "Oooh, or *Skee-Ball*."

"Skee-Ball? Bring it on." His laugh felt a lot less forced, despite the lingering taste of regurgitated coffee in the back of his throat. Ethan took another long drink of Sprite, emptying the cup.

"I got enough tickets for the Power Rangers pencil case once. Best. Day. Ever."

"While that's great and all, we need to up your game for best day ever. It's probably *not* going to be the day you rode the roller coaster with the guy who puked everywhere, though." Ethan made a face. "Sorry you had to be around for that. Thanks for helping me out."

Nick shrugged. "No big deal. It's amazing what wet paper towels and clear liquids can do."

"I feel a lot better. Like I could absolutely hand you your ass at Skee-Ball." Ethan stood, ignoring the peculiar aches that always came with throwing up.

"Yeah, right. All I have to do is spin you in a circle first." Nick wiggled his arched eyebrows as he unfolded their map. After studying it a moment, he pointed them down a path and set off, Ethan in his wake.

The crowd around them thinned as they headed into the area set aside for the midway, the cacophony of voices and rides replaced by tinny carousel music and piped-in country hits. Nick was a step ahead when the first shot rang out.

Something unfurled from the base of Ethan's spine, some instinct he never thought he'd find use for again. He threw himself at Nick, knocking them both to the ground. Ethan's teeth cracked together with the force of their landing, breath crashing out of his lungs as Nick's bony shoulders dug into his chest. A second shot went off, then a third, followed by . . . clapping?

"Let's hear it for the Eighth Division Tennessee Precision Drill Team, folks!"

Nick pushed against him as Ethan struggled to take a breath, but it took several long seconds before the air whooshed into his lungs again. Shaking from the adrenaline rush, he rolled to the side, off of Nick and onto his back. The sky was a bright cloudless blue, filling his entire range of vision. He wanted to close his eyes, but it felt like they were frozen open.

"What the fuck, Ethan?"

Apparently he didn't respond fast enough, because Nick sounded a little more frantic the second time. "Ethan!" The sky was suddenly replaced with Nick's face, close enough, and unexpectedly enough, that Ethan jerked back, head smacking against the concrete walkway.

"I . . ." He started to shake his head, then stopped as flashes of light strobed through his vision, blotting everything else out. He wanted to apologize, to explain, *something*, but the words weren't there.

People around them were turning to stare, a few even moving closer. Along with the pulsating flares behind his eyes, it felt like a haunted house strobe room, monsters lurching closer faster than he could track. He squeezed his eyes shut, rolling to his side and curling up so he could press his hands over his ears. He could smell food nearby, the waxy, pungent scent of fake cheese, just like the cafeteria. It had been nacho day.

"It's okay," Nick said from somewhere close by, but Ethan didn't know who he was talking to. "I think he tripped on something."

It took Ethan a few more seconds before he could speak around his fear, and he didn't recognize his own voice. "I thought . . . Someone was shooting, and . . ."

"It's okay."

He should have been annoyed when Nick repeated the words, but Ethan clung to them, and then to the tentative hand resting on the crown of his head, fingers curling through his hair. The stink of canned cheese seemed stronger as he struggled to sit up. He winced when his abraded palms made contact with the blacktop. Nick's arm under his shoulder helped get him upright, but then he had to pause, head down.

"Dude, you're heavy."

He tried to laugh, but nothing came out. He probably had to breathe in before he could go expelling air all willy-nilly.

"Son, did you hit your head?"

Ethan blinked at the unfamiliar man, whose uniform marked him as one of Dolly's finest. Everything snapped back into sharp focus—the people watching them, the people who pointedly *weren't*, and Nick, who, for the second time that morning, looked like this wasn't a big deal. Like it was normal for someone to keel over in the middle of a sidewalk. Anger and his breath surged at the same time, and Ethan jerked his arm out of Nick's grasp, rearing away from the park employee.

"I'm fine. It's fine. Leave me alone." This was worse than puking on a ride. This was . . . this was it. This was how he had to live, for the rest of his life: fucking shattering apart every time he heard a loud noise. It wasn't even about the humiliation. It was knowing that the fear was always going to be there, waiting. And none of it mattered, because it would always be without Scott.

"I can't . . ."

Somehow Nick caught his whispered words, and suddenly he had a skinny, mouthy bodyguard between himself and the park employee, who had a radio out.

"He said he's fine." Nick looked over his shoulder at him. "We're going to leave. He got sick on a ride a few minutes ago. Must still be a little wobbly. Thanks."

The security guy didn't seem convinced. "Park policy is pretty clear about falls. They need to be reported, and the victim needs to get checked out at first aid. It's for your protection."

Ethan caught Nick's eyes when the security guard turned away to speak into his radio. The man wasn't exactly being discreet, and it was easy to make out the words *drunk* and *underage*. Nick must have been a psychic, because suddenly Ethan was being pulled to his feet and dragged down the path. Once his body got with the program, he sailed past Nick, tugging him left and right through the growing crowds by their joined hands. Nick veered left, and they wound up tucked behind a vending machine. Ethan fought off a case of nervous giggles, almost as amused by Nick clutching his side and gasping for breath as he was by the possibility of getting arrested at Dollywood and having to call his brother to bail him out.

Oh God, no, not Robert. Maybe he'd have Suze PayPal the money. Her Etsy store was doing pretty well. He'd never have guessed there was such a market for fancy hair ties with unicorn charms.

Aaand he was wandering. And Nick was still wheezing, which didn't seem as funny now.

"We should—" Nick huffed another shortened breath, standing up straighter. "They'll probably radio that to every security guy in the park. I think we might have to skip Skee-Ball."

"As long as we're clear that I would've kicked your ass at it. Y'know, if I hadn't freaked out and ruined the chance."

"You didn't ruin *anything*." The calm strength in Nick's voice reached Ethan in a way nothing kinder would have. "Besides, I'd feel bad humiliating you now." A radio pulsed with static somewhere close by in the crowd, and they both jumped. "We should get out of here before we have to run for it again and you wind up dragging my asthmatic corpse to the parking lot."

"I'm only guessing, but I think Dolly's people might be even more annoyed at a corpse being dragged through their park than a couple of drunk and disorderlies." Ethan made a show of peering around the soda machine, then beckoned to Nick. "I think the coast is clear. Remember to duck and cover if you spot a uniform."

He'd never been more happy to see a giant cardboard Dolly Parton with a cartoon balloon saying *Y'all come back again!* Not that he'd ever anticipated a time when he would see one, but this meant they were home free.

The parking lot was an unfamiliar landscape with so many other cars jammed into it. He stood on the curb looking at the mess for a second before Nick suddenly burst into laughter. Ethan had forgotten they were still holding hands until Nick went boneless and heavy against his side, smothering a chuckle in his shoulder.

"Are we . . ." Nick paused, snickering. "Are we in row double D?"

"Oh my God, don't touch me." Ethan shoved Nick away, but not hard enough to actually dislodge him. It was the closest they'd been since they'd met, at least by Nick's doing. And he didn't mind having someone to laugh with.

"We're in row *H*," he said with as much dignity as he could muster.

They made it back to the car without further incident. Nick let go first, and Ethan tried not to be upset about that. He didn't have the right to cling . . . but God, it felt so good to be touched by someone who wasn't afraid of breaking him.

Once in the car, Ethan rested his hands on the steering wheel. He wanted to rest his head on it too, but was afraid if he did, everything would catch up with him and he'd never move.

"Are you okay to drive?" Nick paused in buckling his seat belt to look across at Ethan.

He thought about it, running through the self-check the short-lived therapist had taught him. "Yeah, I'm fine," he finally said. "Are you okay finding a motel and maybe chilling for a little while? I could really use a shower."

"Works for me. Did you have a place in mind?"

"Damn right! Titanic Motel Experience." Ethan pointed to one of the brochures sitting in the console. "The pillows are in the shape of life preservers. And they blast air horns at random times in the middle of the night."

Nick's eyebrows joined his hairline. "Please tell me you're kidding."

"Well. Maybe not the air horns."

"Jesus," Nick muttered. "Well, I hope *you* can draw, because only one of us gets to be the French girl."

Dear Mrs. Raines,

I threw up at Dollywood. Turns out I didn't outgrow motion sickness.

I'm still sorry about the back seat in your old car. :(

I didn't see Dolly Parton, either.

Love,

Ethan

CHAPTER Seven

Pigeon Forge, TN

I t was Nick's turn to wait on the other side of the bathroom door. Ethan still looked shaky, but he'd insisted he wasn't going to pass out in the shower. The door wasn't locked, so Nick figured he could always check if he heard a thump. Any other noise was Ethan's business, as proscribed by the unwritten laws of communal space and shared walls.

Once Ethan turned the water on, Nick stopped his unconscious pacing. He took the bed closest to the door, flopping down on his stomach before reaching for his backpack. He hadn't turned his phone back on since yesterday, but there was no time like the present to be yelled at by his parents *in absentia*. Ethan's claims to the contrary, the motel was sadly lacking in life preserver pillows, which sucked, because he could have used one. At least he'd be drowning in familiar waters.

He listened to Ethan in the shower while his phone went through whatever electronic yoga poses it needed to start. Head cocked toward the bathroom, he strained shamelessly for a mistimed splash or wayward moan. Nothing said he couldn't *hear* whatever Ethan might do; he just couldn't mention it afterward. Nick wasn't blind *or* dead—Ethan was hot, funny, unrealistically kind, and twisted in knots over the death of his boyfriend. That was like, an eight on his personal Richter scale.

His phone started vibrating almost as soon as the screen turned on, buzzing and chirping itself in a weak circle on the comforter.

Focusing on that instead of Ethan's potential grooming habits, he thumbed down the menu to check his alerts. No missed calls, but he'd had the phone off, so they wouldn't show up anyway. Only texts. Thirty-nine unread texts.

Nick cradled the phone in his hands and considered deleting all of them without reading them. He didn't *think* his dad's company could track his phone, but maybe even having it on was sending up a beacon announcing his residency in Pigeon Forge, Tennessee. Too late now, in that case.

He opened the string from his father first, surprised to see only two messages were from him.

The school said you'd made great progress. You can still go back. You aren't in trouble.

A snorted laugh escaped him. Not in trouble. Riiight. With everything he'd done, everything he'd said to get away, there was no way he'd go back to anything less than a week in the Reflection Room, and he'd be lucky not to be on speaking and eating restrictions for a month. One did not simply call Tyler a lying cunt and get a free pass for movie night.

The second message from his dad had come in hours later, almost the middle of the night.

You can call us. If you don't want to go back to Cornerstone, we can talk about it. Just call us. Please. We're worried about you.

There were five messages from his mom, all variations on the theme. They were worried, they wanted him to go back to Cornerstone, he should call. The texts only took a few seconds to read, but he felt them in his chest for minutes after while he stared at the hideous seashell comforter without seeing it. Those five messages were the most his mom had said to him in a year.

That left thirty-two messages, all from a number that wasn't in his contacts. All sent in less than a day, and fuck if he wanted to look at them. He only knew one person that obsessive about keeping in touch.

571-555-8920: *Your dad called me looking for you*

571-555-8920: *I thought you were still locked up on the Island of Misfit Toys*

571-555-8920: *Where are you I can come pick you up if you need help*

571-555-8920: *Your dad sounded pissed*

571-555-8920: *I cant believe you didnt call me right away*

571-555-8920: *Tried to call you pick up.*

571-555-8920: *PICK UP*

571-555-8920: *Nicky this is fucked up Im worried about you*

571-555-8920: *Your dad called again*

571-555-8920: *He said they had to let you leave that camp place because youre 18 now and he cant stop you from being with me but he wants to hear from you*

571-555-8920: *Have to give you a birthday present when I see you*

571-555-8920: *PICK UP THE PHONE*

571-555-8920: *This is pissing me off Nick. You owe me. Your parents tried to get me arrested for fucking you*

571-555-8920: *Least you could do is offer now that its not a crime anymore :)*

571-555-8920: *Should have told them you were MORE than willing*

571-555-8920: *[img attachment - SS05059.jpg]*

571-555-8920: *Should I send that to your dad next time he calls?*

571-555-8920: *You looked pretty happy to have my cock in your mouth*

571-555-8920: *I bet you still make the same noises*

571-555-8920: *Call me Nick we can catch up on missed time*

571-555-8920: *I'm sorry*

The same acidic mirth burned in his throat. "Sorry." Nick spat the word like an accusation, still staring at the message in disbelief. Kyle was *sorry*. He must've been really desperate to get laid. *Sorry.* Nick could remember the way Kyle had always curled his fingers under his jaw, so gentle, so sincere, but he hadn't *meant it*. Sorry he'd gotten Nick sent to Camp Can't-Fuck-You-Anymore, probably.

The rest were more of the same. Peaks and valleys of concern and anger, with a few more pictures of Nick in compromised positions for good measure. Nick had never had the heart (or judgment poor enough) to mention he didn't get off on pictures of himself. Narcissism was Kyle's thing.

"Everything okay?"

Nick jumped, shoving the phone under the edge of the comforter. Apparently he'd been so caught up in Kyle's little messages of love that he'd missed the shower cutting off. "Yeah, fine. How about you, feeling better?"

"Like I never vomited on a ride or collapsed in a theme park." Ethan's smile looked a little weak. "Which is probably better than I should expect."

"You don't look like you're ready to party. Unless by 'party,' you mean 'nap.'" Nick waved a hand at the empty bed.

Ethan scowled, but at the furniture, not him.

"Hey, you want to be ready for the whole *Titanic* experience, right?"

"My baby sister doesn't even take naps. She's seven. This is ridiculous."

"And yet, I can see that pillow has your name on it. Pretend you're sleeping off a hangover. Way more mature than making the choice to recover from being sick so you can enjoy yourself later." Nick's phone chirped from somewhere in the vicinity of his ass, and for a second he wondered if there was a short in the battery. The electric charge that jolted up his scalp had to be real.

"You're bossy," Ethan huffed, brushing past him. Nick jerked away. Ethan's face clouded, clearly catching Nick's involuntary retreat.

The bed squealed in protest when Ethan collapsed face-first down on it, snagging a pillow and jamming it under his head.

"Are you okay?" Ethan bit his lower lip, something Nick didn't find endearing *at all*, thank you. "Is this okay, I mean? I can't really spring for two rooms, but we could take turns sleeping in the car or something?"

Nick opened his mouth to answer, then clenched his jaw shut with a click when the phone went off again. More than anything, maybe even more than feeling it, he hated having to explain why he twitched like a monkey on speed whenever anyone got too close. "It's fine. This is fine. I'm not . . . I'm not afraid of you." He could lie. He had permission and everything. It didn't feel worth it to stretch the truth that much though, not when it was so obvious. "We weren't supposed to touch anyone. In the cartel. Sticky fingerprints, you know?"

Ethan's nodding rubbed his wet hair up into crazy spikes on the pillow. "Got it." His fingers tapped against the bedspread. "You spend a lot of time hungover? In the cartel, I mean? You're awfully good at taking care of people."

The phone again, always the damn phone. Nick pulled it out and flipped it to silent, his hands feeling loose and disconnected from his body as the sparks crept out of his head and into his extremities, seeking escape. "My younger brother died," he said, still staring at the screen. He hadn't meant to say that. "He had cancer, and the treatments made him sick all the time."

If Ethan was surprised at the confession, he hid it well. "I'm really sorry."

That was it. No questions, no *I know you feel*, no overblown sympathy, and the feeling of relief almost hurt. Nick took a deep breath and let it out. "So anyway, the room. Nobody needs to sleep in the car. Unless you start talking in your sleep. Or snoring. Then you're out of here."

"Better prepare yourself, because I can't promise I won't be quoting Rose in my sleep tonight. I'm ready to be inspired!"

"Look, you express yourself any way you want, but if you start singing Celine Dion, I'm kicking your ass out *and* keeping your pillow."

Ethan glared up at him, wrapping his arm tighter around the pillow. "That's cold. See if I hold you up on the ship's bow after dinner."

"I think I can live with the disappointment." Nick snickered. "And no offense, but I don't know I'd trust you not to drop me. We've seen how you handle motion. Ships go up and down. A lot."

"You, uh, do know it's a *pretend* ship, right?"

Nick sputtered, grabbing the spare pillow and chucking it at Ethan's head. "See if I ever bring you wet paper towels after you vomit again." He ignored the messages on his phone, pulling up the clock to set an alarm instead. "Couple hours, and then we can go see your *fake* ship. For some reason. Not even real, Jesus . . ." He trailed off his muttering, lying down on his side. His phone wound up on the nightstand between their beds, and his gaze fell on Ethan, who looked more amenable to the idea of a nap. Hair tousled, damp; eyes half-closed . . .

Nick groaned quietly and rolled onto his back, tossing an arm over his eyes. Yeah, he wasn't blind or dead, despite Reverend Hill's best efforts. That didn't mean it was a good idea to drop his guard. To get attached. To let Ethan down when he was inevitably, irrevocably himself again, and he managed to fuck it all up.

He lingered in self-loathing for a few minutes, riding the edge between thoughts and dreams until someone started running a chainsaw on the other side of the room. Moving his arm away from his eyes, Nick propped himself up a few inches so he could see Ethan molesting his pillow, mouth open and drool smeared across the back of his hand. There. Ethan snored. That definitely wasn't sexy.

"I'm still disappointed the gift shop isn't in the iceberg, man. That's a golden opportunity to sell themed life vests, *wasted*." Nick sighed, hanging on to the railing of the faux tilted deck with one hand while he tried to take a selfie with the other. Maybe he should have picked the one that wasn't at a forty-five-degree angle.

"Seriously. I'm hoping this doesn't ruin the whole experience for me. I mean, think about it. You could get them monogrammed with your name and shit."

"*Language,*" chided a woman behind Ethan, and like the good kid Nick suspected he was, Ethan ducked his head and cringed.

"Stuff," Ethan amended.

Nick laughed so hard he nearly fell off the platform. He flinched away when Ethan elbowed him, but managed to turn it into a spin over the railing. The woman behind them sniffed and turned away.

"Okay, I give up. Take a picture for me? I can't hang on and keep myself in the frame." Nick held his phone out to Ethan.

"Sure." Ethan took the phone with one hand and gestured with the other. "Lean up against the rail and look dramatic. Oh, or lean half over it, like you're about ready to fall!"

He'd had the same thought himself, but no way was he going to admit it. Instead, Nick sighed. "Dramatic? I guess I can." He stepped back until he was against the rail and threw an arm over the top bar.

Ethan nodded, holding the phone up to his face. "Perfect. Now look desperate."

The phone buzzed with an incoming message, and the desperation was real as Nick jumped toward Ethan.

"I think you got a—"

"Don't—" Nick couldn't move fast enough to grab the phone, but that didn't stop him from trying. The phone buzzed again, and Ethan's expression changed, fading from his familiar pinched concern to shock.

"Give me the phone," Nick said, trying to keep his voice steady.

Ethan stared at it a second longer, then reluctantly held his hand out, phone flat on his palm. "Who—" he started, but Nick overrode him.

"It's nothing." He snatched up the phone and shoved it in his pocket without looking at the screen. It stopped his hands from shaking too, as anger and fear curdled into self-loathing. "Just an . . ." Nick dropped his chin, clenching his eyes shut and grinding his teeth together around the words *an ex*, because he didn't know what Kyle had sent or what Ethan had seen. Probably not a picture, if he'd only caught the message previews. That was something. He'd reached a point where his happiness rested on whether or not someone had seen pictures of him on his knees. Swell.

"Just a guy who can't take a hint. Doesn't know he's got the wrong number." Dragging his feet like he was wearing lead Docs, he climbed back up the slanted platform. "You could take a picture with your phone and send it to me, right?"

Ethan's hesitance only lasted a moment before he visibly shook it off. "Yeah, sure. Of course." He fished his phone out of his back pocket and snapped some pictures while Nick faked his way through being goofy.

"Hang on, I want one with both of us." Ethan turned around and leaned against the outside of the platform, holding his phone as far away as he could and tapping the screen a few times to capture them in all their blurry glory.

"Your turn." Nick hopped down and snagged Ethan's phone out of his hand. "Stay on the ship as long as you can, Rose."

Ethan proved to have a disgusting amount of upper body strength, and Nick got a couple of pictures of him hanging off the railing and kicking his feet before a new group of people wandered in and started milling around the platforms, wanting to take their own pictures.

"Ready for the gift shop?"

"Sounds good." Nick waited for Ethan to look up, then tossed him his phone. Ethan caught it with one-handed ease, then flipped it up in the air before catching it again. Nick shook his head. "You'd've been sorry if that fell overboard and you had to dive into icy water for it."

"I don't drop things." Ethan grinned. "I got a trophy for juggling in the seventh-grade talent show."

"Of course you did," Nick muttered, rolling his eyes. The talent show where all of Ethan's numerous family members undoubtedly showed up and cheered him on.

The gift shop, while not housed in an iceberg, did seem to have an abundance of iceberg-related souvenirs. Glass paper weights, ice cube trays, giant posters, iceberg-shaped soap dispensers, and something Nick could only hope was *not* an iceberg-themed vibrator. He let his gaze skim over that quickly, only to spot something startlingly bright yellow on the far shelf.

Ethan must have spotted it first, because he pushed past Nick. "It's the *Titanic* stuffie!"

Nick tried to stifle a snicker. Nobody should get that excited over a neon-yellow stuffed *Titanic*. "Yes. Yes, it is."

Grabbing the closest one, Ethan held it up. "It's kinda awesome."

It was, in the most ridiculous way possible, but Nick kept a straight face as he nodded. "Yes. Yes, it is."

Ethan's mouth turned down at the corners, his disappointment clear. "If you can't see what a fine piece of collectible memorabilia this is, I'm not sure we can be friends."

"It's wonderful. It's the best stuffie I've ever seen. I want to have tiny little plush babies with it. Little lifeboats! We'll run off together and live the life of our dreams, far from the cold Atlantic, only separated when death finally sinks our love."

Ethan set the fluffy boat back down on the shelf, eyes narrowed. "*Humph*. I can tell when I'm being mocked. I'm going to pick out a postcard. You'll be lucky if I don't make you listen to the movie soundtrack tomorrow."

Something about the way Ethan's fingers trailed away from the bright toy made Nick think Ethan wasn't as okay with being teased about it as he was trying to be.

"I'm gonna hit the bathroom. Maybe the urinal cakes are shaped like life preservers. Wouldn't want to miss that." He winked at Ethan, exaggerating it to the point of comedy. "Meet you outside when you're done?"

"Sure. Give me a minute."

Nick waved him off. "No rush. I've got like, 80 Candy Crush levels to catch up on."

He waited until Ethan had turned away to mosey toward the postcards before snatching up the screamingly yellow boat and tucking it under his arm. For one wild second, he considered stealing it, bolting out the door into the Tennessee night with a cursed toy, but he wasn't crazy about getting arrested for petty theft at a tourist trap in Pigeon Forge. As street cred went, that was definitely scraping the bottom of the barrel.

Nick twitched with nerves as a girl with hawkish features rang him up. Ethan was still buried somewhere in the racks of postcards and books, but he didn't know how much longer that would last. He kind of wanted it to be a surprise "I don't know why you're being so nice to me/sorry I made you feel bad about your perfectly legitimate desire to own a stuffed *Titanic* replica" gift.

"That'll be $19.97."

"Are you *kidding*?" Nick slapped a hand over his mouth, his surprised yelp echoing in his ears. Stealthy. "Jesus, do you take kidneys?"

"Cash, Visa, MasterCard, or Discover, sir. No American Express, no internal organs."

Nick pulled out his wallet, digging under the flap he kept his license in for his emergency twenty-dollar bill. Even combined with the few bucks he had floating around in his backpack, it wasn't enough to get him anywhere, so fuck it. He might as well do something nice for Ethan with it. He left his change in the charity jar next to the register, then slunk toward the exit with the toy hugged to his chest.

When Ethan came out of the gift shop a few minutes later, Nick was leaning against the back of his car, destroying brightly colored pixels and covertly watching for the moment Ethan noticed the toy sitting on the hood. His jaw dropped, eyes going wide, and Nick looked down to hide a grin.

"You got me the stuffie," Ethan said, voice reverent. He picked it up, holding the bright-yellow abomination in the air with one hand. "Thank you."

Nick shrugged, trying for nonchalance and failing miserably. "I couldn't imagine you surviving the rest of the day without it. It was obviously necessary to your life." He was thankful Ethan hadn't gone with the *you shouldn't haves*, instead settling on cheerful and obviously heartfelt gratitude.

"The rest of the day? Hell, I'm not sure I would've made it through the next *hour*. Thank you again. It's awesome." He unlocked the car and set the boat on the console between the seats, waiting for Nick to climb in. "Coffee before we head back to the motel?"

Nick thought about it for a second, then shook his head. "Maybe not. I'm feeling twitchy enough. More caffeine probably isn't the greatest idea after the titanic amount of excitement I've experienced this evening."

"I see what you did there."

"Am I going to get the cold shoulder from you now?"

"It's hard to maintain a frigid relationship with someone who buys you a cuddly boat."

Nick held up a hand. "Hey, let's not be going all overboard, here."

"What size hat do you wear?"

Nick blinked at the non sequitur. "Uh . . . what?"

Ethan grinned at him. "You know. Your capsize."

"*Ethan*." Nick held up a hand to beg for mercy. "That was . . . You have to stop now. That was *painful*."

Ethan turned the car on without answering, his blinding smile nearly enough to outshine the headlights.

CHAPTER *Eight*

Pigeon Forge, TN

The *Titanic* had claimed the place of honor on his pillow, and Ethan still got a jolt of happiness every time he glanced over and caught the bright yellow.

Nick leaned out from the bathroom, toothbrush in his hand and a smear of toothpaste across his cheek. Too damn adorable by far, and Ethan tried not to stare. "So what's the plan for tomorrow? Are we setting sail early?"

Ethan blinked, pulling his attention back. "Hang on, let me check Google Maps. I'm not sure how far Nashville is, but I don't think we need to head out of port too early."

"Nashville? Is there something suitably morbid or frightening there?"

"Not that I know of. More about the music. I mean, I'm sure lots of people have died there."

"Oh." Nick jammed the toothbrush back in his mouth, lips tight around it as he started brushing furiously, and disappeared back into the bathroom.

"Doesn't mean we can't look for something, though, if you want."

Nick didn't answer, instead quietly closing the bathroom door. Caught by surprise, Ethan stared at his reflection in the full-length mirror.

The water running in the bathroom was the only answer he got. When the shower turned on, Ethan sighed and flopped back against his pillows. Time to call his mom anyway.

"Hi, sweetie. How was your day?" He heard the TV, or maybe Suze, in the background.

"Good. I went to Dollywood, but it wasn't really my thing. So I went to the *Titanic* museum for dinner." He ran his fingers over the velvety yellow plush. "I might've gotten a stuffed *Titanic*."

"'Might've,' huh? Do they really sell those?"

"Hang on." He pulled the phone away and texted her a quick picture.

"You know I never know how to look at a text without hanging up."

He sighed loudly. "Geez, Mom. Just give the phone to Suze and have her show you."

His mother huffed at him. "You're a horrible child. Won't even humor your aged mother in her twilight years."

"Good night, Mom. Love you."

"Love you too, kid. Brush your teeth."

"Oh my *God*, goodbye." He hung up, somewhere between laughing and rolling his eyes.

His phone battery was getting low, so he rolled over to plug it in. Nick had left his charging. Ethan unplugged it, flinching a little when the screen flashed to life and notified him there were twenty-seven new texts. Guilt made him flip the phone facedown on the shared nightstand before he plugged his in. *Someone* wanted to talk to Nick, that was for sure. To keep himself from thinking about it, he rolled onto his back and stared up at the popcorn ceiling until his eyes crossed.

Ethan jerked awake from a half doze when the shower shut off, disoriented for several seconds. Surreptitiously wiping at his mouth, he was relieved to find out he hadn't been drooling. By the time Nick opened the bathroom door, toweling his hair, Ethan felt conscious enough to give him a tentative grin.

"My mom didn't believe they sell stuffed *Titanic*s. I had to text her a picture."

Nick peered out from under the towel. "Was she properly appreciative of its, uh . . . yellowness?"

"Who the hell knows?" Ethan sighed, shaking his head. "Hopefully she got my sister to help her pull the picture up."

Nick made a noise of possible agreement, moving past Ethan and coming to stop at the foot of the bed closest to the door. "Hey, I'm sorry. I don't have any right to get annoyed with you about your trip."

Ethan weighed his response and settled for a neutral "Thanks." Not knowing what had provoked the reaction in the first place left him feeling like he was on uneven footing. He sat up a little straighter, shoving a pillow behind his back. "Are you hungry? I think I've got a couple of Snickers bars stashed. Plus my mom packed half the snack aisle from Trader Joe's, but I refuse to eat it, just to prove I can feed myself."

"What does the Trader Joe's snack aisle look like? It's been a while since I've seen one. Do they still have that Pirate's Booty stuff?"

Now there was a subject he could get behind with enthusiasm. "They've got this cheddar popcorn now that's even better. Oh, and cat-shaped ginger cookies. But I think you need to try the dark-chocolate-covered espresso beans. I guarantee it'll make up for all your coffee-less years."

Nick's eyes narrowed suspiciously. "If you say so. I'll try them. I'm not really hungry."

Ethan bit his lip, loathing his middle-child eagerness for everything to be okay. "Are you pissed at me for some reason? Or in a bad mood because someone is blowing through your texting limit for the month?"

There was regret, and then there was instantly fucking knowing he'd said the wrong thing. Even apologizing wouldn't help.

Nick's rigid posture contrasted with the very mobile anger twisting his face into a scowl. He grabbed his cell off the nightstand. "Dude, you looked through my phone? What the fuck?"

"I didn't. I wouldn't do that. I saw it when I moved it to plug mine in. But something's obviously going on with you." Blowing out a frustrated breath, mostly annoyed with himself, Ethan hunched over his lap. "Question still stands, though. What did I do that ticked you off?"

"Nashville. Why are you still going? You hate country music. You said as much when you went to—" Nick waved a hand. "That other country music place that's so boring I can't even remember its name."

"Bristol?" Ethan supplied helpfully, then wished he'd learn to shut up.

Nick's laugh sounded anything but amused. "Yeah, there."

The silence stretched out, long and uncomfortable, until Ethan had to fight not to fidget. "There's nothing wrong with Nashville. I'm pretty sure there's some cool stuff there. There's supposed to be good food."

"Like what?"

"I don't know. There's probably a thousand restaurants on Yelp. I'm sure we can find something."

His answers were too fast, too meaningless. Nick wanted him to admit something, but there wasn't some deep, dark secret. Nashville was next on the list. That was all.

"Ethan." Nick stopped, his voice tamped down, hushed. Too soft, every syllable dragging across Ethan's skin, wrapping him back up in the blankets he'd been smothered in for months. "Why are you even going to Nashville if you don't give a rat's ass about seeing anything there?"

"Because Scott can't!"

Nick reared back like Ethan had hit him, and he realized his throat hurt. He'd screamed. Yelled. Something loudly vocal that might cover for the tears that were already stinging his eyes.

"We had a list." Unable to sit still any longer, Ethan scrambled to his feet, swaying dizzily. He shook a finger at Nick, who *definitely* tried to lean away from him. "We had a *list*. For fucking *years* we had a list of all the stuff we were going to do. If I don't care enough to see the things he wanted to see, who will?" Blinking rapidly, he spun away from Nick, staring at the wall, the TV, the door. Anything to distract himself from the pain trying to rip its way out of him. "Fuck it. Fuck it all."

"I'm sorry." Nick was still standing a safe distance away, and Ethan didn't blame him. If Ethan looked half as crazed as he felt, Nick had every reason to hit the parking lot at a dead run.

The thing was, he *wanted* Nick to understand, but at the same time, the urge to lash out was overwhelming.

"Everybody's sorry. Everybody's sad, and sorry, and they're all 'We're here for you, Ethan,' but he's still fucking *dead*. And everyone's

going to forget him, and this . . . this trip is helping me remember him."
He scrubbed at his face. "Sometimes I have this nightmare where I
wake up and I can't picture his face. It's a blank. And I'm so scared that
one day it won't be a nightmare."

Nick started to say something, and Ethan almost darted forward.
If he hadn't been sure that clamping a hand over Nick's mouth
would be the last thing he did before Nick took off for good, he
might have tried it. The thought of hearing one more meaningless
assurance that he'd always have some part of Scott made his heart beat
double-time—he didn't know if it was anger or fear.

"I don't remember what my brother's laugh sounded like. I can
remember him doing it, but it's like a picture, not something real. Not
something I listened to every day for twelve years." Nick's head was
bowed, his buzzed hair looking prickly as he dug his thumbnail into
the soft skin on his bare wrist. "People who tell you they're sorry just
want you to shut up so they can keep forgetting."

Ethan opened his mouth, but nothing came out. In less than
ten seconds, someone he'd known for three days had described what
he hadn't been able to in over a year. "That's it," he finally managed.
"And that's why I'm doing all this." He waved a hand. "To make sure I
don't end up like that—forgetting a little more every day, until there's
nothing left of him at all."

"Do you honestly think that'll be a problem?" Nick's question
held no accusation, and Ethan struggled to not insert accusation that
wasn't there.

"What you said—about people wanting you to shut up? That's
what the whole year has felt like. Even the people who want me to
talk . . . They want me to talk about me, not him. About how I feel
with him gone." Now that he'd started, Ethan felt looser, his words
flowing and light, rather than each admission being a prison break. "I
don't know how I feel without him. I never had to think about who I
was when I was with him, y'know? I was me. But it turns out I'm not.
I'm not myself, because me was . . . Me was *us*. If I forget him, if I forget
who we were, I'm losing myself too."

"I guess you could look at it as a chance to, I dunno, reinvent who
you are. Make choices about who you want to be." Nick ducked his
head in a half shrug. "Because *that's* so easy to do."

"What if I don't want to reinvent myself?" It was harder than it should've been to keep the anger out of his voice. He knew he sounded petulant, but knowing wasn't changing anything.

Nick made a sound that wasn't really a laugh. "Isn't it great how nobody seems to care if we want to or not?" He shrugged at Ethan, but there was nothing dismissive about his intense focus. "You're stuck. If you can't be you without him, you're going to wind up someone else either way."

Ethan massaged his temples with one hand. The circular conversation was more than he could handle without doing something even more humiliating than the day's already stellar examples. He was pretty sure if it kept going, he was going to top vomiting in public *and* panicking over some stupid fucking shooting demonstration. It took every last shred of willpower he had to steady his voice enough to change the subject. "So about those snacks? Did you still want anything?"

If Nick was surprised by the lack of segue, he hid it well. There was always the chance his yawn wasn't faked, either. It had been a long day. "I think I'm going to try to sleep. You don't have to turn off the lights or anything if you're not tired yet. Turn the TV on, whatever. I'm kind of exhausted."

"Nah, I'm okay with some sleep." His afternoon nap had left him more tired than he'd been when he closed his eyes. He'd been afraid of sleeping too hard, jerking awake every few minutes on the cusp of a bad dream he was already living.

Ethan shuffled into the bathroom and briefly contemplated not brushing his teeth out of spite, before fifteen years of lectures from his dentist swiftly changed his mind. He scrubbed at his face with the scratchy hotel washcloth until he felt as raw outside as he did inside.

Nick had crawled under the covers, facing the window that bled light from the parking lot. He didn't say anything when Ethan turned off the lamp between their beds.

"Night." He whispered it, in case Nick was actually asleep.

Nick's breathing never really settled out, and every few minutes headlights from the parking lot would send crazy shadows crawling across the ceiling. Which Ethan was staring at, dry-eyed and completely awake, his fingers curled into the sheets.

A flash of bright green joined the next set of headlights, seeming to pulse at random in the otherwise dark room. It took him a few minutes to figure out it was the message light on Nick's phone.

"Hey, Nick?" He said it quietly enough not to wake someone who was actually asleep, but Nick's bedding rustled almost as soon as he spoke. "I think you're getting more texts. Can you turn your phone over so the light isn't so bright?" *Or answer them*, he didn't add, because even though his curiosity was killing him, Nick clearly didn't want anything to do with anyone who had his number.

"Oh, shit, yeah. Sorry." Nick rolled over, his screen momentarily throwing long shadows across the craggy popcorn ceiling. His frustrated sigh landed heavy into the silence between them, followed by a thump as he fell back against the mattress.

The green light still flashed against the nightstand when Ethan turned his head to peek at Nick, but the phone was facedown. A new set of headlights washed through the window, limning Nick's T-shirt-covered chest as it rose and fell too fast for anyone on the edge of sleep. Ethan tried on a dozen questions in his head, keeping his peace when none of them sounded anything but intrusive.

Another two or three cars had passed them by when Nick spoke, a high, bitter tone lacing his words with anger. "You probably shouldn't listen to a damn thing I say about dealing with . . . with anything. I'd already started fucking up long before Drew died, and I kept doing it until I aced the final." He kicked the polyester bedspread to the floor in a sudden fit of violence that startled Ethan.

"The guy who keeps texting me? My ex? He's . . . he's fucking psychotic. I haven't even seen him in over a year, and it's like he thinks I'm still hanging on his every word. He was my grand love affair that was supposed to make things all better. So don't listen to me. I didn't mean to take anything from you, or Scott's memory. And I don't know shit."

The darkness made it easier to talk. Well, maybe not easier. Nothing was ever going to do that, but maybe less scary. Less something, anyway. "Pretty sure the one conclusion I've come to is nobody knows shit about dealing with—" Ethan stopped, torn between the platitudes he'd been offered of "losing" someone and the stark reality of it all "—somebody you love dying," he continued, voice remarkably steady. "And then you've got a psychotic stalker on top of that. You probably know more than most."

"Tell me something about him? Scott, I mean."

Ethan hesitated over what to share. What first? What was most important? His mouth twisted into a grimace he knew Nick wouldn't be able to see. Realistically, what was the least likely to leave him aching for the rest of the night?

"He had the most ridiculous coffee order in the world."

It seemed safe enough, until he remembered ordering the stupid venti quad-shot double-pump hazelnut caramel latte by rote when he finally went back to school two weeks after Scott died. It was still the first thing that came to his tongue when he shuffled into his neighborhood Starbucks half-awake.

He must have made some noise while he was lost in his head. Nick sounded like he was trying to be gentle when he spoke.

"My parents took us to Disney when we found out Drew was sick again. He *loved* that godawful Small World ride. I went on it three times with him. Same with all the country displays at Epcot. I think he . . ." Nick coughed, clearing his throat. "He said he was going to go everywhere when he died. Fucking ten years old, and he spit that out at the happiest place on Earth. Mom and Dad had let us go through by ourselves, and I think he wanted to tell me he knew what was going on without making them cry."

"He was lucky to have you." As soon as he said it, Ethan regretted the words. They sounded as clichéd and stupid as everything he'd been told. Except that he meant it. Being ten years old and realizing you were dying? It had to have helped to have Nick there as nonadult support. Nobody wanted to hurt their parents.

Nick made a disparaging noise. "Right. I was too caught up in my own angst to be much comfort."

"I think we both know it's not always about comfort. Sometimes it's about somebody being there who *isn't* trying to jolly you along to feeling better when shit sucks."

"Point taken."

Ethan suddenly wished he was a drinker. Besides the obvious obstacle of being underage, he'd always been involved in some team or another, and there were sobriety pledges and all that crap. The few times he'd had a beer or something stronger at parties, he remembered it making him warm and loose-limbed. There was a bottle of Xanax somewhere in the mess of his bathroom kit that was supposed to do the same thing, but he still hadn't managed to take one. It felt wrong to numb himself. If the therapist he'd spent two months hating was right, feeling every jagged edge of his grief was his way of dealing with survivor's guilt. He wondered if Nick felt the same need to let his pain be *painful*, or if watching your brother die slowly left behind fewer regrets than—

"Ethe. Ethan. Breathe, 'kay?"

He didn't know when Nick had gotten up and crossed the distance between their beds, but he also didn't know when he'd started crying again, or when his lungs had stopped working. One panic attack made it easier to have another. He knew that, like he knew he was supposed to take a pill and let his brain off the treadmill when he had one. But he didn't deserve to.

"He got shot. One of our classmates came to . . ." Ethan struggled upright, the blankets lying over his chest a weight he couldn't bear anymore. Nick grabbed his elbow and helped him, then put a hand on his shoulder, holding him up as the room buckled around them.

"One of our classmates came to the cafeteria and started shooting during a lunch period. Scott . . ."

Nick squeezed his neck, the pressure steady enough to settle him back into his body when he drifted. Ethan stretched his fingers out in his lap, flexing them to the point of pain. "I'd just walked in when the shooting started, and Scott was on the other side of the room. I saw . . . I saw him go down, but I thought he'd tried to crawl under one of the tables like everyone else was doing."

Ethan tried to spit out the rest, but it wasn't happening. He leaned forward and pulled his knees up to his chest, hugging them so he wouldn't have to look at his hands and remember them covered in Scott's blood. Nick let go of his shoulder and disappeared, the edge of the overly springy mattress bouncing up and making everything wobble a little more.

Like that morning at the park, Nick returned with a damp cloth, but this time he leaned over to wipe Ethan's face.

"Do I look that bad?" Ethan laughed through a tired sob, horrified when he felt a bubble of snot blow out of his nose.

"I'd still fuck you," Nick assured him, handing over the washcloth.

Ethan wiped at his face, smudging away the raw tear tracks on his cheeks before surreptitiously wiping his nose. Once it was safe, he snorted a laugh, vaguely worried that he was finding anything funny right now. "I didn't know that option was on the table."

"Table, bed, counter . . . your pick." Nick sat down next to him again, the bed dipping dangerously under his weight. "I mean, you were cute before, but now that I know you can blow bubbles with your nose, I'm all in."

Ethan set the washcloth on the corner of the nightstand, then nearly jumped a mile when Nick caught his hand.

"I'm sorry, dude. I'm not trying to joke you out of the shit you must be going through. You scared me a little. You checked out *hard*." Nick rubbed his thumb across Ethan's knuckles for a second before he seemed to realize what he was doing and let go entirely.

"Scared myself a little." Ethan clenched the hand Nick had been holding, but only to keep himself from reaching out for that connection again. He didn't deserve it, and Nick didn't know . . . Nick thought he was nothing more than a grieving boyfriend. He felt his breath stutter, realizing what a liar he was by omission.

A cool cloth touched his face, and Ethan jerked so hard he tipped halfway over and whacked his head on the ugly wicker headboard nailed to the wall behind the bed. Nick shifted back as well, both hands held up.

"You . . . went somewhere, again." Nick bit his lower lip, thick, dark eyebrows drawing together. "Do you want me to call someone? Or do something?" He rubbed the same spot on the back of his head that Ethan was sure had to be softer for all the attention. "I don't have any pot, but I can probably score some if you give me an hour or two. I don't know, dude. Please tell me how I can help."

If Ethan opened his mouth, he was going to start crying again. Or harder, at any rate. He shook his head, trying not to meet Nick's eyes so he wouldn't have to add to the guilt he was already buried under.

"Okay. I'm going to do a thing, and if you don't like it, you can kick me or something."

The next second, Nick's body was over his, a warmth gone too soon as Nick rolled past him and landed on the bed. Nick's hand slid over his again, prying it open and leaving their fingers loosely intertwined.

"This way you can squeeze as hard as you need to, and I can maybe keep you on this side of your head. Is that cool?"

He wanted to say no, he *needed* to say no, if only because he didn't deserve the comfort Nick was offering. Instead, Ethan found himself nodding. "I have . . . The therapist I saw, she gave me pills. It's the panic attacks, and I feel trapped, but I really don't want to take them." He recognized the disjointedness of his words, but couldn't think of how to string them together any better.

"Okay," Nick repeated. "You don't have to do anything you don't want to. Pills don't fix everything. But if you change your mind, I'll get you one."

Ethan glanced over at Nick, who was lying on his side by the far edge of the bed, his arm outstretched between them. Ethan took another shuddery breath, easing out of the cramped position he'd twisted himself into and scooting down the bed so he could put his sore head on the pillow. Whether he should've or not, he kept hold of the hand Nick had offered. That didn't mean he could stand to meet his eyes, though.

Try as he might, Ethan couldn't force the words out. Nick's hand anchored him to the bed. After a few minutes of silence broken only by thready breathing, Nick brought his other hand into the mix, stroking from Ethan's shoulder to his wrist with light, soothing pressure.

"It was my fault. That Scott was there." Ethan added the caveat hastily. He hadn't been holding the gun. "I was supposed to buy the tickets to prom, but I had an assignment to turn in. Scott said he'd do it. And then Trent showed up. But it should have been me standing in line at the ticket table."

Nick surprised him by not pulling away, instead squeezing his hand. "Do you believe in predestination?"

He blinked, casting his gaze sideways for a moment. "What, like there's a reason for everything?"

Nick shook his head, the velvet buzz of his hair scratching against the pillowcase. "More like everything in your life is already decided. But I'm guessing you don't, right?"

Ethan made a face, trying to imagine his life as a script that was drafted before he was born. That didn't make any sense at all. "No. That sounds . . . stupid."

"But then the opposite is that everything—*everything*—is totally random. And either way, you weren't *supposed* to die. But one way, neither was Scott."

Ethan frowned, trying the words in his head, mentally flipping them back and forth like puzzle pieces that would make something meaningful if he could only get them in the right place. In the end, he tucked them away for later. For now, it was enough to take away Nick's belief that it was really fucking random evilness. That Scott wasn't supposed to die. That neither was he.

"Doing okay?" Nick's fingers tightened fractionally.

"Yeah. Still here." His sigh turned into a jaw-cracking yawn. "Just thinking this time."

"Apparently that wears you out."

"I guess so." Ethan grinned a little. "Must be the jock in me."

"You said it, not me. Think you'll be able to get some sleep?"

He blinked, forcing his eyes back open. "I think so?" Provided Nick stayed right where he was, a solid, comforting presence. But he didn't know how to ask.

Nick yawned this time. "Want me to move back to my bed?" His voice was completely neutral, but Ethan grabbed at the opportunity.

"I'm comfortable, if you are." He hesitated a mere second. "Stay?"

Instead of answering, Nick used his free hand to adjust the pillow under him. His other hand stayed curled with Ethan's.

If he maybe rescued the *Titanic* stuffie from under the sheets and tucked it against his other side, Ethan figured he'd earned a free pass.

Dear Mrs. Raines,
Who knew there was a Titanic *in Pigeon Forge?*
Would you believe people get married here? Weird.
Best thing is they sell yellow Titanic *stuffies in the gift shop.*
Love,
Ethan

CHAPTER Nine

Pigeon Forge, TN

It took longer than Nick would ever admit to calm down when he woke up with someone's hand on his throat. There was no pressure involved, only the slight weight of Ethan's fingers loosely resting against his neck, but his semiconscious brain processed threats better than reality. The surge of adrenaline set his heart racing, blood pounding in his ears and . . . other places.

Awkward.

He edged backward, hoping to dislodge Ethan's hand without waking him. It might've worked, except that Ethan's arm hit the bed with a solid thump instead of the pillow. Nick winced and stilled, holding his breath.

Ethan's eyes fluttered open, bright blue and gummy with sleep. "'S'morning," he mumbled, though Nick couldn't tell if it was a statement, question, or protest. His hand flopped back against his face with a loud smack. "Ooooww."

Nick giggled into the corner of his pillow when Ethan whined himself fully awake.

"You hit me!" The childish outrage in Ethan's exclamation probably had a lot to do with how early it was, but it did nothing to curtail Nick's laughter.

"You hit *yourself*, dork. I don't think that's what they mean by 'self-abuse.'"

"It's too early to be clever." Ethan stuck his lower lip out, rubbing his forehead. "And my head hurts."

Nick didn't know what he was thinking when he rolled over and propped himself up on one elbow. Ethan's forehead was warm under his lips, the scent of his hair a little sweaty. "There. All better?" His complexion hid it better than Ethan's, but he was pretty sure Ethan could still see his blush, and he didn't know whether to flop back over to his own side and laugh or wait. For what, he wasn't sure.

"Uh . . ." Ethan, on the other hand, looked like a freckled lobster. "I think so?" He closed his eyes and appeared to give it several seconds thought, then nodded. "Yeah, seems that way."

Nick was fine until Ethan opened his eyes. Almost nose to nose, his entire field of vision was filled by Ethan's face, and when warm, slightly chapped lips pressed against his, he didn't pull away. If he hadn't initiated it, it was all cool, or at least that's what he tried to convince himself.

Ethan moved slightly, and they both froze. There was no mistaking the hard-on pressing against Nick's leg not far from his own raging case of morning wood.

Reality crashed down. Even if he ignored the ghost of Tyler's voice warning him not to touch anyone, the shame of what he'd been doing washed over him like he'd been dunked in an ice bath. Christ, Ethan had spent the entire day before on the edge of panic, driven by grief that hadn't eased much since his boyfriend's death. And Nick hadn't thought twice about exploiting that, taking advantage of their closeness like . . .

Like *Kyle.*

"Sorry," Nick whispered, rolling away so fast he felt a little dizzy when he stood up. The room was small enough that he had to edge sideways to the end of the bed, facing Ethan's confusion the whole time. He spun around the corner into the bathroom and locked the door so he could press his forehead against the painted wood and hate himself in private.

At least his inconvenient erection was pretty much gone. Now he just had to pee, which probably meant Ethan did too, so there went his chances of hiding in the bathroom for the rest of his life.

"Uh, Nick?" Ethan's voice right against Nick's head made him jump away from the door in an awkward leap. "I kinda need to go." He could hear Ethan breathing before he continued. "And I'm sorry if

I made you uncomfortable. I'll buy you coffee or something to make up for it, okay?"

He sounded so miserable that Nick felt his guilt ratchet up another couple of notches. "Nothing to apologize for. Give . . . give me a minute."

The choked noise might've been a laugh. "No problem, take your time."

"That's not—" Nick cut himself off, recognizing a lost cause when he saw one. "I'll be right out."

He made short work of things and flushed, hoping the sound carried. Nothing to see here, just a guy taking a piss. Twisting the knob to unlock it, he was glad to discover Ethan wasn't standing outside the bathroom. Nick turned on the sink to wash his hands, catching movement in his peripheral vision as Ethan snuck past, head tucked down. Maybe they could go a whole day without any more eye contact. Or maybe he could learn not to be a piece of shit who took advantage of vulnerable people who'd done nothing but be unreasonably awesome to him.

This was why he wasn't supposed to touch people. Tyler and Reverend Hill had counseled him endlessly about his "weakness," his inability to understand boundaries and draw the correct conclusions about how he should act. He'd written it off at first, determined not to let them under his skin. The longer he'd been at Cornerstone, the more he'd had to fight tooth and nail to hang on to the shreds of himself he thought were inviolate, the more he'd started to wonder if they were telling him the truth.

He wasn't going to buy into their bullshit about abstinence and following God away from sin (which he was damn sure meant "Don't be queer because Jesus"). But Tyler had told him over and over how he read situations wrong. Filtered everything through a lens that made it seem like his "desires" were returned, when really, he was projecting his selfish, skewed needs.

The edge of the bed caught Nick when he sat down hard, propping his elbows on his knees and burying his face in his hands. They'd never told him what happened with Kyle was his fault. They'd also never told him it *wasn't*. On Nick's better days, Kyle could take his temper and go fuck himself. The rest of the time, it was too easy to believe that Tyler and Hill were right—that Nick's idea of love was so twisted he couldn't even be trusted to comfort a friend. Sometimes he remembered that Kyle had made him feel wanted, and it was usually his own bottomless well of neediness that had set off their arguments.

Being hurt was inevitable. That was life. Hurting someone else, though . . . If he was that person, he probably always had been. Kyle had seen it in him and taken it in stride.

The bathroom door rattled. Nick lifted his head and lunged for the nightstand as Ethan emerged, heading for the sink. It only took a moment of hesitation before Nick opened his phone and turned the ringer back on. Another glance toward Ethan, back stiff where he stood brushing his teeth across the room, and Nick pulled up his texts and started typing without reading anything that had come in while the phone was off.

Hey. Sorry, I've been on the road.

The answering ping came back almost immediately. *Where are you?*

Tennessee, but

The phone vibrated in his hand before he finished typing, generic ringtone loud in the otherwise silent room. Nick couldn't help but glance up. He hadn't thought Ethan could look any more miserable, but he'd definitely been wrong. Disapproval? Discomfort? Hurt? Impossible to tell which had Ethan's shoulders bunched up tight as he brushed his teeth like he was tired of having them and was trying to sand them out of his mouth.

"Be right back," Nick said.

Ethan didn't respond. Nick hunched his own shoulders as he slipped out of the room, quietly closing the door after him.

"H-hey, Kyle."

"Nicky, are you safe? I'm coming to get you as soon as I put gas in my car."

Nick shook his head, bracing himself against the painted cinderblock wall of the motel. He wanted to curl into the smallest space possible, but he was stuck in the middle of the room block, nary a corner in sight. He settled for crouching low, a smaller target for someone who couldn't even see him.

"*Nicky*!" Kyle's sharp voice turned his name into a reprimand, and Nick wondered how long he'd checked out.

"I'm fine, Kyle. You don't have to do that." *Please don't*, he couldn't quite add, even though it lingered on the tip of his tongue.

"Of course I do." Kyle's tone softened. "You disappeared, and I've been worried. You're not safe on your own. I'll come get you."

Nick tucked the phone against his shoulder, freeing a hand that let him pick at the skin on his thumb. "Sorry, didn't get much chance to tell people where I was going. I'm safe now, though." The weak, questioning tone of his voice wouldn't even have convinced *him*.

"Where are you sleeping? How are you eating? How did you get where you are? Hitchhiking?" The rapid-fire questions made Nick shrink back even more, his ass hitting the concrete.

"This was a bad idea."

Kyle didn't answer.

Nick might've been imagining things in the sudden silence between them, but given Kyle's mercurial temperament, maybe not.

"Waiting this long to call me when you need help? Of course it was a bad idea. Or do you mean letting your parents separate us because of an argument we could have handled as *adults*, on our own terms?"

He regretted the laughter as soon it escaped him, but the past year had given him enough perspective to nurture a cynic's sense of humor. "It's hard to make adult decisions when you're unconscious."

"Things got out of hand. But come on, Nicky, you know I love you. I wanted you the first time I saw you, and that hasn't changed. We can make it work now that your parents can't get between us. They were the ones causing all our problems."

Nick's heart clenched when Kyle said he loved him. For a moment, all he could imagine was letting Kyle come get him. Going to sleep in Kyle's bed and remembering the safety of being held, being *wanted*.

Except his bruises hadn't faded yet when his dad had dropped him off at Camp Cut Yourself. Tyler had brought it up during one of his first group sessions, needling accusations about being on the wrong path stinging him but not really hitting home. Not until Tyler flat out told him that if he didn't rethink his sins, getting hit was going to be the least of his troubles. Maybe he'd meant Nick's soul or something, but the nasty glint to Tyler's placid smile hinted at something else. Fuck dudes, take what he had coming to him. Being wanted by Kyle came with a heavy dose of what he had coming to him.

Kyle's voice pulled him out of his head again. "Tell me where you are. Let me come get you so I know you're okay." Nick shook his head to clear it, but Kyle was continuing. "You're really worrying me. Are you in trouble? Is someone there?"

The concern sounded so sincere, so *real*. The need to refute it immediately was every bit as real. "No, I'm by myself." The last time Kyle had gotten jealous had gone so swimmingly. Nick wasn't going to repeat that mistake.

"Okay, good. It's not safe. There's too many crazy people out there. Stay where you are, don't talk to anyone, and I'll be there as fast as I can."

"No." He faltered, resolve fading as fast as his voice. "I mean, you don't need to do that. I'm fine. Pigeon Forge is full of old people and little kids. I'm safe."

"I can be there in seven hours. Find a McDonald's or something and sit tight."

The motel room door opened, and Nick twisted around so fast he cracked his head against the wall. He drew in a sharp breath over the pain, closing his eyes.

"Nick?" It took a second to sort out that it was Ethan's voice, not Kyle's. "Sorry, didn't mean to scare you. I was, uh, going to get a Coke. Do you want one?"

Nick opened his eyes in time to see the worried pinch in Ethan's expression. His heart sped up, his thumb twitching to cover the mic on his phone as he shook his head.

"Who was that? Nicky, is someone bothering you?" Kyle's voice dropped, a rough edge to the words. "Who are you talking to?"

Hunching over the phone, he turned away from Ethan. "Nobody, it's fine. It's . . . I'm sitting outside." Out of the corner of his eye, Nick saw Ethan walk away without looking back. It hurt far more than logic would have dictated.

"I pulled up a city map. There's a McDonald's on Main Street. Do you think you can find it?"

Nick acknowledged the condescension in a back part of his mind, tucked away with all the other ways Kyle had perfected to tear down his self-worth. "I can find it."

Kyle's snort could've been acknowledgment, but signs pointed to disbelief. "Find a seat in the back and stay put. Don't talk to anyone, and I'll be there by one o'clock."

"I—" Nick was talking to empty airspace. He stared blankly at the phone for several seconds before thumbing it off. Kyle was on his way, and if Nick had to hazard a guess, he'd be here well before the seven-hour mark.

Ethan came around the corner, a can of soda in each hand. He silently held one out to Nick, waiting until he took it before stepping back.

Nick slurped down half the soda in one go, lifting the can toward Ethan in a mock salute. "Now that we've had this nutritious breakfast, you want to get out of here?"

Ethan looked a little surprised, but he nodded enthusiastically. "Sure. There's a McDonald's up the street. Want to hit the drive-through on our way out of town?"

Nick shuddered, passing it off as a shrug. "Nah. I'm sure we can find something with a little more flavor on the road, right? And anyway, I've seen your trunk. You've got enough granola bars in there to feed a small city." It wasn't like Kyle was going to teleport there from Arlington in the next five minutes and walk in looking for an Ex-Boyfriend Value Meal, but Nick didn't want to get anywhere near McDonald's. Maybe ever again.

"The granola bars were my mom's idea, not mine. I'm gonna need a *lot* more Coke to choke those down for breakfast." Ethan shrugged easily. "I can get a couple of Snickers from the machine."

Nick raised his eyebrows. "Mmm. Protein in the morning. What every growing boy needs."

Ethan laughed for a second before he choked it off. "Wait a minute. Did you just ... Was that way dirtier than I think?"

Nick bounced up to the balls of his feet, shoving his phone into his back pocket. "How should I answer that? How dirty do you *think* it was?"

He shouldn't be flirting with Ethan, but he knew what he was good for. Good *at*, rather. Kyle had spent a lot of time telling him what he was good *for*, usually when he was already on his knees. Right now, as fucked up and brambled as his head was, he didn't think he was good for much.

"Dirty enough that you should go wash your hands while I spend the last of my change." Ethan made it sound more like a question than a statement.

Easier to agree, especially if it meant they got on the road faster. The sudden sense of urgency shot through him like pure adrenaline, nerves jumping and jittering. "Yeah, that sounds about right. You go do that, I'll grab the stuff in the room." Nick felt a bit of pride at how steady his voice stayed. He even managed to keep his hands behind his back so Ethan couldn't see them shaking.

Ethan stared glumly at the granola bar sitting on the console before starting the car. "You know, these things get recalled all the time for listeria and shit. My mom'll be sad if I end up in the hospital."

"I'm really sorry they were out of Snickers bars *and* Skittles." Except Nick sounded anything but sorry. "Maybe we can find a Wawa or a 7-Eleven, and I'll buy you one of each. How about that?"

"You don't have to sound so . . . so . . ." Words failed him, and Ethan sighed, picking up the rest of the sunflower seed cardboard and shoving it into his mouth.

"Patronizing?" Nick supplied cheerfully. "Solicitous?"

"Oh God, you're one of those people who got a 9,000 on your verbal SAT or something, aren't you? Get out of my car." Ethan pointed at the scenery whizzing past the window.

"If you say so." Nick reached for the handle and popped the door open.

"Close the door! Jesus Christ, do you have a death wish?" The car swerved to the right a little as he leaned over, trying to stretch across Nick and pull the door shut.

"Just following orders."

Ethan humphed loudly to cover the way his heart was hammering double-time. Not that he thought Nick would actually jump out of the car. Well, as much as he could be sure about someone he'd known for all of three days, and who had some serious issues riding him.

"I wasn't really going to leap out to my death like some tragic heroine." Ethan turned to look at Nick, earning a set of raised eyebrows. "You know, since you seem a little worried."

"I didn't think you were." He didn't sound guilty, not when he was a master of innocence. Except that when he risked another glance away from the road, Nick was still staring at him, making no effort to hide his smirk.

"I'm not suicidal, Ethan."

The statement hit him cold, a chill running across his skin lightning fast, leaving him barely enough time to shudder. "I didn't think you were," he repeated.

"Even my worst ideas are all about survival." Nick snorted, turning his head toward the window. "I mean, look at this half-assed plan to hitchhike out of Virginia. It's worked out pretty good."

"Hitchhiking is dangerous, you know. My little sister could tell you all kinds of horror stories about picking up people who won't let you stop for a perfectly healthy grease-bomb breakfast at a legitimate fast-food chain."

"Eat your granola bar, you big baby. You can suck the grease out of a deep fryer for lunch if you want."

Ethan wrinkled his nose, chomping on another bite of sawdust and stale chocolate chips. "Ew." It stuck in his throat until he took a gulp of Coke. When he finished choking, he said, "Use my phone and see what kind of food specialties Nashville has."

"Oh, there's a vegan café that does an FLT—fakeon, lettuce, and tofu. And they've got carob tofu mousse for dessert!" Nick exclaimed as he paged through sites on Ethan's phone.

"I changed my mind. Get out."

"Well I think the bar scene is off the list."

"Oh, hell yeah. It would be nothing but annoying twangy music on the jukebox. Ain't nobody needs that."

"Like you have a fake ID, Mr. Clean. You'd get us caught at the front door before we could order."

"Hey! I might! You don't know me. I could be that guy your parents warned you about."

Something closed down hard in Nick's expression, some land mine Ethan had detonated by accident. "Not even close, dude."

"And I suppose you're a card-carrying twenty-five-year-old? Been buying your own beer since sixth grade?" Ethan took his cues from Nick, playing along with the conversation as it navigated them safely out of the danger zone.

Nick crackled out a laugh that Ethan had already figured out wasn't meant to signify anything funny. "Nah. Getting wasted underage was one of the perks of fucking a twenty-three-year-old."

Ethan covered his surprise with a weak chuckle of his own. "My one serious attempt at getting drunk involved *a* beer. I didn't even finish it . . . Too scared of coach finding out somehow. Or worse yet, my mom." He shuddered exaggeratedly. "Wasn't worth it. Besides, it tastes shitty."

"I'd say you didn't find the right kind, but I'd be lying. It all tastes like shit. You need to step up your game, ditch the beer, and go for the top-shelf stuff."

"Somehow I don't think college lacrosse parties are going to expand my knowledge of top-shelf alcohol. Not if I want to keep my spot on the team, anyway. I'll probably end up confining my wild and crazy experimentation to new brands of candy and exotic-animal beef jerky."

That got a small smile, at least. "You know if it's exotic, it's probably not beef."

"So you say. There could be some genetically superior cows out there, creating new and unique flavors of jerky."

"But they'd still be . . . Never mind."

"Ha!" Ethan felt a little guilty when Nick jumped, but only a little. "Your 9,000 verbal SAT score has failed you now, hasn't it? I win."

"Yes, you win." Nick threw up his arms. "I am defeated. What are you demanding as a prize? Because I have to warn you I'm broke."

"How about a break for some real food?"

Nick's shoulders slid forward. "Yeah. But be sure to save room for all those vegan delights later."

Ethan drove a few miles in tense silence, almost sure Nick was keeping watch on the vehicles behind them in the mirrors. He'd never been great at prodding things out of people, but he framed half a dozen questions in his head before he finally opened his mouth and gave up on subtlety. "I wasn't eavesdropping when you were on the phone earlier, but I got the impression that maybe it didn't go so well. And I was kind of wondering if maybe there was someone else you might want to call. Like a friend or something, who could . . ." *Help.* But he didn't know if Nick was in the kind of trouble that needed help, or his kind, that just needed time.

Nick shifted away from him by a matter of inches, eyes fixed on some point out the window. "I never had a lot of time for friends before. And after . . ." He shrugged, still staring out the window. "Having friends was . . . discouraged."

"After what?" The question popped out of his mouth before Ethan could think better of it.

"After, when I had the privilege of attending a very exclusive private school." Nick dragged his hand over the crown of his head.

Ethan tried not to fixate on how the few semi-accidental times he'd done the same thing last night, Nick's buzz-cut hair had felt like dark, prickly velvet. Now wasn't the time to start thinking with his dick. "Wait, the hair, the rigid posture . . . Holy shit, dude, did you run away from military school?"

Nick turned back toward him, his smile wry and unexpected. "Pretty close, actually. Although the last time I checked, VMI students got day passes to leave campus at least every six months or so."

"Oh."

"I wasn't in juvie or prison. I mean, it was . . . close, I guess." Nick shrugged before glancing at the mirror again. "Anyway, I didn't really make a lot of friends while I was there. There was a guy who was a counselor for a couple months after I started, but . . ."

"Counselors are good, right? There to help you and shit?" Ethan felt a pang of guilt at lying; he'd wanted nothing to do with the counselor he'd been stuck with. But this was the first time Nick had shown any sort of positive reaction, and he was willing to spout absolute crap to keep that going.

"Stef tried a lot harder than anyone else there. He gave me his number and stuff before he left, even though he wasn't supposed to."

"So maybe you could call him?" Ethan took a breath and a mental step back, afraid he'd shot the words out too fast. "Not that I'm trying to ditch you. You know that, right? I mean, I'm looking forward to corrupting you with every form of caffeine available to man. But I don't think . . ." He trailed off, weighing his words. "I'm not sure I'm enough."

"Hey, don't knock your white-knight skills. I mean, except for almost killing me, you've been more than enough."

"It was an accident! You were standing in the road."

"A likely story." Nick pulled his ratty backpack into his lap, unzipping it and flipping the top inside out. Ethan tried to keep his eyes on the road, but he spared a look or two in Nick's direction. He seemed to be trying to squeeze something out of the back of the bag, and finally crowed in triumph as the corner of a piece of paper came into view. Nick's unguarded expression betrayed his worry as he unrolled it. Ethan winced when Nick bit his lower lip again, wondering if it wasn't bruised from similar treatment anytime Nick was on edge.

"I had to hide it," he explained, even though Ethan hadn't asked. "I think he could have gotten in a lot of trouble. He was worried about me, though." Nick put the same hand back in his hair, squeezing the top of his head until Ethan almost told him to stop. "I don't . . . What if . . . What if he *wants* something? What if it was one of those 'Oh sure, if you're in town, give me a call' things?"

"Most people wouldn't risk their jobs for that." Ethan flipped his blinker on to change lanes. "And if he wants something you don't want to give him, then all you have to do is tell him to fuck off and hang up, right?"

"I guess?" Nick unfolded and refolded the tiny piece of paper.

"It's not like he can put a tracer on your phone from a phone call, so I think you're safe."

Nick jerked upright in the seat, crushing the phone number in his hand, and Ethan had to stop his own surprised jolt, gripping the steering wheel tighter instead. Another land mine detonated.

"Maybe I'll text him later. Hell, it's been a year. He might not even remember me anymore." Nick glanced in the side-view mirror, then back at his lap.

Ethan waffled back and forth over saying anything else, afraid to make things worse. "Speaking from experience, I've found the longer you put something off, the harder it is to do. Not that I'm trying to push you or anything," he added quickly.

"That's great and all, except when your choices are shitty ones, sometimes it's better to put them off as long as possible." Nick reached under himself and pulled his wallet out, tucking the paper into it before Ethan could get a better look at it. "I'll think about it." When Nick's attention drifted back out the window, he didn't seem to notice he was tugging a thread that was unraveling his shirt.

Ethan reached impulsively across the center console, laying his hand over Nick's to still him. "If you don't want to call him, you don't have to. I'm not going to make you do anything you don't want to."

"You won't pull over and stop this car until I make a good decision?"

"That's not *really* funny until you have seven kids and two parents in a van on the way to a family reunion. Then it's a constant running joke, because my poor parents ended up stopping every three miles."

Nick smiled a little, making no effort to move his hand. "Vacations with your family must've been one hell of an adventure."

"You have no idea," Ethan said, the nostalgia making him smile. "I would've abandoned us all along some country road and sped away, if I were my parents."

Nick turned his head, eyebrows slowly rising, and Ethan realized what he'd said.

"Oh fuck, I didn't mean it . . . They didn't do that to you—"

"Relax, dude, I'm fucking with you." Nick leaned across the console, making a lightning-fast strike and dropping a damp smack against Ethan's cheek. "It's really, really easy."

He tried for a scowl and failed. The kiss wiped out any potential sting to the insult . . . although was it really an insult if it was true?

"That's me. Easy."

"Oh yeah?" Ethan was startled by the proximity of Nick's voice, the warm rush of breath across his ear when Nick spoke. He shivered, the car drifting before he yanked it back on course. Whether Nick had moved away or been thrown back into his seat, Ethan didn't know, but it was probably for the best. It was really difficult to conceal an erection when he was supposed to keep both hands on the wheel, and he was halfway there from the teasing suggestion in those two innocuous words.

"So, uh, yeah." Ethan coughed, eyes locked on the road. "Think it's time to stop for breakfast? A real breakfast?"

Nick let out a long-suffering sigh. "I suppose. But not McDonald's."

"Great! The sign we passed said there's a Cracker Barrel at the next exit. I can smoke you at the peg game, and we can load up on weird candy."

Nick shook his head. "How are you not dead of scurvy or something?"

"Starbursts, probably. They've got real fruit juice in them."

"Jesus Christ," Nick muttered, sitting up a little straighter as he tried to look in the rearview mirror.

Ethan hit the blinker and moved into the exit lane. "It's okay, I'm pretty sure my mom didn't send the nutrition cops after us." Nick blinked, and Ethan nodded toward the passenger window. "You looked worried, like you were watching for them."

"Still expecting that lady from the *Titanic* museum to track us down and yell at me again. Especially now that we're indulging in lewd semipublic displays."

"If I see a minivan with those little stick figures and eighteen honor roll stickers, I'll try to lose her." Ethan spared a second to grin at Nick, who didn't really look suitably charmed. As he decelerated down the off-ramp, he tried to find a reassurance that landed somewhere between the mercurial shift of dirty teasing and worried vigilance. However someone might do that was kind of beyond him, though. "You know you're safe with me, right? I'm not going to dump you on the side of the road, and I'm not going to make you take help from anyone you don't want it from. You're stuck with me. Which is bad enough."

From the corner of his eye, Ethan saw Nick's face fall. He was surprised when Nick's hand landed on his, heavy, like Nick was trying to give him something with his touch that they couldn't seem to manage with words.

"Best offer I've had all day," Nick said, and it didn't sound like a joke.

Ethan hesitated, hand extended, as he waffled between chocolate and vanilla Moon Pies.

"I swear to God, if you don't pick one soon, I'm going to make you get the banana."

"This is an important decision. Chocolate goes with Coke, but you really want to have vanilla on hand to go with motel coffee. You can dip them in, and it's really good."

Nick raised an eyebrow in what was becoming a familiar expression. "Mmm. Didn't know you were the vanilla type."

"Not all the time, but it *is* a classic—" Nick's laughter cut him off, and Ethan felt a blush climb his face. "Never mind. But see if you get a Moon Pie. Or a giant peanut butter cup. We'll see who laughs last."

"Guess I'll have to occupy my mouth with something else." Nick picked up a ceramic banana from a shelf of cheerfully fat fake food. Waggling it in Ethan's face was . . . unnecessary. He was saved from having to reply by hearing his name over the intercom.

The grandmotherly waitress, Betty, led them to a table and waited for them to sit down before setting the menus on the table. "Can I start you with something to drink?"

"Coffee," Ethan said immediately. "Lots of coffee. I've been deprived so far today."

She patted his shoulder. "Well, no one should be forced to live like that. I'll leave a pot on the table." She turned to Nick. "What about you, sweetie?"

"Uh, a Coke, I guess. I don't feel quite as disadvantaged as him."

"Well, you make sure you stay that way." She patted Nick's shoulder as well. "I'll be right back with your drinks."

"Folksy." Nick's lip curled with distaste, though he stopped short of brushing off his shoulder after she left.

"Don't be a snob. She's very nice, considering she probably thinks we're going to leave her a seventy-five-cent tip." Ethan flicked a packet of sugar across the table with his fingers, nailing Nick in the chest.

"Maybe I can pay her in advance not to touch me," Nick groused, looking around at the plethora of wall decorations.

"Is that a problem? Because sometimes it seems like it is, and sometimes . . ." Ethan didn't know how to finish. Luckily, Nick did.

"And sometimes I crawl into bed with you to spoon?" He shrugged, the loose neck of his T-shirt falling low enough to expose the hollow of his throat. "Yeah, I don't know either. Sometimes it's a huge deal, and sometimes it isn't. Don't ask me to tell you which is when, or when is which, or whatever."

"Maybe you could give me a heads-up when it's one of the not-okay times? I don't want you trying to jump out of a moving car again. Took a couple of years off my life. Uncool."

Nick picked up the sugar packet, folding and unfolding it. "You *told* me to get out, so that hardly counts. But yeah, I'll try. I don't always know until, well, I know."

"I guess that makes sense?" Ethan tried again. "Sure, yeah, that makes sense." He could be supportive even when he was confused. "So what d'you want to eat?"

"I've settled on 'anything but grits,' and I'm working on narrowing the field by what part of the pig I'm most interested in eating. I'm thinking hash brown casserole and bacon. Should be faster than some sixteen-course big boy breakfast."

Ethan didn't have to pretend that hard to be offended, clutching his brown paper menu to his chest. "Oh. You mean what I was planning to order?"

Nick's sigh went on for way longer than it needed to, and Ethan debated flicking another sugar packet at him. Drink arrival blew that plan, but he waited until the waitress stepped away, then grabbed the straw meant for Nick's Coke. Ripping off the end of the paper, he blew on the straw, cheering when the wrapper connected with Nick's nose. "You're sure in a rush for someone who doesn't even want to go to Nashville."

"Very eager to get to the Country Music Hall of Fame. Lemme tell you how eager." Nick leaned halfway across the table, braced on one arm, every gesture as exaggerated as a cartoon villain. "So. Eager."

Ethan fell back on his natural defense against sarcasm—enthusiastically refusing to get it. "Awesome! Let's order, and I'll pull up GPS and check our ETA. And their hours today."

"They'll be closed by the time you eat your breakfast."

"How long have we been together now? You've seen me eat, so you know that's not going to be a problem." Ethan snapped his mouth shut, realizing too late what he'd said. "Traveling together, I mean."

"Smooth." Nick snickered, reaching across the table for the little triangular peg jump game. As reactions went, it wasn't as embarrassing as Ethan had feared.

Their waitress returned to take their orders, friendly as before. Ethan thought of half a dozen inane special requests every time it seemed like she might touch Nick, until her smile looked a little strained and she finally left. "I hope you appreciate that I now have to eat my grits without maple syrup. There's no way I'm asking that poor woman for anything else this entire meal."

Nick rolled his eyes. "I don't see how you could. I don't think my grandmother was that picky when she went out to eat, and service folks around the world hated her."

"Hey, see if I try to save you from untoward advances from our waitress again."

Some of his not-quite-faked hurt must've been conveyed, because Nick glanced up, startled. "Is that what you were doing? I thought you were just being a pain in the ass."

"You're welcome."

"Thank you," Nick amended.

"I'll let you make it up to me by beating your ass in the peg board game." Ethan paused long enough to load up his coffee with four sugar packets and three creamers. "What?"

Nick shook his head. "I thought you *liked* coffee."

"Properly prepared."

"So next time I bring you a cup it should be about half cream and sugar?"

Ethan sipped his coffee, eyes closing as he inhaled the steam. "I'll drink it black if I have to, but this is better. Don't judge me. I need to be fully prepared for our trip to the Country Music Hall of Fame."

Betty came by again with silverware and condiments, setting them down as she cocked her head in Ethan's direction. "You're not trying to go today, are you honey? Didn't you hear on the news? There's been record rainfall in Nashville this past week. There was some kind of sewage backup, and they had to close it so they could move things to the upper floors."

"Oh." His forced optimism left him in a rush so hard he felt dizzy. It must have been obvious too, since Nick looked like he was about to crawl over the table and Betty was patting his shoulder.

"Don't worry, there's still plenty to do in Nashville. I'll go see if your food is ready."

"I . . . Fuck. Now what?" He'd already had the postcard to Scott's parents planned out. Ethan propped his elbows on the table and dropped his face into his hands.

"If it means that much, we could wait a day and see if it gets cleaned up." The words sounded like they were being dragged out of Nick with ice picks and fishhooks.

Ethan shook his head. "No, that seems crazy. And I can't see it taking less than a week or so. I mean, sewage and all . . ." He peered through his fingers in time to see undeniable relief slide across Nick's face.

"So maybe we could eat and head on down the road, see what looks interesting." Nick fished in his bag for his phone, and silence fell while Ethan tried to keep it together.

It wasn't the end of the world. It was a stupid, closed museum that he didn't even really want to go to—except Scott had. Scott had desperately wanted to go, enough to agree to go to the Bell Witch farm even though the story creeped him out. Scott had wanted . . .

Scott had wanted to live to see nineteen.

"How about a replica of the Parthenon? According to their website, they're the 'Athens of the South.' Or there's—"

Ethan's chair scraped across the floor, colliding with someone seated at the table behind them. Nick's sympathetic look told him everything he needed to know about how well he was keeping his cool. Ethan stuttered through an apology, and almost ran into a busboy with a full bucket of dishes, as he tried to escape the table. "Bathroom. Be right back."

He didn't register the world around him again until he'd locked himself in a stall and leaned gingerly against the tile wall. Tinny music played above his head, intercut now and then by the hostess calling a party to be seated. It was so fucking normal it made his teeth ache. Although upon reflection, that was probably the way he was clenching his jaw to hold back whatever was making his throat so tight.

Minutes passed while he stood backed into the corner of a bathroom stall. When he was sure he wasn't going to hyperventilate or vomit, he opened the stall door. Three dragging steps got him to the sink, and he stared at himself in the mirror. Fluorescent lights were notoriously unflattering, but this was ridiculous. He'd give small children nightmares.

Ethan took a breath, then waved his hands under the automatic faucet. It made splashing water on his face a lot harder, but he managed one-handed. He hadn't planned for the automatic hand dryers, either, and rather than stick his head underneath one, he swiped his face on his shirt sleeve. Another deep breath and he made his way back to the table.

Nick looked up, and Ethan managed a wan smile. "Sorry about that."

Their food had come while he was holding a hostile takeover of the single stall in the men's room, and for the first time ever, he wasn't salivating at the sight. He sat down, reached for his fork, and poked at his eggs.

"We could box it up and go, if you want."

Ethan barely had to glance up from his plate to see the death grip Nick had on his own fork, not to mention the covert, nervous peeks he kept directing out the windows.

"There's no reason to hurry. Nowhere to go anyway." And now he was going to sound like a sulky kid. Great. Today was just . . . great.

He got no answer, probably because Nick didn't want to talk to a kindergartener in need of a nap.

Betty chose then to pop up, frowning. "Is everything okay, boys? If something's not right, I can run it back to the kitchen."

Nick saved him from having to put on a smile. "No, ma'am. Eyes bigger than our stomachs, I think. Could we maybe get boxes? My friend isn't feeling great. I beat him at the peg game."

Ethan snorted, but the stack of brightly colored golf tees next to the little triangle board didn't lie. Nick really had gotten it down to one peg. "It's mostly the gloating that's putting me off my food," he assured Betty, who had clearly been lied to by far better men than him. She shook her head, tsking as she went to get their containers.

Once she was out of earshot, he turned to Nick. "Did you cheat?"

"I'm offended, sir, grievously offended. I demand satisfaction for this insult. If I had a glove, I would slap you."

"You can be offended *and* a cheater, is all I'm saying." Ethan stabbed his eggs again, this time managing to swallow a bite.

"Son, I will whip your ass at the peg game any day of the week, with one arm tied behind my back." Nick took a swig of his soda, slamming the tumbler onto the table like a challenge. "Also checkers, Chinese checkers, Uno, Go Fish, and Battleship. I'm not allowed to play Hungry Hungry Hippos anymore. Banned in all fifty states." Wiping his mouth on the back of his hand, Nick tried an arch expression. "True story."

The knot that had been sitting solidly in the back of Ethan's throat dissolved in a burst of laughter. "The truest. I can tell." Leaning back in his chair, Ethan reached for his lukewarm coffee. "Anything else you're banned from doing? Any bench warrants? Secret maple syrup assassins on your tail?" He smiled at Betty when she set down two boxes and left to take care of another table.

Nick popped open one of the styrofoam boxes and started shoveling food in. "Right on my tail, so if we could get going, that would be great."

Ethan set his coffee down, his mood turning serious. "You're not joking, are you?"

Shoulders hunching inward, Nick didn't say anything, and that in and of itself was an answer.

With their food packed up, Ethan led the way to the counter, not even stopping for candy. He paid, making sure to leave Betty a nice tip for putting up with them. They were silent in the parking lot, and Ethan almost expected Nick to bolt instead of getting in the car. Once they were both sweltering in the close air of the sealed car, Ethan felt safe enough to push.

"Can you please tell me what's going on with you? I know I said you didn't have to, and you still don't, but . . . Dude. I need to know *something*. I think you're scared, and that sucks, so if there's anything I can do to help, I'll do it."

"Scared?" Nick stared down at his seat belt, hands twisting together in his lap. "I guess that's a fair description."

"Are you in danger?" It should have been a ridiculous question, but as keyed up as Nick was, Ethan didn't think he was too far off the mark.

Nick leaned forward, his fingers still locked together in front of him as his mouth worked without sound for a second. "Yes— No. I mean, no more than in the past. I talked to my ex-boyfriend, Kyle. He thinks he's on his way to pick me up at a McDonald's in Pigeon Forge, and I'm not there." Nick's voice fell as he addressed the worn floor mat under his feet. "He's going to be so angry."

Ethan's hand clenched around his car keys. "And that puts you in danger." It wasn't a question.

"Yeah." Nick almost exhaled the syllable. "He's the reason I got shipped off to Camp Cornerstone." His mouth twitched, but it was nothing like a smile. "With a black eye and two busted ribs."

CHAPTER *Ten*

Crossville, TN

Nick tried to force himself to meet Ethan's gaze and failed. He didn't want to see the shock or, worse, the disgust. He felt enough of that himself.

"What's Camp . . . What did you call it?"

Ethan's voice pulled Nick out of his own head, and he answered without thinking. "Cornerstone. It's one of those boot camp places." He snorted, wiggling his fingers. "Building stronger youth through the cornerstones of faith, respect, humility, and accountability."

"That sounds like something from a brochure."

"You have to repeat the cornerstones a hundred times every morning before you can pee. I'll probably never see another urinal without feeling *humility*." Yeah, *that* was a memory he didn't want—Tyler standing behind him, making him repeat the cornerstones until he was begging, until it was too late. Having to walk past everyone else in his stained sweatpants . . . But Tyler wasn't looking for him. Kyle was.

"Anyway. After my brother died . . . before too? I was all kinds of fucked up. I knew Kyle from swim-meet stuff. We started hanging out. He was . . . He let me talk about Drew. He was nice to me. And then we started fucking. I was too stupid to see that my boyfriend wanting to know where I was 24/7 and leaving bruises under my clothes so I'd 'think of him when he wasn't here' didn't actually mean he loved me. So then eventually he accused me of cheating on him, left bruises *everyone* could see, and my parents flipped out and sent me off to

Camp Jesusville to get cured of letting hot older guys lead me around by my dick."

Ethan whistled softly. "That's . . . Shit, I don't even know what to say. 'I'm sorry' seems inadequate. That is all kinds of fucked up."

Nick whipped off a three-fingered salute. "I'm a prodigy."

"No, seriously, I *am* sorry. And I honestly don't know what to say." Ethan shook his head. "I'm starting to feel like we should have our own Lifetime movies or something."

Nick shrugged, his hand falling to the window sill, where he traced the tips of his fingers over the sun-bleached plastic molding. "I don't know what to say either. It's what got me here, y'know? I don't think about it that much." Only every second or so, or every time he had to make a choice based on the fear he'd get it wrong, rather than what he actually wanted.

"Yeah? I'd be thinking about it pretty much every waking minute. And watching the rearview mirror."

Ethan released his death grip on the steering wheel long enough to brush Nick's shoulder, and he tried not to jump at the touch. They hadn't even left their parking space, so he suspected Ethan was hanging on to the wheel in an effort not to smother him in supportive hugs or something. Nick appreciated the thoughtfulness. "Well, I *was* watching the mirror . . ."

"With good reason." Ethan visibly hesitated, and Nick tensed. "Thank you. I know it probably sucked to have to drag that up, and I appreciate you trusting me with it."

Is that what it was, trust? Or was it a need to spill it out in a vain attempt to purge himself? Maybe, if he was pretending to be a decent person, it was about warning Ethan away from his swamp of a life. *Beware! Quicksand and moral turpitude!*

"Yeah. Well. You're my ride and all." Nick waved a hand vaguely in front of himself, then instantly felt bad for how it sounded. "And the first friend I've had in a long time. Sorry I cut your breakfast short because I'm afraid . . ." He trailed off, gulping back the first slightly hysterical giggle. "That my psycho ex can . . ." Another giggle rose like a bubble escaping a glass of soda, tinging his voice with deeply inappropriate humor. "Find me in the middle of Tennessee like . . . like a sniffer . . . dog." And that was it, all the tension snapped and maybe he did too. Maybe he had a long time ago.

Ethan shot him a sideways look, eyes wide, and Nick laughed harder. Ethan cracked a smile. "So are you saying he can't? Because I'm willing to, I dunno, spread coffee grounds around the car or something. Isn't that what they do to throw off the drug-sniffing dogs?"

"We probably need a circle of salt to keep him away." Nick coughed, the pinch in his lungs growing tighter with each unpredictable giggle. "I learned how to make those stupid God's Eye things at Cornerstone. Aren't they supposed to ward away evil or something?"

"Or sage. I think I've seen that too."

Ethan's level of enthusiasm made his eyes water with the effort to stop another round of giggling. "We can pick some up at the craft store, when we get the popsicle sticks and yarn."

"Do they sell sage at craft stores?"

"Sure, right next to the holy water and cursed spell books. Hobby Lobby's got a demonology aisle."

"Eh, my mom would kill me if she found out I'd spent money at Hobby Lobby." Ethan tapped the steering wheel with one hand. "Do you think it grows wild anywhere around here? We could pick our own. Wait." He turned toward Nick, grinning. "I'm an idiot. The grocery store sells sage, right in those little red boxes from McCormick."

"I should've thought of that years ago. I'll pop him into a nice hot oven with a little dry rub and be done with it. Suck it, *Chopped* judges. I will *own* the entrée round."

Ethan shook his head. "I'm a little scared right now. Scared, and turned on. It's a weird combination."

"So make sure you stay on my good side, and you won't end up Boyfriend Brûlée."

"You think you'll make it through to the dessert round?" Ethan's eyebrows, which couldn't hold a candle to his own, rose.

"A guy can hope," he said, licking his lips in a way he hoped was at least funny, if not hot. Nick wasn't sure where to go from where they were. At least his hands had stopped shaking. "So. How's your morning going?"

Ethan chuckled at the obvious change of subject, lifting his hand off the wheel and hesitating only a second before he put it on Nick's shoulder, squeezing lightly. Nick leaned into the touch. Nobody had cured him of that yet, of wanting to feel grounded and safe—not Kyle, not even Tyler. Nothing seemed to make him feel less needy. Maybe if he could've fixed that, he wouldn't be hitchhiking across the country, confessing how pathetic he was to near-strangers.

"Honestly, what I think this morning needs is a dozen glazed doughnuts, preferably hot. And I'm pretty sure I saw a sign for Krispy Kreme up ahead." Ethan left his hand on Nick's shoulder while he talked, his voice a comforting rise and fall of kindness and sugar. "We can get it to go. I'm good at eating hot doughnuts on the road. That way we can stay ahead of the ex . . . and, more importantly, keep you out of the local paper as the Iron Chef Killer. That work for you?"

Nick managed a nod, almost too tired for even that small a motion. "That works for me." He settled carefully back in the seat, sliding a little lower so Ethan's hand wouldn't fall off. "I'm sorry I ruined breakfast. I should have . . ." He sighed, closing his eyes for a second against the bright intrusion of the sun. "I don't know. Not fucked a stalker, I guess."

"He's the one who keeps texting you, right? You could block his number."

It wasn't that the idea hadn't occurred to him. His dad had made him block Kyle's old number, and aside from the gnawing worry that Kyle was going to be pissed he wasn't answering, the blissful lack of demands had been almost a relief. He kept his eyes closed, afraid he'd betray something if he had to look at Ethan. He could block the number, sure. But what if? What if he really didn't have any other options? What if he'd already fucked himself up so bad that nobody normal could love him? He couldn't say that shit to Ethan, though, so he swallowed it down and lied. He had permission, after all. "Yeah. I should do that."

"But you won't."

Nick jerked up to look at Ethan. "What?"

Ethan shrugged. "If you do, you won't know what he's doing. I get that. Better to keep an eye on an enemy."

Nick hadn't even considered it in those terms, but as soon as Ethan said it, they made perfect sense to him. If he blocked Kyle, he had no way to know where or when he might show up. If he let the texts and calls keep rolling through, no matter how tense they made him, at least he could ignore them until he had the energy to deal with it. It was the only measure of control he was going to get.

"He . . . he was . . . he was everything, you know? If I wasn't with Kyle, I was thinking about him, or . . ." Worrying about what he might've done wrong, but that was another thing Nick wasn't going to tell Ethan. He was already good for a silver in the Pathetic Olympics. No need to go for gold.

"I know what you mean." Ethan's focus seemed to turn inward for a moment, voice going quiet. "Leaves a hole, huh?"

The realization of what he'd said came too late to pull the words back, and Nick floundered for something to say. "Different kind of hole, but yeah. It's weird that you can miss something so obviously *bad* for you so much."

"I count myself lucky, then. Although there's days when I want to crawl in that hole and pull the dirt over me."

"Getting caught felt like I'd failed somehow. I needed more time to figure out how to handle it, and then all of a sudden I was reciting Bible verses while I moved rock piles from one side of a field to another." Nick sighed. "I know that's fucked up. I think because it wasn't something I got to end, it's hard to figure out if it's really over or not? Or . . . or like part of me wants to believe that it was a mistake. Because I really fucking loved him, you know? And if I couldn't get that right . . . where does that leave me?"

Ethan didn't answer at first, and Nick took a second to angrily wipe his eyes on the sleeve of his shirt. "Fuck, this is stupid. You wanted doughnuts, right?"

"Few things in life that sugar can't cure." Ethan started the car and backed out of their parking space. "And guaranteed to cure when the hot light's on." He nodded toward Nick's phone. "Keep an eye on things, let me know if we have to step it into high gear. I've seen *Smokey and the Bandit*. We're good to outrun an asshole ex."

"Hate to break it to you, but I think Bandit had a Trans Am, not a 1990-what Subaru."

"Don't ever insult a man's wheels, dude. It's like insulting, well, something else."

"Oooh, does that mean you're packing a station wagon in those jeans?" Nick leered, dragging his gaze over Ethan's crotch for effect. Effect that was mostly lost because Ethan was looking at the road, but there was definitely a blush tinting his cheeks.

Nick probably should have felt guilty for flirting with Ethan to make himself forget how bad everything outside the car was, but he'd nearly exhausted his reserves of self-loathing for the day, and it wasn't even ten.

"So if you could call anyone else—a friend or relative, or *someone*, who would it be?"

Nick sat up, the question hitting him out of nowhere. Ethan was a sneaky little fucker.

"Probably Stef, from Camp Killjoy, I guess. He was really good at getting me to be less stupid."

Ethan glanced at Nick when he should have been paying attention to the road. "Would it help if you talked to him?"

Nick didn't know how to explain the instant recoil to Ethan. He'd failed at Cornerstone. Checked out on his responsibilities. His parents had already written him off, and Kyle knew him for what he was—a grand failure in the making. Telling Stef he hadn't been able to handle the program meant letting someone new down. Someone who'd actually had some kind of hope for him. He shook his head, aware that it wasn't enough of an answer. "Nah."

"I'll buy you a doughnut."

"I'm easy, Ethan. Not cheap." Nick pulled at a thread dangling from the hem of his T-shirt, winding it tight around the tip of his finger.

"Two doughnuts? Chocolate milk? Work with me here."

He'd managed to turn the tip of his finger purple before he looked up, straight out the windshield instead of at Ethan. "I'll trade you. I'll send Stef a text if you'll pick somewhere in this stupid fucking town that *you* want to go. And Krispy Kreme doesn't count."

"That's playing dirty." Ethan sounded somewhere between annoyed and admiring.

"And?"

Ethan huffed a sigh. "Fine, I'll submit to your blackmail. Bell Witch Cave. It's about forty-five minutes out of Nashville. As long as it hasn't been flooded, I guess." He poked a finger at Nick. "But no backing out."

Too late to back out. "What the hell is the Bell Witch Cave?"

"It's a haunted farm with a cave where the Bell Witch lives. Duh." Warming to the story, Ethan turned to face Nick at a stop light. "She keeps coming back and, like, knows the past and the future. She haunted this family for years. The daughter got pinched and hit by her. They heard chains being dragged in the house. She came back and haunted one of the sons years later too."

"Right. Sounds . . . enchanting." Definitely too late to back out, Ethan being on a tear and all. "We don't have to spend the night there or anything, do we?"

"I wish. You have to book a year in advance to do one of the overnight tours."

"Darn," Nick said without an ounce of sincerity.

The aggrieved look Ethan gave him, however, seemed real. "If I'd known was a chance of staying here, I would've booked. Maybe we could park in the back of the lot and spend the night if nobody notices us."

"That sounds like a spectacularly bad idea."

Ethan snickered. "You too scared?"

"Only of cops and potential trespassing charges."

"You have no sense of adventure."

"I got in the car with a guy who tried to run me over. I think that counts as an adventure."

"I'm going to have to give you that one." Ethan swung them across traffic into the Krispy Kreme parking lot, where a bright-red neon light greeted them.

Nick swallowed around the lingering tightness in his throat, fumbling with his seat belt to distract himself. "Drew loved these. Mom used to call to find out when the hot light was going to be on a couple days after he had chemo, and we'd all go buy a dozen and eat them in the car." He smiled at Ethan, because it wasn't a sad memory, just a reminder of the happy, sticky kid his brother had so rarely gotten to be.

"Then I say we go eat a dozen in his honor."

"Deal." Nick left his bag in the seat when he got out, his phone shoved back inside it somewhere like a bomb wrapped in clean underwear and tangled earphone cords.

Hunger and imprudence had made half a dozen hot doughnuts seem like a great idea. Between his digestive unrest, Ethan ensconced on a swing set on the other side of the park, and his thumb hovering over an undialed number, Nick was seriously questioning his life choices.

"Call him!" Ethan yelled, kicking the swing up. Nick flipped him off and hit Call before he could spend another ten minutes debating between a call or a text.

"Please take me off your list." Stef's vaguely annoyed voice answering was followed by dead air, and Nick's phone showed the call had ended.

He glanced at Ethan, who'd leaned back and was pumping for the sky, his long legs scraping the ground with every arc of the swing. Did that count? Technically, he *had* called.

With a sigh, Nick redialed, half-expecting Stef not to pick up at all.

"Hello?"

Judging from the first call, he had about two seconds to answer, but suddenly, talking seemed like a skill he didn't possess. Stef hadn't meant *call me if you're ever homeless*. Probably. Except he'd seen Nick at a pretty low point, so maybe . . .

"I'm hanging u—"

"Wait, Stef, don't hang up." The words tumbled out of him in someone else's voice.

"I'm sorry, who is this? I don't have your number saved."

"Nick. Um. Hamilton. From Cornerstone?"

The unmistakable noise of a phone hitting the floor echoed across the call, Stef's voice urgent in the background. "Holy shit! Hang on. Shit. Fuck. Goddamn it!"

Nick snickered, waiting for Stef to collect himself. "That's going to be a twenty-four-hour speech restriction, Mr. Hansen." Nothing like having past abuse to laugh and bond over.

"If you're joking about it, I know you have to be out of that shithole. Are you okay?"

"I think? Depending on your definition of 'okay.'" Nick glanced over at Ethan, who was coming dangerously close to falling off the swing, obviously trying to listen in on the conversation without looking like he was. "I might need some advice or something, though."

"Right. After my poor life choices, that's the one thing I'm not sure I can provide. I mean, I willingly took a job at that place. Doesn't say much for my overall intelligence."

"I'm glad you did," Nick said. "I really needed someone to tell me I was going to make it out of there."

Stef sighed, the sound carrying clearly over the line. "You're out and you sound good. Means they didn't crush you. Where are you? Did you go home?"

"Uh. Not exactly?" Nick turned his back to Ethan, crossing his legs in front of himself on the picnic table. "I was doing kitchen duty, and I saw a calendar in the office, and . . . I don't know. It was my birthday. So I packed up my stuff and told them I was leaving." Nick smoothed his hand over the back of his head, focusing on the prickle of hair against his fingertips. "Tyler and Reverend Hill didn't take it very well, but I got out."

"I'm proud of you, kid. That took courage." It should have sounded cheesy, but something about the way Stef said it made it sound real, like Nick might actually believe it one day.

"Yeah, well. I wasn't going to stay there anymore if I didn't have to."

Stef made a noise of agreement. "So where are you? Did your parents come get you?"

"I kind of haven't called them?" Nick let it be a question, even though he didn't want an answer. "I was hitchhiking, and this guy picked me up, so I'm in Nashville now. And apparently I'm going to some murder farm this afternoon or something."

Several seconds of silence went by before Stef spoke. "Okay. Right. If you're in danger, say, fuck, 'green.' Just say 'green' and I'll call 911, get a tracker on your phone."

"Green? What— No!" Nick choked down a laugh. "I'm fine, really. That didn't come out right, did it? Also, dude, everyone knows you say 'red' if you want help. What kind of counselor are you?"

"The kind with massive student loan debt after getting fired from his summer externship at Jesus Camp because he tried to turn them in to CPS. A bad one, I guess, because you were supposed to be a client, and instead I'm sitting here figuring out if my car will make it to Nashville and back. I'm worried about you."

Nick blushed, hunching down over his lap and curling his hand around the phone to keep the wind out when he lowered his voice. "I'm okay. I promise. I mean, I'm . . . I'm not, you know? I'm still all fucked up, and I feel guilty for leaving, but I'm safe. Ethan's a good guy. He's on this summer road trip, and he invited me to go with him."

"He picked up a hitchhiker. He may be a good guy, but that doesn't say much for his common sense. No offense."

Nick glanced over his shoulder, but Ethan wasn't close enough to hear his good name be disparaged. "He's . . . he's finding his way. And hell, he's not Kyle, so I'm already doing better."

"Ah. I didn't know you meant he *picked you up*."

Nick shook his head, which was pointless since Stef couldn't see his vehement denial. "Not like *that*. He hasn't asked me for anything."

"Yet," Stef muttered, and Nick didn't know if he was supposed to have heard it or not. "I don't care where he takes you or what he says, you don't owe him a goddamn thing, okay?"

"Yeah, okay." He pulled at the same loose thread he'd found earlier, squirming away from the voice of authority out of habit.

"Sorry," Stef said. "I'm not trying to make you feel bad, and I'm not your parent. I'm worried. Is there anything I can do for you?"

Tell me I'm not a lost cause. "I don't know. Ethan was the one who made me call." He laughed. "I think he's afraid I'll let Kyle catch up with us because I don't have anywhere else to go." The hard knot of anxiety in his chest flared, squeezing another laugh out of him that didn't even approach real.

"Yes, you do. Nick, do you want to come stay with me until you figure things out? I can buy you a bus ticket and all you'll have to do is check in at the Greyhound station." Something rattled in the background, and Stef's voice became muffled. "Leave it, it's fine. I'll see you tonight."

Nick twisted the hem of his jeans around in his fingers, fiddling with the cheap denim to distract himself.

"Sorry, I'm back. Just seeing someone out."

"Overnight guests? I'm shocked. I hope you slept in separate rooms and her parents knew where she was."

Stef snorted. "His parents would probably descend on my apartment with holy water and two priests if they knew he was getting the less-lumpy side of my futon, but that's the least of our problems. Which aren't what we were talking about."

Nick's shoulders had developed a wicked kink that he didn't feel until he tried to relax them, sitting up straighter. "No, no, I'd rather hear about how you're doing . . . a guy who apparently comes from a family of vampire hunters. A *guy*."

"I told you there was nothing wrong with your sexuality. I was a counselor. It wasn't appropriate to share personal details with clients. But since you're not my client anymore—hi, I'm Stefan Hansen. I'm gay as a parade."

"A parade? Like marching bands and baton twirling?" Nick didn't try to squelch his grin.

"*Naked* guys twirling batons. Trombones and tubas. So yeah, back to the point. What do you think? Want to come here, stay until you figure out your next move?"

Nick opened his mouth, then took a deep breath. "I think . . . I think I'm okay for now."

"But you'll keep your options open?"

"I will." He felt like he owed Stef some kind of an explanation, but the words kept slipping away. "I like Ethan . . ."

Stef waited several seconds before prompting him. "But?"

"I don't think there is one." It felt stupid to call someone for help and then lie to them. The *but* ran along the lines of, *but I don't know if I'm good for him.* Or, *but I'm afraid I might mess him up as much as I'm messed up.*

The heavy sigh rolled across the phone line. "Dude, I'm a professional. I know a lie when I hear one."

Nick looked over at Ethan, catching a goofy grin and a wave. "I don't want to fuck up his life."

"Why would you think you would?"

"I thought I wasn't a client," Nick said, forcing a lightness he didn't feel into his voice.

"You're not. This is me calling a friend on bullshit. It's totally different. You had some bad things happen. It doesn't make you contagious."

"What if I turn him into . . ." Nick couldn't even finish the sentence. Ethan wasn't like that. But what if it wasn't Ethan who was the problem? What if it hadn't been Kyle? Christ, Nick's own parents couldn't even stand the sight of him. Nobody could miss the common factor.

Stef sighed, and it seemed like he was taking a moment to pick his next words. "Nick, nothing you did made that guy hurt you. Not what you said, or wore, or who you talked to, or anything about *you*. He hit you because he's an abusive shit-stain of a human being. It wasn't your fault."

"Yeah," Nick said softly, breathing the word out.

"Fuck that place *so fucking much*," Stef growled into the phone. "Swear on my coffee beans, if I have to text you that every day for the next decade, I will. It wasn't your fault."

"You could do that." Maybe it sounded a little too eager, but it was already out before Nick had time to rethink it. "I mean . . . Yeah. I mean that. It would be really nice to hear from you."

"I'm serious about the bus ticket. Or if you need anything—*anything*—you can call me, day or night. I'll always listen, even if you're just scared of the dark or drunk or don't know what flavor Pop-Tart to buy."

"Strawberry. Always strawberry. I might take you up on the dark thing, though."

Stef laughed. "I'll send you a nightlight. Or put one in the guest room I don't have yet if you come to stay."

Nick huffed the ghost of a laugh, twisting to look at Ethan over his shoulder. "I'll be okay."

"Will you do something for me?" The seriousness of Stef's tone drew Nick's attention back from Ethan's slow sway on the swing, where he was pretending to be fixated on his phone.

"Depends—I'm never doing another trust fall, dude."

"Ha. Not what I had in mind. But it's something I'm going to ask you as your friend *and* a therapist, which is a terrible combo, so don't report me to the ethics board, okay?"

Nick scowled into the distance, directing his unease at some pigeons who didn't really deserve it. Or maybe they did. Pigeons could be jerks. "I'm listening."

"I want you to say, out loud, that you have options."

Nick ducked his head, the instant rise of shame familiar and unexpected. He didn't even realize he was breathing hard until Stef's quiet voice broke through the buzz in his ears.

"No matter where you wind up, or how bad you think you've messed up. And especially if you're thinking you don't deserve them. I will help you no matter what, okay? So can you say it, even if you might not believe it?"

Brushing hard at his cheeks with the back of his fist, Nick bit his lower lip and curled down into the smallest possible version of himself, his knees pulled up and his head nearly between them.

"I have options," he whispered, and God, that had to be good enough, because he couldn't say it any louder.

"That's it, I promise. No long-distance head shrinking. My license isn't valid in Tennessee anyway. I'll be here, no matter what you want to do."

Nick drew in a shaky breath, shaking his head. "I've got no idea what I want to do."

"I don't think that's true at all," Stef said.

Nick looked over his shoulder again, at the dork hanging upside down under the monkey bars.

"Maybe not."

Interlude
ETHAN DOMANI'S PHONE

Conversation with Scott Raines
Ethan: *You'd know what to do for Nick*
Ethan: *You were always better with real stuff*
Ethan: *I can't even call your mom*
Ethan: *I've been sending her postcards*
Ethan: *I want you to be here, except if you were I probably never would have met Nick*
Ethan: *I kissed him this morning*
Ethan: *I know you don't hate me, because you're dead*
Ethan: *I'm more worried because I don't hate myself, and I know it's because another piece of us is gone.*

CHAPTER Eleven

Adams, TN

"No smoking, climbing, running, or crawling, huh?" Ethan put his hands on his hips. "I get everything but the crawling. Crawling away in fear?"

"I'm more likely to run, but you go ahead and crawl, if that's your thing. At least I know the witch is going to get you first."

"You've never seen me crawl. Don't count your witches before they've pinched."

Nick rolled his eyes. "I have no idea what that means. But if we're going in, let's do it. That gang of Girl Scouts should be far enough ahead now that we won't have to listen to them scream the whole way."

The cave entrance was paved with gravel, and their feet crunched loudly as they started down the incline. The air temperature dropped almost immediately, and Ethan shivered.

"Scared already?"

"I don't need to dignify that with an answer. The only thing I fear is the early cancellation of *American Ninja Warrior* before I get a chance to win it all." Ethan turned on his flashlight, brightly printed with the Bell Witch logo. He was still a little disappointed they hadn't been able to rent an EMF meter, but judging from all the cars in the parking lot, the cave was packed. No self-respecting ghost of a witch would perform like a circus pony in front of a crowd.

"That sounds like a jock thing. Let's concentrate on the witch thing, now. Tell me again why she was so horrible? Turned people into newts?"

"She wasn't really all that terrible." Ethan swatted at a root dangling from the roof of the cave. It had probably been glued there for effect. "She pinched people. Pulled their hair. Made grunting and groaning noises."

Nick snickered. "That sounds more like rough sex than a haunting."

Ethan laughed, leaning toward the damp, smooth wall of the cave to see if there was anything especially creepy about it. In the cool air, the warm gust of breath across the back of his neck felt a million degrees hotter. His shiver had nothing to do with temperature and everything to do with the ghost of Nick's fingers brushing across the skin bared between his T-shirt and shorts.

"Boo."

Ethan yelped and stood up too fast, nearly whacking his head on a rock outcropping. He turned on Nick, rubbing his offended backside with one hand and pointing with the other. "I thought you were just getting handsy, but you *pinched* me!"

Nick raised both hands, blinking wide eyes that reflected the ominous yellow-green lighting in the cave. "Did I? Or was it the witch?"

"Yeah, well, if some long-dead scary woman pinched my ass, I'm not gonna be happy," Ethan grumbled, still rubbing.

"But it's cool if it was me?"

It might've been his imagination, but he thought he heard some uncertainty in Nick's voice. Or maybe he was reading his own uncertainty into it. Ethan rubbed the spot again, pretending to consider the question, when really, he was glad the cave was dim and Nick might not be able to see how flushed he was. "Well, as long as you were in full control of yourself, I guess. If you were temporarily possessed, that would be . . . a shame."

Nick's smile was small, but it looked more genuine than a lot of the expressions he'd plastered on for Ethan's benefit. "Totally myself, I swear." A sliding half step brought them closer, Nick's hand braced against the smooth rock over their heads. His dark eyes were still impossibly wide in the dim lighting, and so damn close—

"Chelsea, stop it! Stop making noises!"

"I'm *not!*"

Nick jerked back, and Ethan made a grab for him, but it was too late to keep his head from cracking against the rock wall.

"Fuck, that hurt." Nick rubbed the back of his head, eyes closed.

"I'm so sorry," Ethan said, fighting down a totally inappropriate snort of laughter.

Apparently he failed, because Nick opened his eyes to glare at him. "Getting a concussion is funny?"

Ethan gave up, gasping between bursts of laughter. "You . . . you jumped like those girls goosed you or something. Dude, you caught *air*."

"I'm glad my pain is so amusing."

"I'd offer to kiss it better, but you saw where that got us already. You might jump and break a leg or something next time."

"There are worse ways to wind up in the ER than sex-related sprains." It must have actually hurt, though, because Nick kept rubbing his head and wincing.

"Priapism, for one," Ethan said.

"*Someone* had an interesting SAT study guide. You'll be all set for that sexual disasters *Jeopardy* category."

The girls had moved on, their voices fading in the distance. Ethan held up his hand. "Okay, giving you warning, here. I'm coming in closer. Don't panic and jump, okay?"

Nick mumbled something that sounded suspiciously like "fuck you" and smacked his shoulder.

"Jerk." Ethan stepped around some loose gravel, his fingers coming to rest lightly over Nick's. The buzz of dark hair under his fingertips felt like angry velvet, prickly enough to mask how incredibly soft it was. "Sorry about your head."

"It's fine." Nick's hand went still. "Not as much padding as when I had hair."

"I guess not. It, uh, it feels kinda cool, though." Ethan snapped his mouth shut. He started to pull away, but at the same time, Nick leaned closer, and Ethan found himself cupping Nick's head.

Nick's forehead fell against Ethan's chest. The slight pressure was enough to disrupt his air supply, leaving him afraid to breathe for fear he'd scare Nick away. Which was silly—Nick wasn't a fuzzy woodland creature. His head smelled like the coconut shampoo from yesterday's motel, more so when Ethan used his fingertips to rub gently.

"Tell me if I hit a sore spot."

He figured a sigh was answer enough, especially when Nick pushed his head harder into Ethan's hand. "Any better?"

Nick nodded, his hair tickling Ethan's fingers. "Might still want an Advil, but better."

"Bet they've got those little travel packets of them in the gift shop." Which brought to mind the bright-yellow *Titanic* in its place of honor in the back seat. Probably not anything equally cute here to buy Nick. A witch plushy? A remote pinching finger? A cursed wishing well to keep his spare change in?

"I think it was mostly books, but maybe they've got potions or something. My mom took us to the witch market in Cusco once, but I can't remember if it was dried alpaca fetus or powdered armadillo for a headache." Nick shrugged, and Ethan couldn't tell if he was being serious or not.

"I think I'd rather deal with the headache. That's kind of disgusting." Ethan paused to reflect. "Actually, really gross. And the poor armadillos."

Nick elbowed him. "Hey, that's my culture, dude. But yeah, I think I'll stick with Advil."

Ethan wasn't sure whether to be glad about their interruption or not. On one hand, Nick seemed pretty chill at the moment, not like the last time they'd gotten a little closer than buddies. On the other . . . On the other, Nick's hair was really fucking soft, and Ethan wanted to know what it would feel like to pet it while they kissed. Except maybe not in a witch cave.

"Come on, let's keep going so I can see this horrifying demon face thing the brochure kept talking about. Maybe it'll scare the headache away."

Ethan was having a hard time remembering that he'd been the one so anxious to tour the damn cave. He stifled a sigh and stepped away from Nick. "Sure, I'm ready to be terrified."

The path was wet under their feet, the rock slick with moisture. By the time they'd reached the supposed Indian grave, Ethan had slipped twice, and his hand was now streaked with slime where he'd grabbed at the wall. The deeper they went, the odder he felt. He must've slowed down without realizing it, because Nick stopped, fingertips brushing his arm.

"You okay?"

"I dunno. I didn't think it would bother me, but does the roof seem closer or something?"

Nick nodded. "It is. The brochure said the cave goes down like fifteen miles, and it gets pretty narrow."

He'd read that too, but hadn't thought it would bother him. Now it felt kind of like the walls and roof were closing in. "Jesus, I didn't think I was claustrophobic, but maybe I am." He closed his eyes briefly, but that made the roof feel even lower. "You mind if we cut this short?" The press of the cave swallowing them wasn't quite the scare he'd been looking for.

"It's fine with me." Nick slipped an arm through Ethan's, entwining their fingers. "If you turn around, it'll get bigger as we go, right? Come on."

It seemed to take them longer to leave the cave than it had to walk into it, but eventually the ambient light got brighter and the mouth of the cave appeared as they rounded a corner.

"So I guess I'm crossing spelunking off my résumé."

"It's okay. Not everyone likes exploring dark, tight spaces." Nick withdrew his hand, patting Ethan on the arm. "I don't think any less of you."

"Gee, thanks." Ethan paused at the base of the rickety wooden steps leading up out of the cave. Maybe it was the relief of not having eighty tons of rock over his head, waiting to bury him alive, or maybe it was the fresh air, but Ethan shivered.

Or maybe it wasn't either of those things. "Did . . . did it just get really cold?"

Nick laughed at him, but only for a second before his eyes widened and he held up his arm, which was covered in goose bumps.

They didn't exactly race each other to the top of the stairs, but Ethan definitely won. And not because he elbowed Nick out of the way and screeched a little.

Definitely not because of that.

They both skittered farther away from the cave, stepping off the main path to recover. Nick bent at the waist, bracing his hands on his knees as he panted for breath. Ethan laughed at him, earning a side-eyed glare.

"Not everybody . . ." Nick huffed ". . . spends their weekends . . . running around on a . . . field chasing a tiny . . . ball."

Ethan grinned, flexing into the most ridiculous bodybuilder pose he could manage while keeping his balance. "Don't be jealous. I have to burn off the junk food somehow."

"Who said . . . I was jealous?"

He was willing to chalk it up to wishful thinking, but it seemed like Nick looked at him maybe a few seconds longer than necessary. "Oh, nobody. Except the person wheezing like a ninety-year-old man with COPD." At least he thought that's what the commercials about wheezing people called it.

Nick stood up, his breathing more even, but still faster and louder than Ethan's. There was a little sweat at his hairline and in the faint shadow of dark hair on his upper lip. Ethan tried really, really hard not to think about those beads of perspiration rolling down under the collar of Nick's T-shirt. Down his chest.

Their eyes met, and Ethan knew instantly that his face was giving him away. Nick's shoulders rolled back, expression unreadable.

Rather than taking the time to overthink it, Ethan took the step between them and tucked his hand around Nick's head, cradling it as he leaned in for a kiss. Nick met him somewhere in the middle. The angle was awkward and their lips were chapped, but Nick's mouth tasted like doughnuts, and he wound an arm around Ethan's back and pulled them closer together.

"Oh my *God*, Chelsea! They're totally making out! That is so cute!"

Chelsea, Ethan assumed, giggled so loudly he was afraid she might hyperventilate.

Nick moved away, ducking his head beneath Ethan's chin and speaking in a low rumble that sent warmth coursing through Ethan's chest.

"You wanna skip the gift shop?"

Ethan, not trusting his voice, settled for a nod and grabbed Nick's hand. Chelsea would have to entertain herself.

The brutal heat of a closed vehicle in the late-afternoon sun rolled out of the doors when Ethan opened the car. He hit the air-conditioning, and they both sat there, the howl of the vents the only sound for a few moments. Ethan wrapped his hands around the steering wheel, not daring to look at Nick.

"So, uh. Where am I driving us?"

"Since I don't want to get arrested, I was thinking a hotel."

Ethan glanced at him, risking the eye contact. "Okay."

Nick lowered his chin, giving Ethan a significant look. "With a bed. So we can fuck."

"That . . . Yeah, that sounds good." It did. Really good. Which made it crazy that he hesitated. Not for long, but it took him another laborious second to shift, step on the gas, and roll them slowly out of the parking lot. "So what changed? Because this morning we were kind of in a bed where . . . where fucking could occur, and it seemed like you thought it was a bad idea."

Nick didn't answer immediately, which left Ethan enough time to castigate himself for being an idiot and vomit anxious words all over the front seat. "I'm not complaining!"

"I have options," Nick said, more to the window than Ethan. "I don't have to be with you."

Ethan bit his lip, wondering what he was supposed to say to that. He jumped a little when Nick reached across the center console and rested a hand on his thigh. That was it—not high enough to be a grab for his junk, but deliberate.

"I don't have to be with you. So it makes it okay that I want to be."

"Did you think you'd have to . . . That you'd owe me sex?" Ethan tried to keep the shock out of his voice, but was pretty sure he was doing a crappy job. "Did I do something to make you think that?" Nauseated at the idea, Ethan flipped the blinker and pulled off the road, the gravel shoulder crunching under his tires as the car rolled to a stop again.

Ethan twisted sideways in the seat. Nick was already shaking his head.

"You didn't. Nothing *you've* done made me think that."

The slight emphasis was impossible to miss. Ethan curled his hand into a fist, wedged between his leg and the back of the seat where Nick couldn't see it.

"I'm glad to hear that." Ethan hadn't expected his voice to come out so angry, and he tried to dial it back. "I'm not pissed at you. I'm sorry. I kind of don't know what to do with how I feel right now."

Nick snorted. "Yeah. I'm familiar."

"You don't owe me *anything*." Vehemence was better than misplaced anger, but something inside him was still shaking. That someone (the stalker-ex, if he had to guess) had made Nick feel like sex was owed, a bill that came due after someone was nice to him, was revolting and horrifying and a lot of other words that should have been in his SAT study guide. "I know you said that's not what's going on, but I need that to be out there."

"You've given me a place to be. Clothing. Food. A tour of the weirdest places in Tennessee. I owe you a lot, dude. But I'm not paying you back in sex. That's just something I think would be fun."

Trying to explain something he felt was so basic was harder than Ethan had expected. "But those are things you *do* for another person when you have the means or the ability or whatever. Except the strange-places tour." Ethan grinned. "That was special for you."

"Thank you. I think? Don't be offended if I'm more in the mood for something completely normal, like a Motel 6."

"But there might be a Bell Witch motel. The soap could smell like musty well water, and the beds could be made of corncobs. Guaranteed haunting in every room. What if we miss out?"

Nick startled him by leaning across the console and kissing him again, a fast press of their lips that ended with a little nip. "If you're still disappointed with the Motel 6 after I hit my knees, we can find the fucking Bates Motel."

Feeling a little dazed, or maybe horny, Ethan settled back into his seat and turned the car back on. Driving with that image in his mind would take maximum concentration, concentration that left Ethan no room for witty conversation. A gulp and a muttered "Okay" was about it. He glanced over at Nick in time to catch what could only be described as a smirk.

Ignoring it in favor of the road, Ethan watched the odometer roll up the miles. One, five, ten, and finally a billboard for a Springfield Inn off of the next exit. He pointed as the sign came up on the car. "It's not a Motel 6, but will that do?"

Nick shrugged. "As long as the room has carpeting, I'm okay."

That was *definitely* a smirk.

Nick wore the same expression while they checked in. Ethan made the mistake of looking at him once as he stuttered out his request for a single bed, only to find Nick's eyebrows raised and his lips parted.

Asshole, he mouthed at Nick, while the desk clerk studiously ignored both of them. Ethan didn't have a clue how much he'd paid for the room when he grabbed the key cards and fled toward the bank of elevators. He heard the clerk laughing behind them.

The elevator buttons had become a mystery to him. He stared at them as though the floor numbers were written in hieroglyphics.

"I, um. What floor did he say?"

"Six." Nick leaned past Ethan and hit the button, leaving a phantom of laughter and heat behind when he settled against the elevator wall. His smirk had softened into an actual smile. "I also took your keys out of the ignition." Nick held them up, the ring dangling from the tip of his finger. "And I hope I grabbed the right bag." He nudged the duffel he'd dropped next to his feet.

"I was *distracted*," Ethan said defensively.

"I gathered. You're not going to pass out or anything, are you? I'm getting a little worried. I can go easy on you if it's been awhile." Nick snickered and gave Ethan's shoulder a condescending little pat as they exited the elevator.

"I didn't know I was signing up for an evening with Mike Mulligan and his steam shovel. I would've done some yoga or something." Ethan pushed the key card into the lock, then stood aside to usher Nick in with a flourish. "After you."

Nick stepped around him, then pulled up short, blocking the door. Ethan tried to look over his shoulder. "Everything okay?"

"It's, uh, it's fine." Nick's voice sounded choked, and Ethan nudged him until he moved out of the way.

"Holy shit." Ethan took another step in, not sure where to look first. "What the hell kind of room did I request? I feel like I'm on a bad porno set!"

Nick doubled over next to him, wheezing laughter. "Dude, you must've looked even more anxious than I thought to that clerk. Is that . . . is that a round bed?" His eyes widened. "And there's mirrors on the ceiling."

"So many people have had sex in this room." Ethan couldn't help his mournful tone.

"Do you want to call down and have them move us? Can we even do that?"

That could take . . . God, *minutes*. Ethan wasn't sure he had that kind of time left. He dropped the duffel bag Nick had brought in for him, and it made a decisive thud when it hit the dark-red carpet. "Fuck it. I bet the soundproofing is good, at least."

Nick laughed at him. For all his swaggering and playful detachment, he suddenly looked a lot less sure of things. "I'm gonna go . . . You know. Bathroom things. Teeth. Whatever." He didn't outright flee, but there was a definite speed to Nick's steps.

"Oh my God, there's a two-person jacuzzi in here. And I think there's some kind of sex shelf in the shower. Are we at a swingers resort?" Nick's voice echoed out of the bathroom, followed by the click of the door shutting and a rattle when Nick locked it. From the sound of it, he then turned on the sink faucet full blast.

"Does the jacuzzi look clean?" Ethan yelled over the sound of running water. He immediately felt stupid for asking, but given what had happened in the room, over and over . . .

The water shut off. "I guess. Why?"

Ethan shrugged before remembering Nick couldn't see it behind the closed (and locked) door. "It's a jacuzzi. How often am I going to be in a hotel that has one? Seems like a shame to waste it."

"Fair point. Um. Can you not stand outside the door and listen?"

Feeling a blush scald his cheeks, Ethan coughed and moved away from the bathroom. He picked up his bag on the way past, tossing it carelessly onto the top of the dresser and unzipping it to retrieve his bathroom kit. No way was Nick going to be the only person with minty fresh breath in this equation. Besides, his mom had conveniently supplied him with a travel-size packet of Clorox Wipes, and it wouldn't hurt to use them on the jacuzzi before filling it up. He couldn't use either one, though, until Nick vacated the bathroom.

He'd managed to toe off his sneakers, when the bathroom door opened. He turned around, pack of Handi Wipes and toothbrush in hand, and found Nick crossing the room. To drop his clothes on a chair. Because he was naked.

"Oh," Ethan said, feeling about as bright as a Christmas bulb. Well. That took care of the awkward *How naked are we getting?* question. *So* naked. So amazingly naked.

"You aren't planning on sanitizing me, are you?" Nick asked, eyeing Ethan's hand. "Because A) that's not how you prevent STDs, and B) there is no way in hell you're getting near my dick with bleach."

Flustered, he stared at his own hand, then tossed the wipes on the dresser. "No! God, that would hurt like hell." Catching himself, he managed a bit of dignity. "And yes, I *did* have sex ed, as watered down as it was."

"I've heard how many brothers and sisters you've got. I'm not sure your parents are qualified to teach sex ed." Nick paused, tilting his head like he was considering something. "Huh. Or maybe they're *really* qualified."

Ethan's lip curled before he could stop himself, even though he was still having trouble looking away from Nick's too-narrow waist and muscled thighs. Amongst other parts. "If you actually want to have full use of *my* dick, maybe less talking about my parents and their sex life. Or hey, *no* talking about it. Ever. That would work for me."

Nick didn't look abashed in the least, his eyes squinching as he grinned. "Sorry."

"You're gonna be when we wind up watching *Jeopardy* reruns."

Clearly Nick had more of a plan than Ethan did, which wouldn't take much. He was definitely not looking for the remote when he closed the distance between them and brushed a hand across the front of Ethan's shorts.

"I think we can find better things to talk about than eighteenth-century poets." Nick pushed the hem of Ethan's shirt up and rested a hand at his waist. "What are your don'ts?"

Ethan stared down at the spread of fingers against the pale skin of his stomach, distracted. "Uh, besides talking about my parents, I don't know that I have any? Or at least I haven't had the chance to think of any?" He struggled to pull his thoughts back. "I'd say nothing too weird . . . but look at where we are. I think we might've passed that point."

Nick rolled his eyes. "That's not an answer, unless you're going to define 'too weird.'"

It felt like the worst pop quiz ever, where if you failed, it wasn't about a bad grade. It was about no sex. Or being humiliated by his lack of imagination. "Uh, no things better relegated to the bathroom," he rattled off quickly.

Nick took pity on him, squeezing his waist gently. "I'll give you mine, if that helps. Don't hit me. Don't put your hands on my throat. Don't . . . don't call me any names."

Sometimes it was easy to tell where Nick's bravado failed him, like the hesitant dip in his voice as he seemed to realize what he was giving away.

In terms of tests Ethan didn't want to fail, this far outstripped the worry that his no-goes would seem tame. He raised a hand, carefully resting it on Nick's bare chest, well away from his neck. "What about kissing you again?"

"I'm good with that."

Nick's smile felt funny pressed against his mouth, but it wasn't hard to find that warm, almost electric current, humming between them like a power line. Or maybe that was the noise he was making in the back of his throat. It had been a while, but thank goodness he hadn't forgotten how to shimmy out of a pair of shorts without breaking a kiss. Some lessons learned at a young and horny fourteen were never forgotten. Kicking them away while standing *had* gotten more difficult, though, and Nick broke the kiss to laugh as Ethan hopped on one foot.

"Need some help?" Nick grabbed Ethan's arm to steady him. "We can take this to the bed, you know. So if you fall, you're not dealing with a concussion."

Ethan stepped out of his shorts and underwear, and Nick's hands caught in his shirt, pushing it up. He tugged it over his head, swinging it in a circle like a lasso before tossing it across the room. If he hadn't been so distracted by Nick's hands, Ethan would've cringed when it hit the floor. Nick had had the sense to put his clothes on the chair.

After a few minutes of the kind of frantic, deep kissing he hadn't indulged in since . . . For a long time, anyway, they broke away, hands braced on each other's chests like it was the only way to keep themselves apart. Ethan looked at the bed and that was all the cue Nick needed to reach for the red velvet bedspread and yank it to the floor.

Ethan knee-walked up the mattress, distracted by the way Nick's cock bobbed as he did the same thing. His skin was much darker than Ethan's, but lighter under his clothes. Ethan splayed his hand against Nick's stomach, appreciating the softer angles there, framed by the sharpness of Nick's hip bones and leading to the dark tripwire of hair that ran from his navel down. When Ethan let his hand follow the path of his eyes, it was as much to fulfill his own fascination with the contrast in color between his fingers and Nick's cock as it was to hear Nick's hissed inhalation.

"This is good?" It felt like a stupid question, but he needed to know Nick wasn't pushing through for him.

"Yeah." Nick's eyes were wide, his smile soft. He curled away from Ethan, down onto his side on the wine-red sheets. Ethan followed, using the angle to explore skin he hadn't touched yet while they kissed again.

They moved together slowly, making new connections and breaking old. Nick's fingers danced a path of blooming heat across Ethan's back, down the knobs of his spine, and ultimately clutched at his hip, scalding him like a brand.

Nick tilted his head back, allowing Ethan greater access to the tender skin of his throat. Ethan pressed his lips against Nick's pulse points, trailing a necklace of gentle kisses between them. He pointedly ignored the thought of anyone before him intruding on Nick's skin with violence.

Ethan's arousal stretched over his body, tightly wound around every nerve ending, but nothing prepared him for Nick licking the palm of his own hand and reaching between them, fingers closing around both of them. Every time, everywhere, anywhere Nick came in contact with him felt nearly as urgent and direct as his cock thrusting into that loose circle of fingers, against Nick.

Given their surroundings, maybe he should have tried for a marathon-fucking session, full of yogic positioning and making use of the sex swing he was pretty sure must be in the closet. Instead, Ethan's orgasm hit him like a freight train to the solar plexus, knocking the wind from him in an unsexy, but heartfelt grunt. Nick's suddenly slick hand moved faster, eliciting a barely bitten-back yelp at the intensity, but only for a second or two before Nick was coming as well.

Nick practically sobbed into Ethan's shoulder, teeth scraping over his collarbone. Nick's body was a stiff weight for a second before he went limp, his climax draining the tension from him. "Ethan." Nick said it like it was a statement, the syllables drawn out and careless.

It felt natural and right to run his hands over Nick's head in slow strokes. Less natural, much less comfortable, was the jolt of protectiveness. Ethan closed his eyes, pushing aside any misgivings. It was better to enjoy the moment and work through the stupid stuff later.

Nick yawned and his head drooped, coming to rest on Ethan's shoulder as a warm, welcome weight. Ethan laughed against his hair. "Not sure we should fall asleep on these sheets."

"Smells like bleach," Nick mumbled. "'S'okay."

"What about the jacuzzi?"

Nick pulled back, and Ethan opened his eyes in time to catch a baleful look. "Is that a hint that you want to get up?"

Ethan winced. "Kinda, yeah. But if you want to sleep, that's fine. I mean, you'll miss out on bubbly hot water, but it's your choice."

"It's gonna take like an hour to fill anyway. Wake me up when it's done." Nick flapped a hand in his direction, rolling further into the bedding with a contented groan.

Ethan slipped out of bed, but stopped to pull a sheet over Nick, unable to ignore that pesky protectiveness. It was just as well to not have a witness when he Clorox-wiped the tub before filling it. There was no reason for Nick to be aware of the neuroses his mom had instilled in him.

Nick wasn't wrong about how long it took for the huge tub to fill up. There was a bottle of rose-scented bath oil and fancy soap in a little basket on the counter, but he settled for pouring some of his shower gel under the running tap. Neither of them needed to chance a weird rash from the adult version of Mr. Bubble. Besides, the shower gel made huge mountains of cedar-scented bubbles.

The hotel air-conditioning had turned him into a walking popsicle by the time the tub was full. He slid across the slick sheets toward Nick, ill-intent in his heart. Ethan laid his icy fingers against Nick's cheek. Nick yelped, scrambling out of his nest of bedding. Ethan immediately remembered why startling Nick awake was more than a dick move.

"Shit, I'm sorry, I was trying to—"

"It's fine. I'm not made of glass." Nick's scoffing tone was belied by his posture, which was as guarded and hunched as it'd been earlier.

Ethan swallowed a couple of self-deprecating apologies. It wasn't about how bad he felt, it was about Nick. "Of course you're not. But I want to be worthy of your trust." He jerked a thumb over his shoulder toward the steaming, bubbly tub. "The bath's ready, if you actually wanted to get in."

Nick didn't say anything, watching him for a second before he broke eye contact and rolled out of the ridiculous bed. Ethan thought Nick was going to walk by, but he stopped, pressing a soft, slow kiss against his temple.

"C'mon. I've always wanted to go swimming in my bedroom."

"Race you." Ethan started running before he'd finished speaking, but Nick was faster, skidding in the bathroom door first. The splash as he hit the tub sloshed a tidal wave of water over the side. Ethan stopped, leaning against the wall for support as he laughed. "Dude, it's not a pool. And, besides, now you've created this dangerous situation. One of us could have a slip-and-fall injury."

Instead of answering, Nick scooped up a handful of suds and threw them in Ethan's direction. "You're jealous I beat your jock ass."

Ethan winced at the water spreading slowly across the tile floor, wondering how much the hotel would charge him for flooding the room below them. He tossed a towel down in the mess, a half-assed attempt at best. Nick's bare chest sinking below the bubbles was distracting.

"Get in the tub already. You look . . . cold." Nick's gaze traveled up and down Ethan's body, pausing significantly below his waist.

He'd never been able to turn down a challenge, and now would be a crazy time to start. Ethan grinned and set both hands on the side of the tub, vaulting in sideways. This time, the wave of water and suds hit Nick in the face first, then washed over the side.

Nick sputtered, spitting out soapy water.

Ethan smiled innocently when Nick had cleared his face enough to glare at him. "I don't know how I did that." Ethan stretched back to lean against the side of the tub. The hot water felt incredible, and he started to sink down lower. Nick said something that sounded like "asshole" but Ethan pretended not to hear, pointing at his head. "Can't hear you. Got soap in my ears."

The jets were on a timer switch, probably to keep people from drowning while they had sex. Ten minutes to get all friendly, and then hot water instead of bubbles being injected into sensitive areas. Ethan stretched out an arm and turned the switch to the max amount.

Nick jumped, eyes going wide. "Some warning would be nice!"

Ethan smiled sweetly. "Don't sit on the spa jets."

"Jerk," Nick muttered, sliding down into the suds.

A few moments later, Ethan yelped as *someone* pinched him. Nick's eyes were still closed, an angelic look on his face.

"So where are we going tomorrow?"

Maybe it was the hot water, or the sex, or the gentle, grounding pressure of Nick's fingers resting on his leg, but the gnawing pit of worry Ethan expected to feel never materialized, and its absence was a relief.

"I don't know," he said.

"That's cool. We'll figure it out in the morning." The water sloshed over the side of the tub again as Nick moved, but they'd lost enough already that it didn't spill much this time. Nick settled an arm across Ethan's stomach and rested his head on Ethan's shoulder. "You were right about the tub."

Ethan hummed his agreement into the soapy fuzz of Nick's hair, too content to gloat. "Thank you for this."

Nick squeezed him, the pads of his fingers slotting into the dips of skin between Ethan's ribs. "Thanks for not letting me drown."

Ethan shifted, slick skin against slick skin, and pulled Nick to sit between his legs. "I make a really good life preserver."

Nick tensed for a second, then relaxed, leaning so his back was pressed to Ethan's chest. "It's like you're made of styrofoam or something," he said, smile evident in his voice.

The jets swirled around them, and Ethan sighed, contentment slowly replacing tension he hadn't even known he was carrying. It felt right, arms looped loosely around Nick, not talking, just being.

CHAPTER *Twelve*

Springfield, TN

"Be right back," Nick told Ethan, who grumbled and rolled away. Nick grabbed his phone off the nightstand, and padded into the damp bathroom. There were still soaking-wet towels piled everywhere. They were going to owe the housekeeper *such* a huge tip.

Nick stared at the dormant phone screen for a few seconds. The toilet was right there, easy distance to "accidentally" drop a phone into. Except he couldn't. For the same reasons he hadn't blocked Kyle—he wasn't ready to give up on his old life entirely, and his phone and the tenuous connections it provided to his family and friends were really the only part of it he had left.

He dropped the toilet lid closed and sat on it, wincing as the cold wood hit his bare ass. It took a minute for his phone to flare back to life, and another few after that for all of his messages to filter in. *All* of his messages. Eight voice mails, and texts into the triple digits.

Nick couldn't stop his hands from shaking, but he managed to get them under control long enough to hit the speed dial for voice mail. His pass code was still Drew's birthday, and he could thumb it in blindly. The automated voice counted his messages for him, like he couldn't see the number displayed over the anachronistic reel-to-reel icon.

Before Kyle could say a single recorded word, Nick pressed the button to delete his message. He did it over and over, the voice mail system finally catching up with him at the end, and then he hung up. All the texts were threaded together under the number he hadn't bothered to save into his contacts. He trashed the entire conversation without looking at any of them.

His head swam, the bathroom suddenly off-kilter as a wave of dizzy relief hit him. He paused on the way back to bed to wash his hands, vaguely amused by the symbolism. His old English teacher would have been proud.

Nick tossed his phone on the nightstand a little too hard, and Ethan murmured something, rolling toward him. He thought about sliding down the bed, about grounding himself in Ethan's inexplicable gravity and all the ways he knew how to make someone happy.

Ethan's arm slipped out from under the hideous sheets, an open hand stretching out to find him. Nick bit his lip and thought about consent, and how much it sucked when everyone was so focused on making you happy they forgot you had a reason not to be.

Eh. Blowjobs were better when you were awake to enjoy them anyway.

Ethan curled around him before he'd finished crawling back into bed, making it almost impossible to get comfortable until he realized he could touch back. He didn't have to lie there like a rock while the blond starfish next to him settled into his fissures. Nick rolled over, tugging Ethan's pliant body with him, and Ethan's nose bumped against the back of his neck, warm breath blowing across his skin.

Anchored and safe, Nick closed his eyes . . . but not before peeking at the mirrors overhead and wondering if he'd always looked like a stranger in his own body.

The sound of Ethan's phone pulled Nick out of a dream where he was buried under a couch after a hurricane. When the couch moved, rolling over to fumble for the nightstand, it wasn't hard to see where the dream had come from.

"Oh shit."

Nick shoved a pillow under his shoulder so he could sit up. "What?"

The glow of the phone lit up Ethan's face, forehead creased. "A text from my sister, Suze." He held the phone up so Nick could see the screen.

Smbdy stalking you. Guy in pics you posted like a million x

His chest clenched, forcing the air out of his lungs and not allowing any more in. Suddenly Nick regretted erasing all the texts from Kyle; maybe they would've told him exactly where Kyle was, or how long he'd been that close to them.

Ethan pulled the phone back, fingers flying over the screen. "Hang on, she must mean Instagram. I'll check."

Ethan frowned at his phone, and Nick's fear ratcheted up another notch. "What? How . . . how did he even . . .?"

Ethan's shoulders slumped, and he waved his phone in Nick's direction. "Here, look for yourself."

Nick took the phone, scanning down the wall of comments.

SuzEQ: *Isn't that the same guy from Bristol?*

RobertthePuce: *Looks like that punk kid who was making faces behind you and the dog statue*

SuzEQ: *Way to stalk, Ethe*

SuzEQ: *Srsly tho—are you following some cute ROTC guy?*

RobertthePuce: *Don't ask, don't tell, Suze.*

SuzEQ: *Oh, I'm telling. I'm telling MOM.*

Nick thumbed back up to the image they were commenting on and found himself dangling from the bow of the fake *Titanic* behind Ethan, who had the world's cheesiest, most sincere grin on his face.

It wasn't Kyle at all. It was *him*.

And Ethan was laughing at him. Or rather, trying not to laugh at him and failing spectacularly.

Nick shook a finger at Ethan, the adrenaline fading a little, only to be renewed when another notification beeped, telling him someone had commented on a photo Ethan was tagged in. He popped up the post and couldn't contain his snort of amusement.

Apparently Ethan's little sister was some kind of Photoshop wizard. She'd gone through at least a dozen pictures and found him lurking in the background of all of them, cropped him out and spread him into a collage entitled *ROTC Dude*.

SuzEQ: *See? Not crazy! That is def the same dude!*

RobertthePuce: *It . . . it kind of is, isn't it? WTF, Ethe?*

Clarasabell: *When did Ethe get a new boyfriend? I missed -one-family dinner!*

WhitnStyle: *Guys, what if this kid is stalking HIM?*
SuzEQ: *-So- telling Mom.*
WhitnStyle: *You'll have to remind her what Instagram is, first.*

"Um. How fast does your mom drive?"

Ethan dropped his face into his hands. "Fast enough to catch us if she thinks I've 'moved on' without introducing her to someone I'm serious about." He stopped and shook his head. "That sounded a lot scarier than I meant it to. She's . . . She worries."

"But she wouldn't, like, want to kill me?"

"Oh, no, that'll be me, as soon as she realizes I broke my promise not to pick up hitchhikers like, three—I'll be generous—five hours after I made it. But she'll love you."

Nick scratched the back of his head, mostly because he didn't know what to say. Ethan's mom would not love him. Ethan's mom would probably look at him like his own did—not the kid she wanted around, but the one she'd make do with because he was what was left. He wasn't the childhood-sweetheart type. But he was totally the guy you fucked to get over one.

"Nick?"

"Huh?" He snapped back to reality, trying to escape the crush of his own head. "Sorry, I don't think waking up is my forte."

"I didn't mean to freak you out. About my mom, I mean. Or the rest of this." Ethan waved his phone between them. "I forget how overwhelming my siblings are if you didn't grow up surrounded by them." His gentle smile took a sour turn, and Nick hated that he was the cause. "Plus, it's not exactly cool to start talking about meeting the family the morning after . . . whatever."

"Don't worry. I never thought you were cool." Nick laid a hand on Ethan's shoulder, kneading his fingers lightly into the muscle there so he'd have an excuse to keep touching him.

Ethan laughed, his eyes closing as he tipped his head to give Nick better access.

Nick was silent for several seconds before asking, "So, uh, what *are* you going to tell your siblings? Your sister seems like she could be pretty determined."

"You have no idea. Ever seen a cat watch a squirrel through the window for hours? That's Suze. She's relentless."

"Well, I'll leave you to figure out what you want to tell her, then. But maybe don't mention me by name? I mean, full name, just in case . . ."

Ethan's mouth quirked, his eyebrows pinched together, and his voice went quiet. "Nick. I don't even *know* your full name. You haven't told me."

"Oh." He didn't yank his hand away, but the awkward pat he gave Ethan's shoulder seemed the kind of touch someone would share with a guy who didn't know his last name. Which was stupid. His name was hiding somewhere, buried under the rockslide of insecurities that were collapsing his windpipe. Nick swallowed hard.

Ethan must have sensed his distress, because he grabbed Nick's hand. "Lie to me."

A cheat, an easy out, but it opened up his throat enough to take a breath. "Ainsworth-Breckinridge. Nicholas Throgmartin Ainsworth-Breckinridge, spy extraordinaire."

"Nice to meet you. Mr. Ainsworth-Breckinridge."

"Oh, sorry, it's *Lord.*"

"Goodness," Ethan said, pressing a hand to his chest. "I've never been in the presence of nobility before. Do I curtsy?"

"Only if you've got a frilly little dress hidden somewhere in your luggage. Otherwise you'd look silly."

Ethan peered down his nose at Nick. "Don't judge me for my ruffles."

Nick grinned. "I would *never.*" He pointed toward the bathroom. "I'm gonna go brush my teeth so I don't have penis breath all day."

"Gross."

"Yeah, well. Worth it." He tossed an exaggerated wink over his shoulder as he headed toward the bathroom. Ethan snickered and fell back against the mattress, phone in hand.

It *had* been worth it, no question. There hadn't been a single moment where he'd wondered what Ethan wanted from him, except skin and sweat and a little honesty.

The cold bathroom tile was slick enough that he could spin without much effort. He turned around so he could lean out the door.

"Hey, Ethan?"

"Huh?" Ethan pushed himself up on his elbows, looking concerned.

"It's Hamilton. Nicholas Efrain Alvarez Hamilton," he said, accenting his name properly, in a way that always made people think he was trying too hard.

Ethan's smile stretched across his face, lighting up his eyes. "Awesome. Now I need your Social Security number and your mom's maiden name, and I'll be able to get that cash advance card I've had my eye on."

Nick stuck his tongue out before ducking back around the doorframe.

Leaving a tip for the unlucky maid stuck cleaning up their mess took the last of his cash. Ethan looked over at Nick before he started the car. "Remind me to find an ATM sometime today."

"Unless you're planning to defile honeymoon suites every time we stop for the night, I don't think you have to worry about tipping housekeeping again."

He waggled his eyebrows. "Would that be a problem?"

"I don't know. What if we develop a strange yearning for taffeta, or one day you realize you can't get it up unless you're lying on ugly satin sheets?"

Ethan gaped at Nick, his brows pinching together. "How does your mind even work? I'm eighteen! I do not have erectile dysfunction."

Nick smirked. "Ah! But you say nothing about the taffeta. I'm on to you, you kinky bastard."

"We already discussed my curtseying dress. Everyone knows you need taffeta to get the proper effect." He glanced at the side mirror, then turned back toward the rearview. Except suddenly Nick's finger was poking his nose. "Dude. If you're not going to help me drive, the least you could do is keep your fingers out of my nose."

Nick, looking not-at-all chagrined, moved his hand away. "I never said I wouldn't help you drive. I thought you wanted to do it all yourself. But the nose thing isn't my fault anyway. You have a cute nose."

Ethan let his scowl deepen, putting the car back into park. "You may not boop me. I'm not into that." After a pause, he relented, unable to keep a straight face anyway. "But you can definitely help me drive."

Nick seemed to consider the offer before nodding. When he said nothing else, Ethan felt safe pulling out of the parking space and guiding the car back toward the interstate.

"So what *are* you into, if booping is out?"

Ethan couldn't stop his groan. "I sucked at this conversation last night." Even thinking about it was enough to make his face heat up.

"This is different. This is what you like."

The blush wasn't fading, and he waved a hand in Nick's direction defensively, without looking away from the road. "What do *you* like?"

He was answered with silence, and when he dared to peek, Nick's face was screwed up in thought. "Well, I mean, getting head is pretty great. And I don't mind giving it, if someone's not trying to give me a tonsillectomy with their dick."

"That's a disturbingly vivid image."

"That's me. Disturbingly vivid." Nick shifted in the seat, tucking one foot under himself and twisting in the confines of the seat belt to face Ethan. Ethan couldn't help noticing it also pressed him into a corner, as far away as he could get in a moving car.

"At the risk of sounding like the most pathetic whiner ever . . . I kind of don't know? I mean, it's sex. There's lots of it I'm sure I'll like. But the sex I've had mostly wasn't about what I liked, or what I wanted. It was about making Kyle happy. And sometimes it was about him blowing me so I'd forget he said something shitty or hit me. So . . . that's it, really. I don't know. A lot of stuff I thought I'd like ended up being stuff I'm pretty sure I'd hate now."

Nick tapped his fingers on his knee, not seeming to recognize that he was doing it. "Other than Kyle, the closest I've gotten to having sex with someone is my group leader at Camp Can't Even trying to watch me jerk off."

He grinned suddenly, which startled Ethan enough in his peripheral vision that he risked a look.

"Until yesterday, anyway. So I'm now a huge fan of enthusiastic handjobs and jacuzzi sex. And blowjobs. Definite yes on those."

Deciding what to react to first felt impossible. Ethan kept his white-knuckled hands on the steering wheel, struggling for words, afraid that if he didn't come up with something fast, he'd end up turning the car around. Retracing their trip to kill someone in Virginia didn't seem productive.

Apparently, he'd been silent for too long. When Ethan glanced over, Nick was staring at his lap, fingers picking at his shirt. "Sorry," he muttered. "That was probably way more than you wanted to know."

"Nah, it's okay. If I'm going to cause serious bodily harm to someone, I prefer to have all the reasons laid out for me." He kept his voice perfectly calm, even managed to drag up a grim smile. "I know you offered to help me drive, but how do you feel about digging holes? Deep ones, out in the woods?"

Nick laughed, the sound choked.

"No, dude, I'm serious. That is not acceptable. A fucking *counselor*? Did your parents even check this place out before they sent you? I'm guessing whoever vets these hellholes would shut it down if they knew." Ethan paused to take a breath. "And that Kyle fuck-head needs his ass kicked."

"I don't think watching us get off was, like, official camp policy," Nick hedged. "It was a thing Tyler did if he caught someone after lights-out. He'd make them . . . you know. *Finish*. And most of us were there because we're fuckups, so it's not like they've never heard a false accusation. He never actually touched anyone. He was just a creep."

"That doesn't make it okay," Ethan muttered, afraid Nick would think the anger was directed at him.

"No, it wasn't okay." Nick sounded surprised by his own admission.

"And, y'know, fucking up doesn't make you a fuckup. It's not, shit, what's that word? Semantics? Pretty sure anybody you meet is going to have done a lot of things they regret. It's human."

The highway unspooled ahead of them, a long thread of gray unraveling into the distance. Ethan's teeth hurt by the time Nick said anything.

"I don't regret sleeping with you. So you know. It's right at the top of my really short list of good ideas."

Ethan had to unclench his jaw to respond, working out the ache before he spoke. "I don't regret it either." He stared straight ahead.

"And if you're into it, I'd really like to help you figure out more of what you like."

Nick nodded, a quick, almost imperceptible movement of his head, and Ethan's jaw relaxed a little more.

"It wasn't always bad. I'm not making excuses for Kyle, I swear—but sometimes it was okay. Sometimes it was even good. I like sex." Nick's snort surprised Ethan. "Revelation there, right? 'Teenage boy likes sex. New study reveals shocking truth.' Before it got weird, I really liked getting backed into corners and kissed. It was hot until I figured out it was about owning every single bit of my attention." Nick's voice shook with a note of bitterness. "Would've been nice if he hadn't fucking ruined it."

Ethan swallowed, wanting to pursue Nick's anger, if only because it was one of the few times he'd seen it flare in self-defense. But he could also see that pushing because he wanted to protect Nick from shit that had already happened to him wasn't going to make either of them happy.

Eyes fixed on the road, Ethan licked his lips and tried to follow Nick's lead.

"Scott and me . . . It was always pretty reciprocal. Like, there wasn't anything either of us hated that the other loved. But the first time I went down on him, I remember thinking, 'Oh, yeah, this.' Like we knew almost everything about each other, but suddenly I knew something else, something even he didn't know, about how he felt and tasted, and . . ." God, his face was on fire. "I like that. Giving head, but also how it makes me feel. Even when it wasn't Scott, there was this kind of intimacy to it. I didn't think it would feel the same with someone else, but that connection is still there."

Yeah. He was going to spontaneously combust at any second. He hoped it didn't set off the airbags. Catching the startled expression on Nick's face, he winced.

"Have you— I mean it's none of my business . . ." Nick trailed off for a second. "I don't know why I assumed there hadn't been anybody besides Scott." Obviously it was Nick's turn to set the car on fire.

Ethan pulled up a smile from somewhere, if only to cover the jolt of pain. That guilt still ate at him on occasion. "Does that seem horrible?"

Nick backpedaled immediately. "No, not at all. Didn't mean to imply that—"

"Nah, you didn't. Trust me, *I* still can't decide how I feel about it." Explaining felt nearly impossible, but the need to defend himself was too strong. "When there's this . . . this place in your life where you've always had someone . . ." Ethan shrugged helplessly. "You get really fucking lonely. And I know it's not wrong—the therapist told me that enough—but I still feel like I have to justify it. Which is stupid."

"You don't have to justify living your life. I'm glad you found someone to make you happy when you needed it."

Ethan thought about it for a minute. "It was a friend of ours, a guy from our lacrosse team. We hooked up at a party. Everybody was doing that thing where they tell you how sorry they are and then avoid you? Ha-joon got me a drink and asked if I wanted to talk, and we wound up in the basement all night. We hung out a few more times, but we weren't dating or anything."

Ethan worked his fingers around the steering wheel, sliding them back and forth across the leather his mom had worn smooth over the decade she'd owned the car before him. "It felt good. We liked each other, but there was nothing going on except what we were doing right then. I'm not sure I knew what it felt like, before that, to be with someone I couldn't see spending the rest of my life with. Which sounds crazy now, but I'd already spent most of it with Scott, so it seemed like it would always be that way."

Nick rested a hand over Ethan's on the steering wheel, squeezing briefly. "Sometimes being in the now, the right then, is good. You needed it. It worked."

That simple explanation resonated in a way all the lectures from his therapist, parents, and siblings never had. Ethan took an easier breath. "Yeah."

"So that offer to help me figure out more of what I like. Does it still hold?" Nick waited for Ethan's quick, emphatic nod before continuing. "Share some more suggestions?"

The innocent expression was a good effort, and Ethan laughed. "You've probably already noticed I suck at talking about sex. The curse of being a pale blond. Everything shows."

Nick held up his arm, his darker skin a distinct contrast to Ethan's freckled white. "I'm kind of enjoying the novelty factor. Besides, it's not like you can't tell when I'm blushing." He let his arm fall back to his lap, where he began fiddling with the thick seam running up the outside of his jeans. "So before . . . Kyle used to pin my arms over my head. Until it started making me feel trapped, I liked it. It was . . . He was taking care of me, kind of, and I didn't have to ask for anything, or get his attention, or *do* anything to be— Fuck. To be worthy of it, you know? It made me feel safe. I don't know if it still would, but maybe that."

"Okay." Ethan grinned. "As long as it doesn't devolve into tickling or anything. Hard limit. Makes me shriek like a toddler, and that's not cool."

"I'll kick you if you try."

"See, that wasn't so difficult. We agreed on something, and nobody blushed." Ethan's face actually stung from all the extra heat it had been exposed to.

Nick hummed his agreement, settling into what had to be a more comfortable position in the seat. "So where are we headed?"

"Depends. Do you think your ex is going to be looking for us? Do we need to drop off the tourist circuit for a while, lay low?" It sounded stupid, once the question was out. It wasn't like the guy was psychic or something.

"I don't know. Isn't that dumb? I'm fucking terrified he's going to pull up next to us at any second and make me come home with him, but I don't even know if I'm worth that much effort to him." Nick inhaled sharply. "Hey, Ethan, I'm going to lie to you, okay?"

"Are those damn maple syrup gangsters tracking you through an implant in your teeth?"

Nick laughed as expected, but Ethan didn't even have to glance over to know it was forced.

"I don't care if he shows up. I didn't spend a year and a half in the Little Psych Ward on the Prairie just to hook back up with him."

"That's not a very good lie," Ethan said.

"Yeah, well, it's all I've got. You're stuck with the truth now, mister. And the truth is I don't care where we're going." He slid a sideways glance at Ethan. "Even if you keep dragging me to murder caves."

Conversation with Scott Raines

Ethan: *I don't know if I'm really forgetting things or pretending not to remember because it hurts less*

Ethan: *This is so fucked up Scott*

Ethan: *Except maybe you'd feel like you were winning every time you made him laugh too*

Ethan: *It was so good to have someone meet me halfway again*

Interlude
NICK HAMILTON'S PHONE

Conversation with Stef Hansen

Nick: *I've got options.*

Stef: *Yup*

Nick: *Just checking.*

Stef: *You okay?*

Nick: *Really fucking great. Makes me nervous.*

Nick: *So what's your boyfriend's name, since I'll be meeting him eventually?*

Stef: *Brian, but he'll break up with me again before you get back.*

Nick: *Um. Okay.*

Stef: *It's our thing.*

Stef: *Where are your options taking you?*

Nick: *Arkansas. Yay?*

Stef: *Sure you aren't being held captive?*

Nick: *Nah, waiting for him to figure out he could do better.*

Stef: *Your options better include condoms*

Nick: *. . .*

Nick: *Exercising my option not to incriminate myself*

Stef: *Latex tastes better than gonorrhea, Nick.*

Nick: *Gotta go. Arkansas. You know how it is.*

CHAPTER *Thirteen*

Gurdon, AR

E than danced along the edge of the train tracks, leaping from side to side, directing searching glances into the darkening tree line. Nick forced himself to uncross his arms and relax, even though he was pretty sure this was how every tragic Southern gothic story about teenage boys went bad.

He could admit, privately, in the part of his head he was frantically trying to wall off away from his mouth, that being stuck in the woods after dark wasn't a pleasant association for him. Tyler had been a fan of "wilderness" trips, which was really dumping his group in the middle of Cornerstone's fenced-off property with a PowerBar and a bottle of water and telling them to walk until they found the camp again. Nick had never achieved any kind of self-sufficient nirvana. Mostly he'd wandered around feeling lost.

Given that he was so familiar with the experience, he didn't have any trouble spotting it in Ethan now.

"Hey, Ethan? Do you know where the car is?"

Ethan waved a hand in the general direction of behind them. "Yeah, right back there," he said, obviously distracted. "I wish they'd been a little more specific about *where* the guy got run over by the train. I don't want to miss it."

Back there sounded entirely too much like it was going to leave them stumbling through the dark trying to find the car. It would be one thing if all they had to do was follow the train line back, but they'd walked at least a mile before even getting to the tracks. Ethan would never have survived in the wild on his own.

Nick sighed. "The website *did* say you could get the same effect by standing in the bathroom in the dark and chewing Wint O Green Life Savers. And it wouldn't involve getting lost in the woods with bears and mountain lions and moonshiners."

"We're not lost. And if it makes you feel better, we'll hit a 7-Eleven and get some Life Savers before we stop for the night. Or . . ." Ethan trailed off dramatically, "we could camp out here tonight, rough it and stuff."

"No!" Nick caught himself. "If you want anything approaching sex, it won't be out here in the fucking wilderness."

"Not a fan of campfires and marshmallows and sex in sleeping bags?"

Nick shook his head, squinting into the trees. "Not a fan of trespassing charges on private property in Arkansas, but sex in sleeping bags is right up there. Too hot, too crowded, and smells too much like feet."

Ethan's face fell, and Nick almost relented. Except really, there was no way he was spending a night sleeping in the woods ever again, no matter how much he wanted to fuck the guy he was with.

"Fiiine. We'll hang out until we see the light, then we can go find a motel. Since *some* people can't handle roughing it. Peeing in the wild, eating bugs for breakfast, sleeping on piles of rocks . . ."

Ethan had stopped to gesture wildly, and Nick used the opportunity to poke him in the stomach. "Not selling it, dude."

Nick turned away, scanning both sides of the tracks for Ethan's creepy light. Heavy footsteps crunched on the gravel behind him. He appreciated that Ethan had learned better than to sneak up on him.

"Hey."

Nick turned around to find Ethan standing a couple of feet away, and smiled in his direction. "Hey yourself."

"What about making out under the stars?"

Nick rolled his eyes, closing the short distance between them and curling a hand into the front of Ethan's faded Captain America T-shirt. "Better, but there aren't any stars out."

Ethan puffed out his chest, bumping against Nick's fingers as he pointed at the large star on his shirt.

"The only thing under that star is your dick, and this was a really long walk for a terrible blowjob pun." Nick leaned in, the word *blowjob* practically whispered into Ethan's mouth before they kissed. He didn't let go of Ethan's shirt, pressing his free hand under it, finding the bare skin he was seeking above Ethan's hip bone.

They kissed long enough to leave Nick light-headed when they broke apart, and he rested his temple against Ethan's shoulder for a second while he recovered some equilibrium. They'd shored up each other's balance while they made out, unconsciously shifting position until Ethan's leg was pressed between his, and one of Ethan's arms was wrapped around his lower back. Nick finally looked up, peering over Ethan's shoulder, and laughed.

"Dude, we found your creepy light."

Ethan jumped away so fast he almost tripped. "Where?"

If he hadn't been laughing so hard, Nick was pretty sure he'd have felt insulted. "Way to ruin a moment. Right over there."

A soft bluish-white light floated at eye level about ten yards away.

Ethan drew a deep breath. "Fuckin' A," he whispered. He started to take a step toward it, but Nick reached out to grab his shirt.

"Whoa, big boy. Don't chase it off."

"Yeah, you're right." Ethan fumbled in his jeans pocket for his phone.

The click of his camera sounded unnaturally loud in the suddenly silent woods. The suddenly, ominously silent woods. The light held steady in the same position for several more seconds, then started moving toward them. The hair on the back of Nick's neck went up as a train whistle, faint, like it was miles off, echoed down the tracks.

"Oh, hell no." Nick's feet made the decision for him, as he grabbed Ethan's hand and started running.

Laughing and stumbling, hanging on to each other to keep their feet, they made it maybe a quarter mile back up the tracks before they had to stop.

Ethan smiled wide, teeth gleaming in the growing dark as he leaned against Nick. "That was awesome!"

Nick's heart pounded in his ears, but the warmth in his chest had nothing to do with how hard it was to gasp for breath and giggle like a hyena at the same time. That was all Ethan, blond and grinning and looking like he'd won an award for Most Adorable Geek.

"If I get murdered by a . . ." Nick panted ". . . ghost train . . . you are going to . . . owe me so big." It took him three sucking inhalations to get all the words of dire warning out.

"I promise I'll sacrifice myself for you. I'll throw myself in front of it before I let you get run over by a ghost train."

"That's weirdly sweet." Nick looked behind them, but there was no light to be seen, no oncoming train, dead track worker, or angry landowner left behind in their mad dash. "It would be even sweeter if we'd run toward the car."

Ethan's eyebrows shot up and he spun in a circle. "We did! I think. Didn't we?" His scowl faded to sheepish sincerity. "We have to follow the tracks back to that rock with the graffiti on it and turn. Uh. Left. Back into the woods. The path was pretty clear from there."

"Right. The rock. How could I forget. Because there couldn't possibly be more than one rock with graffiti on it in an area where stupid teenagers and tourists come hunting for ghosts." Nick shook his head, reaching into his pocket for his phone. He snapped a quick picture of the indignant expression on Ethan's face, the flash washing everything out. Then he pulled up his map program and hit the little walking man button, turning the screen around so Ethan could see it.

"Luckily, one of us was interested in living through this adventure and decided to use the tools God and Google have given us. If we head down the tracks for half a mile, we'll hit the road, and we can walk to the car from there."

Ethan huffed. "I still think going back the other way is shorter."

"It absolutely is, and there's not a fucking chance I'm walking back toward that light, so suck it up."

"Fine. But I'm not going to be happy about it." To demonstrate his unhappiness, Ethan kicked at the crossties on the tracks, except Nick could see the grin he was trying to hide.

"Keep sulking, and I'll leave you out here with the headless train guy."

They were both out of breath and sweating by the time they reached the car. Ethan unlocked the door and dropped into the driver's seat with a groan.

Nick leaned his arms against the roof of the car, waiting until Ethan had the air conditioner running before he opened the door. "I'm gonna vote no more hiking tonight. It's too damn hot. Not to mention pitch-black now." He held up a hand, forestalling Ethan's objections. "And no, your creepy ghost light doesn't help."

Ethan nodded, swiping the sleeve of his shirt across his face. "Motel and shower. Then food."

"Think we could find a place with a pool? I haven't been swimming since forever."

"What, the jacuzzi wasn't close enough to a pool for you?" Ethan waggled his eyebrows. "I know *I* had more fun than I would've had swimming."

"The only record I was going to break in that was holding my breath, though. I'd kind of like to actually stretch my muscles." He glanced down at himself, revising the statement. "The muscles I used to have, anyway."

"And after teasing *me* about being a jock." Ethan glanced toward the woods, which did nothing to help Nick's heebie-jeebies. "I think we can probably find a pool. Pretty sure I've got a swimsuit packed somewhere."

That was a detail that had completely slipped his mind. "I don't."

"No worries," Ethan said with a grin. "It's late enough that we'll be sneaking in after hours. You can skinny dip. I won't tell."

"Eh, nobody'll know the difference between underwear and a swim suit in the dark anyway. Less laundry that way."

Ethan whipped off a salute. "I cannot fault your logic, sir. You okay with going to the Ozark National Forest tomorrow if I promise we aren't looking for decapitated ghosts?"

Nick nodded. "Sure." The warmth of the car seeped into his bones and turned him liquid, and after all the unexpected exercise, it was hard to keep his eyes open. "I'm going wherever you go, dude. I'm here until we run out of gas."

Ethan glanced down at the gauges. "Don't jinx us. We're not far enough away that the headless guy couldn't catch up with us."

Nick found the handle for the seat and leaned it back a few inches, curling into a pretzel under the seat belt. "Tell him to wake me up if he needs me. I'm exhausted."

He was more than half-asleep when Ethan settled a hand against his head, and it was enough like being petted that it pushed him the rest of the way down into dreams.

It was half past too damn late when they finally found a hotel and got checked in. Ethan dutifully pointed out the pool in the courtyard to Nick, who groaned and leaned even more heavily on his shoulder as Ethan tried to unlock the door. The key card finally worked, and they both staggered when the door popped open. Nick made the five whole steps to the bed and collapsed into it face-first. One of his shoes fell off and hit the floor.

"So, laps in ten minutes?"

"I'm too tired to flip you off. Imagine I am, though." Nick's voice was muffled by the drab bedspread.

Ethan's phone rang, saving him from his acute lack of a snappy answer. His mom's cell number popped up on caller ID, and he grimaced. He hadn't called in a couple of nights. That, plus Suze's potential ratting out, didn't bode well.

"Hey, Mom. Kinda late for you to be up, isn't it? Don't you old folks need a good twelve hours a night to prevent shingles and arthritis and stuff?"

His mom's sigh echoed over the line. "You didn't get that smart-ass attitude from me. *Anyway*, I figured if I called later, I might actually catch you, see if you were still alive or not."

It was his turn to sigh. Maybe he was overtired, but the comment rubbed him the wrong way. "Alive and kicking, as you can see."

"See? Am I supposed to be doing FaceGram or something? I don't see anything."

Ethan fell backward onto the bed, landing next to Nick with a pained whimper. "Mom. Come on. We all know you do the PTA and Booster Club social media."

"If I don't mess with you, kid, who will?" There was a weighty, significant pause. "Maybe this naval cadet your sister says you're running away to Canada with."

"He's actually a convicted felon, and we can't leave Arkansas unless we clear it with his parole officer. He only looks like a naval cadet because he got super lice in jail and had to shave his head to get rid of them."

"I was set up," Nick muttered, hopefully not loud enough for his mom to hear. "And everybody had super lice, not only me." That was louder, of course.

"Did I hear someone else's voice? Is he there with you now?" She sounded entirely too enthusiastic. Ethan didn't trust it one bit.

"No, I've got the TV on. One of those ripped-from-the-headlines shows. *Law & Order: Ozark* or something."

His mom sniffed, a sure sign she smelled a rat. Literally, once, but Robert's pet rat had been a very social escape artist. "Ethan Daniel Domani, don't make me break out the car battery and wet sponges."

"I'm incredibly disturbed, yet not at all surprised, that you know so much about torturing the truth out of someone without a warrant."

Next to him, Nick summoned the energy to turn his head and crack an eye open. "My dad knows Dick Cheney. He can probably get her a job."

Ethan snickered, his mom's disbelieving hum cutting through Nick's offer.

"Leaving aside the fact that I can tell you're lying—*and* pretending I'm cool enough not to mind that my teenage son is apparently shacking up with someone I've never met and know nothing about—I'd still like to point out that it's been two days since you called. You promised you'd check in every day. Tweetograms don't count."

"Yes, they do," Ethan insisted, before taking shameless advantage of Nick's proximity to press his face into Nick's shoulder and whine. "This whole conversation could be recorded. Pictures are worth a thousand words. Proof of life, and stuff."

"Ethan . . ." His mom's long pause and suddenly serious tone made him grimace. "I really need you to check in. Your dad and I, we worry. You're a long way from home. And maybe you're alone and maybe you're not, but putting that aside for right now, I have to know that you're safe."

"There's no such thing," Ethan said, because he was tired, and sore, and Scott was dead, part of him in a little wooden box buried in the mess of Ethan's glove compartment. Nick's hand moved lightly against his back.

"Maybe not, but making rash decisions and putting yourself in harm's way to prove me wrong isn't going to help."

Fuck, it sounded like he'd upset his mom. "I'm fine, Mom. I haven't made any rash decisions, or decisions that will give me a rash, or anything. And I have GPS. If I wind up on Harm's Way, I'll have it reroute me and pay the tolls."

There was a long, definitely watery sigh on the other end of the line. "You're a horrible smart-ass. You get that from your father. Here, he wants to talk to you."

Ethan groaned and rolled over onto his back, staring at the stained ceiling while his mom handed her phone over.

"Hey, kid. Your sister says you're using the Facesnap for human trafficking. Remember, don't say anything without your lawyer present."

"Spoken like a man looking to increase his billable hours."

Nick snorted, but Ethan couldn't tell if he was asleep or amused.

"Hey, that's sound legal advice. I think. I mostly steal closing arguments from *Boston Legal* reruns. You having a good time?"

"Yeah." Ethan hoped he didn't sound as surprised as he felt at the admission. He hadn't expected to have fun. Somehow what should have been the trip of a lifetime had turned into a box to check off, something he had to get done before he could move on. Now it was real again. He twisted around to glance at Nick, feeling a grin pulling at his mouth. "Yeah, I am."

"Well, if it helps your enjoyment any, most of your siblings are insane with jealousy. You being out of parental reach, and all."

His dad's pauses were always more ominous. Mainly because they didn't occur very often, and when they did, it was never good.

"So, about being out of touch. Your mom has been pretty worried. She'd like you to check in more often."

Nick turned over, walking his fingers up Ethan's arm, which tickled.

"Dad," he said, infusing his voice with a note of warning.

"Ethan," his dad replied. Christ, he really *did* get it from his father.

"You guys know I'd call you if anything was wrong. I need . . ." Ethan trailed off, distracted by Nick propping himself up on his elbows and scooting closer.

"A blowjob," Nick whispered into his ear, making him choke into the phone.

"Ethan? I told you not to put whole chicken nuggets in your mouth."

"I need some time to think about things, Dad. Without having to check in with you guys and prove I'm okay. I'm not okay. Talking to you makes me feel like I have to pretend I am."

Nick settled over him, a heavy weight pinning him to the middle of Arkansas, and he realized suddenly that he wanted to be here. Not halfway, tugged back to Arlington every night when he called home. He wanted to be where he was and see where he might go.

The offer of a blowjob didn't *hurt*, but gross—he was on the phone with his parents.

"Love you both. Tell Suze she's a brat. I'll talk to you in a couple days." He hung up before his dad could say anything in return.

"So about that blowjob," Nick said, almost offhandedly.

Not *Are you okay?* Not *Can I do anything?* Just Nick, there and solid and real in a way nothing had been for a long time.

"What about it?"

Nick smacked his shoulder, so light he barely felt it. "I feel like we've been talking about sex all day. I'm horny."

Nick hadn't moved away, so Ethan took a chance and wrapped an arm around him, enjoying the closeness they couldn't manage with an emergency brake and three pairs of sunglasses wedged between them.

"Yeah? I thought you were tired?" His hand drifted lazily across Nick's back, the slip of cotton on skin sparking up his fingertips. He lowered his voice to the same whisper Nick had used. "What do you want?"

Nick snuck a hand under the hem of Ethan's shirt, short, blunt nails dragging up his stomach and over his ribs, making him jump in a way that wasn't really unpleasant. "Told you. I want to give you a blowjob."

Nick's fingers skated across Ethan's nipple and back again, and Nick pressed his face against the other side of Ethan's chest. "I want to see if I can feel like you said. Like I'm connected to you."

Ethan didn't know how to respond without turning the moment into something more serious than it needed to be, so he settled for squeezing his hand against Nick's shoulder blade. Nick took it as encouragement, following the path of his nails with his mouth.

The phone buzzed from underneath him where he'd let it drop, and they both jumped. Ethan groaned, reaching a hand to dig under the blanket, and Nick laughed, a vibration against his stomach.

"Just so you know, I'm not planning on stopping, even if you *are* on the phone with your parents."

Ethan finally found his phone and one-handedly tossed it in the general direction of the nightstand without looking at the screen. "Not happening."

"Good. I'd hate for our introduction to be you screaming my name."

As if to prove he wasn't bragging, Nick followed the words with a scrape of teeth across Ethan's nipple. While Ethan didn't yell Nick's name, he didn't quite muffle a yelp.

Nick pulled back, and when Ethan opened his eyes, the concern was obvious. "Sorry. Was that—"

"It was great," Ethan assured him, using the front of Nick's shirt to tug him back down. "But maybe more talking about my dick, and less about my parents."

Nick grinned, dragging his thumb across Ethan's damp chest. "Sorry, talking with my mouth full is rude."

Ethan's snickering turned into something else entirely when Nick went for the waist of his shorts and pushed them down over his hips in one smooth motion.

Ethan brushed his fingers over Nick's hair, wishing it was long enough to card through. "You know you don't have anything to prove, right? If it's not working for you—"

Nick turned his face back up and met Ethan's eyes, and he was smiling in a way that looked more real than the full-speed-ahead cheer he normally used to push through whatever was bothering him. "Ethe, I want to go down on you. *You*, not *someone*. Shut up."

"Oh. Well. Okay, then."

The back of Ethan's head hit the mattress with a thump.

Texas was mile after mile after mile of brown nothingness, and after Nick smacked his head against the window for the hundredth time dozing off, he turned to look at Ethan. "You want me to take over driving for a while? It's boring as hell watching it. It's got to be worse driving."

"Thanks, but I think I'll take my chances. You can't even stay awake long enough to pick a playlist." Ethan cast a quick but significant glance at the phone wedged between Nick's thigh and the center console.

"Not my fault you only listen to old people music," he muttered, surreptitiously wiping leg sweat off the screen with his shorts.

"I have *one* ELO playlist, and it's because my mom likes them. I think you're just tired because I wore you out this morning." Ethan sounded insufferably smug about it. Which, fair enough, Nick wasn't going to argue. Ethan had been a wealth of warm, damp skin after his shower, and Nick had always enjoyed a breakfast buffet.

He chose a playlist called *Away Games* and set Ethan's phone down in the cup holder.

"Is . . . is this Twisted Sister?"

Ethan drummed harder on the steering wheel, out of sync and enthusiastic. "Yeah, and if you don't like it, too bad."

Nick smirked at him, crossing his arms and leaning back in the seat. "Nah, this is good." He hummed along for a few seconds. "So, is this your dad's playlist?"

"This is *mine*, thank you very much. You're a music snob."

"Probably."

Ethan stuck his tongue out. "Maybe that could be your career. Professional music snob."

"Better than the other ways I was considering going pro," he replied without thinking, the warm afternoon sun baking him into a content, filterless idiot.

"Definitely easier than going pro with that syrup-smuggling ring. Or less dangerous, at least."

The easy grin made it impossible to tell if Ethan had picked up on his slip or not. Nick ran with it.

"Yeah, not a lot of professional maple leagues in California, I imagine." It was a good way to admit his plans ran out as soon as Ethan made it to the coast, without making Ethan help him figure out what to do about it. "Did I get you in trouble with your parents?"

"Only in the sense that I'll probably have to shave my head when I get home."

He must've looked puzzled, because Ethan laughed.

"Super lice?"

"Oh, I figured she'd assume I gave you crabs."

"Gross. Is that still a thing?"

"It's not a thing I have, so I'd prefer not to find out." Nick reached up to scratch his neck, which didn't actually itch. It was just that he'd realized how obvious he was when he rubbed his head. "I don't have anything, by the way. Which maybe we should have talked about before you swallowed my dick. But since we didn't. Uh. Mandatory STD and pregnancy testing at good old Camp Crazytown, so I know I'm good."

"But are you pregnant? I mean, come on. Let's get to the serious side of things."

Nick didn't bother trying to stifle his sigh, and Ethan laughed, a little uncomfortably.

"Sorry, trying to lighten the mood, since that was . . . well, really stupid, honestly. I'm always big on the whole safe-sex thing."

Nick moved in the seat, cursing himself because he knew it was another tell. Why was it so easy to spot them, but so impossible not to indulge in them? Maybe Ethan hadn't noticed. There was only so much space in the car . . . and yeah, it was probably pretty noticeable when he tried to cram himself into the crevice beside the door. Forcing his hands flat against the tops of his thighs, he wiggled until he was situated firmly in the middle of the leather bucket seat.

"I wasn't. But I guess I was lucky. So yay, condoms." He didn't light up like Ethan in all his cherubic glory, but Nick knew he was blushing. "I mean. If you want them, or we need them for . . . Damage is kind of done with the . . . You know what? Texas is really interesting. Look at all that brown."

"So many shades," Ethan agreed earnestly. "But, on the other hand, I've seen some pretty promising taco joints. Lunch'll be good."

"We should look up Peruvian chicken places along our route. Not that tacos aren't awesome. You just reminded me that there's all kinds of food I've been missing."

"Pregnancy cravings? Shit, I thought Robert had already cornered the surprise-grandchildren market when he told us about the twins." Ethan reached across the front seat to pat Nick's stomach. "Don't worry, I bet Mom's still got a bunch of her old maternity stuff."

He sniffed, poking his belly out in front of him. "You're mocking me, but I'd be fucking adorable in a baby doll dress, and you know it."

"Oh, totally. You've got the legs for it."

"So you'll still want me when I have cankles and I have to pee every five minutes? Which is really all I remember from when my mom was pregnant with my brother."

Ethan made a face. "Can we go back to you in a dress? That was less weird than talking about your mom's bathroom habits."

Nick kicked his feet up onto the dash, crossing his ankles and trying to look smug. He probably looked constipated. "So does that mean you've got a thing for girls too? Because that would be . . ." Mildly uncomfortable, because Ethan's jeans were already a little tight on Nick, and there wasn't much space for his sudden interest in a threesome. "What's a word when something's hotter than you have language for?"

"Um, shit." Ethan's face fell. He shot Nick a quick glance, then focused back on the road. "I don't want to ruin your fantasies and all, but no." He paused for a second before rushing on. "I mean, no on the girl thing. Sorry?"

"Nah, it's cool, I was only curious." And a lot turned on by a few filthy mental images. "I mean, if *you're* ever curious, I used to know a few girls who would totally be down for the whole threesome-with-two-guys thing, but no pressure. And, you know, boobs are pretty great. The ones I remember from freshman year, anyway."

"How equal opportunity of you." Oh, good, Ethan was definitely pink now too. "You know if we keep talking about sex, even sex I don't really want to have, I'm going to have to pull off somewhere, right?"

"I could pull you off while you drive," he offered, all innocence as he examined his stubby, bitten fingernails.

Ethan groaned. "As tempting as that is, I'm pretty sure I read a Stephen King book about that. It didn't end well."

"*The Shining*?"

"Ew. Not unless you know something about that Danny kid and the creepy twins that I don't."

"I thought it was the one with the clown, so no." Nick stretched over, casually dropping a hand in Ethan's lap. The jump was gratifying. "Horror stories aside, except for the horror of no sex, I saw a sign for some state park a little while back. Wanna stop?"

"Getting arrested for indecent exposure in Texas sounds like a great idea."

Nick squeezed Ethan's leg, and possibly a little more, earning a soft whuff of breath that hit him straight in the libido. "If you park at the back of the lot and we crawl into the trunk, nobody will see us."

Ethan looked at him like he was crazy, eyes leaving the road for long enough that the car started to drift a little. "That is the worst idea I've ever heard. That's like *asking* for a state trooper to haul you out of the car with your pants around your ankles."

"Kinky." Nick sighed and leaned away, trailing his hand across Ethan's very interested cock as he did so. "Fine. I'll embrace the cliché. Find a gas station with a single bathroom, and I'll make it worth your while."

"Oh my God, did you have Viagra for breakfast or something?" Ethan muttered.

Nick couldn't put a name to the persistent need he'd developed to get as much of Ethan's skin against his as he could. Maybe he was making up for more than a year without even jerking off. Maybe the pills he'd taken every morning at camp hadn't been herbal supplements after all, but some weird chemical cocktail designed to kill his sex drive.

Maybe the lure of Ethan—willing, eager, appreciative, *kind* without making his hang-ups a big deal—was a better drug than anything he'd ever tried.

"If you can find us somewhere in the next ten minutes, I guarantee you the best sex you've ever had in Texas, *and* I'll buy you a slushee when we're done. I mean, with your money, but it's the thought that counts, right?"

Ethan's eyes narrowed, and Nick laughed as the car picked up speed.

Or maybe he was just happy.

CHAPTER *Fourteen*

Marshall, TX

"**D**id the car move?" Ethan kept his voice to a whisper, despite the silence of the road around them.

"No," Nick said, at a totally normal volume, and in a tone that definitely verged on pissy. It was a lot to convey in a single syllable.

The full moon overhead made it easy to see Nick's pinched expression.

"Well, we haven't been waiting that long. Maybe we need to roll down the windows or something."

Nick squirmed in the seat, denim squeaking softly across the worn leather. His hand fell to shield the window button, like he thought Ethan was going to lean across the car and let the ghosts in unless he protected it.

"You know I have controls for all the windows on this side, right?" To be a dick, he rolled Nick's window down an inch, filling the car with the faint sounds of crickets. Nick glared at him and rolled it back up.

"How much longer do you want to wait for bored football jocks to come mess with your car? Not to mention the two queers sitting in it?"

Ethan narrowed his eyes. "Don't say it like that. You called yourself queer before, so why would you use it as an insult?"

Nick moved again, and this time there was definitely discomfort in his expression. "Ethan, I have to piss so bad I'm about to wet my pants. Self-aware phrasing isn't my biggest problem right now."

"Why didn't you *say* that? I would've stopped somewhere before we drove out here." It came out sounding more bewildered than he'd meant it to, but really—even Robert's kids would tell him when they had to go potty, and they were three years old.

Nick looked away too fast for Ethan to read anything on his face. "I'm not allowed. I mean, I am. Now. But it was . . . It was a thing. There were times we were supposed to go, and if you had to in between, you held it, or you pissed yourself and had to walk around in soggy sweatpants for the rest of the day. If you asked, the counselors would restrict something." His voice dropped to a whisper, though Ethan didn't think it was the ghosts of Stagecoach Road he was trying not to provoke. "And I'm too creeped out to pee in the bushes."

Ethan stared at him, so shocked he couldn't work up a reply for several long seconds. Shit like that didn't happen in any version of reality he'd ever known. "That's . . . That's completely fucked up. I'm pretty sure I heard about some school doing that to little kids, and they got shut down." He flexed his fingers in his lap. "I'm not one for extreme violence, but if you wanted to go back and burn that place to the ground, I'll drive you. Hell, I'll buy the lighter fluid."

"I mostly want to pee," Nick said plaintively. "And it seemed like asking you to come with me might cross a line."

"Seriously? Cross a line? Given how we spent the afternoon, I don't think watching your back while you take a piss is going to break any boundaries." It earned him a grin, however faint, from Nick. "C'mon, let's go." He reached for the door handle, the dome lamp coming on and flooding the car with enough light to point them out to every ghost within a ten-mile radius.

He stayed away from the splash zone, but he made sure Nick knew he was close. "I don't actually have a kink for listening to people pee. I want that out there."

"Jesus Christ, that's better than sex."

Nick's relieved sigh made Ethan sniff in mock-offense. "Hey! You could at least pretend me accidentally turning on the hand dryer in the throes of passion was the hottest thing that's happened to you today."

"Was that supposed to be a pun?" Nick's shoulders twitched as he tucked himself away and zipped up, the sound loud in the sudden silence.

"I've got Handi Wipes in the glove compartment, asshole."

Nick's laughter drifted over the car as Ethan walked back around to the driver's side. Smudges of dirt on the trunk caught his eye, and he stopped to take a closer look.

"Holy shit, get in the car!" he whisper-shouted.

Nick's head shot up over the roof. "Why?"

"Get *in*!"

Ethan flung himself in the seat, feeling the grin splitting his face as he slammed the door. The passenger door slammed shut as well, Nick staring across the console at him, wide-eyed.

"There's little kids' handprints on the trunk. This is so fucking awesome. If we sit here a few minutes, they might do it again!"

Nick held out a hand. "Give me the keys. I'm not waiting around here to get murdered by dead preschoolers!"

Ethan leaned across and pulled a packet out of the glove compartment, offering it to Nick. "Chill, dude, there's no reason for them to want to kill us. They move cars. No reports of mutilated bodies or anything."

"Yet." If someone could aggressively use a Handi Wipe, Nick was definitely nailing it. When he was done, lemon-scented and glaring, he tossed it in the back seat, then crossed his arms over his chest. "You'll be sorry if I get chewed up by baby ghosts before you get to fuck me."

There was no arguing with that logic, but Ethan wasn't above an aggrieved sigh. "That's fine and all, but I hope it's worth missing out on a paranormal experience."

"Dude. I have *feelings*." Nick pressed a hand to his heart. "Mostly heartburn and regret from the Slim Jim I ate earlier, but also deep sadness and stuff. I offer you the bounty of my ass, and you're more interested in getting your car detailed by the dead? Ow."

"A couple more McDonald's meals, and you can call it bountiful. You're kinda skinny right now, though." Ethan reached across to pinch what he could reach between Nick and the seat. "But skinny or not, it *is* a mighty fine ass."

"Your jeans are too tight. It's squished."

Ethan was busy looking behind them, trying to see anything out the back window, but not so busy he couldn't pause to stick his tongue out at Nick. "You're trying to get me to say something cheesy about getting you out of them, and I refuse."

There was nothing to be seen behind the car, or nothing that wanted to be seen anyway. He twisted around and reached for the ignition. Nick's relief was obvious, his shoulders dropping instantly when Ethan shifted into drive.

They'd only rolled about ten feet down the road when the car suddenly stalled. The radio was off, but static so loud it hurt his ears started pouring out of the speakers. Ethan turned the key, shivering as the engine clicked, but wouldn't turn over. Somehow, the air-conditioning had come on full blast, despite the fact that it barely blew colder than the heater most days. The interior lights blazed on at the same time as the headlights. Then, every bit as abruptly, everything went off again.

"If you can't turn the car on, we're leaving everything and running away. *Now*."

Ethan was inclined to agree. It took him two tries before he remembered to put the car in park to turn it on. When the engine caught, he dragged the shifter back and hit the gas as hard as he could, fishtailing on the gravel and shooting them down the road.

Ethan waited until they were secure in the well-lit parking lot at Donut Palace before walking around to the back of the car. The marks on the trunk were a bit less clear, undoubtedly due to the dust cloud they'd left in their wake. Regardless, there was no denying the tiny little handprints.

Nick leaned in to look. "Maybe it was a raccoon? Don't their paws look like hands?"

"Only if it was a three-foot-tall raccoon. And that's even scarier than ghosts, honestly." He reached into his back pocket and pulled out his phone. Making sure the flash was on, he snapped three pictures, then another three from each side. "Gonna post these to the Weird America forums. These are clearer than anything they have!"

"You'll go down in Marshall, Texas, history, I'm sure."

Ethan spared a sniff as he pulled up the site. "I refuse to acknowledge your sarcasm. And I might buy up the last of the Cap'n Crunch doughnuts and not share them."

"You should be glad I'm *not* having one. Open wounds in my mouth would put your second favorite thing about traveling with me off the table."

Ethan blinked, looking up from the email he was typing. "Wait, what's my first favorite thing?"

"Scaring the crap out of me, apparently." Nick shut the back door and slung his backpack over his shoulder. For a terrifying second, Ethan thought he was going to walk away.

His momentary panic must have shown on his face. Nick hefted his bag. "I want to brush my teeth. That Slim Jim is, like, all over my mouth, and it's gross." He stepped close enough to bump their shoulders together, which Ethan had taken to translating as Nick's version of a reassuring hug.

"I wasn't worried you were too scared to get back in the car." Ethan grinned, not even needing the invitation to lie this time.

"Dork," Nick muttered. Ethan didn't think he was imagining the fond edge to it.

He'd ordered a dozen doughnuts and two cartons of milk by the time Nick got out of the bathroom, and only extreme self-control had kept him from scarfing down a couple. There were no other customers in the bakery, so Ethan didn't feel too bad about taking one of the larger tables by the window.

"You didn't tell me you invited a football team." Nick slid the chair opposite him out and flipped it around, straddling it. "Or is this dinner?"

"Given that it's eleven o'clock in a small town in Texas, I'm going out on a limb and calling this dinner. They don't seem to be into twenty-four-hour stuff around here. I checked." Ethan turned the box toward Nick and opened the lid. "But don't you worry, I got all the food groups covered." He pointed as he named them off. "Meat in the bacon maple, dairy in this cream-filled one here, fruit and veggies in this strawberry rhubarb. I think we're good. *And* I got us milk instead of Coke. Seriously healthy."

"Oh, yeah, it's a regular food pyramid you got going here."

"I paid attention in health class. And I was corn in the food pyramid play in first grade." He fished out the bacon maple, catching a bacon bit as it fell off. "So, after all your recent terrifying adventures, should you call and check in with your friend from camp? Let him know I haven't gotten you killed yet?"

Nick picked through the box before settling on the most boring option, a Boston cream. When he bit into it, a glut of custard oozed out the back onto his hand. Ethan watched him lick it off, covertly spreading his knees a little farther apart. It was definitely the most pornographic spill he'd ever witnessed. It was also definitely a diversionary tactic.

"Is he expecting you to give him an idea of when you might be back in Virginia?" They hadn't talked much about the mysterious Stef, but Ethan had gathered that he lived in Alexandria, and he'd offered Nick a place to stay. Ethan had done his best to keep his anger toward Stef to himself—he couldn't imagine knowing what was happening to Nick and whoever else at that camp and not doing anything about it.

"No."

Nick took another bite of doughnut, effectively nonanswering, and Ethan stifled a sigh.

The girl behind the counter didn't seem to be interested in their conversation. As if to prove him right, she hauled a stool across the floor, metal legs scraping the vinyl tile. A few seconds later, she pulled a tattered V.C. Andrews paperback out from under the counter and cracked it open, thoroughly ignoring them.

"Kyle can text me if I turn my phone back on." Nick spat it out between bites, his gaze firmly on the open box of doughnuts.

"Do you want me to, I don't know, screen them for you? Not that I'm trying to be nosy," Ethan rushed to add, suddenly uncomfortable. "But if it would help. And so you can use your phone."

It was too hard to read the expression on Nick's face, but Ethan preemptively winced.

"I'll think about it."

Ethan reached across the table, resting the tips of his fingers against Nick's bare wrist for a moment. "Lie to me."

Nick took a delicate bite of doughnut, chewing for a long time before he said anything.

"He's part of the maple cartel. I'm..." The way Nick faltered, even coming up with a lie, made Ethan bite his lip.

"They've got pictures of me. Blackmail material, you know?" Nick leaned back, subtly drawing his hand away from Ethan's as he toyed with the remains of his second doughnut. "And sometimes I worry they implanted me with a tracking chip. If I turn my phone on, I could start broadcasting our location to some really unsavory Canadians."

"We could do it in the hotel bathroom. No windows and a giant metal tub to block the signal, right? Just in case." Ethan stared hard at the glittery Formica tabletop. "Plus, you know, I'm only interested in seeing you in your uncompromised state. Fully invested is kind of my kink. So I wouldn't look at those unless you told me to."

"Okay." Nick's voice was barely a whisper.

Ethan hadn't realized he was holding his breath until he let it out in a quiet whoosh. "We'll find a decent place to crash after we finish here." He waved a hand at the box. "Not that we have to eat all of them right now. I mean, we're going to need something for breakfast."

Ethan was glad the bathroom at the motel they'd chosen was relatively clean. Something about the scent of lemon disinfectant felt safe, even though Nick's hands were shaking when he handed his phone over. Neither of them was sitting in the tub, but the bathroom door was safely closed, Ethan's hip leaned against it for extra safety.

"I deleted them the other day. I don't know why I can't do that now." The narrow tub ledge was low enough that Nick looked like he was squatting, hands hanging loose between his legs as he stared up at Ethan.

"The stupid therapist I hated told me we only have so much, like, mental energy every day. Sometimes you use it up on little stuff, sometimes you toss it all at something big. Maybe you're running low today."

The phone was a couple of years older than his, which, given that Nick had been locked up in that hellhole for however long, wasn't surprising. It was scuffed along the edges, the case cracked in a couple of places near the corners. "So how do you want me to do this? Delete them all? Read them? Report them to the nearest FBI field office?"

"I . . . Delete them, I guess?" Nick plucked at the seam in his jeans, staring at the floor.

"Should I read them first?" Ethan felt like shit when Nick flinched at the question. "I don't have to," he hastened to add. "I'm cool either way."

"How about a dramatic reading?" Nick stood, his brows drawing together and his voice deepening. "Nicholas, this behavior is childish. This is why I can't trust you."

"'Nicholas,' huh? Shit, that sounds more like you're channeling your dad or something."

"Oh, it was all very mature abuse." Nick laughed, but there was no humor in the sound.

The screen went dark, and Ethan swiped across it, hoping Nick didn't need to enter the pass code again. He wasn't sure it would happen—Nick might have used up all of his spare courage for the day just to get this far. He opened Nick's texts, two notable entries at the bottom marked *Mom* and *Dad* showing a few unread. Stef Hansen had sent a couple too. And then there were the sixty-seven unread texts from a 571 number with no contact info. Maybe he was jumping to conclusions, but he felt safe guessing that was Kyle.

"Oh, hey, you were wrong! Here, let me try to give this one the proper gravitas." Ethan cleared his throat, adopting a serious expression. "'Nicky, pick up the phone. You know I hate it when you make me wait on you.'" He illustrated his Shakespearean reading by grabbing an imaginary dick and making a jerk-off motion.

Nick laughed, his head tipping back as his shoulders shook. "Nailed it. You sound just like him."

"I don't know if I should be proud or scared. So, uh, am I deleting that one? And the other sixty that probably say the same thing?"

The subtle shake of Nick's head was all the answer he got. Why the hell Nick would want to hear more was beyond Ethan. Nevertheless, he scrolled down a few more messages until he got to one that pushed a sound of startled protest out of his throat without his permission.

Nick was leaning against the sink, arms folded. He flinched when their eyes met.

"Okay, but seriously, fuck this guy. I mean it. This is . . . This is disgusting. This isn't the kind of thing you say to someone who spit in your face and called your mom a whore, much less somebody you love."

"What did he say?" Nick sounded more resigned than curious, and Ethan had trouble forming the words at all. Even acting as a proxy for such an asshole was making him want to shower for a week.

"'I know you ran off like a stupid little slut. When I get you back, I'm going to rent you out on Craigslist to pay me back for the gas I wasted.'" He didn't try to make it sound any less horrifying than it was on the screen in front of him. Nick's laughter, quieter this time, definitely fake, startled him.

"God, he needs some new material." Uncrossing his arms, Nick stepped across the tiny bathroom and plucked his phone out of Ethan's hand. He scrolled down a few messages, snorting as he turned the phone back around so Ethan could read it. "Always followed closely by 'Nobody else would put up with this, Nicky. You're lucky I love you.' and then usually him fucking me until I thanked him for taking such good care of me."

Ethan's stomach turned, the words swimming in front of his eyes. He couldn't read them. Couldn't even imagine seeing them in a bad TV show without changing the channel, much less hearing them so often they'd become a sick joke.

He'd wrapped his arms around Nick before he could think better of it. The stupid phone got wedged between them, and he poured his helpless anger into hugging Nick within an inch of his life. He probably shouldn't have, but he didn't know how to say anything that condemned Kyle's words without yelling, and he thought that might be worse. Nick stood stiff and unyielding against Ethan, except for his hand. He wrapped his hand in the fabric of Ethan's T-shirt and held on so hard the seams at his shoulders were probably in danger.

"I'm so sorry."

Nick didn't say anything, and the air in the bathroom was filled with the sound of ragged breathing. He wasn't sure which of them was trying harder not to break.

"It's not true." Ethan pressed his face against Nick's neck.

"What's not true?" The fact that Nick sounded honestly confused pushed Ethan a little closer to murderous.

"You weren't lucky. And that's not . . . That's not love."

It was the wrong thing to say. Nick broke out of the circle of his arms with a force that unbalanced him enough to take a step back.

Phone still in hand, Nick gestured at Ethan, his voice shaking. "Don't say that. Don't . . . You don't know what it was like. My parents completely checked out on me after Drew died." The phone clattered to the tile, making Ethan jump. "Do you know how it feels to walk into your house every day and know you're the wrong fucking kid? That your parents look at you and wish they could trade you for the better one? Kyle *loved* me! He did! Because if he didn't, nobody did."

"Nick—"

"No! They didn't even care enough to see when I came home limping, or bleeding, or . . . They didn't care. But he did. And if I had to put up with a little weirdness, that was okay. I earned it. I did everything he wanted, and he loved me, and you don't understand."

He'd been disgusted to the point of being sick to his stomach, but now he was scared. Ethan held up a hand, careful to keep it close to himself, nonthreatening. "You're right, I don't understand. I wasn't there. I don't get to make a call on how you felt."

Suddenly, the small space was stifling, the need to get out stronger than anything else. Back to the door, Ethan reached behind himself to open it. "If you need me to delete anything, let me know. I'm not comfortable reading anything else right now, though."

He wasn't afraid *of* Nick, more terrified *for* him. He didn't understand any of this. He wasn't sure he wanted to. People who loved you didn't hit you or use your care against you like a weapon. But he sure the hell wasn't a psychiatrist, and this was so far out of his ability to fix that it might as well be on another planet.

Nick didn't answer him. Ethan backed out of the bathroom and went to sit on the bed. Because staring through the wall was clearly better than actually making eye contact. The bathroom door swung shut a few seconds later, and he tried to pretend he wasn't straining to hear any noise Nick made.

Ethan was in so deep. He knew he'd had a charmed life, with one exception. He'd never wanted for affection, and there'd never been a day in his whole life where he'd wondered if he was loved. His guilt over Scott's death was the only thing even remotely similar to what Nick had described, and even that was different. He felt guilty because he knew it was a coincidence that he hadn't been standing next to Scott when the shooting had started. Nick . . . Nick seemed to feel guilty for escaping someone who'd twisted his grief and loneliness into some kind of choke collar.

The bathroom door opened while he was still trying to find neutral ground they could occupy, somewhere between his unwillingness to comprehend and Nick's insistence that it *could* be understood.

"Can I come out there if I promise not to turn into a complete psycho again?"

"You don't need my permission to leave the bathroom, dude. And you're not a psycho."

Nick had obviously spent some part of the last five minutes poking his fingers into his eyes, which was the only reason Ethan could think of for why they looked so . . . bruised.

"I'm sorry. I don't know what's going on in my head right now. That was totally uncalled for." Nick hung in the doorframe. "I don't even believe most of it. Sometimes."

Ethan caught Nick's eyes. "You were right. I don't understand. And I don't have to. I don't want to read any more of his bullshit, but if you still need help deleting the messages, I can do it."

Nick shrugged. "I deleted them. Well. I hit Delete, and then waffled for a few minutes when it asked me if I was sure I wanted to trash them. But I got there eventually."

Ethan patted the bed next to him. "I do believe that might call for a congratulatory doughnut."

The mattress squeaked when Nick settled on it about a foot away from him. "Can I lie to you? Like, really obviously?"

"If you need to. I've really been enjoying the ongoing story of the maple cartel, but I guess I can deal."

Nick huffed the crust of a laugh. "I never believed him when he told me I was so fucked up that even my own parents couldn't love me. I don't wonder if I should be grateful he still seems to want me. And I don't feel guilty about taking advantage of you when you're obviously so far out of my league I'm not even sure we're playing the same sport."

Ethan scowled, but he didn't let his anger stop him from sliding over and resting the tips of his fingers on Nick's arm, like Nick had done for him so many motels rooms ago. "I'm glad to hear that. Because none of those things are true, and I object to your use of a sports metaphor to self-deprecate."

He'd agreed to be lied to, but he found himself stuck with honesty in return. "Grief warps everything. I love my mom. She's the best. We're *friends*, which I know is, like, the least-cool thing ever, but she's always been there for me. Didn't bat an eye when I told her I was gay. Never treated me and Scott any different than my brother and his girlfriend, or any guy one of my sisters ever dated. Which was actually kind of annoying, but that doesn't matter." He took a breath, forcing his confession out in a rush so he couldn't change his mind. "I'm so fucking angry at her sometimes. She's happy I wasn't killed, and I . . . Sometimes that feels like she's happy Scott died instead of me. It's not real. It's not logical. But it's how I really feel when I feel it."

Nick made a small sound, grabbing Ethan's fingers and squeezing lightly.

"I don't think your parents wish you were dead. Nobody's parents wish they were dead. But maybe they aren't any better at telling the difference between grief and reality than I am."

Nick shrugged, looking far from convinced.

They sat in silence for a long time. It wasn't that Ethan's mind had wandered so much as blanked out everything but the present. He didn't have anything else useful to say, and Nick didn't seem to be interested in talking any more.

Car headlights from the parking lot washed across the room, and Ethan roused himself. "It's pretty late. I think I need to call it a night."

He didn't get an answer, and he blinked hard, trying to clear away some of the sand in his eyelids. Nick was still there, still warm and unmoving under his touch. Ethan rubbed his hand up and down Nick's arm until Nick finally shook himself free of whatever cobwebs had ensnared his thoughts.

"I might go for a walk. I don't think I can sleep, and I don't want to keep you awake."

There was only one bed. Ethan hadn't hesitated when they'd checked in, but now he wasn't sure he should have presumed. "I can take the floor."

Nick shook his head and got to his feet. "No need." Ethan followed the dip of his Adam's apple as he swallowed, forcing a brief smile. "I've got options, remember?"

"One of those is not going for a walk in the middle of the night. It's . . . You're . . ." Ethan faltered, at a loss for how to say what he meant without sounding like a big-city snob.

"Brownish and young?" Nick looked longingly at the door and sighed, shoulders slumping. "Yeah, I know."

Ethan leaned back on his hands, looking up at Nick. "You can keep me awake if you need to. I don't mind." He kicked his foot up, hooking the toe of his sneaker behind Nick's ankle. "Plus then you wouldn't be alone."

"Didn't the sign out front say there was free HBO? Maybe there's a movie on." Nick waved in the general direction of the flat-screen mounted on the wall while he toed off his shoes.

"Okay, but nothing above PG-13. I don't want to be responsible for the corruption of a just-recently-minor."

Nick gave a short laugh. "The big treat at Camp Kill Me Now was *Veggie Tales* episodes. Or sometimes, if we were really good, some terrible biblical epic with bad special effects. I might not even be able to handle PG-13 without some adult supervision."

Ethan scooted back toward the headboard, stuffing one of the many pillows behind his back, then patting the empty spot next to him. "Get comfortable so I can put my hand over your eyes if we see anything too scary. Or boobs."

Sighing heavily, Nick crawled the short distance across the bed and flopped down with his head on Ethan's thigh. "'S'okay?"

"Yup." Ethan reached for the remote on the nightstand with one hand and let his other rest lightly on Nick's head.

He scrolled through the on-screen guide, coming to an abrupt stop. "Damn, you're in luck! It's not HBO, but look what's on. The original *Ten Commandments*! We're all set for the evening."

"What idiot ever gave you the idea that you're funny? Because they didn't do you any favors."

Nick's cranky scowl was a million times better than anything Ethan had seen in the last twenty minutes or so, and he felt some of the tension ease out of his shoulders and stomach. "Nobody had to tell me. I know I'm fucking hilarious. Now shut up and watch my favorite crazy, gun-toting actor do his thing."

Nick's quiet chuckle rumbled against his leg.

Interlude
NICK HAMILTON'S PHONE

Conversation with Stef Hansen

Nick: *I don't know what to do when I get home.*

Nick: *Besides get a job and somehow turn into an adult, I mean.*

Stef: *Do you want to be in contact with your parents?*

Nick: *Maybe?*

Nick: *Except I can't live with them. I can't. I don't trust them.*

Nick: *If they send me back to that fucking place*

Nick: *I can't.*

Stef: *Okay. You can always stay with me.*

Nick: *I'm afraid I'll freak out and go back to him.*

Stef: *You're kind of an adult so you make your own choices*

Stef: *But you don't have to make them because you think you've got nowhere to go*

Stef: *Mi futon es su futon*

CHAPTER Fifteen

Roswell, NM

E than looked alarmingly natural in his new bug-eyed alien sunglasses as he and Nick sauntered down Roswell's historic main drag. The doodle boppers were a bit much, but Nick didn't have the heart to tell him. He'd settled on a glowing "alien wand" himself, complete with flashing LED lights and a tag that warned him it was intended as a toy, and meant for external use only.

"I wonder how many lawsuits it took before they added the disclaimer?"

Ethan arched a skeptical eyebrow at him. "Dude, anyone with any sense knows you don't go around putting stuff made in China up your butt."

"Buy American." Nick waved the wand at Ethan, much to the consternation of the father trying to herd three kids out of a nearby shop.

"You're ridiculous." Ethan's doodle boppers swung wildly when he shook his head, shedding bright-green glitter all over the sidewalk.

"You seem awfully tall for a man who doesn't have a leg to stand on."

Instead of replying, Ethan hopped up and down on one leg, coming dangerously close to falling off the curb and into the street. Nick grabbed his arm with a long, drawn-out sigh.

"I was fine. I have excellent balance."

"I'm sure you do." Nick reached into the pocket of his jeans and pulled out his phone, using his grip on Ethan's arm to hold him in place long enough to take a picture. "That one's going in the Christmas letter, for sure."

"Awesome. My mom does one of those really irritating letters . . . except, you know, sarcastically. She can put that one in, while sharing that her middle child picked up a felon on his coming-of-age trip."

"I hope she mentions the probing you received in Roswell."

"Didn't we talk about how my parents and sex are never to be mentioned in the same sentence?" Ethan scowled. "Besides, I've been probe-less since we got here."

"Hey, *you* were the one who insisted on a trip to the gift shop. I refuse to be held accountable for your lack of probing." He opened his texts with one hand, shaking the wand at Ethan with the other.

Stef: *Mi futon es su futon.*

Nick: *I'm offended on behalf of the Spanish language.*

Nick: *Thank you. Promise I won't be there long.*

Stef: *Not worried. BTW, apartment smells like cabbage.*

Nick: *Careful. Might never leave*

Ethan's eyebrows had climbed into his hairline by the time Nick looked up from his phone. Maybe because Nick had unconsciously been poking him in the chest with the glow wand to punctuate his typing.

"So. I texted Stef this morning while you were in the shower." He tried to keep his voice neutral, even though it was the first time he'd felt even mildly hopeful about his future prospects.

Ethan took the tip of the probe in a firm grip and angled it away from his chest. "Yeah? Was he glad to hear from you?" Ethan sounded blandly curious, but Nick figured he had about ten seconds before the information was dragged out of him.

"He said I could stay with him, if I wanted."

"And?" Ethan was practically vibrating.

"I dunno. He said his apartment smells like cabbage. I *really* hate the smell of boiled cabbage."

"Oh, well, I'm sure you can find the one totally nonskeevy roommate ad on Craigslist. No worries."

Nick laughed dutifully, but Ethan wasn't very good at playing things close to the vest. He tapped Ethan's chin lightly with the wand. "When you get sick of me. I wasn't going to hop a bus today, no matter how tempting a studio apartment that smells like my dad's Irish granny might be."

Ethan also failed at hiding relief. "If you're sure. I know you've known Stef longer."

"I'm sure. Probably be bored out of my mind within hours, what with no visits to terrifying places where my life's in danger and all." Nick paused a beat. "And that's just small Texas towns at night."

"What can I say? Only the best locations make it on my itinerary." Ethan shrugged. "Who else in your life was going to take you to see the giant red fart button in Houston?"

"God, nobody, I hope." Nick snickered to take some of the sting out of the words. "You only get one first time."

"I'm glad we could share it." Ethan batted his eyelashes at Nick.

Nick tucked his phone into his back pocket. "So, what other unearthly delights await us in Roswell? Not that anything can really top the museum. Genuine alien artifacts. I was very impressed."

"The flying saucer McDonald's. They have a giant mural with a planet brain thingy I want a picture of."

"Okay, but we're driving. I'm afraid my probe will melt in this heat." Nick gestured broadly, the probe flashing multicolored lights with the sweep of his hand.

Nick sucked up the final sip of his shake, making loud slurping noises as he tried to get the final drops. Ethan stared across the table, his faux disapproval somewhat defeated by the dripping remains of a McRib.

"If you're quite finished, maybe we can take the stupid picture?"

"Might want to get that layer of barbeque sauce off your face first, before you capture it for all eternity."

Ethan flushed, grabbing for a napkin. "Could've told me sooner, dude." He swiped ineffectively at his face, managing to smear red even farther up his cheek.

"I was going to offer to lick it off, but you know, public and stuff." The stiff plastic cushion creaked when Nick leaned back in the booth. "Maybe you should go wash it off."

Ethan stuffed the final, gooey bite into his mouth, chewing obnoxiously in Nick's direction as he slid out of the booth. Nick stole the last of his fries as revenge.

Maybe he'd been lulled into a false sense of security, trading texts with Stef and snotty comments with Ethan. He was surprised when his phone rang, even though he should have expected something to intrude on the tentative sense of peace he'd been enjoying.

He hadn't expected it to be his mom.

It was his *mom*. He couldn't *not* answer it, but he still had to try twice before he managed to croak out a rusty greeting.

"Nicky?" she said in Spanish. "Where are you? Why haven't you come home? Are you safe? Are you sick? They said you were ill when you left the school. Where *are* you? We're so worried about you. Do you need help? Are you with that Kyle? Do you have a jacket?"

Her voice hit him like a freight train of Spanish and nostalgia, hard enough that he almost forgot her total silence on the trip to Cornerstone. Almost.

"I'm fine, Mom." He couldn't say anything else without letting hurt feelings get the better of him.

"You didn't answer my texts. I didn't call because . . . I wasn't sure you would pick up." Her switch to English was for him. Even though he'd grown up speaking both languages at home, he could barely keep up with her when she got going. At least, that had been his excuse when he zoned out during her exasperated lectures.

"You caught me on a good day, I guess." The lie was easier than admitting he'd been surprised. "So we've established that I'm fine. What else did you want?"

His mother had always been good at glossing over the uncomfortable, and after an indrawn breath, she managed to sound quiet, calm, and infuriatingly reasonable. "We want you to come home. We can buy a plane ticket, or your father can send a car."

"Yeah. And you promise you're not going to send me off to Pray the Gay Away camp again? Because it didn't take."

It wasn't even a fair barb to lob her way. If his parents, in the few minutes a day they spent worrying over his behavior instead of Drew's illness, had ever had a problem with him being bi, they'd never let on to him. Of all the ways he'd disappointed them, he didn't think that had ever been counted in his ledger of failures as a son. To say he'd been surprised by the lessons Cornerstone had tried to grind into him was putting it mildly.

"That wasn't why we sent you there. You needed structure. Rules. Somewhere to be safe while you learned to value yourself. That Kyle—"

"Save it, Mom. He's not in the picture anymore." He'd have to thank Ethan—his lying skills were really improving.

"We want you to come home. Please, baby. Please tell me where you are."

He shook his head, trying to dislodge the lump in his throat. She was crying. He knew how she sounded when she cried. All he had to do was tell her where he was. Stop disappointing her. Stop being so *selfish*, Nicky.

He switched back to Spanish. "I'll be okay, Mama. Don't worry." She drew a heavy breath, and Nick hung up before she could say anything else. He jammed his thumb down on the power button with more force than it required before she could call back.

"Everything all right?" Ethan looked a little worried, thumbs tucked into the pockets of his jeans and eyebrows raised as he looked down at Nick.

"We should go somewhere so you can fuck me. Right now." The Spanish rolled off his tongue.

Ethan's expression squinched inward, confusion obvious. "I took French."

"Let's go." Nick slid out of the booth, skin sticking to the plastic.

"Um, any place in particular?"

"Where do you want to get off?" Nick barely recognized his own voice, but he knew it was too loud. He pushed past Ethan, heading out into the sticky summer air. Anxiety melted like ice from the top of his head down through the rest of his body, and he hoped like hell it would numb him.

"Hey, what's the matter?" Ethan jogged a couple of steps across the parking lot to catch up with him. He reached out to put a hand on Nick's shoulder, and Nick jerked back.

"Nothing. Did you suddenly develop a dislike of fucking?"

Ethan didn't answer him. Nick rolled his shoulders and crowded in closer, forcing himself not to flinch when his personal bubble was breached. He lowered his voice, brushing Ethan's arm with the tips of his fingers in a way he hoped came off as seductive rather than desperate. "It was really noisy in there, is all. I'm a fan of spending my time with you in private."

Ethan took a step back and nodded but didn't look completely convinced. Not his best performance, then.

The thought drew him up short as he stared at the part of the flying saucer–shaped building that canted up forty-five degrees to accommodate a playground. Ethan paused by the driver's side, and with the safety of the dirty car roof between them, Nick tried to unravel his own lies. He'd told Ethan the whole point of lying to each other was not lying to themselves, after all.

"My mom called while you were in the bathroom. It . . . I can't . . . I don't want to *feel* it, okay? So can we just go somewhere, and you fuck me until I don't feel anything?"

"I'm not sure . . . I don't think sex works like that. At least it's not supposed to." The worried crease between Ethan's eyes was becoming familiar.

"Can it now? Please?" Nick's voice cracked, the last of his pride bleeding out of the fissures left by his mom's call.

Ethan beeped the doors open. "Let's not have this discussion in a McDonald's parking lot." His normal athletic grace seemed to desert him as he got into the car, movements jerky.

Ethan turned the car on and the air-conditioning began to leak out of the vents, but he didn't put on his seat belt or even glance at the mirrors as Nick dropped into the passenger seat. Nick swallowed, fighting not to give in to his first instinct, which was to open the door and run like hell.

Spotting people who were angry at him was kind of a specialty.

"I'm sorry," he said, torn by the knowledge that Ethan wasn't going to hurt him and the sense-memory that if someone was angry, he was going to feel it sooner or later. "I shouldn't have asked for that."

Ethan sighed, his hands curling in uneasy circles around the steering wheel. "'That'? Like sex? Is that the *that*?" He made an exasperated sound, not quite a snort, not quite a groan. "Whatever.

The point is, I don't have a problem with you asking for sex. I *do* have a problem with you making it sound like it's a . . . a drug, and we're in a damn soap opera. Not cool."

That reaction was so unexpected that Nick stared silently for several long seconds.

"So wait, your issue is that I was too flowery? Did you want graphic descriptions? I could probably sketch out a diagram."

"My issue is that I'm not reality TV, okay? I'm not something you do so you don't have to think about anything. And if I am, then you need to—" Did Ethan's voice sound thicker? "You need to not pretend this is anything more than a ride. I can deal with being convenient, but I didn't think that's what we had going on here. If anyone with a car and a dick would work as a distraction, don't fucking pretend to care about me in the meantime."

The injustice of it stung. "That's not what I meant."

"No? Because it felt like that's what you meant. Like you could have asked anyone else in the parking lot, and it would have been the same to you." Ethan tipped his head back against the headrest, closing his eyes. "Look, I get wanting to forget shit. I also get using somebody to help you forget. Not like my slate's perfectly clean. But not . . . not with somebody who's maybe more than . . ."

It was somehow worse, not really being able to read Ethan's expression, and Nick sank lower in his seat.

"I mean, can't we do some normal stuff, like getting totally shit-faced drunk?" Ethan still hadn't opened his eyes, but he grinned wryly. "I've heard it works for other people when they're trying to forget stuff."

It was tempting to play along. Ethan had given him an out, again, and the moment was past. There was no reason to keep poking that bruise, except if he didn't, he was letting Ethan think . . . exactly what he'd thought about himself, the first time they kissed. And it wasn't true.

"Hey." When Ethan didn't look at him, Nick pulled himself out of the corner he'd migrated to instinctively and crossed the border between their seats. He squeezed Ethan's arm, leaving his hand there until Ethan finally relented and opened his eyes. "You're not Honey Boo Boo. Or malt liquor, or cheap vodka in a red cup. And I'm really,

really sorry I made you feel like you were anything less than someone I care about. A lot."

Ethan nodded at him, maybe not trusting his voice, and Nick sat back in his seat. "You know what you said, about being angry at your mom? I got angry, and scared, and it's like she and my dad have already been through so much shit—Drew and everything—I shouldn't be so angry at them. I never know what to do with it."

It had been one of the few things Kyle had really gotten about him. Of course, Kyle's usual way of helping involved taking him to bed. And if that wasn't a train of thought he needed to derail with dynamite, he didn't know what was.

"I'm so sorry." Nick was apologizing for something he hadn't even *done*, but Ethan could remain blissfully ignorant of how close he'd come to being used.

"I accept your apology." Ethan relaxed a fraction of an inch, enough anger leaving his face that Nick felt like he meant it. Not *It's okay*, either, which he appreciated. It was rarely okay when someone said that, and it rarely meant he was forgiven. It didn't mean the infraction was forgotten, just stockpiled for later.

The next few seconds of silence, while not exactly comfortable, weren't excruciating either. Ethan finally let out a quiet breath, rubbing at his face. "Somehow I never pictured this part of adulthood. Aren't you supposed to understand your parents better, not be furious with them?"

"I've been trying to forget about that adulthood thing. Maybe that's why I'm not making the connection. Once I land somewhere and get a job, maybe it'll all make sense." Nick wasn't really holding out a lot of hope, but maybe it could happen. Or maybe he'd stay fucked up the rest of his life.

"But, hey, in the meantime we can ignore it and keep doing cool shit, instead."

"Like more ghost hunting?" Nick kept himself from rolling his eyes.

Ethan's smile was quick to appear, but it looked a little more tired than usual. "How often am I going to have the freedom to do a six-week-long Scooby-Doo reenactment? Someone's got to find those ghosts."

"Do you actually *believe* in ghosts?"

"Sometimes. It depends on how I'm feeling that day." Ethan glanced at Nick, then away, staring out the windshield. "Sometimes I want to. Sometimes . . . Fuck, sometimes the thought scares the hell out of me."

A cold finger dragged down Nick's spine, and he shivered.

"You know what they say about ghosts and hauntings, right?" Ethan swallowed hard. "Unexpected death, violent death?"

Oh.

"What if Scott's out there? Stuck? And alone?" Ethan's voice broke on the last word. "I want to know, but I don't too, you know?"

"Maybe they'd let you visit the spot? I'm sure my *abuela* probably knows, like, fifty ways to cast out a spirit." He pursed his lips. "Depending on how well you know your Hail Marys."

A family got out of the car next to them, three kids arguing over who got to shut the minivan door until their mom hit a button on her remote and closed it automatically. Their indignant protests faded away as they trooped into the restaurant.

"I wasn't trying to make a joke out of it." Nick glanced at Ethan, tearing his gaze away from the side mirror.

Ethan shook his head. "No problem, I didn't think you were." He tipped his head forward until it rested against his arms on the steering wheel. "I don't know any Hail Marys, though, unless they're sports ones. I might need help with that."

Nick bit the inside of his cheek to stop himself from making a comment about Ethan hitting his knees. Definitely not the time, no matter how easily the joke presented itself.

"I don't think I believe in an afterlife." He pushed air out his nose, not quite a snort. "Everyone spent so much time telling us how Drew must be in heaven. Like that was supposed to mean something. Like he hadn't spent most of the eleven years he was alive trying *not* to die." He shrugged, shoulders dragging across the warm leather seat. "Personally, I'm hoping for reincarnation. I want to believe there's a kid somewhere who's never heard of leukemia, and never will, and some part of my brother is going to grow up in them."

"I don't know what I believe. All I know is I want Scott to be somewhere good, to be happy." Ethan's voice came out muffled, face still buried in his arms. "I guess that makes me seem kind of crazy, then, huh? Or really shallow. With the ghost hunting and shit?"

"Maybe you're looking for ghosts to prove to yourself whether they exist or not. Maybe it's a way to figure out if you have to worry about it? Or, I don't know, maybe you want to pretend you're Dean Winchester."

Nick watched Ethan's laugh ripple down the tight muscles of his back. "He is really, really hot. For an old dude, I mean."

"My forte." Nick grinned when Ethan looked at him, horror dawning.

"I didn't mean—"

"That guy is probably twice our age. He's old." He pretended to contemplate his fingernails for a second. "I'd still fuck him. But he's old."

The silence between them drew itself out to a fine thread, and Nick gave in first. "I don't think either of us has to figure all of this out right now. You can hunt for ghosts and still hope Scott isn't one." He pushed his thumb into the corner of his eye, focusing on the spots dancing behind his eyelid. "And I can be angry and guilty and want to get hurt to distract me from it. But I can't use you to do it."

"I can't do that for you." Ethan's voice was firm. "I don't think I can hurt someone I l . . . Someone I care about."

Nick turned his attention to the tiny birds jumping back and forth in the mesquite tree they'd parked under, laughing to cover Ethan's near-miss. "You say that now, but one of these days I'll piss you off enough that it'll seem like a viable option."

"No."

All of a sudden, Nick had a lap full of Ethan, gangly limbs locked around him and crushing the breath out of him. His grunt must have conveyed enough pain that Ethan relented slightly, letting go so that Nick could inhale.

"Listen to me, okay? That would never happen. Never. That's not something I would ever do."

"I know that." Nick scoffed, trying to brush off Ethan's seriousness with a laugh that was only semiforced. "It was a joke. I need to joke about it."

"Okay. But it's not. You shouldn't expect it, or think it's just something that happens in a relationship."

Ethan's weight settled around him, and for a change Nick felt safer for the confinement. The soft press of their skin, Ethan's knees bracketing his hips in the seat, brought them closer together than they'd been in bed this morning. Tentatively, he slipped his arms around Ethan's back, one of them skirting under the hem of Ethan's T-shirt and settling against his skin.

"I'm serious. It's not what happens." Ethan pulled away far enough to meet Nick's eyes. "So from here on out, you don't expect it, okay?"

Nick wasn't sure how he felt about Ethan calling him on the easy out of physical contact. Annoyed? A little. Surprised that Ethan would give enough of a shit about him to do it? More than a little, but in an oddly comforted way.

Nick nodded to make Ethan happy, pretending to misread him so the conversation could be over. "Yeah, okay, no expectations. Especially not in a McDonald's parking lot."

"The Hamburglar has eyes, man. I don't know if I could live down the shame of Mayor McCheese watching me fuck." Despite his dire warnings, Ethan didn't make any attempt to climb off Nick's lap.

"You know a disturbing amount of McDonald's mythology. But *I* happen to know this is the only one in the whole world shaped like a flying saucer. We should go be tourists and take stupid pictures in front of it."

"You read that on the wall while we waited in line." The accusation hardly stung, given that Ethan's mouth was resting next to his ear, and the warm wash of his words had nothing on the way his three-day stubble tickled Nick's cheek.

"I still *know* it. I didn't claim it was a secret I gleaned from my Incan ancestors or something."

"Should have. That would've been cooler."

"You got me. The Nazca lines are actually an elaborate map to this very restaurant. Don't tell the tourists."

Ethan's laughter rolled through both of them, aided by proximity and the sudden renewal of their previous hug. "You'll have to take me someday."

"You'll love it," Nick said without thinking, like he could hope to offer even the vague promise of a *someday*. It was hard enough to imagine tomorrow.

"So. Stupid pictures. I'm pretty sure my mom smuggled a selfie stick into the trunk when I wasn't looking."

Even though it was too damn hot to be all over each other in a parked car, Nick still felt a pang of regret when Ethan ungracefully removed himself back to the other seat. Regret, and maybe a knee a little too close to parts of him that were feeling a bit sensitive at the moment. He covered the awkward, unsettled feeling with a grin. "Awesome. I'll get the antennae."

It wasn't hard to find the headband, currently leaking glitter all over the back seat. He perched the too-tight plastic band on his head, missing his hair for about the millionth time since Tyler had shaved it off the first day at Cornerstone. The glitter was itchy on his scalp. He came around the back of the car, waggling his eyestalks in a way he was certain had to be banned on Alpha Centauri, and found Ethan being eaten by an assortment of Trader Joe's bags.

"I *know* there's one in here." Some of Ethan's annoyance was muffled by the combination of paper and plastic. Thankfully, so was the shutter sound effect of Nick's camera as he framed a shot that definitely showed off years of lacrosse practice and hockey skating.

God *damn*.

"Found it!" Ethan had to fight himself free of the bags, and even so, Nick swore he saw a couple of strips of fruit leather try to wrap themselves around Ethan's wrist and pull him back in.

"Jesus, I thought you were kidding." It was *lime green*. "Subtle."

Ethan snickered. "That's my mom. Subtle with a capital Not. You'll see. Wait until you meet her." He pointed at Nick's head. "You'll need to wear those when you do. Mom loves a good set of doodle boppers."

"I'm very afraid right now."

"Shut up and go stand in front of the flying saucer."

Nick almost said *make me*, but Ethan was already sticking his tongue out, and one of them had to be a mature adult.

The selfie stick extended far enough that they caught most of the saucer in the picture. Or pictures, since Ethan couldn't seem to grasp the use of the remote button, and the shutter on the phone went off at least thirty times in rapid succession.

"Put that down," Nick ordered, wresting the pole from Ethan's hand and setting it on the wall behind them. "Just hold your phone out in front of you like a normal idiot." He demonstrated with his, arm stretched above their heads and thumb hovering over the screen. At the last second, he turned his head and planted a loud, smacking kiss on Ethan's cheek.

"Cooties!" Ethan scrubbed his face against his shoulder, laughing.

Nick ignored him, thumbs sliding over his screen.

"What are you doing?" Ethan peeked over his shoulder, paying more attention to the selfie stick he was trying to slide closed.

Nick grinned, turning his phone around so Ethan could see the pictures he'd posted to Instagram—the one of Ethan bent over the back of the car, and the one he'd just taken. *Roswell is very scenic, but you have to watch out for weirdos.*

Ethan's gray eyes narrowed, and he bent over his phone, thumbing through what seemed like hundreds of shots. Eventually he handed over his phone so Nick could see his retaliation—a shot of Nick wielding the sparkly alien probe at his own reflection in a window. *Does this guy look familiar to anyone? Someone call Mulder and Scully—I think my stalker has a clone.*

One of Ethan's siblings liked the photo while he was looking. Nick handed the phone back before he could get caught up in another Domani whirlwind. "Well, now you've ruined next year's Christmas card. Thanks, buddy."

Ethan glanced down at the screen again when his phone pinged, smirking at whatever one of his hundred thousand relatives had said. "Well, what about mine? I guess I should thank you for not making a 'junk in the trunk' joke."

Nick giggled, the sudden outburst surprising him. "I really like you."

Ethan's smile was nothing short of dazzling. "I really like you too."

CHAPTER Sixteen

San Patricio, NM

Maybe two Big Gulps in one afternoon hadn't been the smartest move he'd made recently. Ethan tried not to squirm in his seat and failed miserably. "Hey, did you notice the mileage to the next rest area?"

Nick made no attempt to hide his smirk. "Aw, need to make a pit stop? I told you not to get that second gallon of Coke."

"Yeah, yeah," Ethan groused. "Keep it up and I'll think I'm on a road trip with my dad." The familiar blue sign popped up in his peripheral vision, and he twisted his head to look. "Oh, thank God. Two miles. I think I can make that."

He had his seat belt unhooked before the car stopped rolling, and barely managed to toss the keys into Nick's lap before breaking into a sprint toward the restrooms.

There was a line for the urinals. Ethan banged into the nearest unoccupied stall and fumbled with the lock for a second before giving up and planting the sole of his sneaker against the door. Sweet relief overrode modesty, and he groaned. Free refills were the devil.

It took him a few minutes to wash his hands and remember he wasn't supposed to be amused by the way the overpowered hand dryers made it look like a helicopter was landing on his arm. Then, of course, he needed something to drink. And maybe a peanut butter cup.

By the time he made it back to the car, he was loaded down with two bottles of soda, peanut butter cups, pretzels, and eight of the free tourist brochures from the welcome center office.

Nick was standing next to the car, hands raised in front of him, while a police officer talked to him. Another officer was leaning into the open trunk.

"There's nothing in here but a bunch of granola bars and animal crackers. Did they knock over a Trader Joe's or something?"

Ethan cleared his throat. "Um. Is there a problem, officers?"

Jesus, his dad was going to kill him when—*if*—he ever told this story. Or possibly disown him for not coming up with a less clichéd question.

"Sir, we need you to step away from the vehicle for a moment. We're talking to this young man."

"Um. It's my car, though? And I think you need a warrant to search it. I could call my dad to ask. He's a lawyer."

The mood shifted somehow, the two cops sharing a look he couldn't read. Nick was easier—Nick was somewhere between scared and checked out, with a mild shaking in his raised hands and a resigned look on his face that told Ethan absolutely nothing except that he was going to let whatever was happening roll right over him.

The older office motioned to Ethan. "Why don't you set your food down and come with me while my partner talks to your . . ."

"Friend," Ethan supplied. "Who didn't steal my car and isn't a criminal."

"Just set everything down on the hood and walk over here with me." It wasn't a question the second time, and Ethan did as he was told. He couldn't help looking back at Nick, though.

"Neither of you are in trouble. Just stay calm." The cop who'd been going through his trunk stepped between him and Nick, cutting off his line of sight. "I'm Officer Chee. Can you tell me where you and your friend are heading?"

"Single word answers that only answer the question asked." His dad's voice echoed in his head.

"California."

Officer Chee raised an eyebrow. "You're a long way from the West Coast."

"It's a road trip."

"How did you meet Nicholas?"

Ethan wavered, and then went with the truth. "He was hitchhiking."

"Your parents know you pick up hitchhikers?" Chee didn't wait for an answer. "Are you aware that Nicholas is considered an endangered person?"

The burst of anger was sudden and white-hot. "The only *danger* was that fucking school!" Ethan caught himself. "Besides, he's eighteen. He could legally leave."

Officer Chee's sunglasses dipped as he looked over the polarized lenses. "Are *you* eighteen, son?"

"Yes, I am." Ethan almost reached for his wallet and ID before remembering that sudden moves around cops were generally a bad idea. Over Chee's shoulder, all he could see of Nick and the other officer was Nick's bowed head. "Do you need my license?"

"Not yet. We're just having a conversation right now." Officer Chee shifted, cutting off Ethan's narrow view. "Where did you pick him up?"

Ethan hesitated to answer, even though he hadn't done anything wrong. Yes, he was technically helping Nick run away, but Nick was a legal adult, and despite what his mom thought, Ethan wasn't completely oblivious to the dangers of the world. If he hadn't picked Nick up, someone else might have. Someone who wanted more than a mouthy passenger who criticized their musical choices. Chee's glasses dipped again, prompting Ethan's blurted answer.

"Virginia. I think. Or West Virginia?"

"So which is it? You've been on the road that long, that you don't remember the states?" Chee's smile was probably supposed to inspire camaraderie, but it fell short. "I know road trips can get pretty crazy."

As if Ethan was going to fall for that. His smile was equally as artificial. "Only if you count coffee and junk food as crazy. And, honestly, on those back roads, it can be pretty difficult to tell when you cross a state line." He stretched the fake smile even wider. "Even when you're on your fifth or sixth espresso of the day."

"And how is Mr. Hamilton paying his share of the expenses?"

Ethan's jaw dropped as he struggled for an answer that didn't include four-letter words. *Yeah, tell him to fuck off. That'll go well.* He and his dad had done running commentary on way too many episodes of *Cops* for him to give in to that urge.

Ethan closed his mouth, jaw tight. The air coming in through his nose didn't feel adequate, but he forced himself to breathe deeply a few times before answering. "He's keeping me from going crazy thinking about my dead boyfriend, actually."

Chee flinched, whether because of Ethan's flat tone or mention of The Gay, he wasn't sure. The silence between them was ruptured by Nick's raised, but unintelligible voice.

Heart jumping into his throat, Ethan didn't bother trying to be subtle as he leaned around Officer Chee. "Nick? You okay?"

Nick's hands were down at least, arms crossed over his chest and a hip canted toward Officer Chee's partner. To Ethan's horrified amusement, he uncrossed them and made a jerk-off motion. The cop, who was definitely younger than Chee and not nearly as stone-faced, blushed.

"For fuck's sake," Chee muttered, reaching under his sunglasses to pinch the bridge of his nose.

"He's, um . . . not great with authority figures," Ethan said.

Chee turned away from him, stalking across the patchy brown grass toward Nick and the other cop. Ethan followed, fumbling in his back pocket for his phone. Somehow, he'd never imagined calling his dad for legal advice and starting the conversation with, *So my friend told a cop to go fuck himself, with hand motions, and also apparently I've kidnapped someone.*

"Is there a problem, Suarez?"

"No, sir. I mean, Chee. Trying to get some facts straight with Nick here."

"It's a fact that you can kiss my ass," Nick said, nowhere near as quietly as he seemed to think.

Ethan winced.

"My parents didn't report me missing. I talked to my mom, like, two hours ago. And *Bobby* has been telling me all about some poor kid who's been coerced into— I'm not sure. Was it being forced to fuck the guy who gave him a ride, or was he being pimped out at rest stops? If I knew anyone in that situation, I'd be real worried for them."

"'Bobby,' huh?" Chee leveled the same mirror-lensed stare at his partner that he'd used on Ethan. "Well, I'm sure what *Officer Suarez* meant to say was that if you were in any danger, or being threatened in any way by someone transporting you across state lines, we'd be able to help you."

"I'm *fine*," Nick spat out. "And I want to know who reported me missing, so I can give them the same advice I just gave Bo— Officer Suarez."

Chee pinched his nose again. "Since we now have your assurance that you're not in any danger, we can send you on your way. We'll let Mr. Shelton know that we've completed a welfare check. No further intervention was required."

Nick froze, rapid-fire expressions flitting across his face, anger finally seeming to win out over fear. "You . . . He . . ." He opened and closed his mouth, finally managing, "You stopped us because of something *Kyle* reported?"

"We're required to investigate potentially endangered individuals, and Mr. Shelton filed a credible report."

"Mr. Shelton hasn't seen me in sixteen months. Mr. Shelton is a goddamn stalker. Mr. Shelton sent me—" Nick cut himself off sharply, but the ugly twist he put on Kyle's name said almost as much as the words he didn't.

Ethan winced at the suddenly alert look on Chee's face. Another lesson from *Cops*—never attract curiosity.

"Do you feel that Mr. Shelton might harm you?"

Ethan watched as the Nick he'd come to know retreated behind the face of another person. His anger smoothed away, brows falling to level lines over his blue eyes. "No, of course not."

The sound of frustrated disbelief Ethan made escaped without his permission, and all three of them turned in his direction. "Sorry. Nerves."

Chee frowned, but Ethan cranked up the wattage on his innocent smile.

"Right." Chee turned back toward Nick. "If you don't want to file a complaint against Mr. Shelton, then I guess you're free to go."

"You're not going to tell him where I am though, right?" The hesitance in Nick's question seemed to be the first sign of uncertainty Ethan had seen from him since joining this strange, unwanted party.

"No. The only detail we'll relay is that you aren't in any danger, and that will cancel the missing and endangered report." Bobby— *Officer Suarez*—fished in his pocket for a card, handing it to Nick.

"If anything changes and you feel like Mr. Shelton is a danger to your well-being, you can contact me." His careful, neutral expression turned earnest for a moment, and Ethan was certain Officer Chee was rolling his eyes behind his aviators. "It's not okay for someone to hurt you just because you're both guys."

Nick took the card with a minimum of attitude, though he gave no indication he'd heard the rest. "Cool. Thanks."

"Do we, uh, need a copy of your report or anything?" Ethan asked. If word ever got back to his dad, he'd better have some documentation.

"Mr. Hamilton is legally entitled to a copy of the report." Chee pulled a pen out of his pocket, holding that and another business card out to Nick. "Write your address and email, and I'll forward it to you as soon as I finish up the paperwork."

"Sure," Nick said, scribbling something on the back of the card.

Ethan wondered what address he was giving them, but thought better of asking. Something about the carefully exact strokes of the pen and that completely bland look made Nick look more angry than a red-faced, shouting tantrum could have.

Nick handed the card and pen back. "Can we go now?"

"You're free to go, gentlemen."

Nick was in the car before Chee finished speaking, slamming the door and busying himself with something on the floor.

Ethan waffled over thanking them, ultimately deciding to err on the side of caution. "Thank you, Officer Chee, Officer Suarez. We appreciate your concern." He waited until they turned away before walking to the driver's side. "Shit." He leaned heavily against the roof of the car for a second before collecting his melted peanut butter cups off the hood.

"That was fucking nerve-racking," he said as he dropped into his seat.

"And—" Nick snapped his mouth shut without elaborating, turning his head to look determinedly out the passenger window. "It doesn't matter. No harm, no foul, right?"

"Nick, are—"

"I'm *fine*," Nick snarled. One of his hands was resting on the door handle like he might bolt at any second, but the other was fisted in the fabric of the jeans he'd borrowed from Ethan.

"You don't look fine."

"I am. What are my other options? I can be fine, or I can be not fine, and neither one matters, because it's over. Can you drive?"

Instead of replying, Ethan started the car, punching up the air-conditioning. The fan was loud enough to make a reply difficult, but that was just a coincidence.

Ethan pulled out onto the near-empty road. The world's largest pistachio awaited them. He was at least expecting things to be nuts there.

Interlude
NICK HAMILTON'S PHONE

Conversation with 571-555-8920
Are you sure you want to delete these 137 unread messages?
Messages Deleted

—

Nick: *Are you fucking psychotic? You called the cops on me?*

—

You have not sent this message. Save as a draft?
Draft Saved

—

Nick: *You know all those pictures you keep sending me count as child pornography, right? I hope a blurry iPhone pic of my mouth around your dick is worth the jail time, asshole.*

—

You have not sent this message. Save as a draft?
Message Not Saved

—

Nick: *I loved you so much. Why did you start hitting me? Why*

—

You have not sent this message. Save as a draft?
Message Not Saved

—

Nick: *What do you want from me? When will you feel like you've ruined me enough that I can't possibly leave you?*

—

You have not sent this message. Save as a draft?
Draft Saved

—

Nick: *Fuck you, Kyle. I don't belong to you.*
—

Message Sent at 7:56 p.m.

CHAPTER *Seventeen*

Mescalero, NM

They made good time across the surprisingly beautiful expanse of New Mexico between Roswell and... wherever the giant pistachio was. Nick hadn't really been paying attention to navigational details. When life presented him with the chance to tease someone about their desire to see *really big nuts*, that wasn't the kind of thing he ignored.

Everything was going fine. Driving good, tree pretty, etc., etc., etc. Nothing about his day could have gone any better.

Joking with Ethan aside, he'd never been closer to hurling himself from a moving car in his entire life. Every mile marker they passed, every pine tree and scrubby sage bush seemed like it was striking him in the solar plexus. There were steel bars and scratching, prickly pine boughs warping themselves into a fence around his lungs.

Ethan sang along with the radio, offering him tentative smiles with every surreptitious glance.

The notification light on his phone flashed green, and Nick clenched his fingers tighter around the door handle.

"You've gotta pull over. Please."

Ethan cast another worried look in his direction. "Are you sick?"

"Just pull over." He wasn't sick, but maybe he could be. Maybe it would drag him back inside his skin, instead of feeling like he was flying apart atom by atom.

To his credit, Ethan only nodded, glancing in the rearview mirror before swinging onto the shoulder in a cloud of dust and gravel.

Shoving the door open, Nick stumbled out and away from the car at a near run. Somewhere in the part of his brain that was still functioning, he heard Ethan call his name, but he kept moving.

His feet raised puffs of dust as he zigzagged between the scrub, determined to put as much distance between himself and the road as possible before whatever was rising in his chest burst forth like something from *Aliens*.

"There might be snakes," Ethan hollered from the car. The sun wasn't quite down yet, just low enough to make the light weird and the shadows long. It would be his luck to come across a rattlesnake trying to soak up the last rays.

Nick skidded to a stop, gravel sliding under his shoes as he looked around. There was nowhere to hide, the sky huge and open above him. He didn't know what he was trying to escape, anyway. Kyle didn't have a giant flaming eye over the whole world, tracking his movements. Probably.

Footsteps crunched behind him. Definitely not a snake.

"Nick?" Ethan's quiet voice was a question in and of itself, without making him invoke their liar's oath to say he was okay.

"All I did was post a couple pictures of us to Instagram. I haven't even used it since my parents sent me . . . For a long time. I forgot he made me give him the passwords. I forgot he'd see, and I must have posted your license plate." Nick stuffed his shaking hands into his pockets, clenching them into fists so tight they hurt. "I was *happy*, and he's across the fucking country, and he still managed to—"

An inarticulate scream gurgled out of his throat, every bit as weak and timid as he felt, and it was hard to say who was more startled by it. Ethan took a step back, eyes widening, but something tore loose inside Nick, and he did it again. Louder, angrier, but still useless.

He spun away from Ethan and the road, facing the empty desert and filling it with every bit of furious noise he could, until his throat gave out. Somewhere out in the sparse collection of trees, a coyote howled back at him.

"Holy shit," Ethan whispered. "That coyote is talking to you."

It was so crazy, so completely Ethan that Nick choked on something between a laugh and a sob. "It's probably a whole pack, and they'll rip us to shreds before we can get to the car."

"Or—" Ethan paused significantly "—it's a lonely one who's looking for company. I have some beef jerky in the trunk."

"How can you know every creepy thing in the world, but not know this is how werewolves happen?"

Ethan sniffed, nose upturned. "Cryptozoology. Not my area. Besides, wouldn't it be a were*coyote*?"

"Of course, right, my mistake."

He leaned over, resting his hands on his knees, struggling to regain some equilibrium. When that didn't work, Nick gave up, dropping down on the desert floor with a jarring thump.

Folding his legs underneath himself, Ethan sank down cross-legged next to Nick. "D'you want to yell some more? I mean, you'll probably scare off my pet coyote, but that's okay. I understand you doing what you need to do."

Nick spent a second considering it, then shook his head. "I think I'm done. I . . . I'm so fucking *sorry* I dragged you into all this." Fear nibbled at the edge of his mind again, but he pushed it down. He wanted to believe he hadn't put Ethan in danger by bringing him under Kyle's gaze.

"Hey, the whole thing with the cops went down better than it could've. I mean, neither of us ended up with a cavity search. It's good."

"Your definition of 'good' leaves something to be desired."

"It's okay, my optimism will be enough for both of us."

Nick ducked his head, caught between laughing and whatever weird emotional purge he was inflicting on the world around them. His mind kept flinching back to the text he'd sent Kyle, and he couldn't help imagining all the ways he was going to be sorry, even if none of them were real anymore.

"Wait here for a minute, okay?" Ethan's footsteps crunched away across the gravel and dirt.

He must've lost track of time, because he jumped when Ethan dropped a folded bundle next to him.

"Here, can you hold these?" Ethan held out two bottles of water, waiting for Nick to take them before he picked up the bundle again. He shook it, and it expanded into a shiny, metallic material. "Space blanket. Not sure where Mom thought I was going to be cold enough to need one in August, but hey, it works for sitting on."

"Maybe she thought you were going to be crossing Donner Pass or something."

Ethan snickered. "In that case, I'd've been better off with more beef jerky. You're kinda skinny, and I won't have much left after we feed our new puppy. Not sure how long I could survive on you." Leering exaggeratedly, he leaned forward. "We could try, though. Got the blanket now. Shame to waste it."

Rolling his eyes, Nick scooted onto the blanket. "More likely we'll both end up as coyote chow."

"Eh, I'm willing to take that chance." Ethan settled next to him, arms behind his head as he stared up. "If nothing else, the view's worth it."

The sun had dropped below the horizon, and with it, the temperature. The space blanket felt surprisingly warm for a sheet of tinfoil, but he still shifted closer to Ethan.

"What am I looking for?" Above them, the last streaks of pink and gold were reflected off a few puffy clouds.

"Give it a few minutes."

It was less than that, seconds only, before points of light appeared overhead, one by one. He heard a sharp inhalation, and Nick turned his head enough to catch the expression of wonder on Ethan's face.

The light pollution over Cornerstone had been minimal, but they hadn't been allowed outdoors after dark unless they were on a wilderness survival exercise. The sky there had been crowded out by trees anyway. Here, it seemed like there were no edges, and nothing between him and the stars.

He was going to float away, so he scrabbled for Ethan's hand to tether himself to the earth. Ethan linked their fingers but didn't break the silence, and Nick felt his heart rate slow.

He angled his body until his head bumped against Ethan's shoulder, their arms awkwardly pinned between them. He didn't say anything, afraid what had already come out of his mouth had been more than enough to scare Ethan. Picking an arbitrary spot overhead, he started counting the stars.

It would have been nice to suddenly realize his problems were small and the world was vast. Cliché, but he could understand the draw. The problem was, no matter how insignificant his problems seemed under a blanket of stars in the middle of nowhere, they were still real. They were still waiting for him, somewhere beyond the next mile marker, or out at the edge of the hills with the coyotes.

"This wasn't on the plan." Ethan's voice was quiet. "Thanks for sharing it with me."

"Sometimes the plan gets in the way." Nick sounded hoarse, voice catching on odd syllables. "I'm glad I get to see this with you."

Ethan shifted, the blanket crinkling. "Do you . . . do you feel safer out here?"

It was an odd question, one he wasn't sure how to answer. "What does safe feel like?"

"I used to think I knew. I was hoping *you* had an answer." The noise Ethan made, somewhere between dismay and amusement, had Nick struggling for a more flippant response.

"I mean, he probably hasn't recruited your pet coyote to spy on us, so there's that." Nick waved a hand toward the sky. "But it feels really exposed to be out here like this."

"Do you want to leave?"

"Not yet. I'm not done counting all the stars."

Ethan laughed, the sound rumbling out of him and across Nick's skin as goose bumps. "Far be it from me to interrupt an important mathematical event."

"Shhh. I'm almost to the point that I need to take my shoes off."

"Thirty-six. Eighty-nine-ten-eleventy-twelve."

Nick elbowed him. Gently. "This was your idea, you know."

"Fine." Ethan's dramatic sigh tickled his ear. "One."

Nick lifted his free hand, pointing at an arbitrary spot above them. "Two."

Somewhere a little too close for comfort, a coyote barked again. Nick squeezed Ethan's fingers and kept counting.

Predictably, Ethan found them the kitschiest motel in the world when they finally decided maybe the coyotes sounded like they were closing in and it was time to go. As though the neon sign weren't a big enough clue, the yard in front of the manager's office was dotted with carefully manicured Astroturf, pink plastic flamingos, and a miniature windmill. Nick wasn't sure if they were renting a room or playing a round of minigolf.

Ethan walked back from checking them in, tossing a key in the air and catching it one-handed. He leaned in the passenger window. "I haven't seen an honest-to-goodness motel key in ages. Is this cool or what?" He spun it around the end of his finger.

"Judging from the look of the place, I'm guessing they haven't updated since 1952, so a key fits in. Not that I'm complaining," he quickly added, when it looked like Ethan was going to give him sad eyes.

"There's free cable too. I was informed that I'd have to dial in and enter my credit card number if I wanted to unscramble any of the adult channels."

"Or you could jerk it to the giant nut brochure."

Ethan spluttered but didn't reply. He came around the car and dropped into the driver's seat, then pulled them down to the back corner of the motel and parked in front of room 23. He lifted the bright plastic tag again, key dangling like a pendulum beneath it. "I only got one bed. That's still okay, right?"

Nick grabbed the key, grinning. "As long as you're fixating on nuts, I think we can work it out."

"I am all about the nuts, sir. All about the nuts."

The room itself was tiny but spotless. Nick dropped his backpack on the bed, then picked up the TV remote. "What was your credit card number?"

"You are *not* using my credit card to pay for a parade of boobs."

Nick sighed. "How about one or two boobs, then?"

"One or— No. I don't even want to think about a solo boob. Give me the remote."

"What'll you give me if I do? We can work out a trade deal." Nick leered theatrically, raking his gaze up and down Ethan's body. Ethan blushed as pink as the plastic flamingos outside.

"Only if I get favored nation status." Ethan grabbed the Do Not Disturb sign and hung it on the knob before he shut and locked the door. "Like really favored."

Nick waggled his eyebrows. "Are you saying you want the Security Council to look the other way while you violate my human rights?"

"Possibly. Are you interested?"

After pretending to consider for a moment, Nick reached out, grabbed Ethan's shirt, and reeled him in carefully until mere inches separated them. Ethan's eyes widened, locked with his.

"Fuck. Me."

It felt particularly gratifying to watch Ethan scramble out of his clothes, shoes kicked to the other side of the small room, followed by his T-shirt and jeans. Hands on his hips, he grinned at Nick. "Okay, let's go."

"Impressive," he teased, toeing off his shoes at a more sedate pace. He looked up, waving a lazy hand. "I mean, you got your clothes off really fast too."

Chest lifted, shoulders back, Ethan struck a full Superman pose, before visibly deflating. "Damn it, I think I left my bathroom bag in the car."

Nick winced when his jeans hit the floor with a heavy thump, phone still lodged in the front pocket. The moment of distraction gave him extra time to perfect his innocent look. "We both had the same thing for lunch. I wasn't gonna make you brush your teeth."

Nick relented. At a certain point, he was torturing himself too. He dragged his backpack across the comforter, unzipped the front pocket, and tossed the box of condoms he'd boosted from Target on the bed, followed by a handful of lube packets he'd gotten from a machine in a convenience store bathroom. It looked very telling, spread out on the patterned polyester.

"Oh. *Oh.* You meant, like . . ." They hadn't known each other long enough for Nick to be sure if Ethan was babbling because he was nervous, excited, or freaked out. Or hell, maybe all three. Maybe he and Scott hadn't done that. Maybe he didn't like it. Maybe this was a bad—

Ethan cupped the side of his face, pulling him in for a kiss that unseated whatever thought he'd been about to panic over. By the time they broke apart, Nick had lost track of his master plan and dropped his bag somewhere by their feet. Ethan kicked that out of the way as well, before backing up to the bed and dropping backward, arms spread out.

The bed bounced alarmingly, and when Ethan pointed to the spot next to him, Nick hesitated. "If you break it, they're going to charge your credit card."

"I think that sounds like a challenge." Ethan pointed again. "You. Here. Hurry up."

He couldn't decide if it was weird or hot that Ethan's laughing command hit him in the gut, sending a rolling wave of expectation and want straight to his head. And his dick. Definitely also his dick. Nick fought the urge to follow that detached, floaty feeling down and cede control to Ethan, and crawled across the bed toward him instead.

Nick dropped between Ethan's spread legs without warning, and nipped the inside of his thigh because he could.

Ethan yelped.

He froze when Ethan reached for him, purely physical memory making him flinch. But instead of the slap he expected, Ethan ran fingers down Nick's back.

"You bit me." Ethan's attempt to sound shocked failed, especially when he was laughing through the words. "I'm holding you responsible if I get a bruise. Or lockjaw."

"I *was* going to let you fuck me . . ."

"You're still going to." From anyone else—fine, from *Kyle*—it could have been a threat, but Ethan was laughing, and it freed him up to do the same.

"I totally am." Nick dropped his mouth to Ethan's leg again, and worked his way up slowly until he was breathing against the swell of Ethan's cock. Letting himself have another moment in that dreamy, needy place in the back of his head, he pressed a damp kiss over the crown. "If you're really nice, I'll probably even beg."

He felt Ethan's breath catch, and hated the jolt of fear.

"I . . . Yeah." Ethan paused long enough to draw another ragged breath. "What qualifies for 'really nice'?"

Anything you want. But instead of saying it, Nick occupied his mouth in other ways again. Ethan's hips lifted slowly, then fell sharply to the bed when Nick pulled away and sat back on his heels. The pink flush spreading down Ethan's chest was all the more obvious for the way it rose and fell with Ethan's tightly wound little gasps. Nick dragged his thumbs down Ethan's smooth stomach. "You don't have to work for really nice. Touch me, okay?"

It was like Ethan had been waiting for that bit of permission. He pulled Nick down, then rolled over, bracketing him in. He left a trail of wet heat down Nick's chest, pausing to return the favor of a nip on both hip bones, then kissed the inside of Nick's knees.

Nick made a frustrated sound, and Ethan laughed. "You in a hurry or something?"

"God, no." He wasn't, either. That didn't mean he didn't need friction, posthaste.

Ethan's lips curled into an uncharacteristic smirk as he sat up. His hands moved over Nick's legs in light, sure touches that left Nick squirming.

Being the focus of someone's attention like that held more danger than a dirty hot blowjob. The lights were still on, for Christ's sake, and seeing him like that, touching Nick like he was a place Ethan'd always wanted to go . . . Sooner or later, Ethan was going to find the few flaws he'd managed to hide.

He jumped when Ethan's knuckles brushed lightly across his cock, tension he hadn't realized he was holding back uncoiling in a rush.

"You could get this over with faster if you opened some of that lube, you know." As a joke, it wasn't funny. As begging, it wasn't entreating. As a last gasp at keeping the threat of intimacy out of fucking, it was pretty obvious.

"I thought you said you weren't in a hurry." Ethan fit his long fingers around Nick's cock, the slow rub just shy of maddening.

"I'm a conflicted man," he said through gritted teeth, trying not to buck up into the palm of Ethan's hand. Ethan hadn't said he could move.

And Ethan wasn't going to. Because Nick wasn't only there for Ethan to fuck. They were both there to enjoy each other. The realization twisted something up inside Nick, putting him off-kilter enough that he could ignore all the rules he'd learned for Kyle and reach for Ethan, sitting up to kiss him.

The lube and condoms had gotten lost beneath them, so of course when he tried to find one of the miniscule packets, he wound up squirting Astroglide all over his elbow.

"Wow, I don't think I've tried that position," Ethan said, unsuccessfully fighting off a giggle.

"Your loss." Nick shoved a hand under Ethan's ass, feeling around for another packet and groping him at the same time.

Nick managed to open the lube without losing most of it on the bedspread or a less-useful body part. He hesitated, new-found courage flickering for a second, before mentally shaking himself. He wanted this.

Ethan groaned when Nick wrapped a lube-slick hand around his cock, fingers twisting and sliding. This time it was Ethan's turn to push up into his grasp. Nick leaned as close as the awkward angle would allow, voice dipping low. "I don't think you're going to fit in my elbow. Guess you'll have to fuck my ass instead."

"I . . ." Ethan trailed off, the tell-tale blush crawling up his face.

Nick took pity on him, rolling them both on their sides and guiding Ethan's arm over his waist. If Ethan couldn't find the way from here, there was always GPS.

CHAPTER *Eighteen*

Alamogordo, NM

"I t's very..."

The pistachio towered over them, tan hull splitting like a menacing egg casing about to erupt a pea-green alien. Ethan wondered if he could get away with painting his car that color.

"It *is*," he said, with a touch of reverence the occasion maybe didn't warrant. "I'm getting us T-shirts to commemorate it. Bigger is better!"

"So I've heard. I wasn't aware it applied to snack-food monuments."

A bright-green tram vehicle sped past them, and Ethan waved back at the two little boys leaning out the sides, whooping wildly.

Nick sighed. "Did you want to take the farm tour?"

"Nah, we can't drink the free wine anyway. But I want one of the pressed pennies—"

His phone cut him off, the strains of whatever Katy Perry song Suze had chosen as her ringtone screeching up out of his pocket. He hadn't told her not to call, just his parents.

He thumbed it on. "You're interrupting a very serious discussion about nuts, so this better be important."

The pause dragged on for several seconds before his mom's voice came across the line. "Sorry? And really, is that how you talk to your sister?"

"It is when I'm standing next to a giant pistachio. What's going on, Mom?" Ethan struggled to keep his voice composed. She'd called on Suze's phone, knowing he'd answer it. That didn't bode well.

"Your dad and I got a call this morning . . ." She trailed off, and Ethan heard her take a deep breath. "I need you to hear me out and not hang up, okay?"

"I'm not coming home right now, Mom."

"That's not what I'm asking. Listen, please?"

He wavered, finger over the End Call button, but she went on.

"It was from Nick's older brother."

Ethan couldn't stop himself. He shot a quick glance at Nick, then turned his attention back to the phone. "That's interesting, since he doesn't have one."

His mom's pause was again noticeable. "Do you know that for sure? Did he tell you that? Have you met his family or seen pictures of them?"

"Hang on, Mom." Ethan put his hand over his phone, holding his breath for a second before turning around to find Nick, who'd wandered a few steps away.

"Hey, I'm going to take this. Be right back." Maybe he should've asked, but it didn't seem fair to make Nick answer his mom's worries when he didn't even know what she was trying to say yet.

He hadn't seen pictures. Hadn't asked. But Nick had told him plenty. Ethan didn't think he'd have missed mentioning an older brother.

"So yeah. Nick had a younger brother who died of leukemia. No older siblings."

"At the risk of repeating myself, do you know for sure? I'm not your dad, but you've certainly heard him expound on the advantages of not telling people everything. It's not lying. But it's not really the truth either."

"Why would his brother call you guys?" Ethan countered, even though the specter of his dad would have cautioned him against going on the defense. "If he was worried about Nick, why wouldn't he call Nick? How would he even know how to find you?"

"He said Nick posted some pictures of the two of you, and he did a reverse image search and found some of your sports articles and your Instagram account. We're still in the white pages."

Ethan huffed a fake laugh. "Don't you mean he waved his Google wand and Yelped my Facetwitter?"

"Ethan, he said Nick was in a treatment facility, taking psychiatric drugs that he stopped cold turkey. He was worried that Nick might be . . . unstable. That he might hurt himself. Or someone else."

The tightness in his chest had nothing to do with the heat. How many times over the last few days had he been paralyzed by the fear that Nick would hurt himself?

Maybe sensing his hesitation, his mom pressed harder. "We're worried, sweetie. No, I take that back. We . . . We're scared. I know your heart. I know you would never turn your back on someone in need, but it can't . . . it can't be at a risk to your own safety and well-being." Her choked sob hurt on some level so deep he couldn't name it.

Another bright-green farm truck rattled past. The noise and dust gave him a second to think before he answered, even if the deep breath he sucked in coated his tongue with grit.

"You don't know Nick. You don't know how completely ridiculous it is to even suggest he'd hurt someone else."

"Maybe if you'd introduced us to him before you left, I'd feel a little more confident about his character." His mom wasn't usually sharp, preferring droll sarcasm to make her points.

"I didn't know him before I left." Ethan winced, settling in to dig the hole deeper. "I met him in West Virginia. He needed help, Mom. His parents put him in this . . . this fucking *awful* place called Cornerstone. It's one of those conversion-therapy camps. He left the day he turned eighteen, and he had nowhere to go, no money, and nobody in his fucking family cared *then*."

"They care now, or at least his brother does. He wants him to come home, to be safe. Nick was taking medication for a reason, even if it was being done in a place like that. And you can't just stop taking psychiatric drugs without a mental and physical impact."

"It's been two weeks, and he hasn't murdered me in my sleep even once."

A thump and a muffled conversation were followed by his dad's voice. "Ethe, hey. You got your mom pretty riled up."

The mild tone washed over Ethan in a familiar wave.

"She says she explained what happened, about the call from Nick's brother."

"And I told her he doesn't *have* a brother. He did, but he's dead. I'm sorry you guys are worried, but I've spent every day with him for the past two weeks. He's not dangerous or whatever you're implying."

The long pause didn't bode well. In past discussions, it meant Dad was going into lawyer mode. "So let's take a step back and look at it from a purely clinical standpoint. You're with someone who had been taking psychiatric medication, yes or no?"

"I don't know." The answer felt dragged out of him. Nick's story wasn't his to share.

"It wouldn't be unheard of if he was, especially after losing a sibling. But that's information you need. If Nick *was* on medication and isn't now, that's dangerous."

Ethan didn't bother to hold back a sigh. "I know. Mom made that abundantly clear. He might murder me in my sleep and steal my car to go on a tristate crime spree."

"It's dangerous for *him*, Ethan. People can go into withdrawal. It's something that requires medical supervision." His dad's voice went quieter, like it always did when he was trying to make a point. "And you have no idea why they might have been prescribed. He could be diagnosed with bipolar disorder or schizophrenia. Which doesn't mean he's dangerous, of course, but it might mean he's *in* danger."

Ethan glanced around, phone cradled close to his ear as though Nick might overhear and be offended, even though he was a good distance away, reading a marker full of amazing pistachio facts. Nick had bounced between sad and happy a little too fast, but that was probably normal after everything he'd been through. Even if Ethan had doubts about his ability to help Nick, nothing would convince him that *anyone* needed the kind of help Cornerstone was dishing out.

"I'm not saying you were wrong to help him, but his brother made a . . . persuasive case. He emailed us pictures of the two of them, and screenshots from Nick's Facebook account. The other factor you have to consider is, *if* Nick has been declared incompetent, you could be charged with endangering him by keeping him away from needed treatment."

The cops. The haunted, beaten-down expression on Nick's face. It all came flooding back, and with it, his resolve.

"That's enough." He had no doubt that his dad meant his words to have a big impact, but Ethan felt pretty damn sure his reaction wasn't the one Dad had expected. "I appreciate you being worried, and I'm sorry if I'm making it worse, but I'm not dumping Nick. He can stay with me as long as he wants. Until I get to California, if that's how things go."

Mentioning the cops wasn't going to help his case, but it was a way to relieve some of his parents' fears without betraying Nick. He would've called his parents right away if he wanted commiseration, but this wasn't about winning points for his independence. This was someone threatening Nick's safety.

"Besides, wouldn't the police have kept him if he was really a danger to himself?"

"The poli— *Did you get arrested?*"

Ethan winced, holding the phone a few inches farther from his ear. That was Dad-the-Lawyer voice. It was like Ghostbusters. The streams should never be crossed. "At least I didn't tell the cop to go fuck himself?"

A weak attempt to get a laugh, but it was all he had. Dad made a sputtering noise, and Ethan could easily picture him pinching the bridge of his nose, eyes closed.

"Ethan, remember when I told Robert you were our easiest child? I've changed my mind. I'm promoting Suze. Do I have to send bail money to some godforsaken town in the middle of Texas?"

"New Mexico," Ethan corrected, to be not-at-all helpful. "And Suze eats your office stash of Thin Mints. I'm only saying, on a scale of 'didn't get arrested when the cops pulled us over for a welfare check' to 'steals $5 boxes of cookies to eat while she watches *Teen Wolf*,' I think I should still come out on top of the pile here."

"I'll consider it, if only because you remembered to not smart off to the cops." The long, drawn-out sigh echoed in Ethan's ear. "So why don't you back up and tell me exactly what happened when you didn't get arrested."

"We were at a rest stop. I went to pee, came back, and there were two cops. One had Nick pulled aside, one started questioning me."

"And they showed you ID?"

"They were in uniform and in a cruiser. I figured that was enough."

"Warrant? Did they search the car? Touch you?" Lawyer-voice again, shooting out questions like a super slingshot.

"No. Yes. No."

"They searched the fucking car without a warrant?" The crash of the phone hitting something solid made Ethan wince. "Sorry, I had to get some paper. Give me their badge numbers."

"Dad, chill, it's okay. We handled it, everything's fine. If you'll let me finish . . ." He waited for his dad's grunted response before continuing. "Nick has a crazy ex who is kind of stalking him. Called in some missing-and-endangered report on Nick, and that's why they stopped us. We cleared everything up. It's cool now."

Ethan could hear the gears grinding and switching in his dad's head. "So nobody's been charged with anything?"

"Right."

"What about the ex? Did somebody walk Nick through the paperwork?"

"Um . . ."

His dad sighed. "Glad to know all those *Law & Order* reruns we watched together were utterly wasted on you. Does Nick's family know about this . . . person? His brother didn't mention—"

"He doesn't *have* a brother. That's what I'm trying to tell you. His ex-boyfriend is . . . was . . . He's not a good guy. He's stalking Nick. Had his Instagram password, by the way."

Nick himself was leaning against the plaque of pistachio trivia, arms crossed over his chest and face tilted up toward the sun. His hair was longer than it had been when he'd first climbed into Ethan's car, a soft black velveteen that suited his dark skin. He was also pointedly not looking at Ethan, and Ethan turned around to walk farther into the slim shadow cast by the giant nut. His dad was so quiet he checked to make sure the call hadn't dropped, but he had a full signal and the timer was still ticking. When he put his phone back to his ear, he could faintly make out his parents' voices.

"Not to put a rush on this or anything, but I want to make sure I get to the gift shop here before they close. Have you guys decided to accept my judgment that Nick isn't an unmedicated serial killer who takes forever to murder his victims? Or should I expect another check-in with New Mexico's finest?" He could have hung up, given that it didn't matter what they thought. It wasn't their decision, it never had been. Maybe he still had a carryover need to be polite. Ethan had made up his mind about Nick pretty soon after almost making him roadkill.

His mom came back on the phone. "We love you. We miss you. Keep sending pictures." Her voice caught a little, but she recovered. "And your father says to give your friend his number so he can walk him through filing a restraining order. And that you're still going to have to duke it out with Suze, and— Oh for God's sake, Stuart, you can put the forms in Dropbox. They'll deal with them later. Ethan has to go buy a shirt with a terrible testicular pun on it."

"Wow. Thanks, Mom. Love you both." He hung up.

Nick took a break from looking like sex on legs as Ethan approached, pushing his sunglasses up. "Everything okay?"

"My parents." It didn't answer Nick's question, but he needed a few more minutes to decide what exactly, if anything, he wanted to say. "So, hey, about those T-shirts . . ."

"One-track mind," Nick said, letting his sunglasses fall back into place.

"I don't know about *you*, but I want to get a nice souvenir T-shirt to remember pistachios by."

Nick slung an arm around his shoulders. "Anything you want."

Dear Mrs. Raines,
My life may be complete. I've seen the world's biggest pistachio.
I have a T-shirt to prove it.
Love,
Ethan

Ethan made an effort to keep his hands loose on the steering wheel as they passed another sign for Albuquerque. Nick had been patient—entirely too patient—and it was making him nervous. He knew it was a weakness, but people staring at him, waiting him out, never failed to make him panic and spill his guts.

Whatever Nick was playing on the stereo had to have been recorded as brooding music. Some singer was growling about mercy and blindness and searching for truth, and for a second Ethan wondered if Nick *knew* somehow, and was trying to make him talk with lyrical torture techniques.

"So what did your parents want? Couldn't handle being without you for two days in a row?" Nick didn't even glance up from the screen of his phone when he asked, engrossed in crafting the perfect playlist to transition them from giant nuts to the place where cartoon characters made wrong turns. Ethan looked, just to make sure he wasn't being punked.

"Oh. You know. Stuff."

Jesus Christ, he was the worst at this.

Nick's thumb hovered over the screen in Ethan's peripheral vision, his head tilting sideways to fix Ethan with a disbelieving stare. Which Ethan promptly avoided by pinning his gaze on the car in front of them and hoping an armadillo would choose that moment to commit suicide under his tires.

"Did the maple syrup cartel get to them?"

He had permission to lie, and he still sucked at it. It seemed wrong to invoke their shared avoidance of feelings that way, and he wasn't sure why. It was going to upset Nick, so it should count, shouldn't it? Maybe the difference was that people had been trying to protect him from reality since Scott died, and he thought Nick should get to choose what he wanted to ignore.

"It was kinda worse than the maple syrup guys." Ethan took a breath before continuing, buying himself a few seconds. In the end, it was better to spit it out. "Kyle called my parents pretending to be your brother. He sent them pictures and stuff."

"He said he was Drew? Why . . . why would he do that? How—"

"I don't think he said that, exactly. He told them he was your older brother."

Ethan didn't know what else to tell him. Nick seemed to be mulling something over, even making a few false starts before he said anything else.

"What . . . Did they say what kind of pictures?" Nick's voice sounded too small for the words, like he was trying not to say them even while they were coming out.

"I guess pictures of the two of you together or something, to prove he knew you. He tried to convince them you're supposed to be taking some kind of heavy-duty meds and you were a danger to yourself now that you were off them."

Nick set his phone down in the cup holder, freeing up his hands to worry over the threadbare knees of the jeans he still hadn't given back. Ethan tried to keep his eyes on the road. He blamed being a careful driver for how long it took him to catch up to Nick's question.

"Wait. What kind of pictures did you think he'd sent?"

Nick didn't look up as he shrugged. "I couldn't think of any that would make your parents think he was my brother." His voice sounded flat, inflectionless, and yet another warning bell chimed in the back of Ethan's head.

"I can ask my parents to forward them to me if you want," Ethan offered. "Or you. It'll give my dad a chance to lecture you on filing a restraining order. He takes the legal shit pretty seriously."

Nick's head snapped up. "Why would he want me to file a restraining order?"

The accusing stare cut right through him. "I . . . Shit, I'm sorry." Ethan unconsciously hunched his shoulders. "I might've shared that Kyle was stalking you, threatening you, and well, my dad latched on to that and . . ." He trailed off.

"What did your dad say about you being a target too, now that you're with me?"

"Oh, he didn't. He was worried about you. Besides, I distracted him with the cop incident. He was so happy he didn't have to send bail money somewhere, he forgot everything else."

"Except you *are* a target. The fact that he called your parents proves that."

"The only thing it proves is that he's jealous of my ass showing up on your Instagram." Ethan wiggled in his seat, trying to approximate a shimmy. "Which, I mean, yeah. I get that. Hockey butts are the best."

"You mean disgusting, swampy jock butts? Yeah. Nothing hotter than a plastic cup full of ball sweat."

Ethan gagged, the description bringing back visceral memories of team busses and away game locker rooms. "I'll be sure to picture that the next time I get distracted by seminude pictures of Sidney Crosby."

Nick waved a hand. "I don't even know who that is."

Ethan spluttered because he felt like it was expected, but he kept getting hung up on Kyle. He *really* didn't like Kyle. Maybe even hated him, which seemed like a strong reaction to someone he'd never met. "It doesn't prove anything. Him trying to get my parents involved, I mean. Isn't it the same controlling shit he's been trying with you all along?"

"He's great on the phone." Nick propped an elbow on the armrest and turned to look out the window again. "But you're missing the point. That controlling shit was just me. Now it's you. It's your parents. Don't you see the problem?"

"What problem? That Kyle's a fucking asshole? Because I'm pretty clear on that one."

Nick made an exasperated sound. "He got you stopped by the cops. He called your parents and told them who the hell knows what. He knows who you are." The last was delivered through gritted teeth.

He had to be missing something, some big chunk of information, because Nick's shoulders were hunched tight as he pushed back in the seat, and there wasn't a reason for it. At least not one Ethan could fathom.

"It's not a big deal. I got Mom and Dad straightened out. They're pretty sure you're not a psycho killer, so it's cool."

"Yeah, awesome. And all you had to do was tell them I'm a whiny little reject who runs away from his problems."

"Hey! I didn't say that." It stung, after pushing back against his parents on Nick's behalf, even if it wasn't fair to expect Nick to be grateful. Ethan couldn't figure out how to convince Nick that what Kyle did wasn't a reflection on him. "I'm sorry if talking about him was out of line. I should have asked you, but I wasn't even expecting it to be them. They ambushed me from my little sister's phone!"

"Bet me you don't have a new follower on Instagram. Bet me he doesn't know your address." Nick's voice edged harder. "Bet me he doesn't know about Scott. Because he does. Or he will. He'll start showing up everywhere." Nick twisted sideways, the seat belt straining. "Ask me how I know."

Ethan clamped down on the hurt before it came out in some way he'd regret. "I don't need to ask you. Got a pretty clear picture about how he hurt you and messed up your life. But it's over now. You're not a kid anymore. You see him for what he is. That takes his power away."

"You've got a lot more faith in me than I do."

"I've got a shitload of faith in you." Ethan pulled up a small smile. "You got yourself away from that camp from hell, you survived me almost running you over, you've tolerated all my weird roadside attractions. That's earned some faith."

"I let him hit me. For months. My parents thought it was great that I'd found a mentor on my swim team. I'd gotten into trouble for stupid shit a couple times—shoplifting, mostly—and they thought he was going to keep me from embarrassing them again. It's fucked up how great he was at teaching me to hide all the stuff I wanted them to notice. All my teammates thought I was really clumsy. I guess Mom and Dad did too."

A soft noise followed Nick's confession as the thin denim he'd been fussing with tore under his renewed interest. Ethan bit back reassurance and denial. He didn't know which to start with anyway, and it seemed like maybe Nick was circling something, trying to get closer to the end of a story he'd been sharing in terse revelations for two weeks.

"I tried to tell my mom. Said I wanted to quit swimming. That it was too much, and Kyle was pushing me too hard."

Ethan's hands ached, the effort of pretending he wasn't holding on to the steering wheel like a life preserver too much to maintain.

"I don't know. It's not fair to blame her for not getting it. I couldn't . . . I missed practice two days in a row to get away from him, and when I opened my mouth, I could see how *disappointed* she was in me. Here was this fine young man, taking time away from college to mentor her loser son, and I knew she wouldn't believe me. So that's why I made sure he saw me kissing someone the next time he took me to a party. I knew he'd get so mad, someone would have to believe me."

Ethan sucked in a breath. "Nick—"

"Nuh-uh. I'm saying it doesn't matter how I feel about him, or what I know about him. I can live through him. But I can't live through him clawing his way into the lives of everyone I ever come in contact with. And he *will*, because people believe him." Nick snorted. "I think *I* still halfway believe him."

Nick went motionless next to him, all of his fidgets quieting one after another. "It'll be like with your parents. I can let people wonder if I really am crazy, if I'm lying to them all the time, or I can humiliate myself over and over. And even after I tell them I'm this pitiful little victim, they still might not believe me."

Knowing he was treading dangerous waters, Ethan went back and forth in his head for almost a minute before he got the nerve to let loose the words that had been niggling at him. "If I stopped at the next 7-Eleven, and when we got out of the car Kyle was standing there in the door, would you— Would *he* walk up and hit you? Pull out a gun and throw you in his trunk and take you away?" He didn't look at Nick, rushing on. "Because I'm gonna guess no. And if that's the case, then he doesn't have fuck-all to do with the rest of your life." He made another weak attempt to smile. "And you probably wouldn't appreciate it, since I know you don't need me sticking up for you, but if he tried anything, I'd kick his sorry ass all the way back to Virginia."

Nick's frustrated sigh was so emphatic that Ethan risked another look sideways, then started scanning the exit signs to see when they could pull into a hotel. He needed to be able to face this down with Nick, not give him half his attention while they careened down the interstate.

"I know it sounds fucking stupid. But you don't get . . . Hitting me was to show me he *could*, okay? So was taking my phone as soon as he picked me up from school. Telling me if I could eat. Whispering rumors to my friends and driving them off, one by one. Fucking telling me how much he loved me before he ever left a mark, and making me promise I loved him after he did." Nick let out an inarticulate snarl. "I look at texts from him, and no matter how angry or scared I am, I want to beg him to forgive me. I'm more afraid of *me* than I am of him, because there's still this huge, fucked-up part of me that knows how much he can take away, and . . . and sometimes I still feel like I owe him that."

It was so much more than Ethan was capable of fixing . . . or understanding, his mind treacherously whispered . . . that he decided ignoring it might be the safest option for the time being. "I think I'm done with driving for the day. Are you okay with stopping?"

Nick saw through him, if the sideways glare was any sign. He shrugged instead of answering, but that was enough.

"Looks like about ten more miles until the Albuquerque exits start. There's bound to be a Motel 6 or something. Pretty sure they're supposed to leave a light on for me." The joke was force of habit, and he couldn't even muster up a laugh of his own.

The next fifteen minutes took place in uncomfortable silence, and Ethan doubted he'd ever been so thankful to see a billboard advertising a local hotel. He nodded toward it. "That looks decent."

No answer from the passenger seat. He didn't look over, instead pulling onto the exit ramp and merging onto the smaller, two-lane road. Thankfully, the hotel sat less than a block off the highway, and Ethan jumped out of the car as soon as they hit the parking lot, leaving it running.

"Be right back, gonna check us in."

It didn't take long to grab a room for the night, and a menu for a local pizza place that would deliver to the motel. Nick smiled at him when he got back in the car, and he relaxed a little. He held out the menu. "Anchovy and pineapple?"

"With extra green pepper." Nick screwed up his nose, examining the menu while they drove to the back of the lot to find their room.

"I believe you," Ethan blurted out as he turned the car off. "I don't think I understand all of it, but I'm trying. And I believe you." His palm felt clammy, wrapped around his keys.

"That I want extra green pepper?"

Nick's voice sounded thick. His long lashes were clumped together, eyes red-rimmed, and his smile looked tired.

"God, no. That's disgusting."

"You see right through me," Nick said. He grabbed Ethan's arm and squeezed, though, so Ethan leaned across the console and brushed a kiss against his temple.

"Showers. Pizza. We'll watch some TV. You can tell me more, if you want. Or not."

"Yeah." Nick let go of him, retrieving his phone from the console and shoving it into his backpack. "Sounds good."

Ethan let himself have a moment to exhale after Nick got out of the car. And another to breathe in. The kind of deep, cleansing breath his therapist had walked him through after Scott died. It didn't make Nick's fears any easier to understand, but it struck him as he reached for the door handle that he didn't have to understand them to know they were real. Nobody had seemed to understand that he missed himself almost as much as he missed Scott. Even if they had, it wouldn't have cured him of the emptiness he felt every time he looked in the mirror.

Ethan slipped an arm over Nick's shoulders while he fumbled the key card in the door. Nick didn't flinch away. Their bags slid to the floor inside the room, and they held on to each other as the door swung shut behind them.

They wound up with pepperoni and mushroom, with pineapple on half, which Ethan mocked Nick for without mercy. Nick retaliated by trying to steal the remote, but it turned out to have been glued to the nightstand. He settled for changing it to the home improvement channel and vigorously defending his side of the bed anytime Ethan made a move toward it.

Which ended in a careful wrestling match, and then a not-so-careful attempt to get Ethan out of his clothes. When it seemed like he might smother to death in his favorite Captain America T-shirt, Ethan yanked it off himself and waited for Nick to follow suit.

Ethan yelped when the brass button on the fly of Nick's jeans hit his stomach like an ice chip.

"Sorry." Nick didn't look particularly contrite, but there was definitely something lurking in his expression that wasn't about easy sex or granite countertops. Chalking it up as another thing he didn't have to understand, Ethan used a vaguely recalled PE lesson to flip them.

It didn't occur to him until he was kneeling over Nick, grinning down at him, that maybe sudden plays for dominance weren't the best idea he'd ever had.

Nick reached up, warm fingers curving over his cheek and smoothing down his neck to the flare of his shoulder. "It's fine. I can tell the difference."

"And you'd say if—"

Nick squeezed his neck gently. "Ethan. Shut up and blow me."

Ethan tried for arch, which Scott had always said made him look like he was squinting. "You can't rush these things."

To prove it, Ethan spent an inordinate amount of time taking Nick apart, moan by whimper, closer to the edge with each one, until there was actual begging.

"Jesus Christ, please, please— *Fuck*—" Nick's hips snapped up off the mattress, then down again as sharply, his fingers skidding across the thick white sheets as he sought purchase. Ethan sucked in air through his nose and swallowed again, even though he wanted to grin like a madman.

Nick's strings had been cut when Ethan finally crawled back up the bed and flopped down close enough to share the same pillow. He swept his hand across the bare skin of Nick's stomach, no longer so concave.

"I fucking love you," Nick said, rolling over to kiss him.

Which was good, because Ethan's brain short-circuited, and he didn't even know if Nick had meant it as anything more than, *I love that you put your mouth on my dick.* Maybe the fact that Nick didn't look him in the eye before disappearing down between his thighs meant Nick didn't know either.

Like a freshman date in reverse, they made out after, stretched across the bed with the TV low in the background. The faintly bitter traces of come had nothing on their dizzy, languorous exploration, even though there wasn't any unexplored skin between them. Ethan fell asleep hours later with his arms wrapped around Nick and the soft prickle of hair tickling his neck. Nick murmured something against his chest as he drifted off, but he couldn't untangle it from the threads of slumber that had already ensnared him.

When he woke up the next morning, he was alone.

Interlude
NICK HAMILTON'S PHONE

Conversation with Ethan Domani
Nick: *I'm so sorry*

—

You have not sent this message. Save as a draft?
Message Not Saved

—

Nick: *I didn't leave because of anything you did. I have to get away from him.*
Nick: *I'd never forgive myself if he got near you.*
Nick: *I know this is shitty, and you'll probably never talk to me again*
Nick: *But you're the best person I've ever met*
Nick: *You deserve so much better than getting caught up in all my crap*
Nick: *I'm so sorry, Ethan.*

—

Message Sent at 6:03 a.m.

CHAPTER *Nineteen*

Albuquerque, NM

Ethan yanked on his jeans, hands shaking too much to bother with the button at the top. He flung open the motel room door, pacing the length of the parking lot barefoot. He knew it was a useless gesture, but he had to move or he'd go nuts. Nick's backpack was gone. *Nick* was gone.

His parents' words came up on repeat in his head. Drugs. Danger to himself. He pushed them down with every last bit of energy he could muster. Nick would've told him if he'd wanted to hurt himself, right? Except for that whole "more afraid of me" conversation.

At least the motel room door hadn't locked behind him. That would've topped off an already stellar morning. He dropped onto the bed with a groan, staring up at the ceiling without seeing it. The intermittent message flash finally caught his eye, and he rolled over to grab his phone off the nightstand.

Jesus. He'd slept for three hours after Nick left. He'd woken up thinking about pie, and Nick saying things he probably didn't mean but hadn't taken back. Nick could be *anywhere*.

Ethan: *Are you okay?*
Ethan: *You don't have to go to Pie Town.*
Ethan: *Please tell me you're okay*

His phone remained silent. Ethan fought down the momentary desire to throw it at the wall and leave a dent in the fussy wallpaper. He didn't do stuff like that.

Ethan: *Even if I can't help you, keep my dad's #, k?*

Ethan: *703-555-4383*

Ethan: *He can help if you need legal stuff*

Yeah, he didn't do things like that. Throwing things around in frustration didn't change anything. Of course, most of what he did didn't change things, as evidenced by him sitting in a hotel room, alone, with no clue what to do next.

He scrolled past Nick's messages, finger hesitating before he stopped on Scott's name.

Ethan: *So Nick took off. I'm here in Albuquerque by myself. I think I want to go home.*

Ethan: *I don't think I can deal with having to do this solo AGAIN.*

He hadn't had a one-sided text conversation with Scott in almost a week, probably the longest stretch he'd gone since crashing out of the memorial service when the minister tried to say Scott was in a better place. Maybe he should have missed it more.

Ethan: *Which is worse—forgetting you because I was having a good time, or keeping you alive so I don't have to be alone?*

Ethan: *Good talk, man. Your advice sucks.*

Ethan: *I think I might have accidentally loved that guy*

A loud noise outside his door startled him out of his head: a crash followed by squeaky wheels and someone singing an off-key Taylor Swift song. The four steps to the window felt like he was walking through quicksand. He pushed the curtain aside far enough to peer out the window and see a janitor's cart disappearing down the walkway outside his room. A faint whiff of window cleaner made him wrinkle his nose and pull back into the dark room. The white Do Not Disturb sign was hanging on the inside of the door, and he grabbed it, cracked the door, and hung it on the outside knob. The maid walking in on his private little pity party didn't bear thinking about.

Suze was probably in the middle of her robotics class, and texting his twelve-year-old sister for advice about his missing hookup-slash-traveling-companion-slash-totally-not-boyfriend was probably some new height of pathetic he didn't really want to reach.

It didn't matter anyway. When it came down to it, he couldn't convince Nick they were safe. He couldn't make Nick believe that he wasn't responsible for the actions of his crazy ex and that they weren't subject to Kyle's demands for attention.

Ethan rested his head against the closed door. It wasn't his job to convince Nick of anything. That admission hurt, down to some deep, subterranean level. He couldn't fix his own life. Didn't that mean he could at least get the fucking satisfaction of helping Nick fix his? Hooray. Another big fat check in that book of unfairness.

Bullying Nick into doing something against his will, even if he thought it would help, was uncomfortably close to all the well-meaning and stupid advice he'd gotten since Scott's death. Uncomfortably close to Kyle and the people at that horrible camp. Maybe Nick was making a mistake, and it was definitely hurting both of them, but it was Nick's mistake to make.

Hungry but too miserable to face the world, Ethan pushed himself away from the door and trudged to the dresser. There had to be a candy bar somewhere in the bottom of his backpack. Instead, his fingers closed on the small cedar box, tightly rubber-banded shut. He ran his fingers over the rough carving on the lid—closer to gouges, really—but it had been his first attempt after a class in third grade, and Scott had hung on to it ever since. Until he couldn't anymore, and Ethan had taken it back.

Hunger forgotten in the ugly wave of grief, he pulled it out, clenching the box so tightly his hand ached.

Maybe he'd been hasty in saying he couldn't understand Nick's reaction to Kyle. He'd limped through the days after the shooting, trying to regain some kind of equilibrium when the whole world felt like it was tilting wildly. Scott became Ethan's constant companion in a way he hadn't been even when he was alive—every breath, every step, every *thing* was about learning how to do it all over again while his missing limb, the other half of almost everything since he could remember, ached in a ghostly reminder that he'd never be a whole version of that Ethan again.

He *wouldn't* ever be that Ethan again, but during the time he'd spent coming to grips with that, it seemed he'd become another person, another Ethan entirely. The question was, could he deal with being that new person? Was it enough to make giving up Scott worthwhile?

Did he even have a choice, since Scott was gone?

Ethan sat there long enough that the maid passed by again, her cart rumbling in time to his stomach. He wanted to call Nick.

He wanted to call Scott. He wanted to rewind the past fourteen months, remember to turn in his homework, and be there with Scott when the shooting started.

If he couldn't do that, he at least wanted to stop feeling so damn guilty. Standing still, moving on, remembering or forgetting—his guilt consumed him, and the days he forgot it were swallowed whole when it all came crashing down again.

"If I let go, will you forgive me?"

Tiny handprints and ghost lights aside, he didn't get an answer from the little cedar box.

He laughed, but it felt thick, catching in his throat. "Thanks. I thought I was the one who always danced around the tough questions."

"You have to go," said an unfamiliar voice. Ethan jumped a mile, whacking his knee on the bedside table.

"W-what?"

"Checkout is 11 a.m.! You have to go!"

"Oh, sorry, I'll be out in a few minutes."

There was no answer, but a person-shaped shadow drifted past the curtains, singing the most tone-deaf Beyoncé song he'd ever heard.

As far as signs went, that one wouldn't ever reach biblical standards. But it was enough to get him moving.

Packing up didn't take long. There was only his stuff, after all. At least Nick had taken his toothbrush and the clothes they'd bought.

"Huh," Ethan huffed, doing another inspection of the room.

The clothes they'd bought *and* Ethan's favorite pair of jeans. If that wasn't reason enough to keep after Nick, he didn't know what was. It took months to break in a pair of jeans to that perfect level of comfort. Plus, it gave him an excuse to text Nick without seeming quite as invasive and creepy as Kyle.

Dude, you took my fave jeans!

He didn't expect a reply, and didn't get one, so there was nothing else to do but check out and get in the car.

Everything kind of fell apart once he was behind the wheel. He didn't know which onramp to take. Home? Or California, and up the coast after that? Before, their nebulous plans after crossing the country had felt like Christmas morning. Full of endless possibilities—maybe they'd go to Canada. Or South America. Or Alaska. Now, it just felt empty.

Scott had wanted to go to the Grand Canyon. Nick would have wanted him to go anywhere but where Scott had picked. Ethan . . . He didn't . . .

His gaze fell on the brochures he'd picked up in the hotel lobby last night. A handful, snagged on the way out because he'd been too worried about the conversation he and Nick had never had to peruse them. They were still tucked into the console, crammed under the emergency brake.

"I'm hungry," he told the empty car. Hungry was a feeling as good as any other, and it was so much safer than lonely or scared. He could fix hungry.

And he was in the mood for pie.

Pie Town, New Mexico, was exactly as described on their website: a tiny little frontier town exactly 3.14 miles from the middle of nowhere. Boasting a population that barely jumped into triple digits, it wasn't much but a couple of cafés and a post office. It felt left behind. Ethan could commiserate.

He ran the tines of his fork through the sticky mess of apple syrup. He'd never even heard of piñon nuts before, much less piñon nuts mixed with green chilies in an apple pie, but all the Yelp reviews weren't kidding. The Pie-O-Neer Cafe kicked major ass. And best of all? It didn't remind him of any of the ones Scott's mom had baked weekly for them growing up. He was all about pain-free pie.

Well. Maybe if he'd stopped after his fourth flavor, it would've been pain-free. As it was, five huge slices were sitting a little heavy, and he hadn't even gotten to the chocolate meringue yet. Groaning, he twisted sideways on the stool he'd taken at the bar, trying to spot the waitress who was running his tab.

"You ready to go, honey?" She could have been anywhere between thirty and seventy, her short hair dyed a soft bubblegum pink that matched the trim on her vintage uniform. "I can ring you up if you want."

Ethan glanced longingly at the pie bar, at least a dozen flavors he hadn't tried yet calling to him from under the lights. "Yeah, I guess I need to take a walk before my next round. I was going to look in the gift shop."

She stowed her pen back in the wide front pocket of her apron, nodding toward the swinging saloon doors that led to the general store and gift shop. "Go ahead. No sense in me writing out two receipts." She shook a finger at him, her eyes crinkling behind a set of cat-eye glasses she had to have picked to augment her mystique. "Don't stiff me on the tip. Deal?"

"Deal," he agreed, nodding enthusiastically. Too enthusiastically, which sent him tipping off the red vinyl barstool.

"Sugar high," he mumbled, blushing under the waitress's knowing look. He spun a graceful pirouette on his way past the counter, ending it neatly before pushing through the saloon doors into the gift shop. General store. Mercantile. Whatever it was, there was a lot of pie-shaped things and tie-dye going on.

The tie-dye shirts were on sale, and honestly, who didn't need an oversized T-shirt with psychedelic pie on it? Not as cool as the giant nuts shirt, but still an excellent addition to his traveling collection. When he went home and tried to figure out what to do with the rest of his life, at least he'd have a colorful variety of clothes to do it in.

The entire back wall looked like an episode of Top Pie Chefs or something on the Food Network. Canisters and whisks and mixing bowls and cookbooks. Hundreds of cookbooks. Curious, he drifted closer, not quite ready to believe that they were all about pie. It was dough and some kind of filling. How complicated could it be?

He should have known better after buying Scott's mom a new pie cookbook every Christmas for the last ten years. Each year she'd made a fuss over them and picked out a special recipe to bake for him and Scott on New Year's Day.

Front and center, taking up a whole shelf all by itself, was the official *Pie Town Cookbook*. He picked up a copy and thumbed through the pages, coming to rest on the New Mexican apple pie he'd just had. Scott would've liked it. His mom would've made it for them and served it on appropriate plates, probably something with coyotes. Somehow she had always managed to have at least two plates that matched the theme of whatever pie she'd made. He hadn't understood how she managed it until the summer he'd gone to the beach with them and she took him and Scott to what seemed like a dozen thrift stores, hunting for weird dessert plates.

Ethan squeezed his eyes shut. Right now he would trade anything—the rest of his life, whatever—to be buying this book for her, knowing she'd get to hear Scott tease her about her obsession with themed tableware. Knowing that he'd get to hear it too.

"Can I help you find anything?"

He spun around, almost dropping the copy in his hand.

The girl reminded him of Suze: all bounce and smiles. "You looked kinda lost. Is there a particular book you're looking for? Maybe something with . . . pies?"

Ethan laughed with her, unable to stop himself. Nick would have mocked him for it. Scott would have mocked him for it. The girl looked the kind of charmed that usually ended in him awkwardly explaining he was gay.

He held up the book in his hand. "I was thinking about getting this for my . . ." He didn't even know how to describe Mrs. Raines anymore. Best friend's mom? Ex-boyfriend's mom? Both diminished what their relationship had been in a painful way, but what else was there?

He didn't know, because he hadn't spoken to Scott's parents since the day after the memorial service. Figuring out who he was supposed to be for them without Scott had felt impossible, and he'd already had a dozen other impossible things to navigate.

The girl seemed less amused and more worried by the time he looked back up from the cover of the cookbook. "Anyway, so this one, I think. And a medium tie-dye shirt?"

She looked considerably relieved at being able to do something. "I'll grab your shirt. Meet me at the counter, and I'll get you set up."

Ethan thought for a moment, then picked up another copy of the cookbook. His mom hated baking anything that didn't come out of a box, but his oldest sister, Clara, loved to bake. Maybe he could convince her that pies made great gifts for adorable younger brothers.

Once he was done wearing out the strip on his credit card, he glanced down at the bag, then back up at the girl ringing him out.

"I'm gonna go put this in my car, but I don't want anyone to think I'm skipping out on my tab. Is that okay?"

She waived his receipt at him. "Sure. We've got your credit card number now anyway." Her wink was encouraging, and mildly terrifying in its flirtatiousness. Ethan knew he was blushing even without the prickly heat in his cheeks.

"Promise I'll be right back." He wasn't so much fleeing as walking quickly toward the door, books and shirt clutched tightly in his sweaty hand.

The sun didn't do anything to alleviate the rush of warmth as he leaned against the hood of his car and stared down at his phone. It was stupid, probably, to let his thumb hover over a number he hadn't called in more than a year. But there was something about the tiny little café clinging to the edge of nothing that reminded him of how lonely he was. Like they knew everything around them had changed, but refused to let it touch them.

Maybe if he could acknowledge how guilty he felt to be standing there in the middle of nowhere, he could finally let something touch him again.

Ethan mushed his thumb down on the screen before he could chicken out. He'd let this go too long, this corner piece in the puzzle that was Life After Scott. He knew nobody would answer, or hoped anyway. The call would hit voice mail. He'd confess his guilt. Maybe once he did, he could finally forgive himself.

That was a nice fantasy.

"Hello? Ethan?"

Or Scott's mom could pick up and tell him out loud that she blamed him. That was a possibility he hadn't given nearly enough consideration to.

She was still talking. "Oh my God, Ethan, is it really you?" Her voice sounded familiar and strange at the same.

Ethan opened his mouth, but nothing came out. He gripped the phone tighter, fighting for the apology he desperately needed to get out before her accusations washed over him in a flood that would leave him even emptier than he already was.

"Please don't hang up." Mrs. Raines was crying. "We miss you so much. You disappeared, and . . ." She trailed off in an obvious attempt to get herself under control.

"I'm so sorry," he whispered into the phone, the words woefully inadequate and still hopelessly overwhelming. He ducked his head, hoping nobody inside could tell he was about to cry over a fifteen-second phone call. Almost as much as he hoped Mrs. Raines could magically understand everything he was saying without further explanation.

He could hear her take a shaky breath. "No, I'm sorry. I don't . . . I don't have any right to make you feel guilty about moving on with your life. We want you to know that you . . . You're family, and we love you."

His knees buckled and he sank down, squatting over the dusty blacktop. "I thought it would be hard for you to see me. You know, because . . ."

He couldn't say it. Coward.

"Sweetie, I saw you almost every day for over a decade. The postcards are nice, but we miss *you*."

"I bought you a cookbook. For pies." He said it in a rush, like there was some equivalence between a hundred pages of spiral-bound recipes and all the ways he'd let her down.

"Would you maybe think about bringing it by yourself?" It sounded like she was starting to cry again. "Maybe we can look through it together and I'll bake your favorite."

"Are you sure you want me to?" He hated the uncertain quaver in his voice.

"Of course. You're always welcome. Are you back in town? Did you want to come by this afternoon?"

"I'm actually in New Mexico right now." Ethan pinched the bridge of his nose, closing his eyes and leaning his head back against his hot fender. "I sent you a postcard yesterday, but it's probably not there yet."

"Are you having fun?"

Maybe a minute into their reunion wasn't the time to stretch the boundaries of their relationship. He started to give her a generic, easy answer, then stopped himself. There was nobody to fill in the blanks for them anymore, nobody waiting to tell the third side of the story.

"You know, it's been really weird. Fun, and I've seen a lot of cool stuff, but it's . . . it's been weird."

"You'll have to tell me all about it when you come visit. You're doing okay though?"

He shook his head, biting his lip and using the sharp pain to steady himself. "No . . . Yes, but . . ."

"Oh, Ethan," she said, like she'd said when he skinned his knee in her driveway. Like she'd said when he and Scott had a fight over something childish and he'd gone to hide with her in the kitchen. Like he wasn't the reason—

He hit the ground, legs giving out entirely as a wave of dizziness swept him from his moorings. He'd gotten Scott killed. He owed Mrs. Raines the chance to hate him, if it gave her even the smallest measure of comfort. "I'm so sorry. I was supposed to buy the stupid tickets. Scott wouldn't even have *been* there—" Every word took another piece of his soul with it, torn right from the heart of him.

"Of course he would have. He would've been standing next to you like always, and we might have lost both of you." Her familiar voice was far gentler than he deserved, a salve to his fresh wounds. "Nobody is to blame for what happened except the . . . the shooter."

His therapist had said similar things, over and over and over, but her words offered none of the absolution he felt hearing them from Scott's mom. "Thank you," he whispered, knowing she probably couldn't hear him.

"Losing Scott was the absolute worst thing that could ever have happened to us. Parents . . . parents are never supposed to outlive their children." She exhaled softly. "We don't want to lose you too. But we understand if you need to move on— No," she interrupted herself. "You *have* to move on. But we hope we can still be part of your life."

"Yes." Ethan coughed, then said it louder. "Yes. I mean, I want that. I wasn't sure if you blamed me as much as . . ." He took a deep breath, choking on dust and sunlight. "As much as I blame myself."

She'd already told him she didn't, but the long, silent pause hit him. Maybe she couldn't lie to him again. Irrationally, it made him wish for Nick.

"When Scott was eight years old, he looked up from his homework and told me he was going to marry you. Actually, he said he was glad the two of you were already married, because I could teach you to make pies for him."

Ethan snorted despite himself. "Anything to avoid getting his hands dirty, the jerk."

Mrs. Raines laughed too. "But I thought it was cute. When I suggested he might change his mind someday, he got so angry he stomped off to his room and missed dessert just to prove his point." She chuckled again, but it sounded more like she was collecting herself than actually amused.

"I knew he was telling me something important, but I wasn't ready to hear him. We weren't even supposed to have Scott, you know. He was our miracle IVF baby, and there he was, telling me . . . It was easy to pretend it was a childish phase. But he kept insisting. So I blamed you. I don't know why, except I suppose some prejudices you don't want to admit you have until they smack you in the face. I got him involved in some other sports, thought about maybe putting him in a private school."

Ethan swallowed. He only vaguely remembered feeling unhappy that Scott suddenly had a bunch of things to do that he couldn't come over for, but he hadn't known why. He'd thought Scott was mad at him, before getting an eye-rolling indictment of his own intelligence for even asking. *"I dunno, my mom is being weird,"* Scott had told him, and they'd shrugged and gone back to tetherball.

"I'm—"

"There's nothing for you to apologize for. I was being unrealistic and selfish. He was miserable. He wasn't much for crying, you remember? But he was sniffling in his room one afternoon and said you thought he hated you, and it was like getting shocked. I had to ask myself if all of that time, all that trying, was so I could have a baby or so I could raise a child. And then I had to work very hard to let him be the person he was telling me he was, even if it made me feel like I'd left him vulnerable to the world somehow. I don't think a day went by after he met you that I didn't hear your name at least once. My son loved you, and I do too. I will never be sorry you're alive, Ethan. Wishing Scott was here doesn't mean I wish you weren't. You didn't take him from me."

Relief hit him like a concussive force, and he needed something to keep him from floating away. They were both silent for almost a minute, Ethan concentrating on inhaling, exhaling, his breathing the only thing tethering him to his body.

"So when I get back to Virginia," he said, because he had to do something with all that extra air in his lungs. "We should have lunch. And pie."

Mrs. Raines laughed. "We will."

Ethan dragged the hem of his T-shirt over his eyes, wiping them dry enough to pass for respectability. "I'll bring this recipe book I got you. Maybe you can teach me how to make one."

"I'd like that a lot. And you'll be okay in the meantime, right? No more blaming yourself?"

It was honesty time, right? "I think so. And if I slip up, I'll work hard on not doing it. I'll call you—"

"You call me—" she said at the same time, and they both laughed. "You call me; we'll bake a pie and talk it out. Promise?"

Ethan nodded, even though she couldn't see it. "I promise. Thank you."

"I'll see you soon. Enjoy the rest of your trip."

He waited a few seconds after she'd hung up before thumbing the phone off. He knew his lovely, tolerant waitress was probably second-guessing her choice to be nice to him by now, but it still took him another minute or two to compose himself enough for public consumption.

The string of pie-shaped bells hanging on the door jingled when he pulled it open, stepping back into the air-conditioned bakery. The waitress looked up from the customer she was helping and waved him back to his seat. He slid across the worn vinyl, contemplating all the flavors he hadn't tried yet.

"See? I knew you'd come back. What can I get you this time, sweetie?"

Ethan pointed toward something chocolate covered in a mountain of perfectly browned meringue. "That looks awesome, whatever it is."

"Chocolate peanut-butter meringue. You'll love it. I'll get you another glass of milk too." She flashed him a smile he couldn't help but return, and came back a moment later with a monumental slice of pie and a glass of milk so cold it left beads of condensation on the counter.

Ethan slid the tines of his fork into the pie, cutting off the point and holding it up to examine all the layers of deliciousness. Scott would have loved this place. Nick would have tripped over all the sugar, probably spent ten minutes freaking out before he remembered he was allowed to eat whatever he wanted, and then forced Ethan to try something horrible like sour cream raisin.

Except neither of them were there. It was just him.

"Eyes bigger than your stomach?" the waitress asked, raising her artistically precise eyebrows.

"No, ma'am," Ethan said. He was supposed to make a wish. He'd wished on every pie point he could ever recall eating, including the five he'd already tried here.

Ethan closed his eyes, took a bite, and wished for California.

CHAPTER Twenty

Bushland, TX

There weren't a lot of people on the bus with him, and with the exception of a few couples and what looked like a group of Eagle Scouts, everyone had pretty much laid claim to a row and kept a few between for privacy. Nick had slunk to the back of the bus when he climbed aboard in Albuquerque. He still had a row behind him separating him from the bathrooms, as well as two on either side of the aisle in front of him.

He pushed the armrests up and sprawled across both seats, one foot dangling into the middle aisle, bouncing up and down while he played with his phone. So far, he'd run out of free levels in two games, changed his email password, and signed up for new accounts on Instagram, Facebook, and Twitter. None of which he was using to keep track of Ethan, because that would be stupid after ditching him.

God knew, he never did anything stupid.

On the other hand, the pie pictures Ethan had posted made his stomach growl, and he didn't even like pie all that much. Suze liked them too, and she asked if Ethan was planning on taking up a career in baking or cardiac care. But Nick wasn't stalking or anything, because, yeah, stupid.

NotFromROTC: *Did they have sweet potato?*

Nick slammed his phone facedown against his thigh, currently clad in Ethan's jeans. Only the fact that his head was resting on the seat stopped him from banging it against the wall. This wasn't how you kept someone safe from your shit-show of a life. It definitely wasn't how you made sure you stayed only maybe-in-love with them.

The highway hummed under him, the sun through the tinted windows washing everything behind his closed eyes in a warm, golden light. He wasn't sleepy, but he was damn tired of *thinking* so much. His phone buzzed against his leg, an unpleasant tingle on the periphery of his junk, and he dragged himself upright with a groan just as an elderly woman was passing his seats on her way to the bathroom. She shook her head at him, but he couldn't tell if it was his posture, his wrinkled clothes, or his ratty sneaker blocking her path. He hastily pulled his foot out of her way, turning to look out the window so he wouldn't make any accidental eye contact when she returned.

No matter who was making his phone buzz, it was a safe bet he didn't want to talk to them. If it was Ethan, he'd be righteously pissed at being ditched. Or it could be one of his parents, or Stef, or—

Goddamn *Kyle*.

Well, fuck him anyway. Maybe it was the relative safety of an anonymous Greyhound somewhere in Texas. Maybe it was boredom, and stupidity, and anger. Maybe Nick needed to feel like shit because he'd snuck out of bed in the middle of the night and stolen Ethan's favorite jeans. But instead of looking at any of the messages, he hit the button to call Kyle back, waiting impatiently through the two rings before Kyle picked up.

"Nicky—"

"What? What the fuck do you want *now*? Why are you still sending me shit?"

"Are you drunk?"

"No. I'm pissed off."

Kyle was silent for longer than he would have been able to stand, not that long ago. As it was, Nick still felt excuses and apologies filling his head, but he kept his mouth shut. He had the right to be angry. He didn't have to make things between them easy.

Sure.

"*You're* pissed off? I'm the one who drove seven hours to pick you up, after you asked me to, and you weren't there. I don't think you have a leg to stand on, Nicky."

"I didn't ask you for anything. You told me and assumed I'd do what you said. Like always." His stomach flipped itself over and tried a new yoga position, making him regret his nutritious breakfast of teriyaki beef jerky and root beer.

Kyle's voice fell soft, slow and placating like he was talking to a stupid child or a wet cat. "I know that place must have been terrible, but you're out now. You don't have to let it destroy what we've got. I knew as soon as you contacted me again that we could have a second chance. No more sneaking around, no more worrying about your parents."

Nick snorted, kicking at the frame of the seats in front of his with the toe of his sneaker. "Yeah, you win. You pretty much cost me my parents."

"Did I? Because I think if you recall, they always liked me. They all but gave us their blessing, until you decided to make me look like an idiot in front of an entire house full of my friends. Your mom dropped you off that night, remember? Why would she do that, unless she..." Kyle's pause filled him with anticipation, designed purely to make sure he was waiting for whatever poisoned apple he was about to be offered. "Oh. Maybe she was happy she didn't have to deal with you for a while. Maybe it was never me she liked, it was not having you around to remind her your brother wasn't."

"Or maybe..." Nick cleared his throat so his voice would actually be audible outside his own head. "Or maybe she didn't know you were fucking her sixteen-year-old son."

"I never heard you objecting."

"No. You never did." Nick slumped back against the window.

Kyle sighed, the sound managing to convey disappointment and hurt. "You're not stupid. And you didn't use to play games. Can we cut through all this unnecessary shit and admit that it's because you wanted it? That you knew— That you *know* we have something together?"

"Oh, yeah? What exactly is it that we had? Because from my end, looking back, it's pretty clearly a relationship built on abuse. And you know what? Fuck that."

"It was *one time*—"

"No, it wasn't." Nobody was more surprised by the steel in his voice than Nick. "You always had some reason for it, but don't pretend you only hit me once. It was every time you thought I wasn't totally focused on you. Or when you didn't have to actually hit me, because you made damn sure I knew you *could*. When—when you'd wait until I was begging and willing to let you see how much you fucking meant to me, and you'd remind me that nobody else wanted me."

"You needed the reminding." Kyle's voice was flat and cold. "So go ahead, throw away what we have. But don't come crying back to me when you realize that no one else, including your own parents, wants you."

Nick stared at the leather upholstery, breathing in the smell of diesel and sanitizing air freshener while he wondered why this had ever seemed like a good idea. Kyle knew him. Kyle knew all the things Nick was most afraid of, and what he didn't know, he'd created. Well, fuck it. If he was going to do this, he might as well put it all on the table.

"So did you ever actually love me, or did you just get off on messing with my head and realize that was the easiest way to do it?"

"What do you want me to say, Nick?" For the first time, maybe ever, Nick detected a note of hesitance in Kyle's voice, like maybe the thought had occurred to him that he wasn't going to get his way.

"I want you to answer me, yes or no. Did you ever actually love me?"

"Of course I do. Do you think I would've wasted all this time and effort on someone I didn't give a shit about?"

He laughed without meaning to, the sound punching out of him too fast to stop. "I think you could replace me with a video game in that sentence, and it would sound exactly the same."

Twisting his head to look out the window, Nick caught sight of his reflection for a second before his eyes refocused on the dull brown scenery. Ah. It hadn't been laughter. He scrubbed his cheeks dry with the palm of his hand, carefully regulating his breathing because he wouldn't give Kyle the satisfaction of his pain again.

"Jesus Christ, Nicky, I almost went to jail for you. I tried to find you after your parents sent you away. I tried . . . I wanted . . . I was going to apologize. I want to be with you. I made a mistake. Why do you have to make this so dramatic?" When his exasperation was met with silence, the same edge of uncertainty crept into Kyle's voice. "I love you, okay? Is that what you want me to say?"

Nick had always found Kyle's confidence attractive. Kyle hadn't been wrong when he'd said Nick had never complained. Being the focus of that kind of charisma, of the kind of person who knew exactly what they wanted and wouldn't stop until they got it, had been more intoxicating than any of the booze he'd ever filched from his parents' liquor cabinet. Finding a crack in that veneer hit Nick hard enough to falter as he replayed what Kyle had actually said.

"No. It's what I wanted you to *do*. But I don't think you can." His mind bent around Kyle's blame and Ethan's emphatic denials, the contrast sharp enough to seem like day and night.

"You don't love me." It had been his worst fear for so long, and he said it with the kind of awe people reserved for Disneyland or Jesus. Four words that weighed a thousand pounds in his chest, and popped like soap bubbles when they finally escaped him.

"I fucking said I—"

"No. I heard you. It'll always be my fault, and you'll keep saying it." Nick leaned forward, hand gripping the top of the seat. He squeezed his eyes shut, hoping it would fight his sudden wave of vertigo. "This is over. When we hang up, don't ever contact me again."

"Until the next time you crawl across the floor, begging to suck my dick." Derision laced Kyle's words. Derision, and the threat of the monster under their bed that Nick knew was real.

The dizzy spell wouldn't let him go, and his death grip on the seat was the only reason he hadn't slid down to hide under it. He'd gotten too used to having an out when things got twisty. Ethan's tacit permission, *Lie to me*, had left him at a loss. He didn't have a real enough reason for Kyle. *Because I don't want to talk to you again* would never fly, and that was the sum total of his truth, right there.

But he still had Ethan's blessing.

"I've got a lawyer. I'm going to get a restraining order, and if you come after me . . ." His thumb dragged across the grain of the leather while he tried to wet his mouth enough to make a threat of his own. "If you come near me again, I'm going to give all your pictures to the cops. See how much good your MBA does when you're a registered sex offender, asshole." His heart pounded like he was on mile twenty-five of an uphill marathon, but at least the end was within sight. "I'm done, Kyle."

Nick pressed the red button to end the call, and slumped down in the seat. The lights flashing behind his closed eyes had more to do with shock than celebratory fireworks, and he breathed slowly in and out until they faded.

After a few minutes of shaking in silence, he forced himself up out of his seat and staggered toward the little bathroom at the back of the bus. The lukewarm water he had to pump out of the sink into the palm of one hand smelled funny, like the air and the seats, but he splashed it over his face anyway. He scrubbed away most of the damp, the stiff brown paper towel leaving him feeling raw.

He could've sworn he'd already done the whole "looking in the mirror and seeing a stranger" thing, recently even. Maybe he had some kind of face blindness. A form of amnesia that made him forget who he was every few days.

He was kind of proud of the guy he was staring at, though. He looked like he might make it through the day.

The bus swayed between lanes as he was settling back into his row. His phone skimmed across the seat, but he managed to catch it before it hit the floor.

Four . . . No. Five unread texts. Two missed calls.

Before he could forget what the guy in the bathroom looked like, Nick swiped his phone open.

Are you sure you want to add 571-555-8920 to your blocked contact list?

Number blocked. You will not receive future notifications from this contact.

Phone cradled in his hand, Nick leaned back in his seat and looked out the window. The sun caught a strange angle as they rolled through a curve, and he found himself in the glass again, fingertips meeting on the edge of the frame. He looked the same as he had a few minutes ago, except the guy in the reflection seemed to know something he didn't.

Nick stared at his reflection, squinting against the light. It had never bothered him this much in Ethan's car, mile after mile of the same road passing him by.

Oh. That was the difference. That was what the guy he was almost starting to recognize was trying to tell him.

He was going the wrong direction.

Conversation with Stef Hansen

Nick: *If you realize you're making a huge mistake and you can fix it but it might make someone else upset, you should still fix it, right?*

Stef: *Usually. Depends on circumstances.*

Nick: *Is being in love with some random dude who almost ran me over a circumstance?*

Stef: *Prob.*

Nick: *So if I change my ticket to go west, you'll understand?*

Nick: *I'll pay you back for the ticket as soon as I get my ATM card. I've got savings.*

Stef: *I literally don't know what that feels like*

Stef: *Don't have to pay me back. Be safe. You still want to stay with me when you come back?*

Stef: *Wait, are you coming back? Or does Random Dude live somewhere else?*

Stef: *Please don't move to Kansas.*

Stef: *Don't wanna stand in the way of young love, but I draw the line at Kansas*

Nick: *Nah, Kansas isn't on my agenda. You sure you won't mind me underfoot for a few weeks?*

Stef: *Wouldn't have offered if I did. Keep me updated on grand romantic gestures. Brian broke up with me to date his guilty conscience again, so I live vicariously.*

Stef: *Remember you have options.*

Nick: *I remember. Seriously.*

Nick: *I'm sorry about your breakup. And the bus ticket. Sorry.*

Stef: *I accept apologies in the form of coffee and people not being sore losers when I whip their skinny asses at Mario Kart. NP.*

Nick: *Can do coffee. Will own you at Mario Kart.*

Stef: *Challenge accepted. Call me if you need help switching the tickets around.*

Stef: *Is he picking you up somewhere?*

Nick: *No. My turn to pick him up, I think.*

Conversation with Ethan Domani

Ethan: *Dude, you took my fave jeans!*

Nick: *Priorities in order, I see*

Ethan: *And you left me all these crappy granola bars*

Nick: *Took the beef jerky though. And the money you gave me.*

Ethan: *You're OK????*

Nick: *No scurvy yet. Must be the Starburst*

Nick: *Okay. On a bus. There's wi-fi.*

Nick: *So where are you going tomorrow?*

Ethan: *California? Duh.*

Nick: *Ass. I'm stuck on a bus. Fill me in on your itinerary so I can have fun vicariously.*

Ethan: *Scott wanted to see the Pacific Ocean. Taking his ashes to Santa Monica Pier.*

Nick: *Shit. Sorry. Didn't know you needed to do that.*

Ethan: *My choice. Stole the ashes so he could come with me on the trip.*

Ethan: *I would've made a great goth kid.*

Nick: *Sorry, laughed so hard I dropped my phone.*

Nick: *That was a joke, right, Mr. Human Beam of Sunshine?*

Ethan: *I am darkness and the night, fucker.*

Nick: *Sure thing, Batman.*

Nick: *I miss you. I know that's my fault. Can I fix it?*

Ethan: *I get why you left. I still don't think that guy deserves all the time you spend worried about him, but I get that you can't just walk away from what he did.*

Ethan: *I'm sorry if I did a shitty job explaining that*

Ethan: *And there's nothing to fix. I want to see you when we're back in the same place.*

Nick: *I'll make it happen.*

CHAPTER *Twenty-One*

Santa Monica, CA

I-10 dumped him at the end of the continent, in a parking lot where the heat radiated up in shimmery waves that matched the ocean. Ethan rolled down all the car windows and waited for some of the warmth to seep into him, to stop the weird bout of shivering he really wanted to blame on being cold.

The small box sat in the passenger seat (Nick's seat, his mind kept not-so-helpfully saying).

"I guess we finally made it."

He was talking to a box of ashes on a beach in the middle of summer. Fuck Nick; he totally could have been a goth kid. Except for all the screaming laughter coming from the arcades. That was ruining his buzz. Too damn much fun going on.

He got his phone out without looking at the messages and snapped a few pictures. His feet in the sand with the box sitting on his shoes next to them. The giant Ferris wheel. The ocean stretching out beyond all the people, with the pier hemming it in on his left. Ethan chose a few for an Instagram collage, posting it with the caption: *Here at the edge of the world trying to say goodbye.*

It sounded more maudlin than he felt. He'd been saying goodbye to Scott for over a year. Grief didn't keep people alive, though. Somewhere after the Colorado River, after getting gas in a town called Blythe, he'd crested a low rise on the highway and seen two giant dinosaurs in the distance. Maybe it was talking to Mrs. Raines, or driving through the desert by himself, or time, like everyone had kept telling him. Maybe it was meeting Nick, or Nick leaving, or that he'd finally learned how to spend time with himself and not feel empty.

He'd climbed to the top of the tyrannosaurus and peered out the scratched-plastic porthole windows hidden in its eyes. Cars zipped past on the highway. The brown desert, dotted with sagebrush and cactus, stretched away in every direction. And he'd realized Scott was never going to see it. He still wasn't sure of his views on ghosts, or spirituality, or any of that shit, but standing in that improbable place, he suddenly *knew* he wasn't only holding himself back. He was holding Scott back.

So here he was. Here they were. The culmination of their lives together, and the start of whatever else waited over that horizon where the sky met the sea.

The box was all rough edges and unfinished plans in his hands. He left his phone tucked down into the stinky toe of his sneakers, under his new bright-green dinosaur beach towel. The Pacific Ocean, it turned out, was fucking cold. He gingerly waded out with everyone, until the water was splashing against his thighs when the little waves came in and sucking his breath away when the larger swells crested over his waist.

Tossing the ashes in the air might've provided some sort of dramatic finality, but he and Scott had never been dramatic. They'd been . . . Fuck, they'd been inevitable, unstoppable, like the tide. Constantly moving, but always in the same place. Plus, he didn't want to get a mouthful of his dead boyfriend.

Ethan pried the little box open just under the surface of the sunlit water, his cold fingers fumbling with the latch until he finally got it. Scott's ashes swirled into the water around him, dark and glittering as they sank into the ocean.

He stood there until he couldn't see them anymore, letting his breath move with the rise and fall of the sea. He'd loved Scott. But Scott had loved him too. Scott would have wanted him to be happy.

Ethan wanted to be happy. He wanted a corndog, and a ride on the stupidly high Ferris wheel, and to regain feeling below his waist after he got out of the freezing ocean. He wanted his favorite jeans back, and he wanted to kiss Nick once his hair grew back.

He wanted to be happy. So he would.

Even if Nick hadn't heard Ethan's phone ringing under the frankly garish beach towel, he probably would have known who it belonged to. There was no denying Ethan's unique sense of style. Or his potential color-blindness.

He'd taken three busses back from Wherever-the-hell, Texas, each of them progressively more crowded. He was fairly certain if he hadn't gotten off the city bus four stops early and race-walked the rest of the way to the pier, his seatmate would have murdered him to stop his knee from bouncing. She'd looked like somebody's sweet *bisabuela*, but everyone had limits.

And then he got to the beach, and it was huge, and completely filled with athletic blond guys. A sea of potential Ethans if he squinted, and the real one might leave at any second. After his second trip down the sand, he'd given up on surprise romantic gestures in favor of actually *finding* Ethan. Thus the phone and the empty towel, and when Nick compared the view to the pictures on Ethan's Instagram (that he'd *absolutely not* liked, un-liked, then liked again), it looked like the same angles. So he sat down on the edge of what he hoped wasn't some angry surfer's towel and waited, even though every second his bare toes spent digging into the sand was absolute torture.

After some amount of time that was definitely days, a single blond figure waded out of the ocean, and trudged up the beach toward him. The person stopped too far away for Nick to make out their face, lifting a hand up to shield their eyes and stare hard in his direction. So no matter what, the owner of his borrowed towel was returning.

A few more steps, a few more days, and he was grinning wide enough to hurt as Ethan broke into what could only be described as a flat-out run. Heads turned to follow him, and Nick couldn't be sure if it was worry over the crazy guy charging up the beach or the fact that the crazy guy was spraying sand in their faces as he flew past.

"I . . . Nick . . ." Ethan stopped, panting, hands on his knees. "Hey," he finally managed.

Nick laughed to cover his uncertainty. "Surprise."

Ethan opened his mouth a couple of times, snapping it shut again without saying anything. Which, fair. The burden of explanation was kind of on him here.

"You can exchange bus tickets a lot easier than plane tickets." He made himself keep looking up, leaning back a little so he could take in every half-soaked inch of Ethan. People talked about the light in California like it was magical, and the way the early afternoon sun lingered on Ethan's skin was definitely enough to make him believe in things he'd never been sure of before.

"I was really hoping I could hitch a ride back to Virginia with you."

Ethan's mouth thinned to a flat line, but the corners twitched. He was so bad at lying. Maybe Nick could learn a few things from him.

"I don't know. I promised my mom I wouldn't pick up hitchhikers, you know. What if my luck doesn't hold, and you murder me in an oddly specific way?"

Nick rocked forward, grabbed the legs of Ethan's swim trunks, and used the damp fabric to pull him closer. Ethan met him halfway, clammy fingers tangling with Nick's. It left Nick at crotch-height, the perfect excuse to let himself off the hook for all the scary, messy parts of this. He took a deep breath full of salt and sunlight, remembering that he had permission. He could lie, and it wouldn't mean anything.

Except now he had options too.

"What if I'm kind of in love with you?"

Ethan's fingers tightened in his a second before he was knocked sideways, bowled over by six feet of everything he'd been afraid to want. The hideous towel was warm under Nick's back when Ethan rolled them over, propping himself in Nick's line of sight so close that he might have been the whole world.

"I guess that's a pretty good character reference, but I'll still need to see some ID, Mr. Hamilton."

They were close enough to kiss, but Nick put a hand on Ethan's cheek first, the faint golden stubble scratching his palm when he pushed Ethan's sunglasses up.

"Lie with me?"

Ethan's grin softened to something else, some smile Nick knew was just for him. He lifted his head to meet Ethan's lips, and their kiss tasted like the ocean, and the edge of the world, and all the miles they were going to travel together.

Epilogue

Astoria, OR

The chimes on the door of Wandering Whimsies: Art, Magic, Soul rang musically, and Ethan barely waited until they'd stepped onto the sidewalk before turning to Nick.

"Okay, that was seriously cool. I've always wanted to do a tarot reading, and that was . . . just, wow. The things he said were spot on."

Nick knew he'd failed miserably in his role as designated skeptic during their couples reading, if only because he'd been as caught up as Ethan as the cards had turned over one after the other.

"It was . . . a lot. To think about, I mean." He hoped Ethan could tell he wasn't brushing it off, because he still felt distracted and caught up in trying to remember all the cards and where they'd fallen. What they'd meant. The reader, John, had been so sure of them, explaining each card like a story unfolding across the purple velvet table cloth.

"The last card was pretty cool." Nick nudged Ethan's arm as they sauntered out of the tiny garden in front of the Victorian townhouse-turned-occult shop. "The part about finally knowing what you want. Even if The Sun totally blows your claims of being a spooky kid."

Ethan stopped at the crooked iron gate, grinning at him. "Darkness and the night, dude."

Nick did absolutely nothing to hide his disbelieving laugh, tangling his fingers in Ethan's straw-blond hair. "You're *my* sunshine."

Ethan's gray eyes widened. His mouth twisted, perched like a nervous bird caught between amusement and something Nick preferred not to put a name to. His expression twitched fractionally for a few seconds before Nick laughed again and let him off the hook.

"Your *face*, dude. Oh my God."

"*Your* face, jerk."

The street around them wasn't busy, and Nick didn't really give a shit what the good people of Oregon thought of him. Taking advantage of the narrow opening in the fence, he pressed into Ethan's space and kissed him. He took his time, relishing every careless little hitch in Ethan's breathing until someone whizzed by them on a bike, bell ringing.

"It's my favorite face, though."

Ethan rolled his eyes and nudged Nick's shoulder with his. "So, hey, what did you buy in there? You looked all secretive and shit. Because if it was a love charm, I'm gonna be hurt after that reading."

"Damn, I thought I'd been subtle." Nick tried to make it sound like a joke, but he couldn't deny there was a part of him recoiling in embarrassment. Ethan had dragged him to every haunted outhouse in the South, though. The little plastic bag holding his purchases crinkled when he pulled it out of his pocket. He fished inside it for a second before handing Ethan a small velvet drawstring pouch.

"The lady who works there, Renee, helped me put it together. It's supposed to keep your car safe. Ghosts, demons . . . hitchhikers. She said you should leave it out in the sun every month, or in the light of a full moon. That's supposed to, like, recharge it."

"Whoa, wait, not that I don't appreciate the thought, but I'm kind of fond of hitchhikers."

"Dude, I think you've hit your lifetime limit on picking up random drifters. Don't push your luck."

Ethan nodded sagely. "Of course, of course. Why mess with success? I'm happy with the hitchhiker I have."

"You can always trade up once my warranty runs out." Nick glanced up to make sure they weren't blocking the walkway to the store, and also because he felt weird about the other thing he'd bought. He wasn't sure he wanted to show it to Ethan. Except he'd been meaning, trying, and failing to bring up all the shit that crowded up behind his shame, and this was the perfect opportunity.

He honestly would have been less annoyed with himself if he'd bought one of the poppet doll kits. Instead, he uncurled his fingers to show Ethan a piece of glass shaped like a flat teardrop. It was cobalt blue, with rings of white, turquoise, and black in the middle. Nick brushed his thumb across the smooth surface.

"It's a Turkish evil eye charm. It reminded me of the one I wore when I was little, from Peru. I was thinking maybe I'd keep it in my pocket until I can, you know, talk to someone? Like a therapist. About Kyle, and . . . stuff."

Nick could see the emotions flitting across Ethan's face. Funny how they were so easy to read, after what hadn't really been that long together.

"I think that's a great idea," Ethan finally said. He reached out, closing Nick's fingers around the glass with his own fingers. "The evil eye's supposed to scare away the bad stuff, right? Kyle counts as bad stuff."

Super simplification, but that seemed to be one of Ethan's gifts. Or quirks.

"I texted your dad a little, about getting a restraining order, but I figured this would help me remember that Kyle can't actually see me. I can reach for it when I start to give him too much credit."

"And if it doesn't keep him away, it's heavy enough that you can lob it at his head or something." Ethan pursed his lips. "Might even be heavy enough to break his leg if he's chasing you. Or at least give him a painful shin bruise."

Laughing despite himself, Nick made a show of hefting the charm consideringly. "So what about you? Did you find any proof in there that ghosts are real?"

Ethan shrugged, looking off toward the other side of the street for a moment. It seemed more like he was weighing his answers than sad, but Nick still brushed their fingers together. Ethan's focus returned from the middle distance, and the smile he directed at Nick was soft and maybe a little melancholy.

"I don't know if I found proof, but I think I found what I was looking for." His teeth settled on the edge of his lower lip, worrying the tender flesh. "I think we all make our own ghosts, and yeah, maybe some of that translates into apparitions and hovering orbs when it's all concentrated in one place. But, mostly, I think we get so obsessed with missing someone, trying to stay connected with who they were, that we forget they were people. They . . . *Scott* would have changed. He would have learned things, and seen things, and we'd both be different people now than we were when he died. I think that was the ghost I was hoping to find. The person Scott would have been."

Ethan paused after his rush of words, rolling his shoulders back and glancing across the street again, past the weathered picket fence and out to the ocean. "Instead of keeping Scott's memory alive, I was trying to get away from the person I was becoming without him. It scared me. It still scares me. But now I know that no matter how scared I am, I can still keep going. So . . . yeah. I did. I found what I needed to find. And some haunted train tracks."

Nick only had to force himself past Cornerstone's ingrained limitations a few hundred times a day now, and even they couldn't have kept him from wrapping an arm around Ethan's back and settling his hand at Ethan's waist. Ethan leaned into the touch, into Nick, like he believed Nick was stable enough to support him. They stood there staring at the ocean for a long time, until Ethan's voice broke the reverie.

"This doesn't mean I don't still want to go to Fort Worden, though. A haunted *campground*. I already booked one of the little cabins."

"What is wrong with you?" Nick shook his head. "No, wait, what's wrong with *me*? I just sat through a tarot reading where I got told we share a life philosophy, and that we're gonna take a leap of faith that'll bump our relationship to a new level. And I was *happy* about it."

"Aw, you're still happy about it, admit it."

Happy. Hopeful. And honestly, the hope felt even more foreign than the happiness.

Ethan nudged his shoulder, pulling Nick back to the moment. "Hey, you *are* still happy, right?"

The worried squinch between Ethan's eyes got him the sympathy he'd doubtless been angling for. Nick sighed, recognizing defeat when it gave him puppy-dog eyes. "Yeah, I am."

"Good. Me too. It's weird, though . . ." Ethan trailed off. "I haven't really looked forward to anything in a long time. I'm happy. And I'm looking forward to being happy?" His voice rose on the question.

Nick tugged Ethan closer, watching the waves like they could teach him how to rise and fall.

"I think that's called hope."

Dear Reader,

Thank you for reading Michelle Moore and Reesa Herberth's *Detour*!

We know your time is precious and you have many, many entertainment options, so it means a lot that you've chosen to spend your time reading. We really hope you enjoyed it.

We'd be honored if you'd consider posting a review—good or bad—on sites like **Amazon, Barnes & Noble, Kobo, Goodreads, Twitter, Facebook, Tumblr,** and your blog or website. We'd also be honored if you told your friends and family about this book. Word of mouth is a book's lifeblood!

For more information on upcoming releases, author interviews, blog tours, contests, giveaways, and more, please sign up for our weekly, spam-free newsletter and visit us around the web:

Newsletter: tinyurl.com/RiptideSignup
Twitter: twitter.com/RiptideBooks
Facebook: facebook.com/RiptidePublishing
Goodreads: tinyurl.com/RiptideOnGoodreads
Tumblr: riptidepublishing.tumblr.com

Thank you so much for Reading the Rainbow!

RiptidePublishing.com

Acknowledgments

We'd like to thank our cheerleader/beta reader/long-suffering poison taster, Shannon, for hanging tough with these characters since their inception.

Our sincere thanks also go out to John Marani, master tarot reader, who did a spread for the boys that informed the epilogue and sent them on to more adventures.

In the course of our research for this book, we were strongly influenced by the documentary *Kidnapped for Christ*. Many of the incidents Nick describes taking place at Camp Cornerstone are based on survivor accounts from similar youth boot camps. If they seem horrifying in fiction, the reality is much worse.

If you're interested in learning more about what real teenagers (many of whom are LGBTQIA) face in these institutions, we suggest the documentary mentioned above, and the resources available on these sites:

SIA-NOW - www.sia-now.org

Survivorship - survivorship.org

ALSO BY
Reesa Herberth
AND
Michelle Moore

The Ylendrian Empire series
The Balance of Silence
The Slipstream Con
Peripheral People

ALSO BY
Reesa Herberth

In Discretion (Ylendrian Empire)

ALSO BY
Michelle Moore

If Wishes Were Coffee
Beach Patrol

ABOUT THE

Authors

MICHELLE MOORE is a collection of flamingo feathers and milkshake atoms arranged into human form. She lives in Florida, though the people and cities around her sometimes refuse to cooperate. When not writing, she spends her time trying to figure out what the cats have planned (she hasn't succeeded yet).

Connect with Michelle:
Website: michelleandreesawrite.com
Twitter: @MarigotC
Facebook: facebook.com/Reesa-Herberth-and-Michelle-Moore

REESA HERBERTH grew up in Hawaii, tried Arizona for a few years, and eventually settled in the DC area because it turned out moving from a tropical rainforest to a desert was more of a shock than she could stand.

She's held a variety of crazy writer jobs, including book and video store manager for a defunct chain of music shops, office goddess for an artisan ice cream maker, cheese-cup scrubber at an organic goat dairy, and dye-stained proprietor of a small fiber arts business. Her hobbies include collecting art supplies, competitive procrastination, and just about anything that turns wool into clothes.

With and without Michelle Moore, her other works include the award-winning Ylendrian Empire books—science fiction romance with a queer twist.

You can connect with Reesa here:
Wesbite: michelleandreesawrite.com
Website: ylendrianempire.com
Twitter: @reesah
Facebook: facebook.com/Reesa-Herberth-and-Michelle-Moore

Enjoy more stories like
Detour
at RiptidePublishing.com!